~~Dec. 2002~~

Purchased, online, ~~forom~~
from Thrift Book
in the Summer of 2021
by me, [illegible]

Completed 1st reading book - 2021
[illegible]

Review: (subjective)
- engaging and entertaining.
- Sometimes slow moving.
- Interesting twists
- Good characters development.

[illegible]

The Legend

KATHLEEN GIVENS

WARNER BOOKS

An AOL Time Warner Company

Jacket design by Diane Luger
Jacket illustration by Steve Assel
Jacket hand lettering by David Gatti
Book design by Giorgetta Bell McRee

ISBN: 0-7394-2789-X

Warner Books, Inc.
1271 Avenue of the Americas
New York, NY 10020

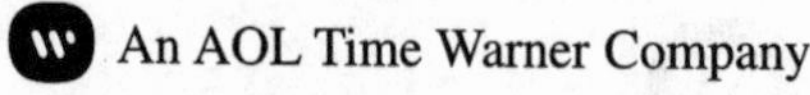
An AOL Time Warner Company

Printed in the United States of America

First Printing: July 2002

This book is dedicated

to Cheryl and Annie, whose courage, grace, and humor under duress has been inspirational;

to Kerry, John, Patty, and Mike, who bring laughter and happiness to our lives;

and to Russ, my love forever.

Acknowledgments

This book had three editors: Maggie Crawford, who inspired it; Karen Kosztolnyik, who saw it through its first incarnation; and Beth de Guzman, who guided with a sure touch. My thanks to all three, especially to Beth, who was in the trenches with me and did extraordinary duty without complaint. Thanks also go to Diane Luger of Warner's Art Department for yet another beautiful cover.

I'd like to thank the Graham clan for their enthusiasm for Bonnie Dundee's cousin's story; and the MacKenzie and MacLeod clans for the temporary loan of Torridon territory to the MacCurries, with special thanks to Stephen R. McKenzie, President and Lieutenant to Caberfeidh, The Clan MacKenzie Society in the Americas, Inc., and to his wife Barbara and daughter Anne. I'm also grateful to Lawrence P. Johnson, Southern California Commissioner of the Clan Gunn Society of North America, and to Nancy and Charles Williams of Tea and Sympathy for the constant supply of resource books and a safe haven at all the Festivals. Thanks also go to Peggy Gregerson and Denise Petersen for invaluable information on twinship.

For reading every word a thousand times and infinite input, I thank my husband, Russ. For critiquing and suggestions, thanks go to Cheryl Becker, Dr. Debra Holland, and Peggy Gregerson. And thanks to other writers who kept me sane: The Loopies, the Ladies of Tea and Sympathy and Deb Cooke. Special thanks go to Virginia Henley for her generosity.

I could not have completed this book without support from Russ, Kerry and John, and Patty and Mike; from my family Violet, Julius, Rich, Jill, Jon, Paula, Nikki, Kim, Ben, Trev, Gwen, Pam, Bob, Greg, Sam, Bev, Carly, and Caitlyn; Aunt Peggy and the Westchester bunch; and from the gang at R.E. Wall & Associates—Forrest, Enrique, Mike, MJ, Jeff, Matt, and Ron.

Thanks also go to Guido and Bean; Susie and Mike; Rick and Mary; Jeanne and Cor; the Lunch Bunch, Georgene, Peggy, Zan, Sue and Ginny and their guys. And for special research in the British Isles, thanks go to Michael The Yorkshireman, Princess Mal, Linda, the Rose of England, and Harry, the Song and Dance King.

My thanks to you all. Life is good with you in it!

Thou art slave to fate, chance, kings, and desperate men.

—John Donne, *Holy Sonnets* X

SCOTLAND
Torridon
Inverness
Loch Ness
Killiecrankie
Dunfallandy
Dundee
Perth
NORTH
SEA
Edinburgh
N
ENGLAND

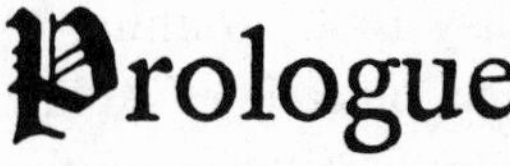

Prologue

February 1660, Torridon, Scotland

Alistair MacCurrie, Earl of Torridon and chief of Clan MacCurrie, pushed the pillow out of the way and stretched his wife's arms above her head, linking their fingers. He shook his black hair back over his shoulder and smiled before he captured her mouth.

"Annie," he said when he lifted his head again. "Are ye ready at last?"

She laughed, her eyes dark in her pale face. "We've only made love for an hour, love."

"I want ye," he growled. "I've been patient. What do ye want me to do?"

She did not answer, but raised her hips to meet him. He moaned with pleasure as his body eased into hers.

"Give me a son," she breathed, then withdrew her hands from his to wrap them about his shoulders and draw him closer. "Give me a son, my love."

Alistair thrust deeper. "I'll give ye a son, my bonnie Annie." He withdrew and thrust again. "And another."

"Enough," Anne said with another laugh. "We have only so many rooms."

He traced a line of kisses across her temple. "We'll build more."

They shared a smile, then fell silent, concentrating on their union. Anne called out her ecstasy first, straining to hold him closer; a moment later his voice joined hers. At last they slept, wrapped in each other's arms. Neither saw the strike of lightning that lit the February night, nor heard the crash that followed.

Nor did they hear the whispers that greeted the first light of morning. "The legend," the whisperers said to one another, then hurried about their work.

Still languid from their night of pleasure, Alistair and Anne came into the hall with linked hands. They ignored the sidelong glances thrown at them, for they were accustomed to comments on their ardor. But when Alistair's small and gray-haired mother saw them, she hurried over. Her words shattered their composure.

"Have ye seen it?" Mairi asked in a tone of wonder.

"Have I seen what?" Alistair shook his head. "Mother, what d'ye mean?"

"Come," Mairi said, leading them outside. She pointed to the huge oak tree that had stood for centuries just outside the gatehouse of Castle Currie. Alistair swore, and Anne gasped as they saw what the night had brought.

The tree, still joined at the base, had been sliced cleanly in two, the singe of fire blackening the bark, the leafless branches stark against the sky. The smell of burnt wood filled the air. Alistair stepped forward to run his hands along the cleft, then turned to his mother, his face pale.

"It's the legend," Mairi said to her son. She glanced at her daughter-in-law, who stared with round eyes. "Anne, ye dinna ken, do ye?"

Anne shook her head.

"The legend of the MacCurries," Mairi said, "tells that three generations of lairds will be born and die on the same date. That to the third laird, twin sons will be born, who will lead the clan to war and then to fifty years of peace. And that the sign of their conception will be this tree—"

She turned to look at the tree, then back at Anne. "And this tree will be split in two. And each half will live." She looked at her son. "Yer father and his father died on their birthdays. It's the legend, as the Seer said it would be. Anne carries the lads now."

Alistair turned to stare at his wife, who put a hand over her flat stomach. For a moment the only sound was that of the waves crashing at the bottom of the cliff, then Alistair shook his head as though to clear it.

"Mother," he said, "it's naught but a lightning strike."

"Alistair," his mother replied in a soothing tone, "if the halves live, will ye believe it?"

"It's superstition."

"It's a prophecy," Mairi insisted. "And a good one, my son." She laughed. "Ye should be celebrating. Fifty years of peace for Torridon. And yer sons bringing it."

Alistair stood silent, then reached for Anne, who slipped into his arms. He looked over her head at his mother. "I canna believe it," he said softly.

Mairi shook her head. "Nor I. But look—" She gestured at the tree. "Time will tell. Peace, Alistair. Yer sons will bring peace to this land."

Anne turned to face the tree, her hand over her middle. "November. They will be born in November."

Chapter One

March 1689, Torridon, Scotland

James MacCurrie looked into his brother's eyes across their father's grave. Blue gaze met blue gaze, the brothers communicating, as always, without words, sharing their grief equally. It would be the last time the brothers would be equals. When they walked away from their father's cairn, nothing would ever be the same for either of them.

James took a deep breath and turned to look at his home. Solid and somber, Castle Currie stood alone on this promontory on the western coast of Scotland, above the waters of Lochs Torridon and Shieldaig, its stone turrets reaching high to the heavens. Above them storm clouds gathered and the wind freshened, but the crowd of people standing outside the fortress paid no notice.

Clan MacCurrie buried its chief this day.

Neil gave the signal to the pipers lining the top of the cliff, their plaids bright against the gray water below them, their movements slow and deliberate as they began the funeral dirge. The untamed music rose, shimmering in the air above the mourners for a moment before wrapping itself around the castle as if in a final embrace, then soaring over the other side of the headland, across the loch, and to the open sea beyond. James closed his eyes, fighting for control, ignoring the stares of the awestruck clanspeople who watched his family.

The Legend, the whisperers said now to one another, just as they had incessantly during the last few months, their talk growing more excited with each passing day. They were silent on the day Alistair, after weeks of semiconsciousness, opened his eyes, talked for a moment with his family, then took his beloved Anne's hand. And died. On his birthday. As his father had, and his grandfather before him, exactly as the Brahan Seer had foretold.

The entire clan had gathered to bury Alistair MacCurrie, coming from the fishing villages that dotted the shores of the sea lochs, from the crofthouses nestled at the base of the sandstone mountains, from Glen Torridon to the east, and from the blue islands that stretched out to sea.

James could feel their stares, could sense their wonder. He felt much the same. He'd been raised with the Legend, had passed the tree that marked his conception every day, had watched his father's birthday celebrations each year with combined excitement and fear. But he'd not believed it would really come to pass.

"There will come a day," the Seer had said, beginning his prophecy as he always did. He had included a wealth of detail in his prophecy. Now James wondered if any more of it would come true. Since his father died, he'd waged a war within himself, part of him believing, part scoffing. Only time would tell.

He felt his throat tighten as the priest placed a hand on the coffin and said a prayer for Alistair's soul. Their father had been an extraordinary man. How could he be gone? How could it be that they would never hear that roar of laughter again, never feel the slap on the shoulder he always gave them before an embrace? Never be teased by him, or encouraged to rise to a difficult task, then praised for their efforts. Never listen to his counsel, his warnings of who to trust and who to watch. James shook his head, denying the death.

His cousin Duncan MacKenzie moved to stand next to him, and James shot him a grateful look. Duncan nodded, his eyes solemn, then bent his russet head as the priest continued. James did not hear the prayers being said, nor the answering murmurs of the mourners. He stared at his hands clasped before him and tried to ignore the waves of grief pouring between him and Neil.

Both brothers turned when their mother slumped to the ground with a wail. Anne lay crumpled at the foot of the grave, her frail shoulders shaking with the force of her sobs. As her sons leaned to raise her, their grandmother stopped them. The prayers paused, and the crowd of mourners watched in silence.

"Leave her," Mairi said, looking from Neil to James. "Ye canna comfort her. Let her weep, lads. She mourns as she should."

"But, Grandmother," James said, his hand on his mother's arm.

Mairi restrained him with a look. "Ye'll leave her. Ye canna understand the grief she feels. Leave her be." Her eyes filled with tears, and her expression softened. "Please, lads, let us mourn as we will. I bury my son today, and your mother her husband. There is no comfort possible for us."

James and Neil exchanged a glance, then stepped back from the women. The wind tugged at James's clothing and tore his hair from its binding, but he ignored it, trying to control his emotions. He met Neil's gaze again and saw his disbelief and sorrow mirrored there in eyes the same shape, the same shade of blue, as his own.

And he saw something more. James watched as his brother steeled himself and put on the mantle of responsibility. Neil was now chief of the Clan MacCurrie and Earl of Torridon. And James was his vassal.

Neil was older by four minutes, and that made all the difference between them. Now, for the first time in their lives, the brothers would not be equals. They'd been raised for this day, had known it was coming closer through the long months of their father's illness, but they'd never discussed it. What was there to say? James knew Neil would lead the clan well, knew he and Duncan would be there to assist him.

Neil's expression lightened, and James knew his message of support had been received and appreciated. They'd always been able to speak without words, even when they were not together. When James traveled, Neil knew when he would be coming home. When Neil, out on the islands, broke his wrist, James had known something was wrong. They'd never questioned this ability. Others found it disquieting, but the twins both treasured and relied upon it. Now they would need it more than ever, for Alistair had died during turbulent times.

War was in the air.

The brothers and Duncan threw the first handfuls of dirt into the grave, then stepped back as clansmen finished the job. When the grave was full, their grandmother helped Anne to her feet, and with her arm around her daughter-in-law looked at the grave.

"He was my son," Mairi said in a voice that carried across the crowd. "And I was proud of him." Her chin trembled, and her tone quieted. "Fifty-four years ago I bore him. I should be long in the ground, and he here to mourn me."

She took a shuddering breath and looked from one grandson to the other. Her voice was much quieter now. "It's yer time now. Make the prophecy come true. Bring peace to my home."

James watched his grandmother place the first stone for her son's cairn with shaking fingers, then stepped forward with Neil and Duncan to finish the job. The sky opened, and the wind howled around them. Torridon bid farewell to its laird with a show of fury that would be remembered for decades.

Early that evening, after the rains had gone, the three cousins walked slowly along the battlements of Castle Currie. Below them, in Loch Torridon' s protected harbor, Duncan's ships lay anchored, bathed in the same dusky light that enveloped the MacCurrie fleet. Fishing boats were tied to the docks that lined the shore, more pulled up on the rocky beach, idled for this day of mourning.

James gazed across the sea loch, his emotions muted. He had been drained by the funeral and the meal, after which he'd stood next to Neil while the clanspeople came forward with their expressions of sorrow and support. He'd thanked them all, moved by their concern, but he'd felt as though he watched himself from the outside.

Easy enough to do, he thought, slanting a glance at Neil. His brother's face reflected James's mood, his dark brows drawn together as he stared down into the harbor. Duncan was quiet as well. The sky had not cleared; the clouds obscured the towering mountains that ringed Loch Torridon, and the wind still whipped around the castle, its rage unabated.

If he turned, he could look up at the tower where his father had died, where his grandfather and great-grandfather had died, where he and Neil had been conceived and born. He could feel the stones behind him, watching to see how he and Neil fulfilled the terms of the legend. Superstition, he told himself. Not a destiny, not a forecast. If only he believed that. He felt like an actor on a stage. He thought his lines were his own, but there were moments when he wondered if another hand were not directing all he did, all they did.

As long as he could remember, James had felt the power of the legend, had known that some day he and Neil would have to face its invisible force. The watchful eyes of the clan had followed the twins as they'd grown, tall and strong like their father, waiting to see what the brothers were made of. Alistair had been respected, but his sons would have to prove their own value.

James glanced at his companions. All three men were tall and lean, but there the similarities ended. Even-tempered Duncan had inherited his father's dark red hair and green eyes, while the twins had Alistair's black hair and blue eyes. And his temperament, James thought with a smile; their grandmother had bemoaned that often enough.

Their mothers were sisters, Anne and Isabel MacKenzie, and when the three had been of an age, all fourteen, Duncan's father had died and he had come to live at Torridon. Alistair had raised the boy as his own, teaching and guiding him as he did his sons. The twins could not imagine life without their voluble cousin. He had been an able ally and partner in crime in their youth, a stalwart companion as they'd grown older.

"It was a good funeral," Neil said softly.

"Aye, the whole clan came," Duncan said. He paused, looking up from his ships to his cousins, each in turn. "The others will be arriving soon."

James nodded. Duncan was right. Representatives from the MacLeods and MacKenzies, the clans whose lands bordered the MacCurries, would come as the news of Alistair's death spread. They'd come to pay their respects. And to judge the mettle of the new MacCurrie chief for themselves. Neil would be no surprise to them, for the clans knew one another well, but the men would still come. They'd bring their condolences and more. They'd bring news of the outside world. Of war.

There had been rumors for months, of troops being raised on the continent, of rebellions planned at home. Neither Scotland nor England had been happy with James Stuart as its king, for he had been a poor leader and was resented in many quarters. Both countries were weary of the turmoil his reign had brought. But few had actually expected William of Orange, King James's son-in-law, to challenge him for the throne. And win, at least in England. Scotland's throne was even now being decided.

"They'll want to talk about the king," Duncan said.

"Which one?" Neil asked ruefully.

William had landed with his army last November. At first it appeared that King James would fight, but within a month James Stuart had fled to France, and by February William and his Mary had been declared king and queen of England. Now the royal pair waited, with all of Britain, for the Scottish Convention, meeting in Edinburgh, to ratify their right to Scotland's throne.

The MacCurries had paid little attention to the uproar. While London and Edinburgh steamed with turmoil and intrigue, Torridon had looked inward, watching its laird decline. Now, whether they wished it or not, it was time to reenter the world.

Neither twin had any desire to be embroiled in a struggle

for the throne, but they might have no choice. The Scottish Convention would decide any day which king to accept, and the Highland clans would then meet to decide to approve or oppose that decision. A gathering of the clans was planned at Dunfallandy Castle to do just that.

"The gathering is in a fortnight," James said.

Neil nodded. "We need to be there."

"Aye." Duncan crossed his arms over his chest. "So which of ye am I going with?"

Neil met his brother's gaze for a moment, then looked back at his cousin. "Jamie," he said.

"Aye, that's best," Duncan agreed. "Ye should be here to greet any latecomers who wanted to mourn his father." But there was another, more important, reason for Neil to stay behind. Transition of power in any clan was a dangerous time, hardly the right moment for the clan chief to leave. With war in the air, it would be even more foolish to leave MacCurrie territory unguarded.

"Too bad we canna sail there; we'll have to ride. Ye ken how I love horses." Duncan sighed loudly as he looked down at his ships. "When do we leave?"

"Ye'll need a week," Neil said, then met James's gaze.

The legend, James thought, catching Neil's unspoken words. The twins will lead the clan to war, then to fifty years of peace. And at Dunfallandy, the clans would be discussing war.

"Ye ken I hate it when ye do that," Duncan said, his tone mild. "Use words."

James looked from his brother to his cousin. "We're thinking of the legend and all the talk that will come if there's war."

Duncan grunted. "There's already been a lot of talk. Everaone's watching ye here and they'll do the same at the gathering. Fergusson invited the clan chiefs, no' just representatives. He'll be expecting Neil, and the man's easily offended."

"Aye," Neil said. "That's why Neil will attend."

Duncan looked from Neil to James. "Ah. Jamie will travel wi' me, but Neil will attend the gathering. Good. No one here will say different, and no one there can tell ye apart except me. It'll work."

James glanced up at the castle tower, feeling the weight of generations. He turned to look into his brother's eyes. The twins held each other's gaze for a moment longer.

Netherby, Scotland

Ellen Graham smiled at her older sister and put her hands on her hips. "Flora, for heaven's sake, stop dancing!"

Flora paused in her twirling to smile at herself in the mirror. Her brown curls settled around her pink cheeks, and her skirts slowly stopped their swaying. "I'm getting married today! How can I not dance, Ellen?"

Ellen laughed. "How can you not? Even the sun has come to help you celebrate. This is the first day without clouds in ages."

"That's because it's my wedding day," Flora said, looking at Ellen over her shoulder. "At last. Do you think Tom will like my dress?"

"Tom will love your dress. He would marry you if you wore a grain sack."

"He would, wouldn't he? He probably wouldn't even notice."

"Tom just wants to marry you. He's loved you since we were children."

"And I've loved him. I just didn't realize it. Father was right."

Ellen sighed. For years their father had told Flora that she'd never find anyone to love her more than Tom Stuart. But Flora, her head quite turned by the attention that the three Graham sisters had received upon their introduction to Edinburgh and Dundee society, had been too busy enjoying herself to remember the boy who had adored her all her life.

Tom, blessed with a patience Ellen never understood, had waited for Flora to grow weary of the parties and agree to be his wife. She finally did, last November, only to have Tom, an officer in their cousin John's troop, march south with King James's army, expecting to fend off William of Orange's invasion. Flora, oblivious to world events, had been shocked, then had been the only one in the Graham household delighted when King James had fled to France and his army dispersed.

Now, six months later, Tom and Flora were marrying despite the uncertain times ahead. No one mentioned it, certainly not to Flora, but most of the family worried what would become of an officer in the army of a dethroned king. Only Flora—and their cousin John—seemed optimistic about the future.

"My wedding will be so different from Margaret's," Flora said. "I still cannot believe she went for a visit, fell in love with a total stranger, and married him! Margaret, the most serious person in the world!"

"The most particular person in the world," Ellen said. "She said her heart stopped when she saw Hugh for the first time."

"That's not love," Flora said smugly. "Love is what I feel for Tom."

Ellen smiled to herself. How different her sisters' marriages were from what Ellen would have thought. Last year sensible, practical Margaret had lost her heart to Hugh MacDonnell and now lived in Glengarry, in the wild western Highlands, about to give birth to their first child. And today flighty Flora was marrying Tom, planning to live near Netherby instead of in town, as she'd always said she would.

Ellen caught sight of herself in the mirror. Flora was the pretty one, Margaret the sensible one. And Ellen? She looked at her dark brown hair and arched eyebrows. I'm all angles, she thought. Her cheekbones were too prominent, her mouth too wide. She was not beautiful, she was not pretty, nor particularly sensible; she was simply the youngest.

"You'll be next," Flora said.

Ellen laughed. "I'm the only one left."

"Who will you marry?" Flora mused. "What about Evan?"

"Oh, please! Who can take Evan seriously? He's just waiting for his grandfather to die and leave him money. Not my idea of a husband."

"When he does inherit, he'll be wealthy."

"But he'll still be Evan."

"That's true. What about David Grant?"

"Oh, not you too! Aunt Bea thinks David is perfect for me."

"He is very handsome."

"So is our stepfather. A man's exterior does not necessarily reflect his interior."

Flora's eyes widened. "Listen to you!"

"Well? We all thought Pitney was very handsome at first. We thought he was charming when he was wooing Mother. And we thought he'd at least be nice to us."

"Instead of horrid. He is a beastly man. I hate it when he tries to be courteous. It's easier when he's his usual gruff self. Is he ever happy?"

"He's very pleased that you're marrying Tom."

Flora's brow creased. "Yes, he has been. I wonder why?"

"Oh, please, Flora! It's simple," Ellen said. "One more daughter out the door. He's giddy with delight. Now all he has to do is marry me off, and he'll be content. Haven't you noticed that he keeps shoving men at me? He can't wait for me to marry one of them and get out of the house. And they're all old enough to be our father or grandfather. There's no one here our age."

"There's David."

"Besides David. Who is marrying Catherine, according to her."

"She says he's all but asked her."

"It'll be perfect for both of them," Ellen said. "She adores him. He adores her money. She'll keep him in the comforts he loves so much. No, I'll stay right here and drive Pitney mad with frustration."

"I don't understand Pitney. Why is he so eager to be alone with Mother? Do they seem happy to you?"

Ellen shook her head. "Not lately. Mother was happy at first, but not in the last year, at least. And where does he go? He's always disappearing." She sighed.

"It's hard to believe they've been married three years."

"They only knew each other six months." Ellen looked into Flora's eyes in the mirror. "Mother was very foolish. She never should have married him."

"No. Why do you suppose she did?"

"She was lonely. Pitney was handsome and charming. It had been years since Father had died. She was tired of being alone."

"I suppose she didn't want to be like Aunt Bea."

"Bea was different. She never married."

"But she would have, Ellen. If her beau hadn't died, she would have married him and had children. Do you think I should change my hair?"

Ellen smiled. "No. It's perfect. And this day will be perfect."

Both girls turned as the door opened and their mother, Rose, and great-aunt Bea came in with Britta, the young girl just recently promoted to Ellen's maid. Britta's eyes were anxious, and Ellen smiled at her. She was fond of the girl, who was very sweet and tried so hard to please. Rose kissed each of her daughters and then laughed as Flora erupted into talk about her dress and hair. Ellen led Bea to a seat by the window.

"I'm fine, I'm fine," Bea said. "Flora, you look beautiful."

"Thank you, Aunt Bea," Flora said.

"Doesn't she?" Rose said. "All my girls are beautiful."

"Oh, they are, madam!" Britta said, then blushed and looked horrified.

Rose laughed. "I quite agree, Britta."

"I do too," Bea said, then sat back against the cushions, speaking in a low tone to Ellen."I'm much better than your mother allows."

"You were very ill," Ellen said.

"I was. I'll admit it scared even me." Bea suddenly grinned. "I even wrote my will; I'm leaving everything to Pitney."

Ellen laughed. "I doubt that."

"So do I. Can't stand the man." She patted Ellen's hand. "It won't be long until you've married as well. You should marry David. I've told you that."

"And I've told you that I will never marry him. He does not care for me, nor I for him."

"He thinks he cares for you, child. He's thought so for years."

Ellen shook her head. "If David cared for me, he wouldn't be courting Catherine as well. He's only courting me to make Catherine jealous."

Bea sighed. "I'd like to see you settled. I'd like it to be someone who will be able to care for you for your whole life."

Ellen smiled. "Wouldn't that be lovely?"

Bea nodded, then moved the curtain aside to see who the footmen were greeting in the yard below. "John is here," she said, then repeated it to Rose. "With ten men. At least he has the sense to know he's a target."

Rose looked from Bea to Ellen. "Go and welcome him, child. You know you want to. We'll be down in a moment."

Ellen smiled as she ran down to the foyer. She was always pleased to see John. He might be John Graham of Claverhouse to the world, the newly appointed Viscount of Dundee, at the center of a political drama that had Scotland fascinated, but to her he was simply her favorite cousin. John had been kind to her as she'd grown up, discussing politics even though Ellen was much younger, never belittling her interest nor refusing her questions.

He'd spent years in King James's army, had been rewarded with promotions and additional duties, some of which had been both unpopular and dangerous. Last November, when William threatened to invade, King James had ordered his army south. John had left at once with his regiment, taking Tom Stuart, one of John's most trusted officers, which meant Flora and Tom's wedding was postponed.

When King James disbanded his army a few weeks ago, John had sent his men home. And Flora had insisted that her wedding be planned at once, despite the talk of war. Few who knew John Graham well expected him to let King James forfeit his throne without so much as a murmur. Speculation as to what he would do had been running rampant since the Convention began, even more so when John suddenly left the meeting. Word soon spread that he had ridden to meet some of the Highland clans who backed King James.

There were even rumblings that once William became king, John's activities would be considered traitorous. At the least, the gossips said, his days in power were numbered. At the worst . . . But Ellen refused to consider that. John and his beloved wife Jean were about to become parents. Surely no harm could befall them now?

She found him in a knot of his men, his back straight, his dark green clothes emphasizing his lean body. She had always thought him very dashing, with his thick dark curls and even features. John did not look like a soldier—he was slightly built and not particularly tall—but he had proven himself fearless, a bold commander, a born leader of men. And a loyal servant to King James, a dangerous habit these days.

He looked up as she called to him, a smile lighting his face. She threw her arms around him, and he laughed, kissing her cheek as he embraced her.

"I am always assured of a warm welcome from you, cousin!" he said.

"I am always pleased to see you. We didn't know if you would come."

"Miss Flora and Tom's wedding? Never. How is the bride?"

"Beautiful. She's very happy. And how is Jean?"

"Very well, considering she's near her term. Weary of the process."

"I'm sure she is." Ellen leaned closer and lowered her voice. "What's the news, John? Where have you been?"

He gave her a wicked grin. "At home with my wife, where else? I am about to be a father."

"Not for weeks yet. And I know you've not been home; Jean wrote that she could not come because of the baby and that you were elsewhere. What will happen now?"

John's expression sobered. "The Convention will decide for William, Ellen. They will offer him the throne."

"And then what?"

"We will wait and see what the reaction is from Scotland. If no one objects, William will be king."

"He is already king in England."

John's eyes narrowed. "There is only one legal king of England, and he is James Stuart. William is a usurper."

"That is a dangerous position to take."

"It is. And more so if I'm successful in my efforts."

"You're going to raise troops for King James!"

"We'll see what support I find."

"John! Welcome!"

Ellen and John turned to find Pitney Malden pausing in the doorway. He moved forward, his hand extended. His wavy dark hair caught the light, and his wide mouth smiled, but his eyes held a cold gleam.

"Welcome back to our part of the world. How is the Convention in Edinburgh? Who will be king?"

"The Convention will decide for William," John said quietly.

"Have you seen King James? What does he say about this?"

John shook his head. "I've not seen him since shortly after William landed. He was like a man in a trance. He could not believe his own daughter and son-in-law would try to take his throne. When Princess Anne joined them, the king burst a blood vessel in his head. He's not been the same since."

"It's such a sad story," Ellen said.

"Enough, Ellen." Pitney frowned at her. "You should not be discussing this."

"It's fascinating." Ellen tried to keep her tone light. "What happens in Edinburgh will change our future."

"You forget that you are a woman, Ellen," Pitney said scornfully. "You should not be discussing politics. You don't know what you're talking about."

The silence was palpable. John's men moved away, many exchanging glances. Ellen pressed her lips together, trying not to say the heated words that had sprung into her mind.

"Ellen knows as much about politics as anyone I know, Pitney," John said evenly. "Few, woman or man, can discuss them as intelligently."

"You are a military man, Dundee," Pitney said. "I expect you to discuss these things. But Ellen should not. It's unseemly. And just one of the reasons she's still unmarried. She is unwomanly."

Ellen felt her mouth drop open and her face flush. She would have said something, but her mother, who Ellen had not realized had joined them, spoke first.

"That's enough, Pitney," Rose said, her tone glacial.

"Ellen is anything but unwomanly. My daughter is perfect." She led Ellen away.

"I don't know what to say, child," Rose said when they were alone on the stairs. "Sometimes Pitney is wonderful; sometimes he is quite dreadful, as he was just now. I am sorry he treated you so."

Ellen forced a smile. "I'm fine, Mother."

"I cannot leave you alone. I won't go to visit Margaret tomorrow."

"Mother! Margaret needs you, and you wanted so much to be with her when she has this child. Go. It's all planned. Both Margaret and Flora will feel slighted if you stay with me. I'll be perfectly fine. Pitney can say what he likes; I choose not to let it affect me."

Rose nodded, but Ellen knew that her mother didn't believe her brave words.

Chapter Two

Ellen stood proudly at her sister's side as Flora married Tom. She loved this beautiful little stone church, with its tall timbered roof and golden oak pews. Flowers and beeswax perfumed the air, tinted blue by the light filtered through the stained glass windows on either side of the chapel. Their parents and grandparents had wed here, and Ellen was pleased that Flora was continuing the tradition. Someday, perhaps, she would as well.

After the wedding, Flora and Tom led the procession back to Netherby Hall, dancing beneath the large trees that lined the path from the chapel, their laughter floating back to Ellen in the sunlight. At the edge of the wide lawns that stretched before her home, Ellen paused to look at the house her great-grandfather had built.

Netherby Hall towered placidly before her, its four stories rising in gray-stoned grandeur to spread its wings on either side of the front steps. The flowers that burst from the urns by the door were the only bright note of color in a landscape still dominated by winter's stark hues. Soon the trees would be alive with new growth. New beginnings, she thought, turning to watch Flora and Tom, linked hands raised high, climb the front steps, then face everyone.

Tom thanked everyone for coming to their wedding, then leaned to claim Flora's mouth in a kiss that caused many to gasp. *I want that too.* Ellen put her hand to her throat, surprised at herself. She wanted what Flora and Tom had, what Margaret and Hugh had found, a passion that transformed those who loved.

And I will not settle for less.

James reined in his horse at the top of the rise. Duncan drew up at his side. The cousins sat for a few moments in silence, surveying the quiet glen below them. There were still no signs of spring here; snow clung to the sides of the rocks.

They'd spent the first night out of Torridon in a crofter's house, sleeping on the floor, the next in a crowded inn. Both days had begun at dawn, both ended at dark, and today would be the same. It would be late by the time they got into Inverness, but they'd have a good meal and a clean bed, which would be welcome. It would be five more days before they'd get to Dunfallandy.

"I can smell the sea," Duncan said with a grin.

"Wishful thinkin'."

Duncan shook his head. "I can smell the sea, Jamie. We're close. And I'll be damned glad to get off this horse. A ship is more comfortable any day."

James saw the weariness in his cousin's face. "Thank ye for coming with me."

Duncan shrugged. "Ye and Neil and I have been guarding each other's backs for a long time."

"And I thank ye for that as well."

"I ken ye do. Besides, I promised yer da I'd look out for the both of ye." Duncan sighed. "Did ye two ever think how grateful I was that ye took me in? Not once did ye throw it up to me that I was a nephew, not a son of yer da's."

"We never felt that way."

"Aye. Exactly my point. I'm trying to tell ye that I ken how much ye're grieving. Even though I loved him, he was my uncle, not my da. And I didna just watch my brother inherit a kingdom."

James shook his head. "I dinna begrudge Neil the title."

"Aye, I ken that. And that, Jamie lad, is another reason why I'm here. We three watch out for each other. So I'm here."

James swallowed hard. "Thank ye."

Duncan straightened his back and lifted the reins. "I'm assuming there are some fine lasses in Inverness. That's why I came, if ye want the truth."

James laughed. "We're still a long way from the sea, Duncan."

"We're close, mark my words. Ye'll buy me a whisky if I'm right."

"Ye're on." James led the way down the hill, looking to the east. Within minutes he saw the glimmer of the water of Beauly Firth in the last of the sunlight. Damn, Duncan was right.

For the first time in weeks, his mood lightened.

John left before dawn the morning after the wedding, Rose left with Flora and Tom in the afternoon. They would all travel together to Glengarry, where Rose would stay with Margaret until the birth of her first grandchild. Flora and Tom would continue their wedding journey, visiting Tom's far-flung family.

Nine days after the farewells, David Grant was making his fourth visit to Netherby, but he had yet to bring news of John. He and Ellen made polite but trivial conversation as they walked across the lawns. The afternoon was cool, but the sun so welcome that she did not mind the breeze. Each day brought more green to the landscape, new growth in the trees, and even the occasional flower.

Ellen watched the shadows of the clouds play across the floor of the valley before them, then stole a glance at David. According to her maid Britta, who'd heard it from the young footman Ned, David was suffering from unrequited love. But David did not act like a man in love; he seemed as bored as she, as though he were waiting for something.

"David," she said at last, "we have known each other for years. We should be able to be honest with each other after all this time. Why are you here?"

His cheeks colored. "I came to visit with you."

"Why?"

He opened his mouth, then closed it.

"David, why are you wooing both Catherine and me?"

"This is not an appropriate topic."

"It is a most appropriate topic. Catherine adores you, and you know it. She deserves your honesty, and so do I. Why are you wooing both of us?"

"Pitney thinks you and I would be a good match."

Ellen stared at him in horror. "I will decide who I marry, David, not Pitney. And what about Catherine?"

David's eyes flickered, and he turned his face away from her, staring across the valley for a moment. "I cannot discuss this with you," he said, spinning on his heel and walking briskly away.

She ran after him. "Why, David? Why can you not discuss this with me? Who is more involved in this than me?"

He did not stop. She stared at his back, thoughts awhirl in her head. Pitney had offered him something—what? She had a sudden vision of Pitney and Catherine bargaining over David and felt ill. David had an heiress on a string already. Why was he wooing her—for gain? Or was her imagination much too strong? No, it was not her imagination. She'd seen something in his eyes she'd never seen before. Calculation. A smugness that unnerved her.

What could Pitney possibly be offering him? Pitney had little money of his own. He controlled all that Rose had brought to their marriage, but that was lands and Netherby Hall itself, not ready coin. And why would Pitney be bribing David? To marry her? Was he that desperate to have her leave Netherby?

She returned to the house with slow steps, groaning silently when she found Pitney in the foyer reading a note. He looked up with a distracted air as she entered, crumpling the note in his hand.

"Ellen, I'll be spending the evening out with friends. Do you want me to send for Mr. Grant to dine with you?"

Ellen shook her head. "No, thank you, Pitney."

"I'm quite sure he would be most pleased to join you."

Ellen put a hand on her stomach. "I feel rather ill. I could not possibly eat."

Pitney nodded. "Fine. I'll tell the staff to stop dinner preparations."

Ellen forced herself to walk slowly up the stairs, her mood much lighter. Heaven, she thought; an evening without Pitney. Missing a meal was a small price to pay.

An hour later the house was quiet. And Ellen was starving. Serves you right, she told herself as she paced her room.

She'd sent Britta off and didn't want to roust the girl, who was no doubt with Ned. She'd have to go down to the kitchen herself and see what she could find.

Ellen opened her door and slipped down the stairs to the second floor. The door to Pitney's study was closed, and she was almost past it when she heard voices inside. She tiptoed past, wondering if Pitney had canceled his dinner plans, then came to a halt as she heard her mother's name.

Two men were on the other side of the door. She glanced around to be sure she was alone in the hallway, then leaned closer to the door to hear more clearly.

"Malden says he hasn't had the chance to discuss it with Rose because of the wedding. He'll talk with her when she returns."

"So this trip was a waste of time."

"Not completely. Did you know that Dundee was here for the wedding? Malden said he thinks Dundee will raise troops for King James."

"We didn't need to ride all the way out here for that. They are saying the same thing in every coffeehouse," said the second voice.

"The Convention has declared him a rebel for refusing to return to Edinburgh. Many of them would like to see him punished. William has men searching for him."

"He's been denounced? Perhaps the bastard will be killed at last."

"Why don't I kill him first?"

Ellen gasped and held her hand over her mouth. Make no sound, she told herself. She glanced behind her at the empty hallway.

"You'd kill him?"

"Yes," said the first voice. "King William would no doubt be pleased, as would many of those at the Convention. James Stuart has no one else trying to put him back on the throne but Dundee, who has now been branded a rebel. Dundee's death would be a gesture of loyalty to William."

"How would you do it? When?"

"There is a meeting of the clans planned at Dunfallandy in three days. It's supposed to be a secret, but many know. Dundee will attend."

"Of course," said the second voice in a considering tone. "King James will want him to sway the clans to his cause."

"All the Highland clans are coming. It will be a large gathering."

"Of Highlanders."

"Exactly," said the first man. "Anything might happen among men like that. Highlanders are notoriously hot-headed. Dundee might say the wrong thing; someone might take offense."

"Do you have men in place?"

"Only one so far. He's from the west. Thinks he's a patriot."

"You could be charged with murder," said the second voice.

"I would do no murder."

"You'd arrange for it."

"You'd pay for it. Dundee is now a threat to the Crown."

"How much would it cost?" asked the second voice.

"More than you've paid me in the last year. Three times, in fact."

There was a long pause, then a brusque laugh. "Yes! Yes, do it. At Dunfallandy. Does Malden know?"

Ellen leaned closer, then spun around as the stairs above her creaked. She jumped to the middle of the hallway as Pitney stepped onto the landing above her. Her stepfather paused when he saw her, his foot dangling for a moment above the step before he took a quick look around the hallway and continued to descend.

"Ellen," he said. "What are you doing?"

"I thought you went out to dine." Her voice sounded unnaturally high. Ellen struggled to calm herself.

"We haven't left yet. I thought you were ill."

"I'm much better now."

Pitney crossed his arms. "So I see. What did you hear?"

"Nothing. Just some voices as I came down the stairs. I was startled because I thought you were out."

"Ellen," Pitney said in a cajoling tone, "if you've heard something that upset you, please tell me."

She shook her head. "I heard voices, but not the words. I . . . I'm delighted to discover we're not being robbed."

"Yes," he said. "So am I."

Ellen forced herself go down the stairs slowly in case Pitney was watching, her heart battering against her ribs. Who were they? She'd recognized neither voice; but the first, the cold one, she'd know again. *Dear God, they mean to kill John.*

She'd have to warn him. Her breath was ragged when she reached the foyer and called for her cloak. The wait seemed forever, but it gave her a chance to make decisions. She'd go to Dunfallandy to warn John. But she'd need help. A woman could not travel alone. She'd need a man to accompany her.

When the footman, unfortunately not Ned, came with her wrap, he eyed her with open curiosity. "Do you need the coach brought around, miss?"

"Yes," she said breathlessly, then reconsidered. The footman might tell Pitney where she went. "No. No, I do not." She forced a smile. "I need a walk."

"It's raining, Miss Ellen. And it's almost dark."

"So it is," Ellen said. "Then I shall walk in the rain." She clutched the cloak. "It's a lovely evening. A lovely rainy evening. A lovely evening for a walk."

The rain stopped while Ellen talked with Evan. As Tom's cousin, he had been the only one she could think of who might help her without an argument. He did not ask many questions, just listened when she told him that she needed to get a message to Tom and that she was afraid Pitney would not let her go. That much, at least, was true. Evan offered to deliver the message to Tom while she stayed home, but she said she must go herself, and outlined how she planned to do that.

Within minutes he agreed. She wrote the letter and left it with him, pushing aside her misgivings at lying to him. He thought they were going to Glengarry. As would Britta, for that was what Ellen would tell her. In an hour, Evan would bring the letter to Netherby. The message, addressed to her, was to seem to be from her mother, telling her that Margaret was having a difficult time, and asking Ellen to come to Glengarry.

It was a flimsy ruse, for Rose had been gone only ten days, barely time to get there and get a message back, but it would have to do. It was the only one she could think of to throw pursuers off her track. She would leave as soon as possible, before Pitney returned from dinner. Before the voices decided to silence her.

It went flawlessly. She was ready before Evan, his manner perfect, arrived, and she pretended to be surprised when the note was brought to her. The staff asked her to wait to leave until morning, but she refused. Britta and Ned watched her with wide eyes when she said Britta would travel with her.

While Britta packed, Ellen wrote to Bea, telling her the truth. Then she summoned Ned, telling him to deliver the letter at once, to give it only to Bea herself, no one else. And he was to tell no one. The boy nodded and left immediately.

Ellen waited in the foyer while her case was brought down and the horses brought round, praying that Pitney and his guests would not arrive yet. The footman who had earlier brought her cloak watched the preparations with narrowed eyes, but said nothing. Ellen tried not to look at him, slipping her hands into her pockets, feeling the pistol she'd taken from her father's chest in one, the charges of gunpowder in the other. She said another prayer for their swift departure.

Ellen and Britta were helped onto their horses, her case was strapped to another horse, and Evan took its reins and his own. And they were off, Evan leading the way down the drive without a word. At the bend, Ellen turned for one more look at Netherby. What will happen before I return? she thought. Will I return? Dear God, be with me on this journey, she prayed. The only thing certain now was that life would never be the same.

Her heart leaped into her throat as a horse thundered down the drive toward them in the dusk. As he came closer, she could see it was Ned, and she let out her breath in relief. Behind her Britta gasped in surprise as the footman, red-faced, threw himself from the horse at Ellen's feet.

"Miss Graham, I must go with you. I love Britta, and I cannot let her take this journey into the Highlands without me to guard her." He held out both hands and waited for her answer while Britta beamed at him.

Ellen smiled at the boy. "We're delighted to have you, Ned," she said, then turned her horse and her thoughts to the west.

They stopped in the wee hours at a small inn to eat and rest, then rose midmorning to start the journey again. She told Evan and Britta and Ned the truth after they'd ridden a mile from the inn. Britta and Ned listened with shocked expressions, exchanging several glances.

Evan thought for a moment, then shrugged. "At least it's not Tom."

Ned swore on his honor, on his departed mother's soul, that he would guard Ellen with his life and help her warn her cousin. Britta looked from Ned to Ellen, then said she would too. Ellen thanked them, trying to pretend she was comforted. And then she picked up her reins.

She rode looking over her shoulder every few minutes, telling herself that she was being absurd, that no one could have followed them already. Perhaps no one would follow them at all. It was even possible that no one had mentioned her departure to Pitney last night, that he'd discovered this morning that she'd gone to Glengarry, that he'd believed her ruse. But she doubted it. He'd known, when they stood together in the hallway, that she'd overheard something that had shaken her badly.

She despised her stepfather, but could Pitney have been so duplicitous as to welcome John at Flora's wedding, slap him on the back, and mere days later, plan his murder? Ellen shook her head; it did not matter now whether he'd known of the plot beforehand. The voices had known.

She had chosen a less-traveled route to Dunfallandy,

skirting the roads one would normally take to the west, but anyone knowing her destination could find them easily, by simply waiting for her at one of the crossroads she'd have to pass.

Would she be in time? John, she thought, do you feel the danger?

Evan had proved to be an unflappable companion, if little company; Britta and Ned had been solicitous and eager to please. And unintentionally amusing. She'd been fond of Britta before the trip and now felt the same for Ned. He truly cared for the girl, and she for him. Ellen watched their camaraderie with quiet enjoyment and not a little envy.

One more day. They should reach Dunfallandy by nightfall. Ellen frowned and looked behind her again. There was no one there. It must be her nerves. She glanced at Evan, who rode ahead of them, then at Britta, who sat glumly astride her horse, her head bobbing as though she dozed. Ned was staring at the landscape around them.

The trip had been without incident. Surely if they were being followed, the pursuers would have appeared by now. Why then was she so uneasy this morning? Why was she looking over her shoulder every ten minutes? She told herself to stop it and enjoy the lovely countryside, the rolling hills that disappeared in the north into the mist, hills that grew taller with every mile they rode west.

It was spring, she reminded herself, despite the cold wind and the snow that had arrived during the night. The snow had melted; the roads were muddy, but still passable. Ellen wrapped her cloak tighter and raised her chin. In just a few hours she would warn John, and all would be well.

She watched a farmer tilling his field, then looked for

flowers along the side of the road, for the buds of new leaves on the trees they passed. She turned to look behind her again. Nothing. She was being ridiculous.

An hour later Ellen turned in the saddle to look behind her again. They were riding through a dense stand of pine trees that hugged the road, undergrowth thick between the trunks. It was cold here in the shade, and she looked forward to the brilliant sunlight that would greet them in another few feet. Then she heard the muffled sound of horses. She looked behind her; the road was empty.

She convinced herself the noises were her imagination, but just when she was thinking of something completely different, she thought she heard it again. The stretch ahead was rocky and flat. On one side of the road the land climbed sharply, dotted with boulders and clumps of small trees. On the other side was a ditch, then an empty field with a stone barrier around it, then another beyond that. The horizons were empty, as were the fields.

She heard it a third time, from behind them, in the pine trees now. Evan, just ahead, was humming. She looked behind her again, past Ned and Britta, who talked quietly to each other as they rode, their voices calm. The road was empty. Ned gave her a smile. Still . . . Ellen moved up alongside Evan.

"I hear something," she said. "Horses."

Evan looked behind them. "I don't see anyone," he said. He stopped his horse and listened. Ned and Britta stopped, too, watching Evan with puzzled expressions.

Ellen could hear the bees along the flowering vines that lined the ditch, and the wind rustling in the pine trees. There was no one visible.

"Perhaps it's your imagination," Evan said.

Ellen was about to agree when she heard it again. Evan

met her gaze with a nod, then turned his horse around and leaned forward to hear better.

There was no need. The clatter of horses was clear now as the men burst from the shadow of the trees. Ellen stared in horror. She had not been wrong. There were four men riding hard, straight toward them, weapons drawn. She screamed and called to Britta and Ned to run.

Evan drew his sword. "Run!" he yelled, slapping Ellen's horse to speed it. "Run!"

The horses did not need a spur. They leapt forward and raced along the road. Britta, the girl's face a mask of terror, leaned low against the animal, clutching its mane. Ned was a pace behind Britta, his head twisted to look at the attackers. Evan, in the rear, shouted for them to keep going.

The men were gaining, almost upon Evan. Ellen felt her throat tighten as their cries of triumph reached her. She drew her father's pistol from her waistband and turned her horse to face the attackers. Ellen lifted the pistol and aimed at the man closest to Evan, and fired. And missed.

She screamed as the man struck Evan a terrible blow across the temple, then again as a second ran him through with a sword. Evan slumped in the saddle, slowly sank to the horse, then to the ground. One attacker leapt from his horse and thrust his sword into Evan's fallen body while the others watched. And then they turned to look at Ellen.

She breathed a prayer as she spun her horse away from them, gasping when she saw how close they were. The world seemed to halt for a moment when she met the gaze of the man in the lead, a blond man with a savage expression. He stared at her with a feral intensity, then waved another man past, gesturing at Ellen. The new man lifted his sword high and spurred his horse toward her.

Britta's screams mixed with the shouts from the man behind her. She could hear his harsh breathing, could smell the sweat of his horse as he drew alongside. His leather-covered arm, holding a long knife, reached for her. He leaned closer, grabbing her cloak, tearing it away from her. And then reached for her again.

Ellen turned her head. She would not watch that blade break her skin, would not look into the eyes of the man who would kill her. She closed her eyes.

An angry roar made her open them in time to see a flash of blue and green charge between her and the arm that reached for her. A large chestnut horse pressed against Ellen's mare, forcing her away from her attacker.

She looked up at the dark-haired man in Highland clothing atop the chestnut, a long blade of glinting steel held high above his head. He roared again, and his arm fell. Ellen watched, fascinated and horrified, as her rescuer slashed at the attacker, forcing him off his horse, then sliding to the ground to dispatch him with a simple plunge of the blade into his chest.

The Highlander pulled his blade free and stared at her for a moment, his chest heaving, his black hair flying around his head. Then he leapt back into the saddle and whirled his horse around.

He was not alone, she saw now, staring openmouthed as a red-haired Highlander hacked at the other pursuers. One fell immediately under the rain of blows, and the others backed away, one of them the blond man.

Ellen gasped as strong fingers curled around her arm. She turned to look into the eyes of her rescuer. Blue eyes, dark brows, drawn together.

"Are ye aright?" he shouted. He gave Ellen one more glance, then turned after the fleeing attackers. He caught one, killing him quickly, but the blond-haired man disappeared into the trees.

Ellen spurred her horse toward Evan. He was dead. She'd known that as he fell, but still she stared at him, waiting for his lifeless eyes to blink, for the hand that lay so still beside him to move. For him to give her his lazy smile and tell her it was all a joke. Dear God, Evan was dead. What had she done?

She sat motionless, fighting her hysteria, while Britta and Ned drew up behind her and the Highlanders joined them. They said something to each other in Gaelic, and both men slid to the ground. The red-haired man leaned over Evan.

"He's dead," he said. He opened Evan's jacket and rifled through it.

Ellen leveled the pistol at him. "Get away, you scavenging pig," she said through clenched teeth. "You'll not rob him now."

The man looked at her in surprise, then slowly straightened, moving to stand next to his companion. They were both big and heavily armed, their chests crossed with baldricks that held their swords, and bandoliers loaded with individual charges of gunpowder. Each had a pistol stuck in his belt and wore the long dagger called a dirk.

No wonder Highlanders were considered savages. These two seemed capable of anything. The dark-haired one slipped his sword into its scabbard as he took a step toward her.

She aimed the pistol at his head. "Stay where you are."

He shook his head. "For God's sake, lass, we just saved yer life. Put the damned pistol down."

The red-haired man moved to his right. Ellen glanced at him, thinking to tell him to stay where she could see him, but the dark-haired man knocked the pistol from her grip and wrapped a strong hand around her wrist.

Ellen screamed and struck him with her fists and feet. He ignored her blows, pulling her easily from the horse and against his body. She felt her feet touch the earth and spun away. He yanked her back against him.

She tried to lurch to the side, but her skirts wrapped around her legs and she fell with a cry. He landed heavily on top of her.

Chapter Three

Ellen lay on her back, her chin tucked down, her cheek in the mud. Her body was pressed against the rocks and wet earth of the road by the heavy man on top of her. The Highlander was very large, his shoulders at her chin, his legs enclosing hers and extending well past her feet.

He had her pinned to the ground. When he took a breath, his chest moved against hers. He watched her with a wary expression. As she tried to take a deep breath, his eyes narrowed, and he lifted himself off her shoulders, shifting his weight to his hips. And hers.

She took a shuddering breath, willing herself not to feel the details of his body, nor the warmth of his breath on her cheek. The gunpowder charges clinked against each other as he leaned back even farther and frowned at her.

"Ye have a strange way of thanking a man who just saved yer life," he said, his voice low. "What are ye thinking, to treat us so?"

Ellen stared at him, then swallowed. He had a straight nose and a wide mouth; his cheeks and jaw were dark with stubble, his very blue eyes surrounded by dark lashes. A very handsome man.

"You were robbing Evan," she said.

"The hell we were," he growled. "We were trying to figure out why ye were attacked. If it wasna robbery, why did they chase ye? Who are ye, lass?"

She raised her head and looked to her right, where Ned and Britta stared, mouths agape. Her father's pistol glinted in the sun, not five inches from her hand. Ellen looked at the Highlander. He followed her gaze and shook his head at her.

"Dinna even consider it." He flicked the pistol out of her reach, then closed his hand around her wrist. "Now, tell me. Who are ye? Why does someone want to kill the lot of ye?"

"Please let me up," she whispered.

"Who are ye?"

Ned flung himself from his horse and scrambled across the mud to snatch up the pistol. He pointed it at the man atop her. "Get off her!" Ned snarled.

The man snorted. "Put it down, laddie, before ye kill yerself or yer mistress by mistake."

"It's you I will kill, sir," Ned said, both his voice and his arm wavering.

"Oh, aye?"

"Yes," Ned said, his voice firmer now.

Britta screamed a warning and slid from her horse, but the red-haired man was faster. He took two strides, grabbed Ned's wrist, twisting the gun from his grasp, then forced him to the ground.

"Ye're safe enough now, Jamie," the red-haired man said mildly.

The dark-haired Highlander rolled off Ellen and leapt to his feet, reaching a hand down to her. She scrambled up on her own and faced him while he watched her, brows drawn together in a scowl. Ellen felt her heart lurch with fear as he took a step toward her; he seemed much larger than he had earlier.

"We are not highwaymen," he said to her, then nodded to the red-haired man. "Let him go, Duncan."

The red-haired man released Ned, who got to his feet, his face scarlet.

"What's yer name, laddie?" asked the giant next to her.

"Ned."

"Ned," the dark-haired man said. "Well done; ye show spirit. But no more heroics, aye? If ye point a gun at me again, Duncan or I will kill ye. Understood?"

Ned nodded slowly. The Highlander turned to Ellen, letting his gaze drift from her face to her neck, then lower, then back to her face. He met her gaze, and she reddened under his scrutiny.

"Why did those men want to kill ye?"

"I . . . I have no idea," she said.

"I think ye do." His voice was low, almost caressing.

Ellen stepped back, flinching as though his words had been harshly spoken. She would have preferred that they were. At his sympathetic tone, she'd almost blurted out the whole story. Don't be a fool, she told herself.

James frowned at her, troubled by the fear he saw in her eyes. Surely she must know he meant her no harm. Did she not realize that he'd just saved her life? Her color was very high, and she turned her face from him, as though she were confused or embarrassed. He studied her again.

Her dark brown hair, loosened from its pinnings, floated down to her shoulders, framing an oval face with even features and arched eyebrows. And beautiful eyes, green, shot with blue and gold, surrounded by thick dark lashes, eyes that now watched him apprehensively.

She was a very lovely woman, and hers was a particularly lovely body, with full breasts, a trim waist, and a line to her hips that made all those layers of silk flare nicely. She pressed her lips together and wrapped her arms around herself.

"I'm sorry about yer husband," he said softly and saw her surprise.

She moved to stand over the body, pressing a hand against her mouth. Her shoulders shook; she was crying again. Duncan swore quietly and plunged his sword into its sheath.

James watched her face. He saw the effort she made to calm herself, wiping her eyes and taking a deep breath, then another. She turned to the maid and the lad.

"Are you two all right?" she asked. They said they were, and she nodded, then turned back to James. "I thank you for helping us, sir," she said stiffly.

"Ye're welcome," James said. "I'm sorry we were no' able to save yer man."

She shook her head. "He was not my man. Not my husband," she said, her voice low.

James looked into her eyes. "No' yer husband?"

"No."

"Ah," he said, as though he understood. "Who was he?"

"His name is Evan Stuart. Was Evan Stuart." The tears ran down her cheeks again, and she wiped them away with an impatient gesture.

"Stuart?"

She nodded. "He was escorting me. I asked him to escort me."

"Why were ye attacked?"

"I . . . I don't know," she said, with the same hesitation she'd had before.

She was lying, he thought. Why? "I think ye do," he said and watched the fear flash in her eyes. "Where are ye going?"

She paused for several moments. "West."

"Really? I did notice that. Where are ye going in the west?"

James crossed his arms over his chest. She did not trust him, that much was obvious. He looked away, to the north, at the mountains disappearing into the gloaming, then back to meet her gaze, keeping his face impassive. Let her decide if he was trustworthy. He'd already proved himself.

"Dunfallandy," she said at last.

"Dunfallandy? Why?"

Her color rose again, two bright spots on her pale cheeks. "Why?"

James raised an eyebrow. "If ye are going to make me ask every question twice, this will be a long conversation." He saw the flicker of anger in her eyes. Good, he thought. Better angry than weeping. He knew how to handle anger. "Why are ye going to Dunfallandy?"

"I . . . I need to talk to someone there."

"Who? Who d'ye need to talk to?"

"My cousin. I need to talk with him. Please, sir, I thank you for your help . . . thank you for saving our lives . . . but we must go."

"Aye. It's getting dark, and we dinna want yer blond friend to come back to finish the job, do we?"

Something else flickered in her eyes, something he couldn't figure out. Determination? He leaned forward and dusted mud from her cheek, watching her eyes grow wide as his fingers moved across her skin.

His touch was surprisingly gentle. Ellen stared at him for a moment, feeling very vulnerable as his hand brushed softly down her face. How easy it would be to lean into that hand, to feel his strength against her for just a moment, to share her task of warning John. She willed her body not to react to his contact.

"Ye had mud on yer cheek," he said, pulling his hand back, his cheeks suddenly suffused with color. "Who are ye, lass?"

"Ellen Graham."

She saw the flash in his eyes as she spoke. He knew the names she'd spoken—Dunfallandy, Graham, Stuart—but then, who would not know them these days?

"Graham," he said. "One of the Claverhouse Grahams?"

Ellen heard the tension in his tone, the slight emphasis on Claverhouse. Be careful, she told herself, not everyone loves John as you do. "I'm from Netherby."

"I dinna ken any Grahams of Netherby."

"Should you?"

He let his gaze slip from her face to her waist, then back. "I canna think of any reason before now to make a note of it."

"And who are you, sir?"

He bowed slightly. "MacCurrie of Torridon." He gestured to the red-haired man. "My cousin Duncan MacKenzie. Also of Torridon."

"Torridon? I don't know it."

"Should you?"

She ignored his echo of her tone and looked at his clothing. "Torridon is in the Highlands?"

"Aye. On the western shore. We're going to Dunfallandy as well."

He turned to the man he'd called Duncan, saying something rapidly in Gaelic. Duncan nodded, and MacCurrie turned back to her.

"We'll take ye there," he said, then gestured to Evan. "And him. And the others as well. Fergusson needs to ken that ye were attacked on his lands."

They rode for almost an hour in silence, Duncan MacKenzie ahead of them, leading the horses loaded with the bodies of the attackers. MacCurrie rode behind her, holding the reins of Evan's horse. Evan's body had been wrapped in a plaid and laid gently over the horse, the others just thrown over their mounts.

Ellen had not had more than a moment to talk with Britta and Ned, but they both seemed to be fine, despite their obvious shock and horror at Evan's death. Evan's death. How could Evan be dead? But he was. And it was her fault.

If she had been wiser, Evan would still be alive. She knew they would be followed; she should have protected them, should have prevented this. She was sure the voices had arranged for this attack, had hired the blond man to kill her. Or was the blond man one of the voices? She'd seen her death in his eyes.

The first voice had said he was going to Dunfallandy. He could be the blond man; his voice fit the cold stare of the attacker. Whoever he was, he'd only been prevented from completing his quest by the grace of God—and MacCurrie of Torridon.

MacCurrie of Torridon. She'd heard the name before, but could remember very little except that the MacCurries were one of the wild clans who ruled the west of Scotland. MacDonalds and MacGannons, MacKenzies and MacLeods. And MacCurries.

Barbarous, her stepfather called the westerners, and he'd not been alone. Many feared the westerners, and if only a tenth of their stories were true, with good reason. But just now the Highland clans were feared most by William of Orange. Any rebellion against him would need those clans to succeed. Which was what the gathering at Dunfallandy was all about.

Who was this MacCurrie of Torridon? He was well dressed, even if dusty from travel, his clothes and weapons of obvious quality. And his arrogance marked him as a man accustomed to being obeyed. No stranger to violence either; his quick reactions and composed demeanor afterward let her know this was not the first time he'd picked up a sword.

From the west. From the west. She rolled the phrase around in her mind, then suddenly remembered the first voice in Pitney's study, talking about the man who had offered to kill John on his own. "From the west," the voice had said. "Thinks he's a patriot."

She looked at MacCurrie again. He was from the west. Did he think he was a patriot? How could she tell? What did a man who would murder another look like? Should the mark of Cain be obvious to her? Or could he look like this man, big and lean and handsome, like a warrior out of the ancient stories?

Surely MacCurrie could not be the man sent by the voices to spy and kill. He'd saved her life, not threatened it, even when she told him her name. He'd killed the attackers; there had been no sign of recognition between the parties of men. And there had been only surprise and concern for her. The Highlander had cared that she lived. No, MacCurrie was not the threat.

The blond man was. He'd meant to kill her, would have watched as his henchman butchered her. She shuddered, feeling her back tighten with the memory of that hand reaching for her, of the cruel knife glinting in the sun. The danger was not over; it had only just begun.

And it was not simply danger to her. Britta's and Ned's lives were at risk as well. She should have come alone. She should have realized that men who discussed murder so callously would not scruple at adding another life to their tally. She'd chosen to risk her own life to warn John, but she should not have asked anyone else to share that risk. She hadn't even told them the truth of where they were going and the danger involved, and now Evan was dead.

Ellen Graham, James thought. Of Netherby. What the hell was she doing, riding across Scotland with one man, a maid, and a boy? Did she have no sense at all? Surely she had to know how dangerous the countryside was, how close to war they might be. A woman who looked as she did should be traveling with a man who could protect her. Obviously Evan Stuart could not.

Why was she going to Dunfallandy? It would be a gathering of men, some very rough. A lass like her, obviously gently raised, had no place among them. To talk to her cousin, she'd said. Or was she going to meet a man? She'd worn no ring, but that meant nothing. Many women left their jewelry at home when they traveled.

She must know how beautiful she was; she'd have had men clamoring to bed her. Was that what she was, someone's mistress, off to spend an illicit day or two while war was being discussed? He frowned. Her manner had been that of an innocent, not a paramour. And now she was crying again.

She said she needed to talk to her cousin. Graham, he thought.

"Are ye related to John Graham of Claverhouse?"

She did not answer. He pulled his horse next to hers and

asked the question again. She looked at him in surprise and wiped her cheek.

"He is my cousin, sir."

"John Graham, Viscount of Dundee, is your cousin?"

She nodded again. "Yes, Dundee is my cousin."

"Why are ye going to Dunfallandy, Miss Graham? Or are ye a mistress?"

She met his gaze without flinching. "Miss."

"Ah. Well, Miss Graham? Why are ye going to Dunfallandy?"

"I've told you, I need to talk to my cousin."

"Ye must be very . . . close. Affectionate, perhaps?"

Her cheeks colored and her eyes narrowed. "John is my cousin," she said coldly. "Nothing more. You're very presumptuous, sir."

"What must ye discuss with Dundee? Or is it someone else ye're meeting? Someone in yer cousin's regiment perhaps?"

She glared at him.

"Well?"

Her mouth drew into a thin line. He'd managed to make her quite angry.

"Is that all you can imagine?" she asked, her tone very controlled, "that I am meeting some man for a lovers' tryst? At a time like this, with William of Orange likely to be declared king and rebellion being discussed? Who has time for love now, Mr. MacCurrie?"

"Many would."

"Not me."

"That's a pity, Ellen Graham."

She opened her mouth, then closed it again. She was truly furious now, he thought. Still better than weeping.

"Is that why you're going to Dunfallandy, MacCurrie?" she asked. "For a lovers' meeting?"

James watched her enraged expression, then laughed loudly enough to make Duncan turn and look at them. "Nay, lassie. I'm off to Dunfallandy to talk about the future of Scotland, as ye verra well ken. And I'm wondering why Dundee's cousin is wandering about the countryside without adequate protection."

"I had two men with me."

"Ye see how well they did."

She kicked her horse into a trot. James let her go in front of him, watching her hips move. Who had time for love? He smiled to himself, then caught sight of the bodies slung across the horses. She was right. He spurred his horse and drew alongside her again.

"I apologize for insulting ye, Ellen Graham," he said.

She ignored him.

"I am sorry. Truly."

At last she nodded. "Thank you."

"Now, lass, why are ye going to Dunfallandy?"

"I need to talk to my cousin."

"Aye, we're all hopin' to do the same. What is it that brings ye out here, risking yer life, Ellen? And why would someone want to kill ye?"

"I don't know why they wanted to kill me."

He looked into her eyes for several moments. "I think ye do."

James let his horse drop back behind her and watched her. Ellen kent much more than she was saying. He shrugged. He'd find out soon enough.

Dunfallandy Castle rose against the sky in a formidable mass, its towers barely distinguishable from the heavily fortified walls in the last of the twilight. There was no grace in its design, but an imposing strength that must have discouraged attackers over the years.

The entrance to the castle was through massive gates, closed and watched from above. Torches lit the drawbridge; more ringed the battlements where armed men silently watched their approach. MacCurrie gestured for Ellen and the others to wait, then rode forward alone to stop before the gates. He looked up at the sentries and squared his shoulders.

"I am MacCurrie of Torridon," he said in ringing tones, "come to attend the meeting. I bring dead men with me, killed on these lands. Get Fergusson."

He waited, motionless, his hands relaxed on his thighs, his hair gleaming darkly in the torchlight, while the battlements buzzed with conversation. Only the stiffness of his back betrayed his tension.

Ellen watched him with wonder. Who was this man who seemed to feel no fear? Her own bravery was deserting her. She glanced at Britta and Ned. The girl's eyes were wide and her mouth tremulous, but her gaze was even when she met Ellen's eyes. Ned was watching the crowd of villagers who had gathered around them. She should have come alone.

Ellen ignored the curious stares thrown her way and watched MacCurrie and Duncan. MacCurrie of Torridon. He said it with such assurance that she knew it meant something more to Fergusson's men than to her. She looked at his back, his wide shoulders and slim waist. A very memorable man, a very handsome man. If she'd met him in other circumstances, she would have been entranced. She looked up in surprise when a voice came booming from the battlements.

"Torridon, ye bastard, what's this about ye bringing me dead men?"

"I'm no' the bastard, Fergusson," MacCurrie called to the grizzled man whose head was now visible in the torchlight. "Whoever is murdering travelers on yer lands is. I thought ye'd want to ken about it."

"Oh, aye, I do, though I'm no' overfond of bad news. Hold a moment, lad, whilst we open the gates."

MacCurrie looked at Ellen, gave Duncan a nod, then turned back to face the castle. When at last the gates swung wide, he led the group into a large courtyard lit by the torches ringing its sides; more lined the wide flight of stairs that led to the castle doors.

The courtyard was full of men, most in Highland clothing, many staring at her and her companions with unabashed interest as they came to a halt at the foot of the stairs. Ellen searched among the crowd for John, but saw only strangers and tried not to hear the comments being made about her.

Ned dismounted and helped Britta down. Duncan slid from his horse. She jumped when a hand touched her thigh and looked down to meet MacCurrie's blue gaze. He held his arms out to her.

"Come, Ellen, let me help ye."

Ellen nodded, putting her hands on his shoulders and feeling his hands circle her waist. He pulled her forward and swung her against his body, letting her slowly slide down the front of him. Before she could protest, her ear was next to his mouth, and he was speaking in a low tone.

"Be careful what ye say, Ellen. Tell only Dundee all of what happened and who ye think the men who attacked ye are. And mind yerself; the men who attacked ye might be here. Fergusson can be trusted with the bare bones, but tell no one the whole of it until ye talk with yer cousin."

She was pressed against him, his hands still tight on her middle, for another second, then abruptly brought to the ground.

"Tell me ye understood, Ellen," he said as he slowly took his hands from her waist, his gaze holding hers. "Tell me ye'll be careful."

"Yes," she whispered. "I understand."

She stood at his side as Fergusson came through the crowd to greet them, his eyes darting from Ellen to MacCurrie and back.

"Torridon!" Fergusson said, clasping MacCurrie's hand. He looked Ellen up and down, then reached past her to shake Duncan's hand. "MacKenzie." He gestured to Evan and the others. "Ye lost some, eh? What happened?"

"I'll tell ye the story over a whisky," MacCurrie said.

Fergusson glanced at the men around them, then back at MacCurrie. "Och, of course, lad. Good idea. We'll have yer unfortunate friends taken care of, eh?"

"Thank ye, sir," MacCurrie said.

Fergusson clapped him on the back. "Come then, won't ye?" he asked and walked away. At the foot of a stairway, Fergusson paused and pointed to Ellen. "I'll have someone get yer woman settled whilst we talk."

MacCurrie shook his head. "She stays with me. All of them stay with me."

"Oh aye?"

"Aye. Has Dundee arrived?"

"No' yet. I expect him any time. Why?"

"I need to talk wi' him."

Fergusson laughed. "Ye and the rest of us, laddie. Ye'll wait yer turn, I expect. Come on in," he said and led the way up to the castle itself.

The hall was large, high ceilinged, and square, a practical space, unadorned and functional. It was noisy, crowded with men standing and lounging at the long tables that filled the room, most dressed in Highland clothing, all armed. At their feet dogs squabbled for the remains of the meal while menservants cleared the tables. There was not a woman in sight.

Fergusson led them through the throng, but many stopped MacCurrie to greet him, calling him Torridon. He must be the Earl of Torridon, she realized. No wonder he was so arrogant; he'd been bred to it. He looked the part, just what she would have imagined a western earl would be like, a mixture of swagger and real physical threat.

Many of those who greeted MacCurrie smiled and waved as though they knew him well; others leaned forward to speak in low tones, or said they were sorry to hear the news. What news? Ellen wondered, as she watched him thank each one, his expression betraying nothing.

He put a hand on the small of her back to guide her through the crowd, but he did not introduce her to anyone, not even when an older man, a tall Highlander with graying blond hair, put a hand up to stop him.

"I'm glad ye came, lad," the older man said quietly. "It's good to see ye." He nodded at Ellen, his gaze taking in the details of her appearance. He smiled at her, then looked past to Duncan. "And ye as well, MacKenzie. I didna ken if ye'd come."

MacCurrie shook the man's hand. "We had to be here, Kilgannon." He gestured to the room. "We all have to be here."

Kilgannon nodded. "Ye're right. Important times, aye? I was sorry to hear about yer father, Neil." He smiled suddenly. "Or is it James I'm talking to?"

Fergusson laughed brusquely. "Kilgannon, do ye think

Neil MacCurrie wouldna be here? I asked each clan to send its chief. Ye're here. Now Torridon is."

"I am here," Kilgannon said. "But if I were Neil, I'd want to be in both places. I'm glad to see the MacCurries represented, lad."

"Thank ye, sir," MacCurrie said, the corners of his mouth quirking as though he fought a smile. He put his hand on Ellen's arm and guided her through the throng in Fergusson's wake, up the spiral stairs at the corner of the hall.

Their host led them to a small room off the first landing, telling Ned and Britta to wait outside with his guards. They looked at Ellen for instructions, and she nodded at them to wait, then let MacCurrie usher her into the room.

It was a surprisingly comfortable room in the spartan fortress, furnished with a large desk and full bookcases. Tapestries lined the walls; heavy draperies encased the large window in the corner. Fergusson poured a whisky for each of the men, then settled himself behind his desk and looked at MacCurrie.

"Now, Torridon," he said, "speak to me."

MacCurrie offered Ellen a chair, then sat in the one next to her. Duncan stood by the door, his arms crossed over his chest.

"What happened?" Fergusson asked. "And where are the rest of yer men?"

"It's only Duncan and me this time," MacCurrie said.

Fergusson's eyes narrowed. "Ye're the chief of a mighty western clan, and the two of ye ride alone? And ye bring yer woman?"

MacCurrie shook his head. "She's no' my woman. We came upon them being attacked on the road from the river."

Fergusson studied Ellen impassively, looking from her

muddy skirts to her face, then turned back to MacCurrie. "She's no' yers?"

MacCurrie's mouth quirked. "No. She's no' mine."

"Ye're very friendly for strangers, laddie. Who is she?"

MacCurrie sipped his whisky, watching Ellen over the glass. "She is Ellen Graham of Netherby."

"Netherby, eh? Where's that?"

"Near Dundee."

"Any relation to Dundee?"

"He is my cousin," Ellen said.

Fergusson winked at MacCurrie. "Dundee's cousin! Right."

Ellen bristled, but tried to keep her tone calm. "I am Dundee's cousin, sir."

Fergusson took a slug of whisky and put the glass down on the desk with a thump, looking at Ellen with new interest. "What brings ye here, Miss Graham?"

"To see my cousin, sir."

Fergusson leaned back against his chair. "Ye rode all this way from Netherby to see Dundee, aye? I'm thinkin' ye could see him at home, lassie. And lookin' at the way Torridon took ye off yer horse, I'm thinkin' ye've come for a different reason. Perhaps ye came to meet Torridon away from home, eh, away from yer da's eyes? A last visit before Torridon marries the MacKenzie lass?"

Ellen's cheeks flushed. Both Fergusson and MacCurrie watched her, and probably Duncan as well. "I did not know Lord Torridon before two hours ago, sir. I am here to see my cousin John."

Fergusson laughed. "Miss Graham, why are ye here? And dinna tell me some concocted tale. I need to ken who is staying under my roof and why. How do I ken ye're no' a threat to Dundee?"

"Ask Dundee who I am," she said.

"I ask ye again, Miss Graham, why are ye here? Ye have ten seconds to tell me the truth before I throw ye out."

Ellen took a deep breath. She would not tell Fergusson why she'd come. In fact, she did not have to speak to him at all. She pushed the vision of the blond man from her mind and rose to her feet.

"That will not be necessary, Lord Fergusson. I'll find my cousin myself." She picked up her skirts and began to move toward the door.

Duncan watched as she approached him, his face impassive, but his eyes dancing. MacCurrie stood, and Fergusson laughed.

"Sit down, Miss Graham," Fergusson said. "Ye'll wait here until Dundee comes, and then we'll have the real story of why ye've come."

Ellen gave him an icy look. "Thank you, sir, but—"

"Sit down, Miss Graham!" Fergusson roared. "I'll no' let ye go out the door. Tell yer woman to sit herself down, Torridon, or I'll see to it that she does." He poured more whisky for himself.

"Ellen," MacCurrie said quietly. "Will ye please stay?"

She shook her head.

He took a step toward her. "I'm asking ye to stay here in safety, Ellen. Let us protect ye until Dundee gets here."

She didn't know just what it was she saw in his face or heard in his tone that convinced her, but at last she nodded and sat down again, feeling both foolish and comforted.

Fergusson grunted. "What am I to do with her, Torridon?"

MacCurrie sat down and sipped his whisky. "Let her talk to Dundee."

"This is no' a place for women, ye ken, leastways a woman like her."

The Highlander shrugged. "I agree. But what was I to do, leave her on the road? Find her a room, Fergusson, a safe room."

"I have no more rooms. There are already three to four in them now."

"Ye have one for me, aye?"

"I do."

"She can stay there and be safe."

Fergusson laughed. "Ye'll be the only man here with a woman in his bed, Torridon. And she'll only be safe if she stays in the room. I have three hundred men here. I canna be responsible for one lass's virtue."

Ellen opened her mouth to reply, but MacCurrie answered before her, his tone untroubled. "I'll take responsibility for her, at least until Dundee arrives. I'm only asking for a safe room in which she can stay for a bit. Surely ye'll no' begrudge the lass a corner of yer castle."

"Enough of them saw her, lad. They'll be sniffing out where she is."

"They'll have to get past me."

Fergusson gave a boom of a laugh, then leaned back, smiling smugly. "I kent it was that way between the two of ye. Good. She's yer responsibility then. Now, how's the west?"

"The west is trying to find out what's really happening. And here?"

"Tense, lad. We'll ken more when Dundee arrives. And before ye ask me again, I dinna ken when that will be. He keeps his travel arrangements quiet these days." He sighed. "I'm sorry to hear about yer da's passin'. He was a fine man. When did he go?"

"A fortnight ago."

"So now ye're the Earl of Torridon, eh?"

"Aye."

"Haven't seen yer brother in a while. How is he?"

"James is well. And yer family?"

"Sent away from here so the likes of ye dinna bother my own sweet lassies." Fergusson gestured at Ellen. "This is no place for a decent lass."

"Who is here already?"

"Kilgannon. Keppoch, MacDonald of Sleat, Lochiel. Seaforth is coming. I'm hearing that ye're marrying a MacKenzie, like yer da."

"It's been discussed."

"Do ye really need more alliances with them?"

"I've signed no contract yet."

Fergusson glanced at Ellen. "I guess ye have yer hands full just now, eh?"

MacCurrie sipped his whisky. A knock sounded on the door, and a young boy stuck his head in. "Sir," he said to Fergusson. "New arrivals."

Neil MacCurrie looked out over the water and told himself James was fine. It was not danger he'd sensed for his brother, but a disquiet, a flicker in the bond between the twins, as though an impediment had stopped the flow of emotion, or caused it to change course. Something had happened, something that had never happened before. He felt no sense of urgency, no need to throw on arms and find James. But something had happened.

He shrugged off the mood and watched the sunset. Winter was waning at last, although the weather had given few signs of that. It was still unusually cold, but the sun was making its journey toward the west, setting each night a bit closer to its summer solstice position. Spring would come eventually.

Neil slid his hand along the stone of the parapet, telling himself that James was safe. He'd know otherwise.

The men's boots slammed against the stone steps, echoing in the small space. Fergusson led a furious pace as he pounded down the stairs. MacCurrie followed a few feet behind, then Ellen. She held her skirts high, trying not to fall. Duncan was behind her, and somewhere behind him were Britta and Ned and Fergusson's four guards.

Her host was annoyed at her refusal to be locked up in a room while the men came down to see who had arrived. She didn't care. Fergusson had made a disgusted sound when she'd refused to go with his men, then strode across the room, throwing his words over his shoulder.

"She's yers to deal with, Torridon. Come or stay as ye choose."

She'd turned to look at MacCurrie then, but the Highlander had said nothing, just nodded at her and followed Fergusson. She'd watched him, wondering if he would abandon her here, but he'd stopped at the doorway and turned, smiling.

The transformation was startling. He was no longer the severe giant whose expression she could not read. The smile had changed him from warrior to charmer. He had a dimple that creased his left cheek. His smile widened and he gestured to the door.

"Come, Ellen. Let's see if Dundee is here," he'd said.

She'd followed him, bemused by this man, so different from how he'd been just a moment before. Neil MacCurrie was certainly intriguing. Or was it James who was intriguing? Obviously the brothers looked so much alike that people confused them. Neil was the Earl of Torridon, and this man had let people assume he was Neil, but Duncan had called him Jamie. Why would he lie about who he was?

She looked at down at MacCurrie, at his wide shoulders that filled the stairwell, and his dark hair catching the light of the torches they passed. He glanced back at her, his blue eyes dark in the dim light. He smiled and faced forward again. Neil or James? Did it matter?

From the west. The phrase hit her like a blow. She'd forgotten the westerner. Could MacCurrie be that man? She didn't want to believe it. But—Was he keeping her close because he feared for her safety? Or because it was the simplest way to get to John?

Evan's broken body was testimony to the cruelty of the men who threatened her cousin's life. Could MacCurrie be one of them? Could he be that duplicitous? She looked at his straight back. Neil or James? Why lie?

At the base of the stairs she followed Fergusson and MacCurrie into the crowd, where the new arrivals, twenty or so Highlanders, were being greeted. John was not with them.

Chapter Four

James nodded at Glengarry across from him. "Aye," James said, "but there's no provision for a peaceful assumption of the throne. We ken how to deal with a violent one, but no' one like this."

Glengarry, the chief of the MacDonnells, was young. Too young, James thought, for the responsibility he had in leading the MacDonnell clan.

"They've chosen William," Glengarry said. "Now they're making it legal."

"What will ye do?" James asked.

"Same as ye. See if I am in good company, then side with King James. But William has an army at the ready. King James has disbanded his."

"He can reassemble it quickly if need be," James said. "He may have already begun to do just that. Why else is Dundee coming?"

He glanced at Ellen. She sat quietly at the end of the table, seemingly staring into space. But he knew better. She was listening to every word he'd spoken to Glengarry, just as she'd listened while Kilgannon had talked with pride about the exploits of his three-year-old grandson Alex, apparently the bonniest lad ever born.

She'd listened, but she'd said nothing, nor had she looked at them. She sat next to her maid and the footman, watching the men move around her in the hall, her face pale and her expression drawn. What was she thinking?

"Is she Dundee's cousin?" asked Glengarry, nodding at Ellen.

James shrugged. "She says she is."

Glengarry slid down the bench toward Ellen, who looked up at his approach, her expression wary. The MacDonnell gave her a smile.

"Miss Graham?" He extended his hand and introduced himself. "I understand ye are from Netherby."

"Yes," Ellen said.

"Ye have a sister—Elizabeth?—who married a MacDonnell of my clan."

Ellen shook her head. "My sister Margaret is married to Hugh MacDonnell."

"And they have two children, aye?"

"No. Are we talking about the same Hugh MacDonnell? My sister and her husband have no children. Had no children. That may have changed by now."

Glengarry gave Ellen a wide smile; apparently she had passed his test. "Of course, what am I thinking? I must be more weary than I thought. Hugh isn't here because the bairn is due any day."

James watched as the young MacDonnell chief talked quietly with Ellen, telling her how charming her sister was, how pleased he was that his kinsman had married so well. She smiled, the lines of worry disappearing from her brow. James crossed his arms and frowned. He'd not seen her smile before.

* * *

"I'm sorry about your father."

James looked at Ellen in surprise. He and Duncan had been watching the hall for the last hour, noting which clan chief was talking with whom, and who watched, as he did. The MacCurries had been away from the Highland gatherings for over a year. It was time to see who had aligned with whom.

Glengarry had talked with Ellen for quite a while, promising to bring home a letter from Ellen to her sister and her mother. After he'd left, she'd sat quietly with Ned and Britta until a moment ago, when she'd slid alongside him, putting a hand on his arm.

"I couldn't help but overhear what everyone said to you," she said. "I'm sorry for your loss."

"Thank ye."

"I lost my father several years ago."

"I'm sorry to hear that."

"I still miss him."

James fought the emotions that her quiet words had summoned. "Aye," he said at last.

"You have a brother?"

"I do."

"Just one?"

He fought his smile. "Aye, just one. And you?"

"No brothers. Two sisters."

"One of whom is married to Glengarry's kinsman."

She nodded, recognizing his admission that he'd been listening.

"And the other?" he asked.

"Married to Tom Stuart, who is one of my cousin John's officers."

"Stuart? Evan's kinsman? And King James's perhaps?"

"They share only the name."

"But a loyal soldier to the king, no doubt, if he's in Dundee's troop."

"Tom and I never discuss politics," she said.

"But you and Dundee do?"

"Yes."

Such beautiful eyes, he thought. Such a beautiful woman. He conjured the image of her discussing politics with Dundee. She'd be very intent, he knew. And Dundee quite voluble. Now that he thought about it, he could see the similarities; she looked like her cousin, her features even and her jaw soft but well defined.

"Are you James or Neil?"

The question caught him off guard, and James gave a loud laugh that turned heads toward them.

"Well? Kilgannon asked if you were Neil or James," she said. "Fergusson said Neil was the Earl of Torridon, and you said you were Torridon. But Duncan called you Jamie when we were on the road."

"Are you no' a surprise, Miss Ellen Graham? When did Duncan call me Jamie?"

"When you . . . when we . . . when you were . . ."

"On top of ye? Ah, yes, I remember lying on top of ye. I don't remember Duncan speakin' to me, but . . . I might ha' been a wee bit absorbed in what I was doing." He turned to his cousin. "Duncan, could ye ha' called me 'Jamie' then?"

Duncan shrugged and yawned. "I could ha'."

James turned back to Ellen. "Ye see, he could ha'."

"Why would you hide who you are?"

"Why indeed?" James studied her for a long while. "A slip of the tongue, lass. Do ye never call someone by another's name by accident?"

"Do you and your brother look so much alike that no one knows which is which? How can that be?"

"We're twins."

Ellen pressed her lips together.

"And since we're asking questions, Ellen, why have ye come here?"

"I've told you—"

"Aye, but why d'ye have to talk to Dundee? Ye see, lassie, I'm wondering just what it is ye're doing. Are ye bringing news for yer cousin from King James?"

Ellen shook her head.

"I didna think so. I'm thinkin' the king has other ways of communicating with yer cousin than through ye, so what else could it be? Something about yer family? Something so important that ye felt ye could not wait for a letter, ye had to deliver the message yerself?"

She looked away.

"Ah," he said. "I got close, aye?"

"No," she said, turning back to him.

"Is there no one else who could ha' come? Could ye no' have sent Evan on his own? Or are ye here perhaps to see yer brother-in-law Tom?"

"Tom is on his wedding journey with my sister."

"A wedding journey at a time like this?"

"No more absurd than a wedding at a time like this."

"Who has time for love now, eh, Ellen?" he said, repeating her words. "So why not send Evan with yer message?"

"I had to come myself."

"But ye're afraid."

She took a deep breath. "Evan is dead, Mr. MacCurrie. And I will not pretend to be unaware that, except for Britta and Ned, I am quite alone here."

"Ye're no' alone, lass," he said quietly. "I'm wi' ye. And Duncan."

"I don't know you, sir."

"D'ye think I would save yer life and then throw ye to the wolves?"

"I would hope not, but I know very little about you, sir."

He felt his body react as she toyed with her necklace, twisting the thin gold braid with a pendant hanging from it. He'd not noticed it before. The Graham badge. Family meant a lot to this lass, obviously.

"I'm not even sure of your name."

"I ha' told ye, lass. MacCurrie of Torridon."

"There are two MacCurries of Torridon."

"Actually, many, if ye're bein' that particular." He leaned over Ellen, so close that she could feel his breath on her brow, could see the shadows his lashes threw on his cheek. His voice was low. "I am Alistair MacCurrie's son, Ellen. Ye have my word on that."

Ellen felt her body respond to his closeness, and her eyes lingered on his lips. What would they feel like on hers? "Both Neil and James are his sons," she whispered. "Which are you?"

He grinned suddenly, his teeth white against the dark stubble. "Both."

Ellen sat back away from him, sudden anger suffusing her. "You are obviously enjoying this, but I don't think joking is appropriate, Mr. MacCurrie. Evan is dead."

"Several men are dead," he said calmly. "What of it?"

"Are you not affected by any of this?"

"By what, lass? Ye rode off across Scotland with a maid, a lad, and one man. And ye were set upon. Ye should have had ten men with ye at least."

"I didn't have time to get ten men."

"Why?"

Ellen stared at him; she'd almost blurted the whole story out. Do not be a fool, she warned herself. Do not trust him; do not trust anyone. She took a deep breath and stood up. Britta and Ned did the same.

"Good night, Mr. MacCurrie."

He rose to stand before her, blocking her way. "Where are ye going, Ellen?" He crossed his arms over his chest, his anger apparent. She glanced around them, seeing the curious stares thrown their way, hearing the sudden silence as conversations paused.

"Please let me pass, Mr. MacCurrie," she whispered.

"Ye have nowhere to go. We have only the one room." Ned took a step forward, but MacCurrie shot him a glance. "Get back, laddie."

"There has to be somewhere else we can go," she said.

"Ye heard Fergusson. There is not another room not spoken for."

"Then we will sleep in the hall."

"Oh, aye, Ellen. Ye, yer maid, and two hundred men. That's a braw idea."

"Have you a better one?"

He smiled slowly, letting his gaze drift down, then back to her face. "Aye."

"I will not sleep with you."

"Have I asked ye?"

"You told Fergusson I could stay in your room."

"I did. But I didna say I'd be there. Fergusson assumed that, lass. And so did ye."

Ellen felt her cheeks redden. "Where will you sleep?"

MacCurrie shrugged. "I dinna ken yet." He stepped to the side and gestured for her to pass him. "We'll find Fergusson and ask."

* * *

Fergusson grumbled, but he found a room for MacCurrie. "Not as good as the first, which you insist upon giving to Miss Graham, but it'll do."

MacCurrie simply nodded and let Fergusson's man lead them to the room that would now be Ellen's. He closed the door behind them all and watched as Ellen considered the room. Britta and Ned looked around with wide eyes. The room was small, but clean, with two chairs drawn before the fireplace. A table stood against the wall, sconces above it. And in the corner was a bed. Ellen gave it a glance, then turned to face MacCurrie and Duncan. They looked large in the cramped space. What would their room be like?

"Imagine what they would ha' given ye if ye were no' an earl," Duncan told MacCurrie.

"It's clean," he said. Duncan then spoke in Gaelic, and MacCurrie nodded.

"You should take this room, Mr. MacCurrie. I'll take the smaller one."

He shook his head. "No. We'll take the other, lass." He looked behind the curtains and under the bed, then turned to her. "We could share it."

"I think not," she said.

"Then we'll take turns guarding ye."

"I'll sleep across the door," Ned said.

"If ye sleep ye'll be of little use," Duncan told him.

"Then I won't sleep."

"This is not necessary. I'll bolt the door," Ellen said.

MacCurrie shook his head. "Ye'll need more. Duncan, ye take the first watch. Ned, get some sleep; ye'll take the second. I'll take the third." MacCurrie strode toward the doorway. "Get some sleep, lass. I'll talk wi' ye in the morning. Ned, dinna sleep on yer watch, aye?"

Ned nodded and closed the door, then faced Ellen and Britta. "I'll sleep here," he said, leaning to pat the floor.

Ellen raised her head. She'd surprised herself and slept for several hours, although her dreams had been full of tumult. She shook off the sleep and listened, tensing when the door creaked open, then relaxing as she heard Duncan's whisper and Ned's answer.

She threw the covers aside and rose, crossing the room to join them. The room was dimly lit by the dying fire. She had slept in her clothes, only removing her outer bodice and side skirts, but still threw on her cloak as she approached the two men. "I'll bolt it," she whispered to them.

Duncan nodded. Ned gathered his blanket and went into the hallway, and she closed the door, throwing the bolt and listening while the latch was tried.

"My cousin will relieve ye," she heard Duncan tell Ned, then the soft click of his boots on the stone. Then silence.

Ellen stirred the fire back to life, then crawled back into bed next to the still slumbering Britta. She wrapped her arms around herself and thought of all that had happened since she'd left Netherby. Where was John? She refused to consider whether the blond man had found her cousin on the road. No one knew his exact movements, she told herself. The blond man could only guess when and by which route John would travel. He could be coming from anywhere, east or west.

From the west. Who was the westerner who would meet the blond man? Was he here already, waiting as she did, as they all did, for her cousin to arrive? The very thought chilled her, and she pulled the covers closer.

Could it be MacCurrie? And did it matter if he were James or Neil? His evasions were unsettling. She'd expected him to mingle with the other chiefs in the hall, but he'd kept himself aloof and simply watched them. And he'd watched her. He'd listened to every word of her conversation with Glengarry. Of course, she'd done the same with his talk with Kilgannon and Glengarry.

She shouldn't trust him, but he and Duncan did seem intent on keeping watch over her. When John gets here, she thought with a yawn, he'll sort it all out.

She woke with a start, sitting up in the bed and staring across the room. The fire was still smoldering but gave out little light. Shadows moved across the space between the stone floor and the stout wooden door, and she heard a sound as though someone were dragging something, then the scrape of boot on stone. She slipped out of the bed. Ned had not worn boots.

Ellen ran for the door, pressing against the bolt just as the latch was tried once, then again. She gasped, pushing the bolt down with all her strength.

"Miss Graham?" The whisper was low. He must be right on the other side of the door. "Miss Graham?"

Ned had never called her Miss Graham. She stared at the light coming under the door, trying to see any more movement, then, slowly releasing her grip on the bolt, bent to the floor and pressed her face to the stone. She could see two dark shapes just outside the door. Feet, no doubt.

As she watched, the shapes moved quickly away. And then the light went out. She huddled on the floor, staring into the darkness. The torch that had been just beside the door had been extinguished. The hallway was in darkness. Where was Ned? There was a scuff of leather on stone.

"I know you can hear me, Miss Graham," came the whisper. Her blood ran cold. It was the voice from Pitney's study.

She was sure of it. "Please let me in, Miss Graham. I'm afraid."

She pressed her hand to her mouth and looked wildly around for a weapon, remembering that Duncan still had her pistol. All that stood between her and the murderer was one door. Where was Ned?

"Miss Graham?"

She closed her eyes and began to pray.

James cursed as he turned the corner from the stairs. The short hallway was in darkness, and he held the torch he carried higher. Ned, wrapped in his blanket, his back to the hallway, was stretched out some five feet from the doorway. The lad was worthless; he'd even let the torch that had been in the sconce near the door go out.

Then James saw that the torch lay on the floor. It had been stabbed out, the end of it thrust into the stones where the wall and floor met. He bent low to examine it. Why would someone have extinguished the light? He looked up at the door, half-expecting to see it pried open, but it seemed intact. He tried the latch, which held, then turned to Ned, flinging the blanket back.

Ned was alive—but only by the grace of God. His thick hair was matted with blood where he'd been struck. He was unconscious, his breathing ragged. James cursed and knocked on the door.

"Ellen," he whispered. "Are ye awake? Ellen?"

She must have been just inside the door, for her reply came immediately. "Who is it?"

"MacCurrie," he said, cursing yet again the subterfuge he'd agreed to. James, he'd almost said. Duncan had already slipped once. Lying did not come easily to either of them.

She opened the door, her eyes wild. She looked from him to Ned. She gasped. "Is he—?"

He shook his head. "No, but not for want of trying. Help me pull him in."

She did so without words, shutting the door quickly behind them and slamming the bolt across. He bent over the lad and gently searched through his hair to find the wound. Ned moaned, moving his head away as though to escape James's touch. James smiled grimly. Moaning meant the lad was alive.

Ellen stoked the fire and lit the candle while Britta stirred in the bed. Ellen came to kneel next to him, looking at Ned with worried eyes. James found the wound and glanced up at Ellen. "Have ye a handkerchief, lass?"

She jumped to her feet and rummaged in her case. "Will he live?"

"Aye, I think so. But he'll have a grand headache."

Ellen handed him a square of cloth, which he pressed against Ned's head. "Did ye hear anything?"

He'd expected her to say that she'd slept through whatever had happened to Ned, but instead she nodded tightly.

"Yes," she whispered. "Someone was here. He wanted me to open the door. He called me Miss Graham, and he said he was afraid. He tried the latch."

Britta stumbled across the room. As she neared them, she threw herself to the floor beside Ned, calling his name.

"Miss Ellen? What's happened? Ned? Ned!"

James rose to his feet and handed Britta the cloth. "He's been hurt. Press this to the wound, but don't move him anymore." He pulled Ellen away from the footman. "Tell me again," he said, clasping her arms. She was shaking so hard that he was afraid she'd crumple to the floor.

He listened quietly, letting a cold rage build inside him

as she told him of huddling on the floor while a murderer tried to trick her. He pulled her against him, wrapping his arms tightly around her.

"I will protect ye, lass," he said. "I swear that he willna hurt ye."

Ellen could hear his heart pounding as he bent his head next to hers, resting his cheek on her hair.

"Ye're safe now, Ellen."

She wasn't sure how long they stayed like that, her head on his chest, his hand stroking her hair. Eventually she stopped shaking and began to realize how closely he held her. He felt so very solid, so safe. So male. She could feel his ribs through his shirt and plaid, could feel each breath he took, could feel his reaction to their embrace.

He shifted his weight, moving his hips from hers. Ellen took a deep breath and pulled away, looking up at him with an embarrassed smile. There were two bright spots on his cheeks; he rubbed his hands on his thighs and took a step back.

"Thank you," she said, brushing her hair from her face. He nodded and followed her gaze as she turned to look at Ned. Britta gave her a tentative smile.

"He's awake," Britta said.

Ellen and MacCurrie bent over the boy, but did not touch him.

"Ned," Ellen said. "How do you feel?"

He looked at her with bleary eyes and frowned. "Like a failure."

"Your hair saved your life."

Ned gave her a weak smile. "My mother said I'd be glad of it one day."

"Were ye awake?" MacCurrie asked. "Did ye see them?"

Ned nodded vigorously; his face clouded and he put a

hand to his head. "There were two of them, sir. One came from each end of the corridor."

"Two of them?" MacCurrie asked, his voice tight. "Did ye recognize them?"

Ned nodded. "The blond man from the attack on the road. And another man, a Highlander, sir. He was dressed like you, but his plaid had more brown in it. And he had a sprig of juniper on his bonnet."

"Juniper?" MacCurrie's tone was sharp. "Are ye sure it was juniper?"

Ned nodded. "Yes."

MacCurrie sat back on his heels and frowned.

"Do you know him?" Ellen asked.

"I might, lass. If he's got juniper in his bonnet, he's a MacLeod. The only MacLeods who dinna wish Dundee well are from Assynt. If I'm right, he's no friend of mine, nor of yer cousin's."

"Why not?"

"The MacCurries and the Assynt MacLeods have been enemies since Neil MacLeod betrayed James Graham, Montrose, back in yer grandfather's time. If the second man is from Assynt, he's no friend to the Grahams. Any Grahams. Nor of mine. We ha' that in common." He leaned back and studied her. "Now we have a MacLeod and the blond man after ye. Why? Ellen, ye need to tell me why ye're here."

She refused to tell him, saying only that she needed to talk with her cousin. He became angry, but stayed with her through the rest of the night, helping to care for Ned, sitting before the fire with her. They spoke only when necessary, but through the long hours, when they sat before the fire together, she was aware of his every movement, of the frequent glances he threw her way.

When he leaned back against the wall and closed his

eyes, she studied him, watching the flickers of firelight play across his cheeks and gleam in his black hair. She looked away, annoyed with herself. She should be feeling gratitude, nothing more.

When the first gray streaks of light appeared, James waited for her outside the door while she and Britta readied themselves for the day, then walked her downstairs, as though they were accustomed to greeting the day together. It had not occurred to her the night before how curious this all was, how trusting she'd been. But now, in the thin light of morning, she knew she'd been a fool.

This man was a stranger, a stranger who had behaved admirably, with a concern and kindness that had comforted her, but still a stranger. He held back from her as much as he gave. And she was doing the same.

MacCurrie left them at a long table, then moved through the hall, greeting the other men, his manner relaxed as he talked and laughed with them. She saw the respect with which he was addressed, and saw men he talked to turn to look at her; she had no doubt she was being discussed. And then MacCurrie disappeared behind a group of men.

Ellen sat with Britta and a very pale Ned, watching the chiefs joking and laughing. They were cheerful, but the Highlanders were obviously growing restless. Duncan sat with her, had been her shadow all morning. She did not ask him, but was sure his cousin had asked him to stay close to her.

"Ellen?"

She turned to find MacCurrie standing over her, his eyes unwavering as he watched her. He had shaved, revealing lean cheeks and a well-defined jawline. His hair was combed and drawn back neatly behind his neck. He smelled like soap. His lips, previously hidden under stubble, were beautifully drawn, wide and full, sensuous but very masculine.

How could the man look so beautiful? she wondered as she took in his clean white shirt, his blue jacket, slashed to show the white silk lining underneath, the large jeweled brooch that held the plaid to it. His kilt was blue and green, the same blue as his jacket. He looked like a man of wealth and power. He was armed, as were most of the Highlanders, even here in the hall, a pistol in his belt and his sword at his waist. His eyes showed that his anger was not gone but banked.

"Yer cousin has no' arrived yet?" His tone was polite, nothing more.

"Not yet."

"I'll wait with ye," he said.

He sat next to her, leaning back against the table. He put a hand on his knee, and she looked at it rather than into that cool gaze again. His fingers were long and tapered; he wore one ring. A signet ring, the kind worn by many of the Highland chiefs.

She felt a sudden wave of doubt. Had she been wrong? Was he Neil after all? He certainly looked the part. But then the brothers were twins; James would look the same. He looked around the room, his expression calm. Say something, she told herself.

"Mr. MacCurrie, who are all these men?"

James told himself he should be insulted that she wouldn't trust him. And he was. How many times must he prove himself? But it was difficult to hold on to his wrath. She was pale, her lovely face showing her tension; her cheekbones stood in stark relief against her hair. She was afraid. She's naught but a defenseless lass in this gathering of men, he thought, and felt something in him relax. He might be just as wary if he were she.

He gestured to the hall full of Highlanders. "Ye're looking at some of the most powerful men in Scotland, lass. See the tall man watching us by the fireplace? That's Alexander MacGannon, the Earl of Kilgannon. The man on his left is the MacKenzie chief, the Earl of Seaforth."

"The one who wants Neil to marry his kinswoman."

"The same. The man on the other side of Seaforth is Lochiel, head of the Camerons. They want yer cousin to ken their thoughts before the general meeting begins. They all want to ken what King James will do."

"What are their views on William of Orange?"

"Aye, and isn't that the heart of the matter?"

"What do you think?"

"Of William of Orange coming to claim King James's throne when he doesna have a legal nor moral right to claim it? No' much."

"And what do the others think?"

"Most likely the same."

"So they—and you—will back King James?"

"No' necessarily. It depends."

"On?"

He assumed Dundee's cousin would share Dundee's politics. And if not? Was she here to bring the tale of which clan chiefs supported King James back to William's camp? He shrugged; no matter. William would have his own men here to report to him. In two days everything said here would be discussed in Edinburgh.

"It depends," he said, "on whether most of the other clans will do the same. On what France does. On what Dundee does. We've none of us any wild desire to lose our lives or lands."

"But surely that wouldn't happen."

"It could. If we lost, it would."

"Do you think King James can rally enough support to fend off William?"

"Lass, that's why we're all here, to find out just that."

"What will you say?"

"I'll listen at first, then decide. Before I commit the MacCurries to war, I need to ken we'll be in good company."

"Ellen!" The voice came from across the room.

She turned to see David Grant stalking toward her. She rose to greet him.

"Ellen!" David said as he came to stand before her. "Thank God I found you!"

At her side MacCurrie stood and watched with narrowed eyes. "What are you doing here?" she cried. "Is something wrong at home?"

"No. Bea sent me. She said you'd come to warn Dundee of a murder plot. Where is he?" He gave MacCurrie a sharp glance. "And why are you in the middle of all this rabble?"

"Ellen," MacCurrie said, his voice cold. He moved his hand to the hilt of his sword. "Do ye ken this man?"

"Of course she does," David said. "She's going to marry me. And who, sir, are you? Where's Dundee?"

"He's not here yet," Ellen said. "David, I am not marrying you."

"We'll talk about it privately," David said. "Aunt Bea changed everything. I'll tell you about it when we're alone."

MacCurrie stepped to the side. "I'll leave ye then."

"No, please stay," Ellen said, putting her hand on his arm. She met his gaze, saw the anger there, then withdrew her hand. "Lord Torridon, this is David Grant of Dundee. David, Neil MacCurrie, the Earl of Torridon."

David inclined his head. "Torridon."

MacCurrie nodded, but said nothing.

David leaned over her. "What the devil is going on? Why are you here with him?"

"We were attacked on the road; Lord Torridon rescued us."

"You were attacked on the road?"

She nodded. "Yes. Evan was killed."

David's face flushed. "Why did you come here alone? What were you thinking? Why did you not tell me?"

"There wasn't time."

"But it's true that you came to warn Dundee of a murder plot?"

Ellen looked from David's angry face to MacCurrie's cold eyes. Both men waited for her answer.

"I—" she began, but turned as Britta stood up and moved next to her.

"Miss Ellen, look! Your cousin John has arrived."

Chapter Five

John was pacing the length of the hearth, Fergusson watching from his chair behind the desk, when Ellen was shown into the study, followed by David and the Highlanders.

"Ellen!" John cried, opening his arms. "Fergusson's just been telling me you were attacked on your journey. Are you all right?"

Ellen ran into his arms and kissed his cheek. "Oh, John, thank God you're here! Are you well?"

He tightened his embrace. "I'm well, but I cannot believe you—" He paused to turn to MacCurrie, keeping his arm around Ellen.

MacCurrie gave John a wide smile and extended his hand. "Dundee. It's been a long time. Ye were Claverhouse the last time we met."

John took his hand and smiled in return. "Torridon. Yes, it's been a while. I'm sorry to hear about your father; he was a good man."

"Aye, he was, thank you."

"Thank you for saving my cousin's life. MacKenzie, you as well."

Duncan took John's hand. "I'm glad we were there, sir."

"As am I. If you had not been, this would have been a sad day for my family," John said as he released Ellen. "I cannot imagine life without this cousin of mine. Grant, good to see you again. What brings you here?"

David shook John's hand. "Miss Bea sent me to find Ellen, sir."

"And how is Aunt Bea?"

"Worried about both of you. Who is trying to kill you?"

John laughed ruefully. "Who is not, these days?" His expression sobered. "I saw Evan's body downstairs. Do you know who attacked you?" he asked Ellen.

She shook her head. She'd kept her silence this long; she'd tell him everything when they were alone, not before.

"Tell me what happened," John said, settling into a chair.

Ellen gave an abbreviated account of the attack and rescue; then MacCurrie and Duncan told their version. MacCurrie's manner was calm, but his eyes flashed when he described the man reaching for Ellen with a knife. He then told of the attack on Ned, which made Fergusson lean forward and ask pointed questions. Their host was obviously displeased at MacCurrie's story.

When they had finished, John steepled his hands. "Torridon, MacKenzie, I owe you an even greater debt than I realized. I am grateful, sirs."

MacCurrie nodded. Duncan smiled.

"Fergusson," John continued, "I thank you for protecting my cousin."

"It was Torridon, not me," Fergusson said. "He's been caring for her. Spent the night with her."

Ellen began to protest, but was interrupted by MacCurrie.

"After the lad was hurt," the Highlander said, "I stayed

to help care for him. There were four of us, sir, and nothing improper about it."

"I saw ye take her off her horse, lad," Fergusson said. "And I see the looks the two of ye give each other. Ye dinna act like strangers."

MacCurrie shrugged. "Ye have quite an imagination, sir."

Fergusson snorted. "Aye, must have." He rose to his feet. "A toast, gentlemen," he said, pouring a glass of whisky for each man. "Torridon. MacKenzie. Grant. Miss Graham, will ye join us?"

"No, thank you, sir," Ellen said.

Fergusson raised his glass high. "To a successful gathering." The men repeated his words. Fergusson glanced at Ellen. "And to cheating death."

Ellen felt a chill run down her back.

"To cheating death," John repeated, followed by the others.

Ellen met MacCurrie's eyes as he lowered his glass.

"To cheating death," MacCurrie said again softly, saluting her with his glass.

After another few minutes, John and Ellen were left alone in the study. He walked back from closing the door behind their host and stood looking out the window, then moved to bend over her, taking her hands in his.

"Ellen, what happened? Why are you here?"

"Oh, John," she said, suddenly close to tears. "There is a plot to kill you! I was at Netherby—"

By the time she had finished her story, John was sitting opposite her, his chin on his hand. He had listened without interruption, watching her with an untroubled expression.

"It is not the first time someone has wished me dead," he said in a calm voice. "Nor will it be the last, I imagine."

"John! You are in danger every moment you are at Dunfallandy!"

"I have been in danger for years, my dear. And I'm sure I won't be surprised when we discover who these latest plotters are. I have a fair idea myself."

"You must leave at once! Tonight!"

"I cannot leave, Ellen. I came to talk with the Highland clans, and I intend to do just that."

"They can talk without you. Someone can tell you what they decide. You do not have to be here. John, there are at least two men here who are trying to kill you! They've already killed Evan and tried to kill Ned."

"And they tried to kill you, Ellen. Don't think I'm not mindful of that. I am very aware of the danger. And I'm very angry that you have been exposed to it. But I need to be here with these men. I need to hear who says what and how he says it. I cannot leave now."

Ellen stared at him in disbelief. "You are putting yourself in danger!"

John patted her hand. "I'm not a fool, Ellen. I am guarded at all times—as you will be now. I know I am in danger; I've known since the moment I left the Convention that I was a marked man. There is a price on my head, my dear, did you know that? You could be rewarded by telling where I am."

He laughed softly. "Dunfallandy is as safe as anywhere, probably safer. Most of the Highlanders are loyal to King James, not to William of Orange. I need to be here, talking with them, deciding what we will do. Ellen, my dear, these men are watching me. If I run away because someone wants me dead, do you think they will follow me to war? Would you? Why would anyone follow a man who is afraid to do what he asks of you? If I run now, then everything I've worked for will be undone. I will have no credibility."

John leaned back and studied her. "Ellen, it is I who should be upset that you came here on your own! Now you are in as much danger as I. But for Torridon and MacKenzie, you would have been killed and none of us would ever have known what happened to you."

"I wrote to Bea before I left."

"How could you have simply ridden off in the night, Ellen?"

"How could I not? Who could I trust to bring you the message?"

"Evan."

"I could not ask him to risk his life while I stayed home in safety."

John shook his head ruefully. "You use my own arguments against me."

"Yes. But tell me, in my place, would you have let someone take the risk that was properly yours?"

"Ellen, I am a soldier. I am a man."

"And I am a woman. My gender makes no difference. I had to be certain you got the message; the responsibility was mine. And once they realized that I had overheard them, I was in danger at home. I would have been foolish to stay in that house. I don't know whether Pitney is involved, but even if he weren't, would he protect me? Could he, even if he chose to?"

John's expression grew grim. "That's true." He met her gaze. "You cannot return home until we discover who the murderers are and whether Pitney is part of the plot. I'll send men to start the process." He shook his head. "You were very brave, Ellen. Foolish, but brave. It's the Graham blood."

"Which gives us the foolishness or the bravery, John? Or both?" She smiled with him, then sobered. "I had no choice. If I had come alone, Evan would still be alive."

"And you might not be. You are not responsible for Evan's death, Ellen. Others are. Thank God for Torridon and MacKenzie." He studied her for a moment. "What is this between you and Torridon? How well are you . . . acquainted?"

Ellen lifted her chin. "I met him when he and Duncan rescued us."

"And since?"

"I've spoken with him, that's all. He stayed with us last night to be sure Ned had survived. Fergusson reads too much into very little."

"Then why are your cheeks so flushed?"

"He's been very kind." She pushed the memory of his embrace away. "John, I hardly know the man. In fact, I'm not even sure who he is, if he's Neil or James. Duncan called him James, but he's letting everyone assume he's Neil."

"Neil is Torridon, Ellen, and only the chiefs were invited."

"Doesn't it bother you that he may be lying?"

John shrugged. "It really doesn't make a difference which brother is here. If he's James, he surely has Neil's agreement to be here; they are very close. And for my purposes, it doesn't matter. I've known the MacCurries for years; Tom went to school with them. Both are loyal. Distrust is a two-edged sword, Ellen. One must be careful, true, but one can also lose a good ally by not trusting."

"Perhaps, but one is alive to regret it."

He leaned to kiss her forehead. "Don't worry about the MacCurries, my dear. Does it matter which brother he is?"

Ellen paused, considering. "No," she said, realizing with a start that it didn't matter. All she'd wanted was the truth. "But I think he's James."

John laughed. "I'll find out. In the meantime, I need you to listen and watch while you're here, and tell me what you learn. Perhaps you will find the men you overheard." He rose to his feet. "Ellen, I'm going to have you guarded every moment, but I need you to promise me you'll be very careful."

"I promise."

"Good. Now I must get downstairs. Everyone has waited long enough."

Ellen nodded, unhappy but resigned.

James saw Dundee and Ellen enter the hall, surrounded by Dundee's men. Good, he told himself. Dundee was here; she was no longer his concern. He should feel relieved. Why, then, did he feel a sense of loss? He watched as Dundee was welcomed by the other Highlanders, noting who greeted him with a smile and who was wary.

Dundee would find much support here; he'd already learned that much in the few conversations he'd had with the other leaders. But not all would back him and King James. There were those who were here only so they could report to William what they'd learned. There were also at least two men who wanted more from the gathering.

After last night's attack on Ned, he'd be looking for a MacLeod. But which? Many MacLeod families still lived on the lands that bordered Torridon. A handful of those had never recognized the MacCurries' ownership of certain properties.

There had been many violent incidents between the MacCurries and those MacLeods over the decades. His father had been ambushed by some MacLeods years ago, and had killed one of them as he defended himself. The death had never been forgotten, nor avenged, though vengeance had been threatened many times. Could one of those MacLeods be here among them now? But Ellen Graham was no longer his concern; he didn't need to solve this one.

Dundee settled at a table near the end of the hall and was immediately surrounded by Highlanders. Ellen, sitting a few feet away, was looking around the room. She didn't see him. James watched for a moment, then he thought of something to say to Dundee.

Ellen watched as MacCurrie approached the table. The Highlander nodded at her but stopped before John, bending low to talk earnestly with him. John listened, his expression serious. Both men turned to look at her, and MacCurrie said something that made John smile. What was he saying?

"I need to explain."

She turned to see David standing over her. MacCurrie watched as David settled next to her on the bench. "Yes, David, you do. Whatever possessed you to say we were marrying?"

"Your Aunt Bea asked me to find you and bring you home."

Ellen spread her hands. "What does that have to do with your telling MacCurrie we were marrying?"

"I watched you, Ellen. He takes too many liberties."

"He has taken no liberties."

"He calls you Ellen."

"So do you."

"I've known you for years. He has no right to speak to you that way."

"If I objected, I would have said so."

"You spent the night with him."

"We spent the night caring for a boy who had been struck on the head. David, answer the question. Why did you say we were marrying?"

"Your aunt wants us to marry. Your stepfather wants us to marry."

"You have talked to Pitney?"

David nodded. "He wants you safely home."

I'm sure he does, Ellen thought as she stared at David, fighting her rising temper. He might be right. Bea had certainly been his advocate the last time they'd talked, and Pitney had made no secret of his approval of a suit from David. But she and David had never discussed marriage. It was absurd. And fiscally improbable; between them, she and David had nothing with which to make a life, even if she wanted to.

"It makes no difference whether Aunt Bea and Pitney want us to marry."

His face flushed. "I would be pleased to marry you, Ellen."

Pleased, she thought. Not exactly a vow of eternal devotion. Unrequited love, Ned had said. "What about Catherine?"

"What about her?"

"She thinks you love her; you've told her you love her. She thinks you are going to marry her."

He looked at his hands.

"David? Did you let Catherine think the two of you were marrying?"

"She might have thought that."

"Because you led her to believe it."

He looked into her eyes, his voice pleading. "Everything's changed now. Trust me, everything has changed. We can marry now."

"David, I don't understand."

"You don't need to, Ellen. Just know we can now marry."

"David—" She tried to keep her tone courteous. "I cannot marry you."

"You can. And you will."

Ellen stared at him, trying to collect her thoughts. David was obviously not telling her all of it. She would ask him again, but first she needed to control her temper. What had changed? What had Pitney promised him? Money, it seemed, enough to enable David to marry her and spurn Catherine.

Or was it Bea? Her great-aunt was very wealthy. Perhaps she'd given some of this wealth to David. But no, that would not be like her. Bea must have promised money to them, or to her, if she and David married. The more she considered it, the more likely it seemed that Bea had done just that.

"Did Bea promise you money to marry me?"

David looked away, and Ellen felt her temper rise again. Bea *had* made promises; perhaps Pitney as well, and David had accepted their offers. She rubbed her arms, feeling suddenly unclean. And humbled. Apparently no one believed Ellen Graham capable of marrying without money being exchanged. There had been no mention of love, no pretense of affection. Why else then did he want to marry her?

Fergusson stepped to the dais and called the meeting to order. He welcomed everyone, saying that he was sure they knew, as he did, how fateful these next days were for Scotland. He asked John to come forward. John smiled at her as he passed, then gestured to the men he'd left to guard her.

She put David out of her mind as John was greeted by resounding cheers from the Highlanders. He raised his arms and thanked them, then told them he was grateful for their attendance.

"As is your king," John said. "He thanks you for all your past loyalty. And asks for your help now."

"Are ye here to raise an army, Dundee?" called a Highlander.

John nodded. "Give me enough men, and we will take the throne of Scotland back." He smiled as the chiefs shouted their approval.

"How many do ye need?" called the first man.

"How many do you have?" John waited until the laughter subsided. "First I have another, a more personal request of you. My cousin Ellen Graham was attacked on her way here to warn me of a murder plot against me. But for Lord Torridon and Duncan MacKenzie, she would be dead."

A current of murmurs went through the gathering.

"We are looking for a blond man," John continued, "about six feet tall, wearing Lowland clothing. And for a Highlander who helped him attack my cousin's footman in the night. He wore a sprig of juniper on his bonnet."

"A MacLeod?" asked Glengarry.

John shrugged. "Or someone masquerading as one. If anyone knows who either man is, please bring him to me alive. I will take care of him as he deserves."

"He's in William's pay, no doubt," came a voice from the back of the room.

"We'll find out," John said grimly. "I ask for your help in finding the men who would have killed my cousin. And in raising an army to fight William of Orange."

"Will ye lead the army yerself?" It was MacCurrie's

voice, and Ellen craned to see him. He sat near the front with Duncan, Alexander MacGannon on his left.

John nodded. "It would be my honor to lead the Highland clans for the king."

"Who will lead our men?" asked Kilgannon.

"Each chief will lead his own men. And I request each chief to sit on the war council. We must be in accord."

There was another round of applause, then more questions as the Highlanders pressed for details of how the army would be organized and what the plan would be. After an hour of discussion most of the chiefs were nodding their agreement, and John, who had appeared relaxed and confident throughout, was smiling. Ellen couldn't be more pleased. Or prouder of her cousin.

"Gentlemen," John said. "I have come to ask for your assistance for the most noble of causes, for king and country. Our nation has been shamed by this usurpation of the throne. Help me to win it back for our king, for our country. For ourselves. I ask that you risk your lives and your futures. I will do no less. I am about to become a father; I would like my child to be raised in a Scotland that is ruled by men of conscience, not men of will. Who among you is with me?"

MacCurrie rose to his feet. He had shed his jacket; his white shirt stood in sharp contrast to the gray stones behind him as he raised his sword high above his head. The blade caught the light from the window above him and glowed above him. Ellen caught her breath. His voice rang out across the gathering.

"The MacCurries are with ye, Dundee."

"And the MacGannons," said Kilgannon, raising his sword as well.

"For Scotland," MacCurrie said. "And King James!"

The Highlanders leapt to their feet, roaring their approval.

The rest of the day was spent in endless discussions. Ellen sat with Britta and John's guards for most of it, then asked if she could walk in the gardens. The guards were not pleased, but received John's permission, waiting while Britta brought her cloak, then followed Ellen silently to Dunfallandy's walled garden. Britta, who had forgotten her own cloak, shivered, and Ellen told her to wait inside. The girl gave her a grateful smile.

It was sunny outside, but the air, trapped in the enclosure, was numbingly cold and the gardens almost empty. There were two men working in a far corner, planting despite the frost that still lay in shady corners. A few hardy evergreens were the only color within the stone walls.

Ellen walked slowly on the path, listening to the crunch of her shoes on the gravel, followed a heartbeat later by that of the guards' boots. She walked twice around the perimeter, then across the middle before she surrendered to the chilled air. Wrapping her cloak tighter around her, she made her way back to the stairs that led inside.

MacCurrie stood at the top, watching her with his usual intensity.

"Lord Torridon," Ellen said, aware of the guards who had stopped behind her.

"Ellen."

She walked up two steps, then stopped. His eyes were a glacial blue, his jaw set. He's still angry, she thought. The wind pulled at her cloak, swirling icy air around her ankles. She climbed another three steps.

"Why did ye no' tell me about the plot against yer cousin?"

"I—" She glanced at the guards. "Come inside, please. We can talk out of the wind." She climbed the last steps, then past him. He followed her into the small square room that served as the side foyer.

"Wait in the hall," he ordered the guards.

"We cannot do that, sir," said one.

MacCurrie glared at him. "Ye'll do it. Ask Dundee for permission, if ye must. Go."

"We cannot leave Miss Graham alone, sir."

"She's no' alone, man! She's wi' me. I'll keep her safe. Now go."

"I'm fine," Ellen told the guards. "Please wait for me in the hall."

The guard nodded, clearly unhappy. MacCurrie waited until they were gone, then crossed his arms over his chest. "Why did ye no' tell me, Ellen? Did ye think I was part of it?"

"They talked about a westerner."

"Am I the only man here from the west?"

"No, of course not. But I didn't think I should trust anyone."

"No' even someone who saved yer life? No' even someone who missed a night's sleep to guard ye? No' even when I asked ye? I dinna understand."

Ellen raised her chin. "I wanted to, but there was more at stake than my desires, sir." My desires, she thought. Wonderful choice of words.

"So ye desired to trust me, but thought better of it?"

She flinched at his sneering tone, but met his gaze. "Yes," she said quietly. "That's exactly it."

He was silent then, watching her with an unreadable expression.

"Mr. MacCurrie, John is more than simply my cousin,

and there is more at risk than just his life or mine. He is one of King James's most trusted advisers. The future of a kingdom is riding on his success or failure. How could I trust anyone?"

He raised his gaze to the ceiling, then back to her as he considered. "Ellen," he said at last. "Ye're right. I'm sorry." He caught her hand and brought it to his lips, kissing her palm, then releasing her.

She felt her body tremble, her skin tingle where he had touched her. "I . . . I was afraid I wouldn't be in time."

"So now Dundee's been warned. What will ye do, Ellen? Will ye go home?"

She paused before answering. "I cannot."

"Why?"

"The plot to kill John . . . I overheard it at Netherby. In my stepfather's study."

"So he kens of it."

"I don't know. He wasn't in the room. But I will not go home while that man is there. He may not be part of the plot, but he had those men in mother's house and he knows I overheard them. I disliked him before; now I despise him."

"So where will ye go?"

"I don't know. I'll have to talk to John."

"He'll be leavin' soon, lass. We'll all be leavin' soon."

"Yes."

"Are ye marrying Grant?"

"No."

"He says ye are."

"Yes, but I'm not."

"Then why does he say this?"

She shook her head. "I don't know. Truly, I don't."

"That makes no sense."

She sighed. "Mr. MacCurrie, there is much in my life

right now that makes no sense. I don't even know to whom I am speaking. Are you Neil or James?"

James smiled down at her. Tenacious lass, wasn't she? He should tell her nothing. But he couldn't ignore her question. He looked into her eyes.

"Ye are speaking to Torridon, lass. Neil became laird just a fortnight ago, ye see. It's important that he appear to be a strong leader. There are those who would test him; if they find him lacking they'll move in and take the lands that have belonged to MacCurries for generations. So he must stay at Torridon and be ready for the challenge."

"You really think his leadership will be challenged?"

"Oh, aye, it will be. But he also must be here at Dunfallandy, to represent the clan and be part of the decisions. And only the clan chief may make the final decision to join Dundee or no'. So Neil must be here as well."

"Which one are you?"

"I am here, lass. Does that no' tell ye I'm Torridon?"

"No. It tells me one of the brothers is here. I think you're James."

"Do ye?"

Ellen nodded. "Duncan called you Jamie."

"That's what ye said."

Her eyes flashed. "Trust, Mr. MacCurrie, should be extended both ways. To whom am I speaking? Neil or James?"

James, he answered silently. I'd like ye to ken it is James ye speak to. But he could not say that. He could not risk someone finding out Torridon had not attended the meeting.

There was another reason, and he faced it now. Neil was chief of the clan, the Earl of Torridon. James was not without resources, but Ellen had her choice of men. For the first time in his life he felt the sting of being the younger brother. He did not begrudge Neil his inheritance; but to go from an equal to a vassal was a transition he'd not yet made. It would take some time.

He looked into Ellen Graham's eyes. How he hated this game.

"Ye're speaking to Torridon, lass."

"Am I?"

He could see the disappointment in her eyes. He almost told her then but was stopped by the rapid footsteps that approached them. Ned came flying around the corner.

"Miss Ellen, Lord Torridon! I saw him—the blond man! He's in the minstrel gallery now! Hurry!" He ducked back through the doorway.

James grabbed Ellen's hand, pulling her after him as he followed the boy. They entered the hall, skirting the room, ignoring the curious glances thrown their way. At the end of the hall was a small loggia, the stairs to the minstrel's gallery leading steeply up from it. He paused at the foot of the stairs, dropped Ellen's hand, and drew his sword.

"Stay here," he told her and Ned and started up the stairs.

"Be careful," she whispered.

He looked over his shoulder. "Aye," he said, then continued to climb.

Ellen stepped into the stairwell, watching him take three steps at a time until he disappeared around the curve of the staircase.

She waited then, leaning forward and closing her eyes, listening as hard as she could. She could hear his boots against the stone, could hear him pause at the top of the stairs, then take a step onto the wooden floor. Laughter from the hall, where John still held court, drowned any other footfalls. She straightened, twisting her hands together.

A moment later someone was rushing down the stairs. Ellen backed away to stand with Ned. If it was the blond man, they'd have no defense, she thought. She looked around for a weapon as MacCurrie burst out of the stairway.

"He's gone," he said.

"But I saw him, sir," Ned cried.

MacCurrie held his hand up to stop the boy's protests. "Dinna fret, laddie. Someone was up there. There are footprints in the dust."

Ned took a breath, giving Ellen a satisfied look.

"What is going on?" Duncan stood in the doorway to the hall, his hand on his sword hilt.

"The lad saw our blond man in the gallery, but he was gone when I got there," MacCurrie said. Duncan said something in Gaelic, and MacCurrie answered him in the same language as he sheathed his sword. He turned to Ned. "Keep watching, laddie. He kens who ye are now, so guard yer back as well as Miss Graham's."

Ned's eyes grew wide.

"Dundee wants ye back in the hall, Ellen," Duncan said. "He's no' happy ye sent yer guards away."

"I'll go and talk to him," Ellen said.

Duncan nodded and turned back into the hall, Ned at his heels. As Ellen moved past him, MacCurrie gripped her arm and turned her to face him.

"Ellen," he said, his voice low. "Ye are in danger. I trust ye ken that, lassie. Tell me ye will be careful."

She looked into his eyes. "I will be careful."

Chapter Six

Neil MacCurrie slammed his sword back into its scabbard. They were too late. The crofthouse was a smoldering ruin now; the crofter lay lifeless in his yard, staring at the sky. His family was coming out of hiding, wailing as they gathered around the dead man. Neil felt sick as he watched; he turned away to look up at the towering mountain above.

The runner had done his best, but the attackers had had the advantage of surprise. It was over before Neil heard of it. Three attacks in three days. Far-flung, but all on the border of MacCurrie lands, each more violent. And in each case the victims had identified MacLeods, the same few MacLeods who always made trouble.

He swore as the crofter's weeping wife placed a kiss on her husband's forehead and her children leaned over their father, wailing. By God, the MacLeods would pay for this.

Ellen sat for hour after hour with Britta and Ned while John led the discussions. Each clan's resources were discussed, supplies and ships and guns endlessly talked about. She had been fascinated at first, but as the topic switched to things she cared little for, she let her attention wander. MacCurrie sat with Duncan near the front; David sat down the table from her. She'd spoken to neither since she came back into the hall.

MacCurrie made a comment that provoked general laughter, and her attention focused on the Highlander again. She wasn't sure what to think of their talk, but she stared at her hand, remembering him holding her palm to his mouth. Just the memory of that touch affected her now, making her body feel warm all over. If her reaction to a simple kiss on her palm was that strong, what would a kiss on the lips be like? She'd never know. After this meeting she'd probably never see him again, never know which brother it was who had caught her interest so thoroughly.

Had there ever been a man more beautiful? She smiled; there were two of them. God had blessed the women of Scotland when He'd created two men so superb. She sighed, knowing she'd miss him. Would she hear in a few months that Torridon had married a MacKenzie girl? Would he remember being with her at Dunfallandy? Or would the army being raised here change all that?

War. No one had said the word, but it hovered above them all, the unspoken echoing from the hammered ceiling. War, to try to put King James back on the throne. Ellen believed that William had usurped his father-in-law's kingdom, that Parliament and law—and King James—should have prevented William from invading and putting himself and Mary on the throne. But—war.

She leaned to her left and could see MacCurrie's profile, his expression solemn. He would go to war. With his brother. And Duncan. And John. Would they return home? Would John's child be fatherless? Would the MacCurrie clan lose these splendid men? She shivered and wrapped her arms around herself. She'd come to try to save John's life, but there were forces much more powerful here than even the blond man and his partner.

Fergusson raised his arms high, halting the talk, announcing that his staff had food ready at the back of the hall. John said they'd continue the talks after the meal. The hall full of Highlanders agreed, climbing to their feet. Ellen did the same.

James stood and stretched. He was not accustomed to such long periods of inactivity; he needed a long swift ride, but he couldn't leave Dunfallandy. Perhaps he'd walk around the castle grounds again, as he had before. Perhaps he'd find Ellen. He glanced back at the table where she'd spent the last few hours, but there was a sea of men between them.

She was no longer his concern, he told himself again, but he knew he lied. He'd been worried about her when she left earlier to go to the garden. He'd followed her, not sure Dundee's men knew just how real the danger to her was, had stood at the top of the steps, ignoring the cold, as she walked along Fergusson's unplanted garden paths. She had looked very small against the high stone walls, a frail woman caught in a web of violence.

He'd seen the men who had attacked her on the road. She'd not been a person to them, she'd been an obstacle. And it was just that attitude that he feared. Dundee was a trained soldier who would not hesitate to give as good as he got, but Ellen was unprepared for the ruthlessness of men who murdered for political gain. Or greed. Were they simply hired killers, or was someone of wealth and power behind this?

Not his concern, he reminded himself. Like hell. For whatever reason—and he suspected those eyes and that face and that body just might have something to do with it—he was not going to walk away from Ellen Graham. In a few days at most, perhaps much less, she'd be off with her cousin, and he'd never see her again. Until then, well, he'd try to see that she was well protected.

Duncan was talking to MacGannon. James waved as he strode away. He found Ellen easily, standing with her maid and Ned next to the table where she'd spent the afternoon. She was repinning a lock of her hair that had drooped onto her neck. He studied her hands as they moved to recapture the lock, remembering her hand in his earlier, the feel of her fingers against his lips. What would that long slender neck feel like to touch? To kiss?

He moved toward her, then stopped as Grant reached her first, leaning over her and smiling. She looked up at him with a grave expression, then nodded. Grant bent his head close to hers. James spun on his heel.

He walked quickly to the stables. His stallions were well, and he paused a moment, enjoying the sight of the beautiful horses he and Neil had brought back to Torridon. They'd been scoffed at for importing the tall strong Spanish stallions, which dwarfed the Highland ponies, but they were faster than any horses he'd seen. They were one of the reasons that Ellen Graham was still alive. If he'd been on a Highland pony, she'd be dead now; he'd never have gotten there in time.

She would marry David Grant. It shouldn't matter to him. It didn't, he told himself. He walked slowly back to the hall. This bond he felt with her would be broken when they parted. There were other women.

It was noisy in the hall, the conversations of the clan chiefs excited and cheerful. Some had left already, quietly stealing away as it became apparent which way the discussions were going. The gathering would disperse soon. If Dundee's actions had not been considered traitorous before, this meeting would be, and all those who had attended it would be suspect.

James stood by the door, scanning the tables. Duncan was still where James had left him. Ellen was nowhere in sight, but David Grant sat with Ned. Britta was gone as well, he saw. Perhaps Ellen had withdrawn upstairs. James headed toward Duncan, then froze as he saw a man dart through a door to his left. He knew that man; he was a MacLeod of Gairloch. James ran after him.

The stone corridor was dim, not all the torches lit, and the shadows thrown by the fleeing man danced on the walls. James called his name. He'd not expected the man to stop, and he was proven right. MacLeod skidded around a corner, then another, down a flight of stairs, and into the kitchen.

The sudden bright light and warmth made James blink and hesitate. The kitchen, a huge vault, was well lit by the countless torches that lined the walls and by the ovens that illuminated the worktables. MacLeod faced him now, his sword drawn. Behind him the kitchen staff scattered with harsh cries, many running away.

MacLeod waved his sword. "Torridon, get back!"

James took a step forward as he recognized the other man—Angus MacLeod, whose father had been an Assynt MacLeod. "Why are ye here, Angus?"

MacLeod sneered. "Can only earls attend such gatherings?"

"Only chiefs were invited. Why are ye here?" He took another step.

"Get back!" MacLeod lunged, his sword reaching into the air between them.

James drew his sword and leaned forward. "Ye dinna want to do this."

"No? Why not?"

"Because I'll kill ye."

"Try, MacCurrie," MacLeod said.

James parried his blow, feinted, and lunged, slicing MacLeod's thigh. "Why did ye attack the lad with Miss Graham? Why did ye try to lure her out of her room?"

"I dinna ken what ye're talking about," MacLeod said, moving to his right.

"Aye, ye do, man. Why? Who is the blond man ye're working with?"

MacLeod charged forward with a roar, his sword aimed at James's heart. James batted it away, knocking it out of MacLeod's hand and forcing him against the wall.

"Who is he?" James asked, his blade at MacLeod's throat.

The man spit in his eyes. James held his sword steady, but stepped back and wiped his face with his sleeve.

"Who is he?" James demanded, pressing the blade tighter against MacLeod's throat. "Who is he? Did he pay ye for this, or did ye volunteer to terrorize the lass?"

"He paid me."

"Who is he?" MacLeod twisted and tried to duck below James's sword, but James leaned to his left and blocked his escape. "Who is he? Tell me, ye bastard!"

"Fraser. Cecil Fraser."

"Why does he want her dead?"

"He wants Dundee dead, ye fool! She just got in the way."

"Then why—"

MacLeod twisted again and drew a knife from his belt, slashing at James. James leapt back, and MacLeod slashed again, the tip of the knife scoring James's left hand. MacLeod swiped at him once more and James ran the man through. MacLeod stared at him for a moment, then slowly slumped to the floor, lifeless.

Ellen heard the shouts, saw the men running toward the door. John moved to stand next to her, his men closing around them in a phalanx. They drew their swords and faced the room. All around her Highlanders were unsheathing weapons and looking for the threat. David drew his sword and looked around him warily.

Where was MacCurrie? Duncan, who had been talking with several other Highlanders, met her gaze across the room and started toward her, his russet head towering over the others, his handsome face creased with worry.

"What is it? What's happened?" she asked John. He shook his head. Ellen saw Duncan stop and stare at a side door. She couldn't see what he was looking at; the men around her were too tall.

"Ease yerselves, men," Fergusson shouted, jumping to stand on a table. "We're no' under attack. All is well."

"What happened?" John called.

"Torridon killed a man in my kitchens."

Ellen paced the room again. She and Britta had been rushed up here by John's men, two of whom guarded the door now. John had brooked no argument. He'd told her to go with them; he'd come and tell her what had happened later. Britta was asleep, curled up on the bed, but Ellen was wide awake, wondering if the blond man was dead. And MacCurrie? Had he been hurt?

Two hours later, Ellen heard the guards greet John; she lifted the bolt to let him in.

"John, what happened?"

"Torridon found one of the men who attacked Ned and killed him."

"The blond man?"

"The Highlander."

"Is he all right?"

"No, he's dead."

Ellen put her hand to her throat. "MacCurrie is dead?" she whispered.

"No, Ellen," he said softly, moving to the fire. "The other man is dead, the MacLeod."

"Oh." Ellen felt her cheeks flush.

John sat down in one of the chairs, stretching his feet before him. She sank into the other chair.

"What happened?" she asked again.

John's eyes were amused when he met her gaze. "Torridon is well, my dear. Answering to Fergusson just now. The gathering is over. Most will leave in the morning."

"Are you pleased? They pledged their men, didn't they?"

John nodded. "Some did. Several are going home to prepare for war. Others will wait and see if those who said they'd join us actually do. But we did well, Ellen. We have the start of an army."

"John, can you succeed?"

"Don't I always?" He smiled, then his expression sobered. "I will leave tomorrow. I must go to talk with several clans who did not come here. Then I must go home. Jean's confinement is almost over and I must be there with her."

"Of course."

"I'll leave in the morning."

"I'll go with you."

"No. I cannot put you in more danger, Ellen, and where

I'm going, I cannot guarantee your safety. I want you to stay here with Fergusson."

Ellen looked at him in horror. "Oh, please, John! I can't stay here!"

"It's the safest course. Unfortunately, everyone now knows you are my cousin, and that makes you a target. Fergusson's not a bad man, my dear, just gruff."

Ellen's mind was spinning. She knew she couldn't go back to Netherby. But stay here with Fergusson after everyone else was gone?

"I could go to Glengarry," she said. "Mother is there with Margaret. Perhaps Flora and Tom are still there as well."

"I've sent for Tom. He'll meet me on the road." John considered. "But Flora will probably stay with your mother and Margaret."

"I'm sure Tom would not let Flora travel with him. When he hears that you're gathering troops, he'll want Flora somewhere safe. Glengarry's a long way away from Edinburgh."

"It may not be far enough. But yes, that's what we'll do, get you to Glengarry. Too bad Glengarry himself has already left. You'll have to stay here until Hugh can send men for you."

"I could go myself. I could travel at night with Britta and Ned."

"You cannot be serious, Ellen! Look what happened on your way here."

"Perhaps you can lend me two or three men, John."

"What about the men who attacked you?"

"They were after you, John, not me."

"They attacked you."

"Only to keep me from warning you. I'm no longer in danger, John."

He studied her for a moment. "Do you know a man called Cecil Fraser?"

She shook her head. "Who is he?"

"The man who hired MacLeod to attack Ned. And you and me, apparently. You don't know this man?"

"I don't know the name, but I'm sure he was one of the voices I heard, the one who said he'd come here."

John nodded. "I thought the same. We'll just have to keep asking questions. Someone will know him." He steepled his fingers. "We'll bury Evan tomorrow."

"And then you'll go."

"And then I'll go. I'll talk to you in the morning. Get some sleep, my dear," he said, rising to his feet. He gave her a kiss on the cheek, telling her he'd leave his men outside her door all night.

"Your footman is out there. I'd like him to sleep in here. The boy's been hurt once. We don't need any more incidents."

She let John out and Ned in. The boy's weariness showed in his eyes, but he smiled as she closed the door behind her cousin with a sigh. Stay here until Hugh could come for her? If Glengarry was joining John, Hugh might be too busy for months to come and get her.

"Your cousin has two men out there, Miss Ellen," Ned said, "and no doubt Torridon will come back as well."

Ellen looked at him in surprise. "Come back?"

Ned nodded. "He was here earlier, twice, until just before Dundee came out, as a matter of fact." He thrust out his chest. "We talked for a long time."

"You did? About what?"

"About Mr. Grant. He was most interested in Mr. Grant."

"What did you tell him, Ned?"

Ned flushed. "He kept asking, Miss Ellen."

"I understand. What did you tell him?"

"I told him Mr. Grant wants to marry you, but you don't want to marry him because you think he should marry Miss Catherine because he already asked her."

"I see. And what did he say?"

"He didn't say anything, miss. He just listened."

David was waiting for her when she came downstairs just a few moments before the funeral. He nodded to the men who had escorted her, then fell into step beside her, his expression serious, his tone low.

"I'm sorry, Ellen," he said. "Evan deserved better than to die on a road."

"Yes."

"You shouldn't have come here."

She looked up at him then. "What are you saying, David? That if I'd stayed home, Evan would be alive?"

David's face flushed. "Well, he would be, wouldn't he?"

She opened her mouth to speak, then changed her mind. She had no defense; David was right. Evan was dead because of her. She'd told herself the same many times already. David cleared his throat and she turned to him again.

"I've come to take you home, Ellen."

"I'm not going home. But I wrote a letter to Bea." She pulled it out of her pocket and handed it to him. "Would you take this to her for me?"

"Not going home? Where are you going?"

Ellen explained quickly, and David turned to glare at John. "Your cousin takes too much upon himself. The Highlands are never safe, least of all when war threatens. I will take you home to Netherby."

"I'm not going home while Pitney is there, David. I cannot."

"I can protect you!"

"I cannot stay in the same house."

"Then stay with Bea. Or with me."

She shook her head. "I will go to Glengarry."

David slapped his gloves against his thigh and narrowed his eyes. "Ellen, I disapprove of this."

"Yes," she said mildly. "I know."

"I'll talk to Dundee. We'll leave right after the funeral."

Evan's funeral was a paltry one. Ellen stood with John and Fergusson as the prayers were said and Evan's body was lowered into the ground. In her hand she clasped his ring and the Stuart badge he'd been wearing when he died; she'd give them to Tom when she saw him, when she explained why his cousin was dead.

She tried not to cry; behind her Britta sobbed loudly while Ned patted her hand awkwardly. Fergusson had been kind enough, Ellen thought, with a glance at her host, had even told her he was sorry about the mishap. Mishap, she thought. This was no mishap. It was murder, plain and simple.

MacCurrie and Duncan stood on the other side of the grave, next to David, and with them several of the remaining clan chiefs. MacCurrie had not spoken to her, nor had Duncan, but both had nodded when she'd arrived at the graveside.

David's face was pinched and flushed as he watched her. He was still angry. Obviously his talk with her cousin had not gone well. David watched John with narrowed eyes, and she had a momentary qualm. Could David have known about the plot against John?

Ellen wiped her cheeks again and dabbed at her nose. None of this seemed real. Evan was not dead, John was not going to war. But it was all true, and she had to face it. First she had to stop her tears. She looked away from the grave, to the valley below, blanketed now, in the rain, by clouds that drooped low over the landscape. In the sunshine it was green. She'd looked at it from the window of her room as she'd thought about MacCurrie.

He stood in the rain now, bareheaded, his hat in his hands. One hand had a bandage wrapped around it, but he seemed to be all right. The rain poured from his hair, to his shoulders, down the front of his short jacket and plaid. She could see his skin where his shirt was plastered against his collarbone. He looked wonderful. And after today she'd never see him again.

When the service ended, John took her arm and guided her back into the hall, where Fergusson had breakfast waiting for his guests. She sat on a bench, looking at her hands while the men talked around her and Britta sighed as she wrung the water out of Ellen's cloak.

"Ellen. How are ye, lass?"

She looked up into MacCurrie's blue eyes, and her tears started again. "Thank you for coming to Evan's funeral." She gestured to the bench as she wiped her tears away. "I'm sorry, I just can't seem to stop crying."

He sat next to her. "I don' mind, lass." He waited while she calmed herself. "I'm sorry ye are so sad."

"It's my fault Evan is dead. But for me he would be safe at Tom's house. It's all my fault. I knew we could be followed, but I never thought they'd kill him!"

"Ellen," MacCurrie said, leaning toward her, his voice warm. "This is no' yer fault; ye didna threaten yer cousin's life. But for ye, lassie, yer cousin might be in that grave instead of Evan. Ye were verra braw to come halfway across Scotland and warn him. It's no' yer fault that there are men who would kill him, nor that they would kill ye to stop ye from warning him. Ye did what ye thought best to do. Look at Dundee." She followed his gaze to where John stood talking with Fergusson. "Scotland is better for yer cousin being here, lass. And if there's any blame, I must share it. If we'd been a few minutes earlier—"

She waved his words away. "How can you even think that? You saved our lives. Evan is not dead through your fault; Britta and Ned and I am alive because of your valor. I want to thank you, sir. And Duncan."

"It was our pleasure," he said softly. He looked at her hair and then her mouth, then into her eyes. "I wish ye well, Ellen. I wish ye a long and happy life."

She blinked her sudden tears away. "Are you leaving?"

"Soon."

She stared at him, wanting to reach across the small space between them, to touch his cheek. Instead, she nodded and tried to memorize his face. "I wish you well too, Mr. MacCurrie. I will always think of you with gratitude."

"Thank ye, lass."

She traced a finger along the bandage on the back of his left hand. "Who did you kill last night? Did he do this?"

MacCurrie nodded. "A MacLeod. He wasna alone, apparently, so his companions will have gone on home to spread the word that I killed him."

"They'll make trouble at Torridon?"

James shrugged. "They'll try. My brother will take care of it."

"Guard yourself on your journey, Mr. MacCurrie."

"I will, and ye as well, Ellen Graham." James lifted her hand to his lips for the briefest of touches. He wanted to pull her into his arms and kiss that bonnie mouth, but he'd caused enough of a fracas last night. Kissing Dundee's cousin in Fergusson's hall would endear him to no one, Ellen Graham least of all. Who had time for love? "Keep yerself safe on yer journey home, lass."

She brushed her hair over her shoulder. "I'm not going home. I'm staying here, then going to the MacDonnells, to my sister."

James thought of Glengarry leaning over Ellen, of the way she'd smiled at him. Glengarry, he knew, would welcome her warmly. How near to Glengarry did her sister live? "How will ye get there?"

"John wants me to wait here until my brother-in-law can send men for me. But I'll go to Glengarry myself if need be." She raised her hand to stop his protest. "My cousin has already warned me, Mr. MacCurrie. Here's Fergusson with him now."

"Are ye still here, Torridon? I thought ye'd left aready," Fergusson said.

"I'm saying my farewells now." James rose to his feet and extended his hand to Fergusson. "Thank ye for hosting this, sir."

Fergusson took his hand and shook it, his grip very tight. "Ye're welcome, Torridon. Dinna come back soon, aye? Trouble is followin' ye, lad. No offense, but I'm glad to see the back of ye. First ye bring dead men to me, then people are bashed on the head in my halls, then ye kill a man in my kitchen. God only kens what would happen next."

"I'm leaving. Things will be calmer soon."

Fergusson gestured to Ellen. "She'll be here, so who kens what's to come."

James glanced at Ellen. "Ye will guard Ellen well?"

"I told ye they didna act like strangers," Fergusson said to Dundee, then turned back to James. "The lass will be safe enough, Torridon. Ye need no' worry. I ken what it is to care for a lassie myself. She'll be fine here, lad, dinna fret. Go home and marry the lass Seaforth's picked for ye and forget this one. All cats are gray in the dark, eh?" He laughed loudly.

James blinked, controlling the urge to punch Fergusson's teeth through the back of his head. Ellen flushed. James met Dundee's gaze and saw his anger mirrored there.

"I cannot impose on your hospitality any longer, Lord Fergusson," Ellen said coolly. "I will get myself to Glengarry."

Fergusson snorted. "Oh, aye, that would be an excellent idea. That way Fraser can kill ye much easier."

"I cannot believe that I am still in danger. It was John whom Fraser was after, not me, sir."

"Ye better believe that ye're still in danger, lassie," Fergusson said. "Isn't she, Dundee?"

John nodded. "I'm afraid so, Ellen. You'll have to stay here."

Ellen looked from her cousin to Fergusson. She would not stay here with this man another night, but screaming at him wouldn't help. She kept her tone calm. "If I am still in danger, then I would be selfish to stay here with you, sir. If Fraser is indeed lying in wait to harm me, then by being here I put your household in jeopardy. Someone in your family might be harmed if he tries to reach me. And when word gets out that Dundee is gathering an army, you might not want to be known for harboring his cousin. It's wiser that I leave. Perhaps you could spare a man or two to accompany us?"

She glanced at MacCurrie, who watched her with a mixture of annoyance and amusement in his eyes.

Fergusson nodded thoughtfully. "Ye may be right."

"No," John said angrily. "Ellen, you must stay here. Fergusson, I'll leave two men with her to guard her. Put her off in a distant room. But I don't want her on the road alone."

Ellen lifted her chin, but MacCurrie spoke before she could.

"I ha' a better idea," he said. "Dundee, if ye give me those two men, I'll take Ellen to Glengarry on my way home."

"It would take you out of your way."

"No' really; a day or so is all. But she'd be safe, and then I'd be off home. And ye wouldna have to worry about her." MacCurrie turned to her. "I'd be proud to escort ye, Ellen."

"I think it's a good solution," John said. "Is this acceptable to you, Ellen?"

"Yes," she said breathlessly. "Yes, it will be fine." She looked at MacCurrie. She'd have a few more days with him. "Thank you, sir."

A brief smile touched MacCurrie's lips, then he said to John, "We'll leave as soon as Ellen's ready, Dundee."

"An hour?" John suggested.

Ellen nodded. Fergusson, looking pleased, said he'd get a meal ready to send with them.

"I'll go tell Duncan," MacCurrie said before striding away.

She watched him leave, his stride long, his chin high. There had been a light in his eyes she'd not seen before.

Triumph.

Chapter Seven

"You cannot be serious, Dundee," David said to John. He'd followed them down from Ellen's room, protesting all the way.

John had discussed it at first, explaining why Ellen should travel with MacCurrie, but David had continued to argue. At last John held up both hands, saying that it had been decided. Ellen shook her head when David applied to her, busying herself with Britta and Ned and their belongings.

David continued saying the same things he'd been saying for ten minutes. Now, however, he said them in the middle of the busy courtyard where John's men were readying their horses. And in front of MacCurrie and Duncan, who exchanged amused glances as they listened.

"Enough, Grant," John said, raising his hands. "Ellen is going with him."

"Then I will come too," he said.

John sighed and turned to the Highlander. "Torridon?" John asked.

MacCurrie shrugged. "Unless Ellen objects?"

Ellen shook her head.

"Get yer things, Grant," MacCurrie said. "We'll no' wait for ye."

James watched Grant scurry away. Damn, he'd not expected that one. He frowned to himself, then saw Dundee gesturing to him to walk a few feet away from the others. James followed Dundee to the outer wall.

Dundee thrust out his hand. "I thank you again, Torridon. My cousin is very dear to me. I'm glad she's traveling with someone I can rely upon, someone who can protect her. I was afraid she'd attempt the journey herself."

"I think she would have," James said as he gripped Dundee's hand. "I'm grateful for yer trust. I'll keep Ellen safe, ye ha' my word on it."

"I trust you will also keep my cousin's reputation intact."

"She will no' be harmed in any way, Dundee, including from me. I dinna give that lightly, sir."

Dundee nodded, apparently satisfied. "Good. I will hold you to it."

"And Grant will be along to chaperone us, ye ken."

Dundee laughed. "Which will make it very interesting."

They left just after the midday meal, when the rain had stopped and Dundee was ready. The two parties rode together to the river Tummel, where they would part. She kissed John's cheek and wished him a safe journey, then watched as he and his men headed south, wondering when she would see him again.

She was amazed that John had agreed to let her travel with the Highlanders. Was this wise, to have MacCurrie escorting her? She closed her eyes, remembering the feel of his lips on her hand. She probably should be running from this man; it was a very good thing that David was along.

Ellen watched MacCurrie give orders to the soldiers who were accompanying them north, and tried not to see that Ned held Britta's hand openly, his expression daring anyone to challenge his right to do so. She felt suddenly alone. David didn't love her. And MacCurrie? Best not even to think of him. Their journey would end, and MacCurrie would hurry home to tell his brother what had happened, to prepare for what was to come.

James cantered to the head of their small group, pulling alongside Duncan. Grant rode a little behind them, then Ned and Britta, then Ellen. Behind her were Dundee's men.

"No' the trip home I'd expected," Duncan said.

"I didna mean to just spring the change of plans on ye."

"I warrant ye didna ken it yerself until ye spoke, Jamie. Did ye?"

James grinned. "No."

"I'm no' surprised that ye'd no' let her stay with Fergusson, nor let Grant take her home."

James gave a snort of derision. "Grant! And Fergusson canna protect her."

"Let's hope we can, laddie. I dinna care for how many people saw us off."

"Nor I." He watched Ned reach across to Britta and hold her hand for a second. "D'ye think the wee lad can fight at all?"

"We should find out tonight, eh?"

"Good idea." James gave his cousin a long look before he spoke. "Duncan, I need ye to go home. Neil needs to ken that war is comin'."

Duncan raised his eyebrows. "And leave ye alone?"

"I willna be alone. I've Dundee's men. And Grant."

"And two women and a laddie. I dinna like it."

"Neil needs to ken, Duncan. A week can make a difference. And—" James ran his hand through his hair.

"And what?"

James frowned. "I keep havin' the feelin' Neil needs us, or will soon."

"Do ye?" Duncan asked quietly.

"Aye."

"A 'feeling'? Like when Neil broke his arm, and ye kent something had happened? Or when ye got set upon in Inverness, and Neil kent ye were in danger, and we found ye before ye were killed? That kind of 'feeling'?"

"Aye."

Duncan let his breath out in a huff. "Damn." He looked at the sky, then back at James. "A'right, I'll go. But there had better be a good reason."

"I think there is. Maybe I'm wrong."

"Ye're not. I dinna ken how ye two do it, but I've seen it too many times not to trust it m'self. When d'ye want me to go?"

"Tomorrow. Ye can leave us when we get to the crossroads."

"Aye. That's what I'll do."

"Thank ye." James nodded at Ned. "D'ye think he's armed?"

"I dinna think so. And what of Ellen? Shall we give her back the pistol she was waving around? I have it in my bag."

James frowned. He'd forgotten the pistol. "I dinna ken. I'll ask her," he said as Duncan handed it to him.

Ellen watched MacCurrie approach her. He rode as though born astride a horse. He looked formidable outside the castle, even more dangerous with all his weapons strapped to him and his shield tied to his horse. A Highlander, she thought, a warrior; and he was protecting her.

"How are ye doing, lass?" he asked as he joined her.

"Fine, thank you. I'm admiring the scenery." Most of the trees were still bare, but some were in bud, the new green bright against the dark green of the scattered pines. In a few weeks this glen would look very different.

"This? Wait until summer."

"It's beautiful now. Look how steep the sides of the hills are. And the trees go all the way down to the river. Where are we? What is this place called?"

"Killiecrankie Pass. And ye're right. It's a bonnie place." He gave her a sidelong glance. "Ellen, d'ye want yer pistol back? Would it make ye feel safer?"

She looked into his eyes. So blue, she thought, then forced herself to concentrate on what he'd asked. The pistol. She'd forgotten all about it.

"Yes, thank you," she said. "It was my father's."

He handed it to her. "D'ye ken how to use it?"

"Of course." She tucked it into her belt.

"Would ye really ha' gone to Glengarry on yer own?"

"Yes. I hope I would have thought to get the pistol back first, though."

"I'm glad ye agreed to come with us."

"I'm glad you suggested it. Thank you, sir."

"My pleasure, lass. I also came to tell ye which brother I am."

She stared at him. "Really?"

"Aye, really. I couldna tell ye at Dunfallandy. I've a'ready explained why Neil had to be both places."

"Yes. You're James, aren't you?"

He smiled slowly, letting his gaze drift from her eyes to her mouth. "Aye."

"Really?"

"Aye."

"Thank you for telling me, Mr. MacCurrie."

"James, lass. I've been calling ye Ellen; I'd like ye to call me James."

"James," she said. "Who looks like Neil, but is not Neil."

"Does it make a difference?"

"Yes."

He nodded, fighting a wave of disappointment. Of course it made a difference to her. It would to everyone. "I'm no' the Earl of Torridon."

"No, Neil is. But James saved my life and is protecting me again now."

His mood lifted.

"Did you think I'd be disappointed?" she asked.

He couldn't answer while his thoughts tumbled. Grant turned to look at them, and James gave him a glance before returning his gaze to Ellen. She tilted her head.

"You are who you are, James. It makes no difference to me if you are an earl or a crofter. You saved my life, more than once, and I am very grateful."

Grateful, he thought. Aye, the proper emotion. It was fruitless to be feeling more, to be wondering what other emotions he could cause her to feel. It made no difference to her which brother he was, nor should it. Ellen might be caught up in a dangerous situation and grateful for his protection now, but she'd forget him once she was safe again.

"Do you think we will have war?" she asked.

"Aye."

"So what will happen? Who will win?"

"I dinna ken, lassie," he said as Grant turned to join them. "I'll just speak with yer cousin's men, Ellen." He pulled his horse away from her and let Grant ride alongside her.

They spent the night in a tiny inn. Ellen lay awake in the room she shared with Britta, thinking and listening to laughter from the public room. James MacCurrie. She'd known it all along. She was glad he'd told her without her asking again. But something had happened during that conversation; she'd watched him withdraw from her. No matter, she told herself. He was probably wise. It would be a short journey, and then they'd part.

She turned restlessly in the bed, then heard the creaking of a bed in the next room, where James slept with Duncan, David, and Ned. Or did he sleep? Was James MacCurrie awake, just inches from her, moving as restlessly as she was?

The next day was dry and clear, with a strong breeze that rustled the new leaves of the trees they passed. The pines were surrounded by birch and rowan and oak trees that stretched their new limbs to the sky as if to welcome the sun. Ellen basked in the warmth and kept her thoughts to herself.

David barely spoke to her, although he rode next to her. James had not said anything since wishing her good day at breakfast. He'd interrupted Ned's endless conversation with the landlord, glowering at the boy before ordering him outside. It had not affected Ned much. He was still talking.

Last night, after she'd retired to her room, James and Duncan had given Ned some lessons in swordsmanship. Ned now told Britta in endless detail how one lunged and parried and thrust and defended, and how important a shield, or targe, was. Britta listened with wide eyes and appropriate responses.

Duncan bid her farewell in the midmorning, and she listened in surprise. She'd assumed he would be traveling with them to Glengarry and said as much, but Duncan explained that he'd return to Torridon to give Neil the news from the gathering. Ellen gathered her wits enough to thank him again for saving her life.

A few moments later he rode over the hill that would take him north and eventually to Torridon. James watched until Duncan was out of sight. And Ned talked. Ned was still talking when they stopped for a meal at the side of a small stream, far off the main road.

John's men took their food, which the landlord at the inn had provided, and settled under a tree; Ned and Britta shared a rock next to the water, holding hands and talking in low tones. James, David, and Ellen sat on boulders that overlooked the stream and blocked the wind.

She fought the urge to curl up on the warm rock and bask in the sun like a cat while James stretched his long legs out before him and leaned back against the stone. David sat primly upright, flicking his hand at a bee that hovered near him. They talked of the view, of the mountains that loomed to the north, of the trees here and at Netherby, how winter might at last be over.

"This valley will be lovely soon," Ellen said, gesturing to the view before them. "The trees will be full of leaves, and the mountains full of heather soon."

James smiled. "We're just on the edge of the Highlands. It gets better as we go west."

"Isn't the west all barren land?" David asked James.

"Some is," James said. "Glen Torridon is fertile, and there are many farms near the shore. But the land just outside the castle is rock. We have walled gardens, of course, but only one native oak tree."

"One oak tree?" Ellen asked.

James nodded. "Aye. A very ancient one."

"Netherby Hall is beautiful," David said. "It looks out over the valley. And Ellen's Aunt Bea has a house that has an even better view. The land is very fertile, very profitable. A man could be very comfortable there."

Ellen had never heard that tone in David's voice before, that hint of ownership. Had Bea promised him merely money? she wondered. Or something more? Ellen felt a chill. Something had changed while she was gone, something significant. She couldn't bear to listen to David talk about her home as though it were his, and turned to James, choosing the first topic that came to mind.

"Do you travel by ship?" she asked. "I've heard Highlanders often do."

James laughed. "It's easier than land, lassie. Aye, we use ships all the time, for trade, for fishing, and for protection."

"I hear that you have little choice, since there are no roads," David said.

"No roads like in the east, aye," James answered. "But we like it that way. Keeps all but the most tenacious away."

"Makes travel slow," David said.

James looked at Ellen, smiling into her eyes. "Some things are worth the wait."

They rode until dark, then made camp in a narrow valley next to a small river. James had been quiet for most of the afternoon, and remained that way as he built a fire in the middle of the clearing. He told John's men to take the first guard shift, that he and Ned would take the next one. Then he settled under a tree and watched as Ellen and Britta prepared their makeshift bed. David unfolded a blanket and laid it nearby. When Ned asked James for permission to go for a walk with Britta, James shook his head and pointed to the other side of the fire.

"Sleep now, laddie. Ye'll no' be sleepin' later, I guarantee ye that."

Ned did not argue. Ellen wrapped her cloak around her. The afternoon had been warm in the sun, but night had brought cold temperatures. James got up to stir the fire but said nothing to her.

He'd dozed, waking often to look around and assure himself that all was well, but now James was wide awake. It was time to relieve the others. Ned slept soundly on the other side of the banked fire, snoring softly next to David. Britta slept with her back to James.

Ellen faced him, one hand under her cheek, the other tucked against her chest. He watched her side move with her breathing and the light play across her cheek. Had Grant ever touched that cheek? It was an unpleasant thought, and he turned away to look into the dark.

He started to stretch his arms, then froze as he heard a snap, then another, and then a whinny from the horses, who were suddenly moving restlessly. The hair on the back of his neck rose. He leaned forward, pulling his sword from its scabbard. There it was again. Someone was trying to creep up on them. From the sounds of it, several someones.

He stayed in his crouch and moved toward Ellen. Behind him, where Dundee's men should be, he heard a man's scream cut short. Everyone was awake now. Ned looked at Britta, who scrambled on all fours over to him while David blinked into the darkness. Ellen reached for her pistol and started to stand.

James leapt to his feet and sprang to Ellen's side. "Stay down!" he shouted to her. "Grant, arm yerself!"

From behind him he heard the first war cry and spun around. Four, five, six men ran toward him, arms raised and weapons gleaming in the firelight. Ellen screamed, and Britta started to wail.

James rose to full height, putting a foot on either side of Ellen. She screamed again when the first man lunged for him, and again when the man fell into the fire, sending sparks high into the air.

It was a blur then. He fought another man, then grabbed Ellen's arm and pulled her to his side. He couldn't see Ned or Britta, but could hear Ned's shouts mingling with those of the attackers.

Somewhere behind him he heard one of Dundee's soldiers shout, and then a loud crashing through the bushes and shrill whinnies of alarm from the horses. He kicked at what was left of the fire, bouncing the body off into the darkness, then spun around as a third man charged toward him.

Ellen swung her pistol up and fired into the man's side, her face a mask of horror as the man fell writhing to the ground. James quickly dispatched him, grabbed Ellen's arm, and pulled her into the trees with him.

He heard Britta's shrill scream and Ned's cry. And then nothing. He held Ellen to his chest and listened, then slowly moved away from the clearing.

Neil paced the room, stirred the fire in the hearth, then turned to pace again. It was only a nightmare, he told himself. But he knew it wasn't. It was a warning. James was in danger. He did not know what or who from, but James was in danger. He stood before the window and battled his compulsion to find a horse and ride like hell for Dunfallandy.

James, he thought, be safe. Come home. He stared out at the water, at the thin moon just barely illuminating the mountains across the loch. I should have gone, he thought. I should have gone.

The legend told of going to war, then fifty years of peace led by both brothers. Not one, he told himself. Not one. The younger son was prophesied to bring home a lass from the east, then follow her when she left. He would marry her. And Neil would marry a girl with the same name.

He frowned. For the first time in his life, he prayed that the legend was true, that James was not lying dead or injured somewhere in the east. He wrapped a plaid around his shoulders. He'd go and see the oak tree, the only tangible proof of the legend. And then he'd go to the chapel and pray that the Seer had been right.

Ellen tried not to cry. James had thrust her beneath these fallen branches with a hissed order to stay there and be quiet no matter what, then had left her. How long ago? It seemed hours, but it couldn't be. She strained to see, but there was only a darkness full of horrible sounds of fighting.

David had run. James had rushed to her side, had defended her and dragged her into the bushes. Ned had fought off at least one man, Britta behind him wailing and waving a knife. But David had run, his eyes wild as the men attacked James. He'd held his pistol in his hand and could easily have picked off one of them, then drawn his sword and helped. But he hadn't. He'd met her gaze, then dashed off into the dark.

Ellen jumped when something ran across her hand, then calmed herself and listened. There were shouts from the other side of the clearing, then a shot.

"We got Torridon! I saw him fall!"

"Find him!" called a voice very near her. "Bring him to me. And find her. She can't be far."

The voice was not ten feet away, and Ellen clasped her hand over her mouth, trying not to scream. It was the voice from Netherby, the man who was going to Dunfallandy. The blond man. And somewhere out there James was hurt.

"He's no' here!" called the man across the clearing. "But I saw him fall!"

She heard the man near her swear, then a rustling to her left. She crouched lower and tried to see through the branches. The movements stopped, and she waited, closing her eyes and praying.

"We got both the soldiers, Fraser," called the first man.

Fraser, Ellen thought. Cecil Fraser was the blond man. Evan's murderer.

"I got the laddie," the man said.

"And the maid?" Fraser asked.

"I cannot find her."

Ellen stifled a sob. James, Ned, Britta. And David gone.

"Never mind her. We came for Ellen Graham," said Fraser. "Where is she? And find Torridon!"

"We hit him. I saw him go down."

"How many did we lose?"

"There's only you and me left, Fraser," said the man. "Seven of us, and only you and me left. I thought you said this would be easy. Except for one, all of them fought. You said the boy was too young to be a factor."

"Relight the fire," Fraser said coldly. "Let's find them."

Ellen backed out of the branches and crept away from the clearing. If they came through the trees with torches, they'd find her. She stayed low, in a crouch, looking all around her as she tried to move silently, to stay under the ferns and the bushes. She could hear the voices growing quieter as she crawled across the ground.

The earth sloped uphill, and she tried to remember the clearing and how it had lain in the terrain, then froze as she heard a movement in the bushes behind her. Someone was moving stealthily toward her. Her father's pistol was still in her hand, but the gunpowder to reload it was by the fire, far out of reach.

Ellen turned to face the new danger, holding the pistol before her, straining to see in the darkness. She gasped when a hand clamped over her mouth. Another hand held her motionless in a tight grip, and she was pulled toward her assailant. She writhed in terror, trying to bite the hand that kept her silent.

"Ellen," James whispered.

Her breath came out in a wheeze, and he released her.

"Say nothing. Dinna make a sound. Follow me."

He slipped through the trees in a low crouch, and she did the same, gathering her skirts into a ball before her. After a while he turned to her and pointed.

"Two of the horses are over there," he whispered. "We're going to get on them and walk away very quietly. Dinna make a sound."

"James, it's Fraser!"

"I ken. Go."

"What about Britta and Ned?"

He put his mouth to her ear. "I'll come back, but now ye must go. Please."

"But—"

"Go!" He pushed her forward.

They walked the horses at first, then galloped for at least two miles before he stopped and turned to her. She saw his face now in the dim early morning light, grim and streaked with dirt. And blood.

"Are ye a'right, lass? Are ye hurt?" he asked her.

She shook her head. "Are you all right? You have blood on your face."

"I'm fine," he said, wiping his cheek.

"Why is he after us?"

"He's after ye, Ellen. I wish I'd killed the bastard instead of wounding him."

"You wounded him?"

"Aye. Put my sword through his arm. If I'd been fighting only him, he'd be dead. They weren't soldiers, Ellen, nor even well trained. Fraser was the only one who kent what he was doing."

"They said they'd hit you!"

He smiled then, almost a sneer. "Did they?"

"They said they killed both of John's men. They knew who we were, James!"

"Aye, we were followed."

"But how?"

"I suspect Ned told the landlord where we were goin'."

It was possible, Ellen thought. Ned had not stopped talking, and despite James's warning to the contrary, perhaps the boy had let their destination slip. She shook her head, the horror of the attack still sinking in. John's men were dead. And Britta and Ned?

"We have to go back to look for Britta and Ned."

"Did ye see them?"

"Only at first. Ned was fighting."

"Good lad. And Grant?"

"He ran away."

"Did he?" He looked away from her. "I didna see either Ned or Britta on the ground, lass. Maybe they got away."

"There were seven attackers. Only two lived. James, we have to go back."

He shook his head. “No’ now. I’ll go when it’s full light.” He led her horse away from the road, into the trees. “When I can see, I’ll go back.”

“I’ll go with you.”

“Ye’ll stay here.”

“Then I’ll go back without you.”

“Ellen,” he said, his voice weary. “I canna risk ye again, lassie. Let’s wait for the light, then we’ll argue it.”

She nodded. He slowly slid from his horse and helped her down.

They waited for what seemed like an eternity. James lay back and closed his eyes, and Ellen stared at the sky, watching the dawn arrive. Daylight had been slow to arrive this misty morning, but it was here at last. She turned to James, only to find him watching her.

“I’ll come with you,” she said.

He nodded.

Chapter Eight

The clearing was empty except for their belongings, which were strewn everywhere. James had insisted on going first, then coming back for her, telling her no one was there. Ellen looked around her in disbelief. Just a few hours ago seven people had had a meal here.

Now grass and ferns lay pressed against the earth, matted and broken, and dark spots marked where blood had seeped into the ground. Ellen's bag had been ransacked, her clothing flung onto the mud. James's bundle had been opened and left under a bush.

Britta's and Ned's horses huddled warily nearby with those of John's men. Fraser had taken his own horses. And his dead. They found the bodies of John's men, one near the road, the other almost to the clearing. But no Britta, nor Ned. And no David. Ellen stood next to the remains of the fire. She'd shot a man here, watched as James had killed him. Surely this was a nightmare.

"Do you think Fraser took Britta and Ned?" she asked James.

"Why wouldn't they have taken their horses?"

"Perhaps they were in a hurry."

"If they took Ned and Britta, they would ha' taken their horses. Grant's horse is gone."

She nodded.

"Did ye look under the bushes over there?"

"Three times, James. They're not here."

"Aye." He sighed. "I'll bury Dundee's soldiers while ye gather yer things."

"I'll help," she said.

He looked into her eyes, then nodded.

They buried John's men beneath a large oak tree, digging as deeply as they could in the thick soil. The ground was no longer frozen, but it was soggy. When at last they rolled the soldiers into the makeshift grave and covered them, James said a prayer in Gaelic and Ellen one in English.

They returned to the stream and washed, side by side, bending over the water. Ellen caught a glimpse of their haggard faces in the still water at the shoreline. James washed his hands, then his face, closing his eyes and letting the cold water drip from his cheeks before he wiped his face dry. Then he helped Ellen gather her things; he wrapped his in the old plaid they'd been bundled in.

Ellen stood in the middle of the clearing, looking around one more time. "Britta? Ned?" she called, then again, louder this time. And again. She listened, but heard only the sounds of the horses' restless movements, the rustling of the trees, and the murmur of the stream.

"Britta! Ned!" She waited, praying that they'd hear her and answer. There was no reply. She looked at the sky, where the mist still skimmed the tops of the trees, then turned to James. "Now what do we do?"

"Now I'm going home."

"Home."

"Aye."

"Not Glengarry?"

"No."

Ellen stared at him, her shock numbing her. He was going to leave her here. She opened her mouth to protest, then closed it. He'd saved her life more than once; she had no right to ask any more of him. David's running had shocked her, but somehow, even though she'd only known him for just a few days, she'd expected so much more from James MacCurrie.

He watched her, his hair unbound, his shirt opened to show the dark hair on his chest. This splendid man was going to abandon her in the middle of a strange country with only her wits for protection. She felt for the pistol in her pocket and tucked the gunpowder horn under her arm. So be it.

"I'll go ready the horses," he said.

She looked into the trees. "Fine."

He gave her a sharp glance, then brushed past her through the undergrowth. She sat down on a rock.

James frowned as the sun blinded him. His head ached from the blows Fraser's men had delivered after they'd knocked him down. Three men against him, and he was still standing. He should be proud, but he was too tired to feel anything except grateful that both he and Ellen were alive.

The lass was not pleased that they'd go to Torridon instead of Glengarry, but he'd explain it all later when he didn't hurt so much. He leaned his head against his stallion's flanks, closing his eyes for a moment. They'd been extremely lucky. Had Fraser had another man as good as he, James would be dead.

Their attackers had meant to kill them all; they'd not even stopped to take weapons. Death had been their goal, not robbery, just as it had been in the earlier attack on the road. But why? Why was Fraser still after Ellen? Dundee had told everyone of the attack, of the plot to kill him. The man James had seen in both attacks was not an idiot. There was a reason he was still looking for Ellen. Revenge? Money? Or both, as it had been with the MacLeod?

There was little evidence of all the death, Ellen thought. A few dark stains that would fade with the first rain, two shallow graves that would eventually sink into the ground, their occupants forgotten. And where were Britta and Ned?

How could David have left her? He'd looked at her wildly, then leapt into the darkness, knowing he was leaving her to her fate. Perhaps, she thought with a wry smile, perhaps he was still running. And now James was doing the same. She wouldn't think about him, wouldn't wonder how she could have been so misled by his bravery. He had saved her life again, and then he'd had enough. She sighed. They were strangers to each other; he'd already done more than most people would. It was not his fault that she'd assumed he would continue to do so.

She'd go to Glengarry on her own. What choice did she have? She could go back to Dunfallandy with her tail between her legs and wait until Hugh's men could come for her, or she could go to Glengarry by herself. It would be dangerous; it would be lonely. Cecil Fraser aside, the journey would be long, but not impossible. She had coins in her purse and a gun in her pocket. She would ride as quickly as possible during the day, hide somewhere at night.

She didn't turn when James came back to the clearing, nor did she look up at him when he came to stand before her.

"Ellen?"

She did not move.

"Ellen? What are ye doing?"

"Waiting."

"For?"

"For you to go."

"For me to go." He said each word slowly, distinctly.

"Yes." She looked up at him, a mistake. His eyes were narrowed. He crossed his arms over his chest. "You're going to Torridon."

"Aye."

She rose to her feet. "And I am going to Glengarry."

"To Glengarry. By yerself."

"Yes."

"Ellen, what are ye thinking? Surely ye have no' already forgotten that Fraser wishes ye dead?"

"No, I've not forgotten," she said. "But that's what I'm doing."

He took a step toward her. She'd thought she was prepared for anything, but an enraged James MacCurrie was intimidating. Terrifying. He looked as though he could strike her dead.

"Ye damned fool! What are ye thinking?"

"Do not shout at me!"

"I am no' shoutin'! If I were shoutin', they'd hear me in Edinburgh! What in hell do ye think ye're doing?" He stepped closer.

She held her ground, speaking coldly. "Going to Glengarry, James. What are you doing?"

He swung away from her, staring into the trees. "What am I doin'? I dinna ken what I'm doin'. I'm worrying about a lass who risks her life without a thought." He turned back to her, his lips thin. "Are ye really that witless, Ellen, that ye'd ride off by yerself?"

She lifted her chin. "Apparently."

"I ken ye're no' stupid, Ellen. But I dinna ken why ye think to go to Glengarry alone."

"Because you are going to Torridon."

"So ye're goin' to ride across Scotland by yerself, thinkin' that somehow ye'll fend off Fraser if he's a mind to come after ye! One shot, Ellen, that's all ye'll get; one shot! And Fraser will have not only a gun, but a sword and a knife against ye. Do ye truly no' understand how vulnerable ye are? Do ye care so little for yer own life? I dinna risk my life for everaone, ye ken, but I did for ye, Ellen Graham—the more fool I—and it means nothin' to ye!" He raised his chin. "Aye. Well, go then! Put yerself stupidly in danger. Godspeed to ye. Ye'll need it."

"Thank you," she said coldly. He opened his mouth, then closed it. "James," she said in a softer tone, "I am grateful for all your help, very grateful. I know I would not be alive except for you. But now you're going home."

"Aye. So?"

Despite her effort to remain calm and distant, she felt her lips tremble, and put her hand over her mouth to hide her weakness. How had she been so blind? He moved next to her and reached to touch her, but she shook her head and turned away.

"Ellen, lassie, look at me. If ye dinna wish my company, at least let me find someone to accompany ye. I beg ye, dinna go off on yer own."

"You said you were going home!"

"Aye! So?"

She felt a wave of anger and closed her eyes as she prayed for control; then opened them, all risk of tears gone.

"You are going to leave me on my own, James. What am I to do? I can't go home, I won't go back to Dunfallandy. So I will go to Glengarry while you go home. I thank you for your earlier assistance."

His eyes were wide with horror. "Ye thought I would leave ye here? By yerself? That I would abandon ye?"

She nodded.

"What kind of a man d'ye think me? How could ye think that I'd leave ye alone and defenseless?"

"You told me you were going home."

"I am, but no' alone! *We* are going home. How could ye think I'd leave ye?"

"I . . . I thought . . . You said 'I.' "

He stared at her for a moment, then spoke in a quiet tone. "So I did. But I would never leave ye on yer own. Never." He took her hand in his. "Never, Ellen."

"Oh, James—"

"Hush, lassie," he said, his voice gentle. He put one hand on her shoulder, then slid it to her neck, pulling her against him.

Ellen moaned, leaning against him, feeling his chest move against hers and his body respond. A warmth spread from the very center of her; her skin tingled and her body ached for him. She gave a sighing shudder.

But then he drew back, releasing her, his gaze lingering on her mouth for a moment before rising to meet hers.

"Lass," he said. "We have only two choices. We can go back to Dunfallandy, and ye can stay with Fergusson." He shook his head as she began to protest. "Hear me out, please. I ken ye dinna want to go back there. Our only other choice is to go to Torridon."

"We could go to Glengarry."

"It's too dangerous. Fraser's out there, lass, and he kens

where we were goin'. There's only ye and me now, and I dinna ken how many men he has with him. I canna protect us if he has many men with him, no' by myself. And I must go home as soon as I can. Neil needs my help."

"Why? What is it?"

"I dinna ken yet. I'll find out when I get there."

"I don't understand. If he needs you—?"

"I dinna understand it either. Ellen, my brother and I . . . we ha' a way of communicating sometimes . . . with just a feelin'. And I have had one since Dunfallandy, that I need to get home and help Neil."

"A feeling?"

He looked slightly embarrassed. "Aye. I canna explain it, but it's happened enough so I trust it. And so does Duncan."

"What do you think has happened?"

"I think the MacLeods are testing him. We ha' a parcel of land that both clans claim, and I think they're goin' to see if they can steal it away."

"Will they, do you think?"

"No' if Neil can help it, and he's verra good."

"So you wanted to go to Torridon all along, not Glengarry."

He shook his head. "I meant all I said, Ellen. I was goin' to get ye to Glengarry and then go home after I had ye safe there. That's why I sent Duncan to help Neil until I get there. I promised Dundee no harm would come to ye, and I mean to keep that pledge, but I'm no' sure I can if we go to Glengarry. Fraser is waitin' for us, I feel it in my bones."

"I see."

"Do ye? Do ye understand, Ellen? I canna explain it, but I ken I'm right no' to go to Glengarry. There is something verra evil about that man. He enjoys hurting people, lass, enjoys terrifying them. I dinna think he has any . . . I dinna think he's right in the head."

"He's not. I saw his eyes, James. I saw his pleasure in my fear." She sighed. "I don't see what choice we have."

"Nor I."

He leaned forward, just inches above her. "Ellen, ye are a verra braw lass, ye ken that?"

"What does that mean?"

"That ye're brave, lassie. Verra, verra brave."

She reached a hand up to stroke his cheek. He caught her hand and kissed her palm, as he had done at Dunfallandy.

"Ellen Graham, will ye trust me to keep ye safe?"

She nodded. "Yes."

"Then will ye come with me to Torridon?"

"Yes."

They spent the night at a crofter's house at the base of the Monadhliath Mountains. She couldn't stop watching him. Ellen slept in a bed with three children while James slept on the floor with the dogs.

When she woke in the night, she saw him silhouetted against the fire. His shoulders were straight and wide, his torso long and lean, and she felt a wave of longing that shocked her. She watched him from her dark corner until he pulled his plaid over his shoulders and lay down on his back. She eventually went to sleep, only to dream of her hands on that muscled chest, of her fingers on his taut sides, of his hands on her.

As they rode out of the crofter's yard, James looked up at the sky, squinting into the hazy sunlight. "We'll ha' rain later."

Ellen saw the first wisps of dark clouds coming over the

mountains that loomed above them. "We may have to find shelter."

"Aye, but without children and flea-bitten dogs."

"Perhaps with a bath."

"Och, ye're dreamin', Ellen. Ye'll get a bath at Torridon, lassie."

"What is it like, Torridon?"

"Spectacular," he answered without hesitation. "The castle itself is verra large, and it's built out of the red Torridon sandstone, so it looks like it springs from the very rock around it. It's on a headland that juts out into the waters of the loch, protected on three sides by the cliffs. Behind it are Beinn Dearg and Beinn Alligin and Liathach, and the other mountains. To get there from here, we'll go through Glen Torridon, some of the bonniest land ye've ever seen, and then we'll come to the lochs, Upper Loch Torridon and then Shieldaig. Ye'll see the outer Loch Torridon from the castle."

"You're very proud of your home."

"Aye, I am. It's Neil's home now, though."

"Does that bother you?"

"No. I have my ships—three of them—and several properties, lass. I may be a younger son, but I'm no' penniless."

"What will happen now? Will you stay at Torridon?"

"Of course."

"Will Neil marry the MacKenzie girl Seaforth wants him to?"

"I dinna ken. That's Neil's decision."

"And what will you do?"

James looked into her eyes, and she felt her body respond. He grinned suddenly, and his dimple appeared for a moment. "The same thing I ha' been doin' for years, guardin' my brother's back and protecting Torridon from the sea."

"You move like a man who is accustomed to the sea."

"And how is that?"

She shook her head. "I don't know how to explain it. You move like a man who is very accustomed to his body." She felt her color rise at the images her words conjured. "And who will protect Torridon from the land?"

"Neil. He'll have to do something to earn his keep, aye? We've the mountains to protect us for the most of it. Unless the MacLeods misbehave." He was quiet for a moment. "What will ye do about going home?"

"I'll decide that with Mother. Pitney is her husband; he has control of Netherby lands, but I will never live under the same roof again with that man. We could live with Aunt Bea, my father's aunt. She lives nearby."

"Ye're sure she'll have ye?"

"I think so. She's always been very good to us."

"She wants ye to marry David Grant."

"Probably. But I won't."

"What will happen to ye when yer Aunt Bea . . . when she's gone? Ye'll have to go back to yer stepfather's house."

"Netherby is my father's house, not his, but no, I will never go back there while Pitney is there."

"Perhaps ye'll marry someone from nearby."

"No."

"Is there no one ye care for in all of Dundee?"

She felt her cheeks redden as he watched her. "No, and even if there was, I have no dowry. My father died before he could arrange all that. I bring nothing to a marriage but myself."

"For many men that would be enough. With yer beauty, Ellen, and yer family's connections, ye could have any man ye wish. A titled man, a wealthy man. Ye could marry verra well."

She pretended to be unaffected by his words. "I will not marry where I do not love."

"But ye see yer life at Netherby."

"It is my home." She watched as his eyes flickered. "And you? Will you marry? Do you have a—?"

"No."

"No one at all?"

"No one, lassie."

"But you'll stay at Torridon?"

"Where else would I go? I'm a younger son, Ellen."

"But not penniless, I'm told."

He smiled. "No, no' penniless."

"With your splendid looks and your family's connections, you could marry quite well. You could marry a wealthy woman, a titled woman."

He laughed and looked away, his cheeks bright with color. She smiled; she'd managed to embarrass him thoroughly.

Her mood sobered then as she thought of Britta and Ned. Where were they now? She'd been praying for them since the attack, but feared she prayed in vain. Had they been captured? If so, they would have been questioned and would have told Fraser that Glengarry had been their goal. What would he do to them, this man for whom life held so little value? She knew the answer. If Fraser had captured them, they'd not lived long.

Aunt Bea would be worrying about her as she worried about Britta and Ned. She'd given her letter to Bea to David, but who knew where David was and if he'd ever deliver it? She'd have to write to Bea again, and to her mother, to let them know she was alive, to explain where she was, and that

Britta and Ned were missing. But all that could wait until she was safely at Torridon.

She'd not be there long; she would have to go to Glengarry, to her mother and her sisters. And then where? Not to Netherby, obviously, but where? She glanced at James, remembering the thoughts that he'd inspired, thoughts that would not leave her alone. Yesterday, when he had pledged to keep her safe, he'd stirred something in her that she'd never experienced before.

He rode beside her, frowning at the pack of horses he led, his long arms straightening the tangles of reins. What would life be like with this man? She really didn't know him at all. She knew he was breathtakingly handsome, brave, and fearless, that he'd risked his life for hers. And that she wanted him to touch her again. Beyond that, she refused to think.

James bought food for three days in a small village. They ate their midday meal at the side of a loch, sitting under pine trees that rustled in the strengthening wind. Above them, russet against the sparse green of the mountain, a herd of red deer grazed, the large buck watching them while the does and young ones fed.

In the darkening sky the birds were active and noisy, as though they had to get all their work done before the storm came. James looked at the clouds, then at Ellen. Her hair was tied back loosely, and strands had come loose, falling around her temples and cheeks. Her skirts were dirty, her short boots scuffed from the trip. She was the most beautiful woman he'd ever seen.

This morning he'd watched her move about the tiny crofthouse, gathering their things and laughing with the children, and he'd watched her kneel by the burn outside and wash her face and hands, then comb her hair before tying it back. For the first time in his life he wondered what it would be like to have a wife, to watch his woman do these simple tasks every day.

To watch Ellen every day. To wake at dawn and see her long lashes dark against her milky cheeks, to watch the sunlight find the many shades of brown and cinnamon and chestnut in her hair, to kiss that bonnie mouth and to touch those round breasts. And in the night, to feel her wrap her legs around him while he plunged deep into her.

James shook his head to clear his thoughts. He needed distance between him and Ellen. They'd be alone now for several nights. Closer to Inverness he could find inns, or crofthouses, but the stretch ahead, through the mountains, had few villages. He'd promised Dundee that she would not be harmed in any way, but the memory of her response to his touch was all too fresh in his mind.

A woman who looked like Ellen would have her pick of many men, dowry or not. She could marry a wealthy man, a titled man, a duke or an earl. Like Neil. If he had a title, he could claim a woman like Ellen, he could woo her and not fear that she'd laugh at his suit, nor that her family would try to dissuade her.

He wouldn't think now of what the future would bring. She was one of the powerful Grahams of the east, and he inseparable from the powerful MacCurries of the west. They would have no shared future except the few days left on this journey and the trip to Glengarry, where he'd deliver her into the care of the young chief of the MacDonnells who had looked at her so warmly.

She fascinated him, this beautiful, brave woman. If things were otherwise, he'd be thinking about a life together. But things weren't otherwise, and he'd bring her to Glengarry as she wanted, then probably never see her again. He took a deep breath. Best to face it now. She needed to be with her family. And he needed to get to Torridon to be sure that Neil was all right, that his earlier worry, long since faded, had been groundless.

"Looks like rain," he said. "We'd better be goin'." He moved to gather the horses and left Ellen staring after him.

James said little as they rode that afternoon, barely answering her questions. Ellen fell silent, watching him and wondering what had altered his mood. Had she said something wrong, offended him in some way? He was polite, but there was none of the blaze she'd grown accustomed to seeing in his eyes.

Perhaps he was worried about Neil and whatever was happening at Torridon, or thinking of his father and grieving. Or perhaps . . . Her musings were cut short by the first drops of rain. She looked up and saw that the gray clouds that had been inching over the mountains were now overhead, and much darker.

There was no shelter here. This was a wild land, filled with trees and streams and towering mountains. They'd passed only a handful of villages all day and fewer houses off on their own, and none in the last few miles. A rugged land, where only the hardy survived. Ellen pulled the hood of her cloak over her head as the rain intensified.

They rode another mile, then James called to her to stop, handing her the reins of the horses he'd been leading, saying he'd be right back. He guided his horse up between the trees, disappearing behind the branches. She waited, wondering what he was doing. After several minutes he returned and pointed up the slope.

"I dinna think the rain is going to stop, Ellen, and it's getting late. There is a cave up there we can stay in," he said, wiping the rain from his face. "It's large and dry. Are ye willing to stay there?"

She nodded.

The trail was steep, the rock slippery in the rain. Ellen gritted her teeth and closed her eyes when the horses had difficulty finding firm footing, but eventually they made it up to a small clearing. James slid to the ground, then parted what seemed to be a small thicket, throwing branches behind him, then led his horse in, returning a moment later to reach up for her.

"I'll help ye down," he said.

He held her next to him for the briefest of moments, then released her and took her horse's reins, motioning for her to follow. She stepped through the branches and up onto a small ledge, then through a cleft in the rock. It was a large cave, tall and narrow but long. She stood between her horse and James's, blinking into the darkness while he went back out into the rain for the other horses.

When her eyes adjusted, she saw the three terraced steps that led into the darkness. She climbed to the top step, pulling her hood off her head. The cave was dank and cold, water dripping somewhere out of sight. But where she stood was dry and out of the wind. There was a passage to the left, and she leaned into the dark opening, but didn't dare go any farther.

When James returned, Ellen helped him undo the saddles and bridles, stacking everything neatly while he rubbed the horses down. When they were finished, they went back out into the rain for firewood. The storm was worse than before, the wind blowing Ellen's cloak away from her and plastering James's plaid to him. Within minutes both were soaked to the skin, but they had enough dry wood to start a fire.

Back inside the cave James led the way into the passage she'd seen earlier, disappearing into the dark. Ellen followed slowly, feeling her way gingerly along the ribbed floor of the passage, wrinkling her nose at the smells of wet horsehair and leather and wool. It would be an uncomfortable night, but better than outside.

Chapter Nine

"Everything's wet," James said as he took the firewood from her. "It'll take a while to get the fire going."

It was dim here, but a sliver of gray light penetrated from a back corner. They were in a small, almost round room. The floor was flat; the walls had niches in them, as though for candles. James bent over the wood in the center of the space.

"How did you know this cave was here?" Ellen asked.

He answered without looking up. "I was here with Neil and our da years ago, when we were caught in a snowstorm. I wasna sure I could find it again."

"I'm glad you did."

"Aye, we're out of the rain, and this way no one can tell Fraser about us."

"Do you think he's still following us?"

"I wouldn't doubt it."

"Why?"

He looked up at her then, his face illuminated by the tiny flames that he fanned with one hand. "I dinna ken. I thought ye might."

"No. I don't understand. I knew we could be followed to

Dunfallandy and that we'd be in danger, but it was John whom Fraser went to kill. He was only after me to prevent me from warning John. Why does he still hunt us now?"

James rose to his feet and studied her for a moment. The lass was afraid, and he hated to worsen her fear, but she needed to hear his thoughts. "Ye, Ellen," he said. "The rest of us are incidental. It's ye he's following."

Ellen hugged her arms around herself, her eyes wide. "Why?"

"Fraser meant to kill ye when he attacked ye all on the road. He killed Evan at once, then went after ye. And if we'd no' been right there, I think he would ha' killed ye all." He paused, then continued. "But this time his men didna try for ye."

Her voice was a whisper. "No. They all went after you."

"First Dundee's men, then me. Grant ran, and Ned fought, which I dinna think they expected. I think they were planning to kill all the men first and then come after ye. But I dinna think they would ha' killed ye. Last time Fraser meant to silence ye. This time . . . Ellen, yer cousin John is surrounded by soldiers; he's too well guarded to be an easy target. I think Fraser wants to hold ye for ransom, to lure Dundee to a spot where he can kill him."

Her face went even paler. "I'd not thought of that."

"How many people hate yer cousin John?"

"He's not like that, he's not a man who has enemies."

James laughed ruefully. "John Graham? Lassie, Dundee's enemies are legion. Half the population of the southwest hate him, and now all those who back William. Ellen, yer cousin has many enemies. But I dinna mean them, the obvious ones. Who could want him dead for other reasons?"

"John is a very fair man. He's thorough and honorable and conscientious."

"Traits that would no' earn him love in all quarters."

"No."

"So who comes to mind? Who benefits by removing him from Dundee?"

"Unless King James is restored to the throne," she said, "John's power in Dundee is gone. If he's not already lost his title, he will soon."

"Aye, that's true enough. So perhaps it's just revenge for some slight ye dinna ken about. Or—" He blew lightly on the flames, adding another twig. "Who gains by gettin' ye out of the way?"

"Gains?"

"Aye. Who gets yer income?"

"My income is paltry, a small inheritance from my grandmother, barely enough to buy gloves—" She paused and stared at him.

"But what, lass? Ye just thought of somethin'. What is it?"

"David. He said Aunt Bea changed everything. She must have promised him money to marry me."

"Which would be motivation to keep ye alive, no' harm ye."

"That's why David wanted to come with us."

"To protect ye?" James snorted. "He mucked that up, didn't he? Who inherits yer aunt's property when she dies?"

"Probably my mother, which means Pitney would control it."

"What if yer aunt made ye her heir?"

"And that's why David wanted to marry me?"

James scowled. "Why would he need any incentive, Ellen? Most men would take ye in yer shift." He stared down at the tiny fire, trying to ignore the vision of her naked. "I mean penniless," he added quietly.

"Why is Fraser after us? Could it be you?"

"Me? I dinna think so. It was Dundee Fraser went to kill, and ye he wanted to stop. The part I dinna understand is why he's still following ye. I can only think it's to hold ye for ransom." He took a step toward her, then stopped. He'd been about to wrap his arms around her, to comfort her, and maybe more. He cursed himself for an animal. She needed protecting, nothing else. "Come closer to the fire, Ellen, ye're shivering."

She came to stand next to him, holding her hands out to the flames. He took off his bonnet and shook his hair back, peeled off the baldrick and sword, then the gunpowder bandolier, and laid the pistol atop them all. He straightened and turned to her, pulling her cloak from her shoulders, his fingers grazing her neck.

"Yer hair is wet, lassie. I'll get yer case so ye can change yer clothes."

He turned abruptly away before he touched her again, his boots ringing on the stone floor of the outer cave as he grabbed her case and his bundle. He paused, watching the small movements of the horses. They were content; no one was approaching, then, he thought, though it hardly seemed likely with the rain blowing in sideways through the mouth of the cave. They were safe tonight. Alone tonight.

He counted his heartbeats until they quieted, then returned to find Ellen putting another branch on the fire. She straightened and watched him walk toward her while she twisted her hair, letting the water from it drip on the rock. He put her case near her feet, his bundle next to it, and she gave him a small smile, her cheeks bright with color. He sat on the stone floor to take off his wet boots, aware of her gaze still on him. When he looked up at her, she looked away. He put his boots near the fire to dry, then rose to his feet, holding the food pack high with a smile.

"I'm hungry, lassie. Are ye?"

"No," she said, then realized how empty her stomach was. "Yes."

"Isn't that just like a woman, saying aye and nay at the same time?"

"You say this from your vast experience with women."

"I am no' inexperienced in that realm."

"I'm sure you're not," she said and turned away before he could see her embarrassment.

He handed her the food bag and spread his second plaid out on the floor. "Miss Graham, will ye join me for dinner? Our choices may be limited, but there's much of it. Whist, lass, ye're dripping on our table. Change yer clothes while I serve our dinner." At her hesitation, he laughed softly. "I willna look at ye."

Ellen nodded and moved behind him, pulled her wet boots off, then her stockings, turning away as she reached under her skirts to undo the garters that held them. She looked over her shoulder at James. He was busy unfastening the bundles of food. She slipped out of her sodden clothes.

James was right; it did feel much better. She stood for a moment, naked, letting the warmth of the fire dry her skin, then she dressed quickly and sparsely, wearing only a chemise, bodice, and underskirt. Barefoot, she spread her clothes to dry on the other side of the fire and settled herself on the plaid.

"Better, aye?"

Ellen nodded. He handed her bread and meat wrapped in a napkin, then rose to his feet, stepping back to stand on the stone. He undid the brooch that held the top of his plaid and removed his jacket, letting the end of the plaid drag on the stone while he pulled the wet wool from him and dropped it. Then, with one swift, smooth movement, he pulled his shirt over his head.

She caught her breath. His shoulders were wide, his chest lean, with dark hair at the center that spread across the width of him, then tapered into a line along his well-muscled stomach, disappearing under his belt. He dropped his shirt atop his jacket and bent to pull another from his bundle.

"I never get used to bein' wet through, do ye?" he asked her.

Ellen shook her head and watched the muscles move under the skin of his arm. Smooth skin, long arms. He behaved as though he'd peeled his clothes off before her a thousand times before. He met her gaze, his eyes amused. James MacCurrie knew exactly what he was doing.

"Look away, lass," he said softly.

She did, but not soon enough. She saw him unbuckle his belt, saw the soggy plaid slide down his hips. She lowered her eyes, fighting the urge to look up at him. She could see his feet in front of her, his lean ankles and strong calves, as he kicked the wool away.

She pictured him standing naked before the flames as she had done, letting the warmth caress his skin. If she looked up again, she'd see the firelight play across his stomach, his chest, his legs, see him watching her as she'd watched him.

"Ye can look now, lassie," he said, and she did. He wore an oatmeal-colored shirt that reached midway down his thighs. He'd left it open over his chest, and he was laughing at her.

"You might try to be a bit less amused," she snapped.

"We're no' in a drawing room, Ellen. We're alone in a cave. I canna see a reason to sit in wet clothing."

"James MacCurrie, you are truly amazing!"

"I ha' been told that."

She stared into his eyes for a moment, then decided that she was not angry but embarrassed, both by his words and by her reaction to him. He swept up his wet plaid, draping it across the ledge at the back of the room. The blue-and-green pattern melted into the dim recesses of the cave, like draperies around a very large bed.

He came to sit on the dry plaid and reached for the stone bottle between them, pushing his dirk into the cork. As he twisted it, he looked up from the task to give her an appraising glance.

"Ye're beautiful, Ellen."

She couldn't breathe, just stared at him as his words spread warmth through her. "Thank you," she said at last.

"Ye've no' been told that often, ha' ye?"

"What?"

"That ye're beautiful. Why has David Grant no' been tellin' ye daily?"

"David!" Ellen felt her brain clear.

"Has he told ye that ye're beautiful?"

She shook her head.

"Strange way for a man in love to behave, d'ye not think?"

"David doesn't love me. He's pretending to care for me, but he's only doing that because he wants Catherine to be jealous."

"He came after ye."

"Because Aunt Bea asked him to."

"How well d'ye ken the man?"

"I've known him most of my life."

"And ye can read his mind?"

"No, of course not. What do you mean?"

"I dinna think ye ken yer David Grant as well as ye think, lass." He twisted the cork slowly. "Either he does care for ye, or he's watchin' ye for another reason."

"Which would be?"

"Perhaps yer David Grant heard the news that ye'll come into wealth and suddenly finds himself in love wi' ye."

"Wealth from Aunt Bea?"

"Perhaps."

She shrugged.

"He's always been attentive to you?"

She nodded.

"He's been trying to make Catherine jealous for a long time, eh?" James drew the cork from the bottle with a satisfied expression. "If he does care about ye, why did he run? If a woman I cared about was facing danger, I wouldna run away."

"James, there is no comparison between the two of you. You didn't run away. I'm very grateful to you for protecting me. Enormously grateful."

He smiled. "Tell me again, Ellen. I do love a grateful lass." He held the bottle up to sniff it. "It's whisky! I thought we were gettin' wine."

"Is that bad?"

"Depends. Let me taste it." He held the bottle to his lips, waited a moment, then handed it to her. "No' bad at all. Have some; it'll warm ye right up."

She gingerly tasted the whisky, closing her eyes as the fiery liquid slid down her throat. Then she took another sip. "Not bad," she said, handing it back.

"Ye've had whisky before?"

"You are not the only Scot here, James. Of course I've had whisky. Aunt Bea taught me about whisky."

"My da taught me."

"My father taught me its uses. Aunt Bea taught me how to drink it."

He raised one eyebrow. "Ye drink whisky?"

"She does. I do not make a habit of it."

James stretched his long legs out in front of him. "So what did yer da say are the uses of whisky?"

"Well, you can drink it, obviously. Cook with it. Use it to cleanse wounds or to clean your hands. Or even to clean furniture."

James gave a roar of laughter.

"It depends, of course, on the quality of the whisky."

"Lassie, be warned, ye'll no' live long if ye try to use whisky to clean furniture at Torridon."

"I'll remember that." They ate in silence for a few minutes while Ellen stared into the fire. He passed her the bottle again. "If I have more of this I may get very silly," she said, taking a sip, then another, then putting the bottle down next to her.

James drank deeply. "And I may ha' a difficult time keepin' my promise to yer cousin."

"James, you promised that you wouldn't let anyone harm me. There are only you and I here. I cannot believe you would ever harm me."

"I kissed yer hand, Ellen. Twice."

"Which did not harm me."

He raised an eyebrow. "It left ye unaffected?"

"Not unaffected, but not harmed."

"Not unaffected, but no' harmed, eh?"

"No," she said.

He leaned forward, pausing when his lips were just inches above hers. "Do ye wish to see if you continue to be unaffected?"

Ellen lifted her mouth. "Yes."

He slid his hands onto her cheeks and pulled her to meet him, his mouth soft and demanding. She put her hands on his chest, feeling his heart beating against her palm, his skin warm through the fine linen. She slid her hand higher, feeling the outline of his muscles, the intake of his breath as she wrapped an arm around his neck.

So this was what Margaret had meant, this sense of floating, of her heart not even beating and yet pounding, of wanting a man to touch her and possess her and to possess him. And this was only a kiss. She could feel his body respond to her, and hers to him. Her breasts tightened, and she pressed them against him.

His lips brushed hers, once, twice, then claimed hers with a fierceness that stirred her more than his gentleness. When his tongue searched for hers, she responded, feeling the melding of their breath. At last she drew back, her hand to her mouth, staring at him while he watched her with dark eyes.

"Not harmed," she whispered, looking at his lips. She stroked a hand along his cheek, letting it linger on his jaw, tracing it down his neck, then resting at his collarbone. "And not unaffected."

"Nor I, Ellen." He leaned forward again, drawing her to her knees as he rose to his. His mouth descended on hers as he pressed her against him, his hands roaming down her back to cup her buttocks.

She knew they should stop, knew she should pull back, should tell him not to touch her this way, but as he moaned again and pulled her even tighter, his hand caressing her waist, her hips, her thighs, she knew she wouldn't say anything.

He widened his stance and pulled her between his thighs, her hips resting against him. His heartbeat accelerated as he swooped down on her again, lacing his hand through her wet hair, tipping her head back, slipping his tongue between her teeth.

Ellen wrapped her arms around his neck while they explored each other. She knew she should tell him to stop, but she no longer cared. For the first time in her life she lost herself in a man's touch and deliberately shut her mind to all the consequences. She wanted this; she wanted him; she would think no further. Her heart was pounding. Or was it his?

His breath was ragged, his arousal hard and firm against her stomach. His hand was on her breast now, stroking her, then moving higher to the neckline of her bodice, dipping below the lace to explore, his fingers warming her skin.

She arched back to allow his kisses to descend from her mouth to her neck and then lower still, to just above her breasts. She slid her hand inside the opening of his shirt and felt his response immediately as she drew her fingers across his chest, feeling the dark hairs there encircle her fingers.

His hand at last found her breast, cupping it, exploring its contours. She moaned, lifting herself to his touch, then moaned again as his other hand circled her ankle, slowly moving higher, pulling the chemise away from her skin and replacing it with his fingers.

Ellen did the same, reaching down his leg to find the hem of his shirt, then sliding her fingers along the hardened muscles of his thigh. He shifted his weight with a soft groan as her hand explored the planes of his hip, then his buttocks, his skin smooth and warm.

James slid his hand behind her knee, pushing back her skirts, lifting her leg against his, bare skin against bare skin. He moved his hand higher with a slowness that was both torture and delight. He lifted his head and smiled at her.

"Ellen, from the first moment I saw ye, I felt as though

we were linked somehow, as though we were meant to be together, as though we'd already been together. I canna explain it, it makes no sense to me, but there it is."

"I feel the same," she whispered. "And it makes no sense to me either."

"But it's there."

"Yes, it's there."

He smiled. "Kiss me again, lassie." He claimed her mouth again with a ferocity that left her breathless. He tasted like whisky, like nectar. Like heaven. When he lifted his mouth from hers, she gave a whimper of protest.

"James," she said. "Don't stop."

With a swift movement, he lifted his shirt over his head and threw it behind him, kneeling naked before her. He was beautiful, his body long and lean and ready for her, his eyes a deep blue as they watched her study him.

She put a hand on each of his wide shoulders, letting her fingers glide down his chest, tangling her fingers in the dark hair there, then stroking lower. She followed the line of hair to his waist, tracing the contours of the muscles of his stomach, then to his hips.

He pulled her against him for a long searching kiss, then lowered her onto the plaid, leaning over her with a smile. "Ellen," he said as he traced a line of kisses down her neck. "Ye are so beautiful, so bonnie."

He undid the laces of her bodice, pushing her chemise out of the way and covering her breasts with his hands. He smiled at her, then bent to replace his fingers with his lips, his touch sending thrills through her. She laced her hands through his hair and closed her eyes, concentrating on his lips on her breast.

At last he lifted his head. "Oh, lassie, ye're sweeter than I imagined."

She smiled up at him. "Did you imagine this?"

"Oh, aye, from the moment I saw ye."

She slid her hand up his left thigh. "So did I."

He laughed softly, the sound rumbling though his chest. "Did ye now?"

"Yes, I—"

His mouth covered hers before she could finish her sentence, his hands no longer hesitant as he reached under her skirt and stroked his way up her leg. He separated her knees with his, then pulled her skirt high. He leaned back and looked at her, smiling.

She half moaned, half sighed as he ran his hands up her thighs, his fingers sliding along her skin, leaving a trail of sensations that warmed her more than whisky. When his hand cupped her, she arched to meet him.

He bent to kiss her, parting her lips with his tongue, sliding easily inside her. Ellen gasped, closing her eyes and letting his touch ignite responses she'd never dreamed of. His breathing grew more rapid.

"James," she said, stroking his back, then reaching between them. She wrapped her fingers around him and smiled as he moaned. She sighed his name. "James."

From far away, there was a whisper of noise, a rushing of wind that grew louder. Ellen opened her eyes; James lifted his head, his hands suddenly still. The rushing continued, like hundreds of pieces of paper being rubbed together, a thousand leather purses swishing through the air. What was it?

The horses began stamping, their whinnies at first restless, then quickly alarmed. James took his hands from her and leaned up on his arms, staring at the opening to the rest of the cave. When his stallion snorted and gave a shrill call,

James rolled off her, leaping to his feet and catching up his sword and shield.

"What is it?" she whispered.

He listened for a moment, watching the door of the inner room for a moment. "Bats."

"Bats!" She scrambled up, pulling her chemise over her breasts and yanking her bodice closed, her skirts falling in a tumble around her legs. "Bats?"

James came back to the fire. He laid his weapons down, then gave her a sharp glance.

"In the back of the cave," he said, picking up his shirt, "where we didna go, there's a huge room, full of bats. Thousands of them. They leave through a big hole farther back, but ye can hear them all through the cave."

"Can they get into here?"

"I suppose they could, but I think they're after food, lass, no' us."

Ellen watched as he pulled his shirt over his head and put his arms through the sleeves, covering his wide shoulders and tapered sides, his taut stomach and long thighs. She took a deep breath. What had they been about to do? And what would they do now? She wrapped her arms around herself as he pulled on his boots.

"D'ye want to see them?"

She nodded, then stepped into her still-wet shoes. He reached down to the fire, taking a branch that was alight, and led the way through the door to the outer cave. The horses moved restlessly. The rustling sound seemed to come from behind them, then above them. Ellen stared fearfully around as James stuck the branch into a crevice in the wall. He led her outside.

The rain had stopped, the wind lessened. The moon lit the wet landscape with rays of cold white that deepened the shadows and turned the rocks and trees gray. Overhead the living cloud darkened the sky, blanketing the tops of the trees, then faded. The rustling sound was much less now, only a whisper, and a moment later the moon was left alone in the sky.

"Have ye ever seen the like?" he asked.

"No."

"Nor I, though there are lots of caves at home." Home, he thought. The simple word brought his responsibilities back to him. Ellen shivered as the wind wrapped around them. "Ready to go inside?"

She led the way, then waited while he stopped to pat the horses, who were quieter but still wide-eyed. He took the almost extinguished branch from its crevice, holding it high so they both could see their footing.

Back in the inner room Ellen added wood to the fire while James bent to pull his boots off. Then she did the same, putting her shoes neatly on the other side of the fire. Her hair was disarrayed, her eyes dark, her clothing still askew. A beautiful woman who should be cherished and loved properly, not tumbled in a dank cave and left behind by a man going to war. Who had time for love?

What had he done? What had he been thinking? He'd almost compromised her despite his promises to Dundee, to himself. She'd been willing, yes, but only because of the whisky and her ignorance. The blame was all his.

"I thought at first that it was Fraser," she said.

The bitter taste of shame filled James. He'd protected her from Fraser, only to prey on her himself. "Aye, for a moment, so did I. Then I remembered the bats."

She held her hands to the fire. "I wonder where Britta and Ned are."

He didn't answer.

"You think they're dead," she said.

"Aye, I do."

"Then where were their bodies? Fraser left John's men behind."

"I ha' no answer for that."

"If he took them hostage . . . do you think he'd keep them alive?"

"If he took them hostage, it wasn't for long. A slip of a lass like Britta couldna outlast Fraser, Ellen." He sighed. "They're most likely dead."

Her eyes filled with tears. "Ned was fighting."

"Aye."

"Do you think Fraser's still following us?"

"Could be. That's why we're back here, and the horses are near the entrance. Fraser could easily have talked to the crofter we stayed with and discovered our direction. It would ha' been hard for him to follow us in the storm, though, and it's unlikely he'd ken this cave. But we shouldna relax our guard."

"James, what happened before we heard the bats . . . I—"

He held up a hand to stop her. "It willna happen again, Ellen."

"I—"

"Lass, it willna happen again."

Her tone was cold. "Are you sorry it did?"

"Aye."

Ellen bit her lip and looked away, fighting her tears. She couldn't blame him. She'd had too much to drink; he'd forced neither the whisky nor himself on her. She'd all but begged him to make love to her. Her cheeks flamed as she remembered her words. Had she gone mad?

What had she been thinking? Had the fear and loneliness she'd been trying not to face overwhelmed her? Or had she proven to herself—and to James—that she was a wanton who slipped into a man's arms the first time they were alone? Was the whisky the cause, or just an excuse to do what she'd wanted to anyway?

His face was lit by the glow from the fire as he looked down into the flames, his jaw set and his lashes lowered. She still wanted him. She'd heard about such women, had listened to her mother and friends discuss them when they thought Ellen wasn't listening. She'd looked at David, at Evan, at the older men Pitney had brought to meet her, wondering how anyone could be so carried away by passion.

She no longer wondered. She'd desired James MacCurrie almost from the first moment she'd seen him, and no less now, even when he had so clearly rejected her.

He was beyond handsome, that was true, but it was more that just that. There had been an attraction between them so strong that she could almost have touched it. He'd felt it too, she'd known that at once. And obviously others could see it. Fergusson had been candid; others more discreet.

How could she not have desired such a splendid man, have wanted him in her arms, in her bed, even if only for once?

What now?

Neil stroked his hand along his horse's neck, hoping to quiet himself with this mundane task. Something had happened, something that had woken him from a sound sleep and sent him roaming through the castle, the memory of a woman sighing still ringing in his head.

Who was she? And why was the memory of her sigh enmeshed with his thoughts of James? It was not danger that he'd sensed for his brother, not fear, but an emotion that he'd not experienced before; he wasn't even sure what it was.

Was the woman real, or a spirit guide sent to warn him? Of what? He'd not seen her face, nor did he know what she had to do with James. And it was not merely the woman who had unnerved him, but the break in the bond between him and James. It had been a waver last time, the tiniest change of course. But this time the interruption had been lengthy, as though James had been removed from him for some time.

Why? They'd both had women before; it had never affected the bond. But this . . . Whoever she was, she was changing them. And Neil was not pleased. Part of him was jealous of whatever James was experiencing, a strange and disquieting emotion. He'd never envied his brother the freedom from the duties that had landed on his own shoulders.

At a very young age he'd realized that James had his ships and properties, but he'd never have the title, nor the castle. Neil had always thought it a reasonable compromise. James had been given the means to make his own wealth and the independence to do so, while Neil had been given a fortune in land and the obligations that went with it.

Until their father died, the twins had been equals, had shared everything. But now James was experiencing something Neil couldn't understand, something so strong, so overpowering, that it was taking him to a place where Neil could not go. Neil patted the horse again, then turned to face the night. Would his brother come back? And if he did, would he be changed forever?

Who was she?

They lay on the cold stone floor, Ellen on the far side of the fire, wrapped, at his insistence, in James's plaid; James was nearer the door, wearing a shirt from his bundle, a second thrown across his legs. She slept fitfully, her thoughts tumbling, bringing her to wakefulness time and again.

She was safe here, for the moment. Not happy; ashamed of herself and certain James despised her, but physically safe. She needed to focus on that rather than on her misery. Britta and Ned were out there somewhere—alive, she prayed—and her cousin John was gathering men to go to war.

She said a prayer for John and his wife, and another for her family, for Margaret, who, God willing, had safely had her first child, for her mother and Flora, so far from home. For Aunt Bea, left behind with only Pitney and her imagination for company, and for Hugh, who she knew would be so proud of his first child. And Tom—had he been told of his cousin's death? Did he blame her for Evan dying?

And where was Cecil Fraser?

How could her life have been turned so upside down in such a short time? A fortnight ago she'd been at home with her sister and mother, all of them safe. Now the Grahams were spread across Scotland, in the middle of a struggle for a kingdom. She was no longer even sure who she was, what she was.

James turned on his back. This stone was hard, and he was cold. He moved closer to the fire, looking across at Ellen. She slept huddled under his plaid, the wool wrapped around her shoulder, sloping down to her waist and reaching to her hips. Her lashes were dark against her cheeks, her hair twisted in the blue-and-green folds. MacCurrie colors, representing the land and sea of their home. Torridon.

He wanted her. He'd take her home and keep her safe. Home. Neil. He no longer had that fearful urgency to reach

Neil. It had been replaced by an emotion he didn't recognize, not alarm, but not ease. He frowned into the dark. He'd be home as soon as he could. Then he'd know what was happening to Neil and the clan. And he'd have Ellen within the walls of Torridon, where he would have the whole clan to protect her.

Who had time for love?

Ellen woke to find herself alone, the fire all but burned out. James was gone, his boots and weapons and bundle with him. The bottle of whisky lay next to the food parcel. She picked it up with a grimace; it was still two-thirds full. It apparently had not taken much to remove her judgment. She scrambled to her feet, pulling her clothing into order, relaxing as she saw his plaid still stretched across the rear of the room, his pistol near the door. He was here somewhere.

The morning mist covered the tops of the trees and coated her hair and eyelashes with moisture as she put her case down and listened. Three of the horses were tethered here on the small ledge of stone, the others gone. Water dripped from the trees in a muted cadence while she waited.

Before long, James's stallion raised his head and looked in the direction of the small stream that lay below, and a moment after that she heard his voice, talking quietly to the horses he was leading back.

Ellen saw his expression change as he saw her, guarded now, heard the slight hesitation in his words to the horses. She watched his long legs as he approached her, the line of his shoulders as he turned. When his hands patted the horse's neck, his fingers spread wide, she felt her body remember what his fingers had done to her.

"Good morning," she said quietly.

"Good morning, Ellen. How are ye today?"

"I'm fine, thank you. And you?"

"Good. We need to leave as soon as we can."

"I'll be ready," she said, then lifted her chin. "James, we need to talk."

He shook his head, his eyes narrowing. "No, lass, we dinna."

"Yes, we do." She took a deep breath. "I drank too much whisky."

"That's no' how I'm remembering it."

"I don't regret it, James."

"But I do, Ellen."

Chapter Ten

It rained the next day, a soft drizzling wet that made travel miserable. Ellen watched James as he rode in front of her. She had nothing to say to him, and he apparently nothing to say to her. Had she imagined what had transpired in the cave, the warmth in his eyes, the caress in his touch? She wasn't sure whether she wanted to cry or lash out at him.

Just before dark, James stopped and gestured to the city before them. "Inverness. We'll stay at an inn."

She followed his gaze. Inverness, a harbor for centuries, lay next to the Moray Firth, the huge sea loch that linked it to the rest of the seafaring world. Bisected by the River Ness, the city wound along its banks, the buildings spreading from the river in tight knots of tangled streets.

James knew his way, leading them through the crowded lanes to a small inn, old but well kept. He helped her dismount, asking her to wait inside while he talked to the stable lad. She went through the door he'd gestured to, standing in a snug foyer filled with two benches. A staircase disappeared above her.

"Good evening, Missus," said a cheerful voice behind her.

Ellen turned to see a portly woman who watched her with open interest, blue eyes pale in her ruddy face. She was neatly dressed, her graying brown hair pulled back tightly, her apron clean. She looked at Ellen from head to toe, then smiled.

"Spending the night?"

"Yes, please."

"Is that one of the MacCurrie twins ye're with?"

Ellen nodded, not sure how much she should tell this woman.

"I thought so. They always stay here. We ken them, they ken us. Makes it easy all around." She thrust out a hand. "Janet MacKinnon."

"Ellen Graham," Ellen said as she clasped the older woman's hand.

"Graham, eh? Any relation to Dundee?"

"He's my cousin."

"Yer cousin, eh? Well, well, well." She turned and bustled up the stairs. "Come wi' me, lass. I'll show ye yer room. Is it Neil or Jamie ye're with?"

"James."

"Ah, good thing, that. Neil's been promised, I hear. Jamie's still deciding if he'll take the lass."

"What lass?"

Janet threw a look over her shoulder. "Do ye no' ken? Well, Seaforth wants to cement the alliance between the MacKenzies and MacCurries by marrying both the twins to his kin. Their mother was a MacKenzie, ye see, and this would tie the two clans together by blood forever. Of course, the MacLeods are asking for Jamie too, to smooth over the trouble they're having between them and Torridon. But ye ken all this, no doubt."

They reached a landing, and Janet leaned to look at Ellen's hand. "Ye've no' married him, ha' ye?"

"No."

"So it's two rooms for ye, then. Follow me, then, lassie."

Janet led her to a room on the second floor that overlooked the stable yard. She brushed the curtain aside, giving Ellen a view of the darkening sky, then moved to the bed to plump a pillow.

"Ah, here he is," Janet said as James appeared in the doorway, carrying Ellen's case. "Welcome, Jamie." Janet gave him a quick embrace. "I'll put ye down the hall. Ye ken my rule."

"And what rule would that be, Mistress MacKinnon?"

"No one unmarried shares a room. Ye can ask all ye wish; it'll no' happen."

"We're no' asking to do that."

"Good thing. Now, come, Jamie. It is Jamie, isn't it? I canna tell ye apart."

"It's Jamie."

"Good. Come, lad, I'll show ye yer room. And mind yerself downstairs. I've a room full of Munroes, and they dinna like yer king."

"We'll be careful."

Janet gave Ellen a shrewd glance. "I'll feed ye in the kitchen, both of ye. Much safer. And if anyone asks, ye're no' Miss Graham, lassie. Ye're Miss Sinclair."

"As bad as that?" James asked.

"As bad as that."

"D'ye wish us to go elsewhere?"

"Whist, no! They'll drink themselves into a stupor and never ken ye're here. But I dinna need a brawl under my roof." She shook her head. "As if I'd let ye go elsewhere, James MacCurrie! I've kent ye since ye were a bairn." She turned to Ellen. "When my father was ill, Jamie and Neil brought him oranges from Spain. Can ye imagine? We dinna forget such things. When ye're ready to eat, lassie, go on down the same way ye came up. Come, Jamie."

She bustled away, James following her out of the room. He turned to look at Ellen as Janet pulled the door closed.

Dinner was in a corner of the kitchen near the settle and the door to the public room. James and Ellen sat on ancient wooden benches at a battered oak table while the women buzzed around them. The public room was noisy, fragments of conversation drifting in as the door opened. Janet breezed by them constantly, dropping snippets of information, while her girls gave James sidelong glances.

Janet said that there were twelve Munroes in her inn, drinking heavily and in high spirits. They were on their way south to join General Hugh Mackay's army near Edinburgh. Word had spread from Dunfallandy that the clans were rising for King James. Old alliances were being renewed, old enmities remembered. James sipped his whisky thoughtfully as he listened.

When Janet left, Ellen leaned forward. "Are we in danger here?"

"No' as long as I keep my mouth shut. I dinna ken any Munroes, so they shouldna ken me. We have no argument with them. But I'm surprised it's started so soon, the gathering of the armies."

Ellen had been thinking the same. Dunfallandy had been over only a few days, but the news had traveled north faster than they had. Where was John this night? And Tom? War had never seemed more likely. She'd been trying not to think what would happen after the armies were raised. All the men she loved would go to war—John, Hugh, Tom.

Janet pushed through the door, her arms loaded with dirty dishes. She handed them to one of the girls, then leaned over James and Ellen. "There's a price on Dundee's head. Twenty thousand pounds. Dead or alive. William of Orange sent troops to Dundee's home to arrest him, but Dundee wasn't there."

Ellen put a hand to her throat. "Was his wife?"

"Aye. And Dundee's son. But they werena harmed, thank God. If ye ken where yer cousin is, tell him no' to go home."

Ellen's eyes filled with tears. John was the father of a little boy. What a time to bring a child into the world. What would life bring for this babe?

"Yer cousin Duncan was here," Janet said to James, "flirting with my girls as always. He said ye'd be coming through, but he said ye'd be alone."

He didn't respond. Janet laughed and patted his arm. "He gets silent when ye corner him, lassie. Where are ye from?"

Ellen blinked away her tears. "Netherby, near Dundee."

"Dundee?" Janet gave James a sharp glance, then turned back to Ellen. "From the east, eh? Ye do ken the legend, do ye not?"

"Janet," James protested. "We dinna need this."

"What legend?" Ellen asked.

Janet smiled. "Oh, it's a bonnie one. The legend of the MacCurries. The Brahan Seer said that the old oak tree at Torridon would be split in two by lightning on the night the twins were conceived. And that they would lead the clan to war, then to fifty years of peace. And that each would marry a lass from the east, which is why I ken our Jamie here willna marry the MacLeod lass. Or at least no' the one from Lewis. Everyone else is east of Torridon already."

James shook his head. "It's nonsense. Superstition."

Janet's eyes narrowed. "Did yer da no' die on his birthday? Did yer grandda no' do the same, and his da before him? Was the oak tree no' split into two, and both halves live? And are ye no' leading the clan to war?"

"Neil will lead the clan."

"Ye beg the question, Jamie." She straightened and shook her hair back over her shoulder. "I've been thinking of this every day since Duncan was here. It's the legend comin' true. Ye ken it and I ken it, and all the protesting in the world willna make it go away." She spun on her heel, leaving them.

"A legend," Ellen said.

James met her gaze with stormy eyes. "Aye."

"Which says that you and Neil will lead the clan to war."

"Aye." With a sigh of annoyance, James told her most of the lore about the legend. He was quite sure it had been embellished since their birth, but whether he liked it or not, much of it had come true.

"You don't believe it?"

He hesitated. The problem was that he did believe it. Or most of it. "I like to think that we have some choices in our lives."

"So do I." She looked down at her hands, then back at him. "James, why don't you leave me here in Inverness? I have money, and Janet seems very capable. I'm sure she could find me a way to Glengarry. You could get home much faster without me."

"Leave ye here?" He leaned forward, trying to keep his voice low and his anger in check. "Leave ye here? Ellen, ha' ye gone mad? Why would I do that?"

"It would be easier."

"For whom?"

"For you, James. I . . ." Her voice faded and she leaned back, hugging her arms. "It's best that we part."

"Is it? Why?"

"You despise me," she whispered.

"Despise ye?"

She looked away. James studied her for a moment, wondering what she could possibly be thinking. He'd done everything he knew to care for her, to protect her.

"Ellen? Look at me, lass. I dinna understand. Why d'ye think I despise ye?"

Her lips trembled, and she put a hand over them, then began to rise, her other hand on the table. He clasped her wrist.

"Ellen," he whispered. "What are ye thinking?"

She slumped back onto the bench and tried to pull her wrist from his grasp.

He tightened his fingers. "Lass, ye were right, we do need to talk. But no' here. I dinna despise ye, Ellen Graham." He looked around the kitchen, at the serving girls who were openly watching them now. "We canna talk here."

Janet burst through the door, laden with another armful of dirty dishes. "Take these," she called over her shoulder to one of her girls, then stopped next to their table, taking in James's hand on Ellen's wrist. She looked at him with a frown. "They say ye killed a MacLeod at Dunfallandy."

James released Ellen. "Aye."

"Which will start more trouble between ye and them."

"It willna help," James said with a grin.

"Ye need to keep yer temper, laddie."

"He was trying to kill Dundee."

Janet's eyes widened. "For the reward."

He shrugged. "I dinna ken why."

"And now ye're taking Dundee's cousin home wi' ye?"

"I am."

Janet shook her head as she moved away. "Just be careful, Jamie."

"I will be." He waited until Janet was talking to her serving girls, then rose to his feet, holding out his hand to Ellen. "Let's go upstairs, lass."

Ellen took his hand, and he squeezed her fingers, then led her across the kitchen, past Janet, who watched them with narrowed eyes, past the serving girls, who looked at her with open curiosity and him with open admiration.

James released her as they climbed the narrow stairs. He stood back to let her enter her room first, then closed the door and leaned against it. He crossed his arms over his chest.

"Ellen," he said, his voice low. "How could ye think I despise ye?"

"You've not spoken to me in two days."

"Nor ye to me."

"You . . . when we were . . . I don't regret what we did in the cave, James. You say you do."

He nodded. "Aye, I'll always regret that."

"I think you despise me because I was so brazen."

He stared at her with wide eyes, then gave a bark of laughter. "Brazen? Ellen, ye dinna ken what brazen is, lassie. Trust me, ye are no' brazen." He paused. "I thought ye were angry because I preyed upon ye."

"Preyed upon me? How did you prey upon me?"

"I kissed ye. I forced myself on ye."

"I threw myself at you."

He pushed himself away from the door. "I was verra happy to catch ye."

He crossed the space between them in two steps, wrapping her in his arms, holding her tight against his chest.

Ellen threw her arms around his waist, glorying in the feel of him. Her mind was clear for the first time in days. I want him, she thought, and he wants me. Nothing else matters right now.

"Ellen, lassie, I'm the one at fault," he whispered in her ear.

She raised her face to him. "Hush, James. Kiss me."

James bent his head, his mouth claiming hers with a fierce joy. He moaned as her soft lips opened to his pressure and let him explore her. He knew he couldn't let this be more than a lingering celebration, that he'd sleep alone in the small cot Janet had provided, that Ellen would sleep alone in her bed. He knew there was no future to this attraction, that Scotland was poised to go to war and that he would be in the midst of it. But right now none of that mattered.

Nothing mattered except the feel of Ellen's lips against his, her breasts rising against his chest, her waist trim and smooth beneath his hands. For these few moments he would concentrate on the feel and smell of her, how she tightened her arms around him and ran her hands along his sides and up his back.

"Ellen," he said, leaning back to let his hand slip between them, searching for her breast. She moaned and arched back as his fingers found her soft flesh.

His body leapt in response. No, he'd not been mistaken. He'd not read her glances wrong, nor misinterpreted her touches. He felt a surge of desire so strong it threatened to overpower him. At last he raised his head and clasped her to his chest, feeling his heart beating against her cheek as stumbling footsteps came down the corridor.

Two men were mumbling as they went past Ellen's door, their drunken words slurring into each other. Munroes, talking in Gaelic about killing Dundee with their bare hands. He glanced at Ellen, who had not understood. It was the liquor talking, but it was her cousin they discussed.

"Ellen, I willna leave ye here. Please do not ask it of me. I want to take ye home to Torridon and keep ye safe. Say ye'll come with me."

"Is that what you truly want?"

He nodded, not trusting himself to speak.

"Then, yes, I will."

He loosened his arms and leaned back, smiling down at her. "Ye are the most beautiful woman who has ever lived, lassie. Ye must ken that." She shook her head; he laughed. "Then I'll tell ye every day until ye become accustomed to hearing it." He watched her for a moment. "Ellen, are ye no' angry wi' me for what happened in the cave?"

"No," she whispered. "I'm not angry."

"It willna happen again, lass, although I can assure ye I'm willing."

She stared at him with dark eyes.

"D'ye understand why?"

She shook her head.

"I promised to care for ye, to protect ye. And I willna break that promise."

"My cousin John is not here, James. This is between you and me."

"Aye, I ken that. I'm no' ignoring that ye have as much right to decide what we do as I."

"Thank you," she said crisply.

He cringed at her tone. "War may be coming."

"Yes."

"And if it does, I'll be in it."

"I understand that."

"We ha' no idea how long it will last."

"Nor if you'll win. Yes, James, I know all that. And the

MacKenzies and MacLeods both want you to marry their daughters."

He drew back. "What?"

"Janet said Seaforth wants you to marry a MacKenzie, like Neil. And that the MacLeods want you to marry one of their women to form an alliance."

He frowned. "Janet talks too much."

"It is true?"

"Aye."

He caught her hand in his, but then he raised his head higher, his expression hardening.

"Listen to that, lass."

She had heard the singing from below, but stiffened now, ill with horror, as she recognized the song. It had been written some years before, about her cousin John, asking for his head. The voices rose with the chorus. "On a platter, on a platter, we will have his head upon a platter" they sang. Suddenly everything seemed clear to her. James was right. No matter how strong desire was on both their parts, who had time for love now?

"Ye see, Ellen? It's bigger than ye and me, lass. I want ye, make no mistake, but it's better that we not act on it."

"Yes," she whispered, putting a hand on his cheek.

"Someday all of this will be over, Ellen."

She closed her eyes as he pulled her against his chest. She took a deep breath, listening to the rhythm of his heart. When he tipped her chin up, she opened her eyes, meeting his gaze and then his lips. He kissed her softly, then released her, moving away with a sad smile.

At the door, James turned to look at her again, keeping his gaze on hers until the door divided them. Alone, Ellen let her tears fall.

* * *

Neil watched with grim satisfaction as his men led the cattle away. Behind them the MacLeod crofthouse still burned. He'd reclaimed all the cattle stolen from his crofters, and more. Many more.

He'd killed no one, not at any of the five crofthouses they'd raided, just frightened the tenants badly. This was the only house he'd burned, for this was where he'd found the MacCurrie cattle. Even here he'd been lenient. He'd let the crofter and his family pull their meager possessions from their home before he had it torched. He'd sent the crofter off with a demand that his laird come and pay Neil a visit to end this.

Neil looked up at the peak of Ruadh Stac Mor and considered his next actions. This would have to be played carefully. Duncan had arrived home last night, tired, but not too weary to tell what had happened at Dunfallandy, of the attack on Ellen Graham, of James's apparent fascination with her.

And he'd brought news of the discussions of war. It was as they'd feared: there would most likely be war, and unless James brought home reasons otherwise, the MacCurries would back King James.

This was not the time to start a war with the MacLeods. Neil wanted to prove that he could not be intimidated, nor his people be preyed upon, but he had no intention of fighting on two fronts. For the moment all was under control.

He kicked at an ember that landed near his feet, then looked to the east. Ellen Graham. His brother was falling in love with Dundee's cousin.

Contin, Garve, Achanalt, Achnasheen, Kinlochewe. Ellen remembered the names of the places they'd passed since Inverness now, but she knew in a month they'd be forgotten. Torridon was their next stop. This morning James had told her that they would be at Castle Currie before nightfall.

They'd had no rain since Inverness, and had made good progress, which had pleased James. He'd been polite, cordial, teasing, had watched her with eyes full of desire, but he'd not touched her except when necessary. They'd spent their days talking of inconsequential matters, their nights at small inns, taking two rooms, or in homes where they slept apart. She wasn't sure what was worse, wondering if he cared for her, or knowing he did but would not act on it.

She had only a few more moments alone with him. They'd eat their midday meal beside this lovely loch, the mountains of the west towering above them, and then they'd be off on the last leg of their journey. Soon they'd be at Torridon, surrounded by his family and clan and Duncan. And Neil, with his plans for his brother's future.

Ellen was weary of traveling, but each mile that brought them closer to Castle Currie brought her fears and concerns closer as well. What would James's family say about her? Would they welcome her? She was not his wife, not even his lover. Once among them, would James be hurriedly married for political gain?

And it wasn't just that. She was loath to face the letter she would have to write to her mother. Knowing Rose would be horrified at what had happened to Ellen since she'd left Netherby, she dreaded telling of Pitney's treachery, Evan's death and Britta's and Ned's disappearance.

She'd have to write to Bea as well, to warn her. So much had happened to her since she'd seen her great-aunt. And what had happened to John since he'd left her? Had Tom joined him? She breathed a prayer for the safety of her family, and another for Britta and Ned.

Let William be king, she thought. I want my loved ones safe.

Ellen tried to push aside the knot of dread that formed in her stomach whenever she thought of war and its destruction, but it was also time to face it. Life would never be as it had been just a fortnight ago. Eventually she'd go to Glengarry, to join her mother and sisters, and leave James MacCurrie and Torridon far behind. But she might never go home again, might never stand on Netherby's steps and look across the valley, counting the shades of green in the spring and the gray trees in the winter.

She shook her head to clear her thoughts, busying herself with unwrapping the bundles of food and setting them on the rock they would use as a makeshift table. Their last meal together before Torridon.

James gave her a grin as he walked up the hill with the horses.

"Lassie, ye look as though ye've taken every meal of yer life beside a Highland loch. A verra bonnie sight."

Ellen smiled as he came to stand over her. If he'd been alone, he would have eaten his meal on horseback, but she had spread a cloth on a rock and set their food upon it, as though this were a dining room in a fine home instead of a small meadow overlooking a smaller loch. A meadow with a splendid view, but a meadow nonetheless.

James sat against a tree and stretched his legs out, enjoying the sight of Ellen framed by the trees and mountains behind her. He'd stopped in this quiet spot many times before, but never had he had such a sense of peace.

They'd not been followed, and the worry he'd had about Neil had subsided in the last day, even when he'd paused at the foot of the glen that led to Loch Maree and the

MacLeods. He should be relieved, should be eager to be home, but he found he was in no hurry to arrive. Once there, he'd be surrounded by people who would claim his attention. There would be constant talk of war and endless preparations and discussions. Duncan had no doubt already arrived with the report of the gathering and the clans' pledged support for King James. And Neil would expect James to be in the midst of all of it.

Ellen handed him his food. This woman had become part of his life, and he was in no hurry to share her, or his time, with others.

"Tell me about your family," she said.

"What d'ye wish to ken?"

"Well, who will I meet?"

"Neil. Ye ken Duncan already, of course. My mother, my grandmother."

"What is your mother's name?"

"Anne. She was a MacKenzie, as ye ken. My grandmother is named Mairi."

"What are they like?"

James smiled. "My grandmother is a wee bit of a thing, but she has a way of making us all listen. My grandfather always said she ruled Torridon, no' him. And my mother, well, she's no' herself since my da died. She's quiet; they used to laugh all the time. She's no' the same. She's fragile now."

"It hasn't been very long since your father died. Perhaps she'll get stronger. My mother did after my father died. It took years, but she did come back to the world. And then made the most dreadful mistake."

"Which was?"

"To marry my stepfather. They've not been happy. He's

always gone—and I've heard stories of where he goes. My mother is quite miserable."

"Why did she marry him?"

Ellen met his gaze. "She was swept away by a handsome face and a charming manner."

"Something I'd never be."

She laughed. "I wouldn't expect you to understand."

"I could be swept away by a beautiful face. In fact, I ha' been."

"And did you survive?"

"So far. I've no' kent her long. We'll see what happens."

Ellen blushed and busied herself with her food. James watched her, then looked over her head at the blue sky of the west. Colors were brighter here, the mountains higher, the lochs deeper and bluer. Home, he thought. And having her here to see it only increased the pleasure.

James had been correct, Ellen thought as she followed him along the narrow track. Glen Torridon was beautiful beyond words, thick with trees, rowan and beech and oak competing with the endless firs for the sun. The mountains overhead were truly amazing, tall and gaunt and ancient.

The riderless horses were between James and her, strung together on a long lead, and Ellen let her horse plod along while she looked around with awe. She'd heard of the mountains of the west, had been properly impressed with those they'd ridden through on the trip from Dunfallandy, but nothing had prepared her for these behemoths.

Each was larger than the last, each trying to claim the sky. Gray and brown and rosy stone climbed into the heavens, the bases of the mountains dotted with rocky terraces, green moss and trees dividing the steps. The trees were thick here, the mist hung overhead, slowly lowering over the mountains, making her think of the stories of spirits and faeries her nurse had told her when she was small. It would be easy to believe in creatures from another world here, easy to imagine strange forms hopping from rock to rock, or watching them as they made their slow progress along the track.

James seemed not to notice how lovely it all was. His back was very straight, his gaze shifting from side to side. Obviously he did not share her mood. She watched his careful perusal of the trees above them and felt his uneasiness infect her. She drew her father's pistol from her belt and checked that it was loaded, then carefully replaced it.

It couldn't be Fraser. James had convinced her that the guardians of the road would be sure he had not followed them. That left the MacLeods.

Neil clapped Duncan on the shoulder as he passed. "Let's go," he said. His cousin looked up, then rose to follow him, as Neil had kent he would.

"James?" Duncan asked as they crossed the courtyard. Neil nodded. "And we're goin' to welcome him home, I suppose?"

"Aye. Before the MacLeods do."

In the stables, they found the other men Neil had told to prepare to ride, and a few minutes later they were in the courtyard. Neil's grandmother stood next to his horse, giving him a worried look.

"Is it Jamie?" Mairi asked, her voice low. "Do ye ken something?"

Neil nodded. "He's comin' home."

"Anythin' else?"

"No." Neil sprang into the saddle, then leaned to pat her hand. "I ha' to go, Grandmother," he said gently.

"Which way do ye ride?"

Neil shook his head. "I dinna ken. It'll come to me."

"Go with God, then, Neil. And bring all of ye home."

Neil smiled grimly. "I'll try." He turned his horse to face the gate, gave Duncan a glance, then raced out of the courtyard, his men following him.

He'd been going over the accounts with his factor when a nagging worry had grown into a knot of fear. James was coming home. And someone was waiting for him. He had no doubt that the MacLeods would love to take their revenge on his brother. Jamie, he thought, I'm coming.

Ellen had been silent for some time now, and when James turned to see why, he saw in her eyes the recognition of their danger. He'd brought her up behind him miles ago, letting the other horses trail along in the rear. Now he stopped, holding his hand out for hers. She guided her horse alongside, and he reached for her hand. He brought it to his mouth, kissing her fingers, then leaned to whisper into her ear.

"Get yer gun out, lassie." He gestured at the rocks that towered close to the track before them. "If the MacLeods are planning anything, they'll do it here."

She showed him her pistol.

"Good. Now, I want ye to go back a bit, to where the trees are close to the road. Hide in them, Ellen, deep. Dinna speak or move until I call for ye. And keep yer horse quiet."

"I want to stay with you."

"No. I'm goin' to let the other horses go ahead of us, and if nothin' happens, then I'll call to ye. If there is an ambush, I want ye out of the way. They willna find ye there."

"James, you cannot fight off several of them by yourself!"

"I won't be alone." He gave her a crooked smile. "Neil is comin'."

She stared into his eyes. "How do you know that?"

"I dinna ken. But I do. We've only to hold them off for a bit, then Neil will be here. And probably Duncan as well."

"Then wait with me in the trees."

He shook his head. "And let Neil find me hiding? No' likely!" When she opened her mouth to argue, he put a finger on her lips, then leaned over to replace it with his own. His kiss was deep and long, and he drew back slowly from her.

"Go now, Ellen, before I forget what I need to do." He nodded back along the trail, and after a moment she turned her horse and retraced her steps.

Neil paused, looking at the road ahead as Duncan came alongside him.

"Ye ken the MacLeods would love to take their revenge here," Duncan said.

"It's on our land," Neil growled.

"Aye, but ye ken I'm right." He sighed. "And I suppose this is no' the time to remind ye that ye've just raided five of their crofthouses?"

Neil grunted and watched the glen ahead for any movement.

"Are ye goin' to send some men up the hill?" Duncan asked, shielding his eyes as he looked up the slope above the road.

"Aye." Neil gave Duncan a glance. "Want to take them?"

Duncan nodded. "That way it'll be done properly. What will ye do?"

"Wait a bit and watch, then, when I figure ye're in place, I'll ride along the road. Watch for us."

"I'll send ye a signal. We'll squash them between us. If they're there."

"And if no', we'll have had a bit of training for the young ones."

Duncan laughed softly, then began to pick his men. Neil looked at the road before him. He knew where he expected the MacLeods to be, a blind turn coming the other way. It was coated with trees and rocks that would provide cover for armed men ready to attack an unwary traveler.

It was here that the MacLeods had ambushed young Alistair MacCurrie as he came back from Inverness, here that Alistair had killed the grandson of the MacLeod chief, then barely escaped with his life. It was thirty years ago now, but still not forgotten by either side. The bend of death, the Brahan Seer had called it years ago, when he'd predicted that a day would come when Alistair would kill a man here and that the deed would be avenged years later.

Not today, Neil swore. If anyone were to die today, it would be a MacLeod.

There, among the trees—the movement he'd expected. Three men, moving stealthily lower on the mountain to position themselves above the road, disappearing into the trees. He watched as three more joined them. Not yet, he told himself. Duncan would be only halfway there.

The minutes passed slowly, but then Neil saw the flash of a sword from the rock above the MacLeods. Duncan loved to send that message, loved to stand tall on the rock and defy the enemy. Neil smiled, then picked up his reins. Jamie, he thought, I'm here. He moved forward at a walk, signaling his men to follow.

He saw a riderless horse round the turn, then another and another, and still more. The MacLeods exploded out of their hiding place, their battle cries loud as they raced down the slope, Duncan's men just behind them. The riderless horses reared and screamed, plunging forward in a bunch, blocking the road as the MacLeods turned to one another in surprise. Neil grinned and spurred his horse into a gallop.

Ellen heard the first war cries from her right, then they were repeated from the road below her. James. His voice, loud above the pounding of hooves, grew quieter as he moved forward. There must be an echo, for the same cry came back from across the small valley, where the road climbed into the trees.

She held her hand over her horse's nose, but soon realized that no one could hear it over the noise. The war cries were deafening now, the rock bouncing the voices back around the turn. And then there was silence. She leaned forward, trying to listen. And she prayed. After what seemed liked forever, she heard the sounds of men talking in low tones on the road below her, then laughing.

Two men. One was James.

"Ellen, lassie," James called. "Come out and meet my brother."

Chapter Eleven

Ellen pushed the last branch out of her way and stared at the two men before her. They were identical, both the same height, both standing in the same pose, legs wide. They had the same jet black hair, pulled back from the same forehead, and the same deep blue eyes, which watched her now.

Neil was dressed well, but simply. He wore a saffron shirt, the long leggings called trews, and a plaid thrown over his shoulder. The brooch at his shoulder was jeweled, the sword hilt he rested his hand on was gleaming gold, his boots of obvious quality.

Next to him, James looked travel-worn, and she knew she did as well. She was suddenly aware of her unkempt hair and her muddy skirts. She pulled her cloak around her as she approached them. The brothers watched her with intent expressions, both with that slight lift to the jaw. James moved forward, his smile wide, to take her hand in his and lead her forward while Neil watched them with no visible emotion.

It was astonishingly odd to look from James's delighted expression to Neil's impassive one, to see the same features at the same moment in different modes. She couldn't tell if

Neil MacCurrie was pleased or displeased about her presence. He looked from her face to her feet, then said something in Gaelic to James.

"Ellen," James said, pulling her next to him. "My brother, Neil."

"Lord Torridon," Ellen said.

"Welcome, Miss Graham." Neil's eyes were cold, his tone just short of rude.

James told her that they had been successful, that the MacLeods had been taken prisoner with harm to no one, and Ellen nodded, drawing strength from his touch. She would watch Neil as he watched her before deciding what he was.

Duncan appeared, leading several other men. He called out a greeting, embraced James and then Ellen, his smile wide and warm. It faded as James told about Fraser's latest attack.

"I should ha' stayed wi' ye," Duncan said.

James shook his head. "I asked ye to go ahead, Duncan. I had Dundee's men, and Ned."

Duncan nodded. "Aye, but I should ha' stayed. Ned's a lad. What about Grant. Was he killed?"

James shook his head. "No."

"David ran away when we were attacked," Ellen said.

Duncan gave her a puzzled look. "Grant? I wouldna ha' thought that."

"I would," James said.

"I'm glad ye're both still alive," Duncan said. "Shame about Dundee's men and Britta and Ned. They were good people."

"Britta and Ned might still be alive," Ellen pointed out.

Neil gave a snort of derision.

"One never knows what strange things might happen," she said, matching his cold tone.

Neil's smile was sardonic. "No, one doesn't." He spun on his heel and walked toward his men, throwing a comment over his shoulder.

"What did he say?" Ellen asked James.

James looked after his brother, his eyes troubled. "He said we should go home." He grinned at her. "Come, lassie, yer bath awaits ye."

Duncan patted her shoulder. "Neil's a wee bit testy just now. We've had a bit of trouble with the MacLeods."

Ellen only half listened to Duncan's story as they started away. She was both angry and afraid. Why did Neil dislike her so intensely? How could he be so different from his brother? And what did this mean for James and her?

She rode next to Duncan, James ahead of them with Neil, Neil's men behind them with the MacLeod prisoners. The brothers said little to each other, but exchanged glances so often that she was sure they were communicating.

"Duncan," she said, "do they know each other so well that they don't need to speak?"

Duncan watched his cousins for a moment, then laughed. "Oh, aye. They always do that. Makes me daft. I wish they'd use words."

"So I'm correct to assume they're talking now?"

Duncan nodded. "Aye. Look, lass, Jamie just said something that surprised Neil. Neil's raised one eyebrow. Now he'll look at Jamie, see? Jamie's said something in return—ye can see it in Neil's bearing. And neither has said a word. They've been like this as long as I've kent them." He turned to meet her gaze. "I've always wondered who it would be to break that bond."

"What makes you think it is broken?"

"Neil's verra anxious."

Ellen shook her hair back. "Anxious. Does that mean 'rude' in Gaelic?"

Duncan snorted. "I take ye're no' overpleased with him."

"No."

"Give him time, lass. Neil has a good heart."

"I've seen no evidence of a heart. Or of courtesy."

Duncan gave a bark of laughter.

They rode out of the glen at last, and along Loch Torridon, riding west into the fading sun, its rays highlighting the sides of the mountains that ringed the water. The loch was long and large, dotted with islands, white crofthouses tucked below the dark peaks. Duncan told her that this was Upper Loch Torridon, which would blend into Loch Shieldaig, then turn north and join the sea.

The shingled beaches were abuzz with activity, and many called greetings as they passed. Boats of all sorts lined the harbor; ships were anchored offshore, shore boats hurrying to and from them. Torridon was thriving, its people well fed. And curious. Ellen was reminded of her dishevelment, and tried to comb her hair with her fingers and straighten her filthy skirts.

"Ye look bonnie, lassie," James said as he joined her. He gave Duncan a smile as his cousin fell behind them.

"I look dreadful," she whispered. "They'll wonder who you brought home."

"Ellen," he said, his voice low. "No one else's opinion of ye matters. Only mine, and I think ye're beautiful. Hold yer chin up, lass, and dinna mind Neil's mood. He'll be more polite to ye in the future."

"I don't want to cause problems between you."

James grinned. "Ye dinna. Ye won't. Dinna fash yerself."

He pointed to the village they were about to enter, telling

her its name and some of its history, then pointed out the individual mountains on the other side of the loch. She smiled at him, her mood lifting as he talked.

Many of the villagers called greetings to James and asked him questions in Gaelic. She understood none of it, but gathered that they were curious about Dunfallandy, and welcoming him home. They must have asked who she was as well, for she heard her name and "Dundee" often. The villagers smiled at her, and she smiled back in return, saying hello in English whenever addressed.

Ahead of them, Neil was talking and laughing with his people, his smile wide. He could be James, she thought, as he took a moment to explain something to those standing at the side of the road. The likeness was uncanny. No wonder people talked about the twins.

She heard Neil say her name without inflection and met his gaze. He nodded but did not smile. She felt a thrill of apprehension, followed by a wave of annoyance. Neil was taking her measure. He had made it obvious that he did not welcome any intrusion between him and his brother. She raised her chin. It was time Neil MacCurrie learned to share.

They rounded a headland, and Ellen gasped as she saw Castle Currie. Huge and formidable, the castle commanded the larger headland ahead. It dominated the skyline, the walls of the structure of the same rosy sandstone that formed the mountains behind it; the castle appeared to spring out of the rock itself.

There were four round towers, linked by high walls that rose from the very edge of the cliff, with one narrow road leading up to a gatehouse. The rays of the sun were behind the castle, throwing the fortifications into sharp relief, the tops of the parapet washed with weak light, the shadows black beneath them.

She'd heard about these western fortresses, how impregnable they were, how necessary. Every horrible story about the Highlanders' violent natures and brutal raids came back to her in a flood. It was easy to imagine this harbor full of longboats and warships. Ellen wrapped her cloak tighter as they rode into the shadow of the castle, the air much colder where the sun had fled. What was she doing here, at the end of the earth?

The road up to the castle was lined with houses, then lifted itself for the last steep rise, bordered by long red stones carved with strange symbols, spirals and intricate knots. They paused as the large gates of the gatehouse were opened. Ellen leaned her head back, staring up at the stone walls and the men who manned them, wondering what she would find within. A warm welcome, or more of Neil's chilly reception?

The path turned twice before reaching a second gatehouse, no smaller than the first. Just outside the gatehouse, on a barren square of soil at the edge of the cliff, was the oak tree. Ellen stared at the twin trunks that grew upright, reaching for the sky. Through its still bare branches she could see the water of the loch; between them, the mountain James had called Beinn Currie. There were tiny buds of new growth just beginning to appear, the pale green barely visible against the gray limbs.

She held her breath. In Inverness the legend had seemed amusing, childish almost, but here, in the shadow cast by the twin trunks, she felt part of an ancient pattern. She glanced at James, who was talking with Duncan, then met Neil's gaze. He nodded slowly, as though recognizing her emotions, then turned from her with a half-smile. She exhaled, convinced that somehow she'd just passed a test.

Inside the castle, a large courtyard was quickly filling

with the people who poured out of the buildings. To the left was the ancient keep, built at the edge of the headland, and attached to it were two wings, each four stories tall, each facing the water. On the inland side another series of buildings was surrounded by curtain walls, fortified with parapets and manned even now, when the laird of Castle Currie was home.

Neil began calling orders as he dismounted, and men leapt to take the prisoners and hold horses. Neil and Duncan strode toward a low building at the far side of the courtyard while James helped Ellen down, holding her against him for a moment.

"I ha' to help Neil see to the prisoners, lassie," he whispered. "Just wait here, and I'll be right back. Dinna be afraid, Ellen."

"I'm not," she whispered.

He laughed and squeezed her hand, then followed the knot of men around the prisoners into the same building Duncan and Neil had entered. A groom set her case on the ground next to her and took her horse, leaving her alone in the swirl of people. Curious glances were thrown her way, and some of the women smiled, but no one said anything to her. She held her hands before her and waited.

After several minutes she saw the huge doors into the keep swing open, framing a gray-haired woman. She paused for a moment, staring at Ellen, then walked slowly across the courtyard, her gaze never wavering. She was thin and small, but she walked proudly, her shoulders back and her chin raised. As she got closer, Ellen could see that her eyes were the same blue as James's, as Neil's.

When she was a few steps away, the woman smiled and held out her hands. "Welcome to Torridon," she said. "I am Mairi MacCurrie."

Ellen returned the smile and took the outstretched hands, surprised to feel the strength of James's grandmother's grip.

"Thank you for your welcome, madam," Ellen said. "I am Ellen Graham."

"Ah." The older woman looked into Ellen's eyes. "Duncan told us about you. Dundee's cousin. The lass our Jamie and Duncan kept from harm."

Ellen nodded. "Yes. Again and again."

"Then ye are doubly welcome, lassie, for ye ha' had quite a time. Come inside, come inside. The air grows cold. Ye must be weary after yer journey. Tell me what happened and how it is that ye're here and no' at Glengarry."

James stood with Neil and Duncan, watching while the prisoners were secured. Neil had not thrown them in the old bottle dungeon, but into the cell that their grandfather had had fitted in the end of the stables. The men would be contained, but treated with civility. Which was more than they deserved. Neil had explained his thinking, that a war with the MacLeod families of Gairloch would only distract his attention from the greater threat from the east.

James knew Neil was right, but still he was furious that the MacLeods had planned to ambush him and Ellen; he had no doubt that their intentions had been murderous. He stood outside the cell, looking into the faces of the crofters who had meant to do him harm. They refused to look back at him.

"I like the old days, when we simply killed those who tried to harm us," Duncan said, coming to stand next to him. The prisoners pretended not to hear.

James nodded. "So do I."

"It's no' out of the question," Neil said. "Depends on what happens next." He leaned in toward the bars.

"MacLeods, if I decide to let ye live, and if ye ever threaten a MacCurrie or MacCurrie property again, I'll strike ye down wi' my own hands, and I will be neither quick nor merciful. It was my brother ye tried to kill, and I'll no' be forgetting that soon. D'ye understand?"

The men nodded.

"Good," Neil said. "I want us all to ken the risks ye run." He turned on his heel and walked back to the courtyard, James and Duncan behind him. When he stopped, James came to his side, meeting his gaze.

James knew his brother was trying to make amends for his earlier treatment of Ellen. They'd argued about it on the ride home, when he'd told Neil what he thought of his coldness. Neil had refused to give ground, had not apologized, but neither had he argued. His surprise at James's vehemence had been obvious. And now he was trying to repair the breach. James was not sure it was enough, but he was willing to stop arguing.

He'd been surprised himself by the extent of his anger. He'd expected his brother to be welcoming, or at least polite, not scathing. When Neil had been rude, Ellen had watched him with a fearful expression, her eyes large, and James had felt an instant rage that had shaken him to his core. Rage at Neil. He'd been angry with his brother many times, aye, but rage? Never. It was unbelievable. And unforgettable.

Now Neil watched him, wondering what he was thinking. For the first time in his memory James had shut his brother out, refusing to answer his questions. Neil wanted to know why Ellen was here, and what she was to James. What she was to him. He wasn't sure himself. But he'd be damned if he'd let anyone harm her.

* * *

Ellen looked around her in wonder as James's grandmother led her through the ancient part of the castle. They'd entered through doors that were almost fifteen feet high, opened to welcome James home, Mairi had said, leading her into a hall that must have stood for centuries. At the far end of the room was an arched window that overlooked the lochs below. Mairi paused in front of it.

"This is one of my favorite spots," she said. "I remember standing here the day my son was born—James's father—wondering what my child would be like. I never dreamed I would outlive him." She gave Ellen a sharp glance. "You have come to a house in mourning."

Ellen nodded. "Yes, I know. I'm sorry for your loss."

"It was a loss for all of us. My daughter-in-law Anne is no' herself. If she drifts off in the middle of a sentence, or suddenly starts to weep, ye'll ken why."

"My mother was the same when my father died. It must be very difficult for her. And for you, Lady Torridon."

"When my husband died, I thought it was the end of the world. It took years . . . I've never felt whole since. Losing Alistair is beyond comprehension. I still dinna believe he's gone. I wake in the morn expecting to see him." She sighed and wiped a tear away. "But life goes on, lassie, and that's what we'll do. Neil is laird now, and he's doin' a good job. And Jamie and Duncan will help him."

Ellen smiled. "James takes his responsibilities very seriously."

"Aye. And Duncan as well, although ye'd no' think so, with all his antics." Mairi straightened her back and gave Ellen a smile. "Come, Miss Graham, tell me what's happened since Duncan left ye. And please call me Mairi. Anne is Lady Torridon now, and soon Neil's wife will be. I prefer my own name, lass."

"Thank you. Please call me Ellen, then."

"I intend to. Come now, let's go find Anne."

Ellen was brought to a snug corner of the great hall, where James's mother sat looking into the fire. Mairi led Ellen to stand before Anne, smiling as she bent over her daughter-in-law.

"Anne, dear," Mairi said. "This is Ellen Graham, the lass Duncan told us about, the one he and Jamie saved from the highwaymen. She's come home wi' our Jamie instead of going to Glengarry."

Anne MacCurrie lifted her gaze to meet Ellen's, her intelligent hazel eyes full of sadness. She held out her hand and smiled. "Welcome, child. We didna ken ye were coming, but ye're verra welcome. Where are the lads, Mairi?"

"Comin', love. They caught some MacLeods," Mairi said as she settled into a chair. She gestured for Ellen to do the same. "We'll talk for a bit, Ellen, until the lads come, and then we'll get ye a room. Ye're no doubt wantin' a bath, aye?"

Ellen laughed. "You have read my mind, madam. I would love one."

Anne smiled again. "Then ye shall ha' it. Now tell us, if you would, how ye've happened to be here instead of with the MacDonnells."

Mairi asked most of the questions, about Ellen's home and family, John, the trip to Dunfallandy, and Fraser's attacks. Ellen told them everything, sparing no detail when they asked more probing questions. Neither asked about James, but when Ellen praised his courage and kindness, Anne and Mairi exchanged a look. James's grandmother's eyes gleamed with humor and speculation, his mother's with pleasure. Ellen suspected that she'd told more than she'd intended to.

Anne came to life when James entered. She gave a cry and rose to her feet, throwing her arms around her son, patting his back and telling him how good it was to have him home, asking him how he was.

James embraced his mother fondly. "I'm well, Mother. Dinna fret."

"I was so worried when Duncan told us about Fraser," Anne said. "Who is he? Why does he want John Graham dead?"

James shrugged. "I dinna ken, Mother. But he's quite persistent."

"If he wants another shot at Dundee, he can join the Williamites," Mairi said.

"No doubt he already has," James said. "So ye've met Ellen."

"I went and brought her inside. What were ye thinking to leave the lassie outside by herself?"

James's cheeks reddened. "I was comin' back, Grandmother."

"Aye, well, we've been havin' a chat while we waited. Ah, here're the lads," she said as Duncan and Neil entered.

Ellen saw the glance Neil gave James, saw James meet Neil's gaze, then look at her. She took a deep breath. She'd not wanted to come between the brothers, but it seemed she had.

Duncan settled loudly into a chair opposite her. "Well, Miss Graham, would ye like to stay awhile, or ha' ye developed a taste for travel?"

Ellen laughed. "I'll be quite content to stay for a while."

"And we're delighted to ha' ye," Mairi said.

* * *

Neil watched Ellen all through the meal, watched as his brother listened to her every word, as Jamie bent low over her, as Ellen smiled and reached a hand to touch his arm. Duncan was correct; the lass had bewitched his brother.

Jamie had barely spoken to him since they'd had words on the ride home. Neil couldn't remember the last time his brother had been so angry. James had told him, in so many words, that Ellen was to be welcomed, that Neil was not to be rude again. Neil rubbed his chin. How had this woman become so very important to his brother in such a short time?

His mother was describing now how she and his father had met, smiling through her tears as she told the story. Ellen Graham reached to put a hand on his mother's, receiving a weepy look of gratitude from her. He should be feeling quite pleased tonight, Neil thought. The MacLeods had been routed without bloodshed, thanks to Jamie, and as a result he'd been able to send an outraged demand for a meeting with their chief, a meeting in which he planned to end this testing of him, one way or another.

He'd assumed Jamie would be giving these problems his full attention; he'd never dreamed that the lass Duncan had told him about would be anything more than a memory, never imagined that Jamie would bring her home. And he was even more incredulous when James called the lass out of the trees and she'd come, her skirts torn and filthy, her face streaked with dirt, her hair drooping around her shoulders. His brother had introduced Ellen Graham as though she was the most beautiful, the most precious woman who had ever lived.

She'd cleaned up well, he had to give her that. Ellen was beautiful, he supposed, if one liked dark women. He preferred blondes, or ones with fire in their hair, not drab Lowlanders. Her remarks about the political situation had been both astute and concise, if quite biased toward Dundee. She was extremely attentive to James, kind to his mother, gracious in her comments about the castle, and she laughed with Duncan often. All of which he found pleasing.

Duncan seemed to like her as well. And his grandmother? Neil turned to look at her, startled to find Mairi watching him with a thoughtful expression. He colored. He knew his grandmother had guessed his thoughts. He was jealous—not of Ellen; Jamie could have her—but of the loss of his brother's attention.

Since their father became ill, he and Jamie and Duncan had gotten in the habit of settling down with a bottle to talk about what they should do next, often staying up late into the night, and that was what he'd expected to do when Jamie got home. There certainly was enough to discuss. But he suspected Jamie would not be talking with him tonight.

Neil knew he should be more generous. He should be pleased that Jamie had found a woman who pleased him. There had been no mention of marriage, nor of handfasting, so perhaps this infatuation would pass as quickly as it had arrived. Which would be best. Both Seaforth and MacLeod were pressing for a betrothal with Jamie. Neil would marry a MacKenzie, and he'd been thinking that Jamie should marry a MacLeod, which should help to settle the wayward MacLeods of Gairloch.

He'd never expected Jamie's head to be turned by a Graham. From the east. He heard the phrase as though it had been said aloud. Ellen Graham was from the east. He straightened his back, ignoring the chill the words had brought. He might marry the MacKenzie lass, who was from Kintail, but he suspected Jamie would never marry a Hebridean MacLeod.

He'd have to find a way to get the lass to Glengarry as quickly as possible.

Ellen sighed and turned over again. She was weary; her bed was soft, her room beautifully outfitted. And she was clean. She'd had her bath before dinner. So why could she not sleep? Dinner had been long, but fascinating, with Anne's stories and Duncan's jokes, and tales of what had happened at Torridon in James's absence. The conversation had often turned to the political situation, a good part of the meal spent speculating what would happen next.

None of that was keeping her awake. Neil had watched her throughout the meal, his gaze rarely leaving her. At first she'd not noticed, caught up as she'd been in learning about James's mother and grandmother. But each time she looked at the end of the table, where Neil sat, he'd been looking at her. And soon she was so self-conscious that she found it impossible to ignore him. Neil had almost not spoken to her, asking her only one question: why she had felt it so imperative to go to Dunfallandy herself.

James had slipped his hand into hers under the table as she struggled to explain why she'd had to warn John, and it was James who declared her courageous. Mairi, who also had watched her throughout the meal, though with far less intensity, joined James's praise of Ellen's bravery.

After the meal they'd joined many of the clan in the hall. James had introduced her to everyone there, his smile wide and his hand warm on her elbow, or on her back. He stayed with her all evening, but they'd not had a moment alone since their arrival.

James's family had been generous in their reception of her. Anne and Mairi had both welcomed her, and even their thorough questioning had been handled with courtesy and charm. She was sure they wondered what she and James were to each other, and surer still that James would be the recipient of much sharper questions. Duncan had been Duncan, his grin wide and his laugh infectious.

And Neil? Neil frightened her. He had said all the right things, had offered a toast to James's return and Ellen's arrival, had laughed when he was supposed to laugh. There was no repeat of his rudeness on the road, but there was a reserve, an iciness, whenever he looked at her. And he looked at her constantly. She knew he didn't want her here, but wasn't sure why.

What had she expected? she scolded herself—that James's family would all welcome the stranger she was into their home and their hearts on the same day? She was being ridiculous, she told herself as she turned over again. Tomorrow she would write to her mother, to Bea, and tell them all that had happened.

When would she see her mother and Aunt Bea again? Torridon was so far from everything; she must have been mad to agree to come here. Glengarry was a long way away, and Netherby might as well be on the other side of the world. She parted the bed hangings and looked through the window at the night sky, lit by a hundred thousand stars.

"Ellen Graham," she whispered. "What are you doing here?"

Chapter Twelve

James paced the room. He'd pleaded weariness and gone upstairs instead of retreating with Neil and Duncan to discuss everything. He was weary. And perhaps not thinking quite straight. He was still angry with Neil. And still shocked by his anger.

His brother's behavior had been perfect all evening, but James knew him too well. Neil didn't want Ellen here; that was Neil's problem. James had no intention of letting her go anywhere. If it were up to him, he'd keep her at Torridon, safe with his mother and grandmother, until the war was over.

And then what? He couldn't imagine life without her, couldn't imagine letting her go to Glengarry now, letting her return to Netherby and her stepfather. They'd shared only a few words this evening, and they'd had an audience at all times. He'd watched her, had seen her watching him, but a shared smile was not enough.

She'd looked beautiful at dinner, the blue dress she wore the same color as her eyes, her shoulders lovely above the filmy white lace that covered the tops of her breasts, her hair gleaming in the candlelight. She looked regal, magnificent, glorious. He'd been proud of her as he introduced her to his kinsmen, had seen the men stare at her, the women notice every detail of her appearance.

It was not just her beauty that impressed them; she'd charmed them with her genuine interest in them, her contagious laughter, her good humor at the difficulties of communicating with people who spoke only Gaelic. By the time she'd wished all a good night, most had been won over. His mother and grandmother seemed to like her. Duncan was fond of her already. But not his brother.

He stopped before the window, looking at the moon rising over the water. Loch Torridon was inky in the dim light. Its waters appeared calm from here, but they surged with strong hidden currents; he felt the same. James turned his back on the window and looked at the door. He could feel Neil asking him to come downstairs, to talk. He straightened his shoulders. Why postpone it?

Neil and Duncan were seated before the fire in Neil's study, their legs stretched out to the warmth. Both turned as he entered; neither was surprised.

"Thank you for comin', Jamie," Neil said.

James raised one eyebrow. So they would be formal tonight. Duncan would be pleased; there would be no silent conversations between the brothers. He poured a glass of whisky and sat in his usual chair. The three were silent for a moment, then James turned to Neil.

"What are ye doing about the MacLeods?" James asked. "Besides assuming I'll marry one of them and solve the problem?"

Neil grinned, and James felt the knot of tension inside

him relax. It would be all right between them. He'd been correct to come down.

"I've sent for their laird," Neil said. "We'll see who comes. It willna be Gairloch, I'm thinkin', although I've written to tell him what's been happening. It'll be the local MacLeod tacksman. If I'm right, we'll solve it without bloodshed."

"And if ye're wrong?"

"Ye'll marry a MacLeod," Neil said with another grin.

"Like hell," James said.

Duncan exhaled and swore, and the cousins all laughed together.

It was better, James thought as he climbed the stairs to his room. Not healed, not resolved, but better. They'd said not one word about Ellen, nor discussed Neil's plans for alliances with the MacKenzies and MacLeods, nor anyone's marriage plans. But they'd at least agreed to face the world together, and to be civil to each other. It was a start. He was glad he'd gone.

But through it all, he had been thinking of Ellen. He couldn't stop thinking about her lying below him, how her kisses had tasted, the feel of her breast in his hand, her hand on his thigh. He wanted her, but it was more than that. He wanted to talk with her, to discuss the evening, to gather her impressions of his family and his home. He wanted her in his life.

He stopped before her room, leaning against the door for a moment. He tapped lightly, his heart beginning to pound. He waited, tapped again, and called her name, this time rewarded by the sound of movement within. Ellen opened the door with wide eyes, holding her nightgown tightly closed at her neck. Her hair was down, tumbling in dark waves around her shoulders.

"James!" she whispered. "What are you doing here?"

He leaned forward, cupping a hand on her cheek, sliding it behind her head. "I missed ye, Ellen."

He bent his head, and she raised hers with a sigh. When his lips met hers, she leaned forward. He caught her around the waist, pulling her against him, deepening the kiss.

"I missed ye," he said at last.

"And I you."

"We'll walk in the morning, lassie, and we can talk then." He bent to capture her mouth again.

She put a hand on his shoulder, then wrapped it around his neck, kissing him with a fervor that left him no doubt that Ellen wanted him as much as he wanted her. He lifted his head and grinned, then leaned to brush his lips against hers.

"It's verra bonnie when ye miss me, lassie."

She blushed, and he laughed, releasing her with a smile. Her nightgown had fallen open, exposing the tops of her breasts, round and full. He raised his gaze before he lost the battle with his control.

"I'll see ye in the morning," he said.

"Yes," she whispered, then stepped back. She looked behind him, her eyes growing wide, then quickly closed the door.

He turned around and saw Neil. His brother's eyes told him that he'd not missed any of it. James stiffened, expecting Neil to say something caustic, but Neil simply nodded, then walked down the hallway to his room.

Morning brought rain, a slow drizzling rain without wind, which rolled down the stones of the castle and drained in lazy streams into the gutters. The sky was thick with gray clouds, layer upon layer, which dropped their moisture in unhurried showers, then waited while the next wave got itself into place. And the day brought news from the east, from the runner who arrived early mid-morning.

The Scottish Convention had offered William and Mary the throne of Scotland, the runner announced, and they had promptly accepted. Dundee was still visiting the clans who had not attended Dunfallandy, receiving pledges of men and support, was asking the clans who had already pledged to prepare. The call to arms would come soon.

King James was said to be in Ireland raising troops, meeting with much success. William's forces were gathering as well, his army growing with each day. Edinburgh was alive with Williamite sympathizers; those who favored King James were leaving the capital. The east held its breath to see what was next.

Neil, James, and Duncan listened to the runner's report in Neil's study. They asked a few questions, but it soon became evident that the man had already told everything he knew, and Neil told him to get some food and rest. The runner withdrew, leaving them to discuss his news.

"We'll have to get word to the crofters in the outer reaches," Neil said.

"And ready the ships," Duncan said.

James nodded. The king would need ships to ferry the troops from Ireland to Scotland, and Torridon was well equipped to help. The landing would be farther south, no doubt, but they needed to be prepared. Their father had kept his men trained and armed, so they had a ready fighting force, but this would be a far greater effort than simply keeping Torridon safe. They'd have to leave men behind to protect the clan and castle as well as sending men to join Dundee. Every MacCurrie needed to be ready.

Crops would still have to be planted and tended, fishermen sent out on the sea for extra trips. The stores from the winter were almost exhausted, and Torridon would need food to send with its men and to store in case of a siege, unlikely as that was. There was much to do. They talked for an hour, then joined the others in the hall. James looked for Ellen, while Neil and Duncan arranged for the word to go throughout Torridon. There would be a gathering of the clan tonight, and the household was already responding.

He couldn't find Ellen. His mother was in the kitchen, talking with the cook, but Ellen was not with her, although one of the kitchen lasses said she had served Ellen breakfast much earlier, so she was not still abed. He roamed through the courtyard, wondering if she had gone to see the outer buildings, but he was stopped every few feet by men wanting to know the latest news, and his progress was slow.

Ellen looked out over the harbor, now abuzz with activity. Last evening it had looked so peaceful, the sun lighting the sky over the moored ships, the smaller boats lined up on the shore in long lines. The reds and purples of the sunset had been reflected in the still water. How different the same scene was this morning. The water was filled with craft of all sizes, the beaches all but empty of boats. The village was busy, people hurrying to and fro.

She turned to look at James's grandmother standing beside her. Mairi's silver hair was deceptive; she missed nothing. She'd brought Ellen up here on the parapets that overlooked the village and the loch, saying she hoped Ellen would enjoy the view. Ellen suspected she had more in mind as Mairi settled herself on a stone bench that overlooked the water.

"I had them build this bench," Mairi said. "I used to stand here, watching the loch below, waiting for my husband to come home to me, and I would grow weary. I sat here every time he left. One day he didna come back."

"I'm sorry," Ellen said as she settled herself next to the older woman.

Mairi waved her hand. "No need, lassie. 'Twas a long time ago." She fixed her steady gaze on Ellen. "What are ye thinking?"

"That I have to tell my mother what happened before we decide whether we'll go back home at all. I'd like to get a letter to her at Glengarry."

"Simple enough. We'll see ye get writing things. The runner who's here now can take yer letter south."

"Two, actually. I'll write to my great-aunt at Netherby as well."

Mairi gestured for one of the men on the parapets to come to her. "Tell the runner to wait for two letters from Miss Graham. Dinna let him leave without them." The man nodded and left them, passing the message to another. "Done, lassie. Ye've only to write them."

"Shall I go and do that now?"

Mairi shook her head. "He'll wait." She looked out over the water. "Spring will come eventually, I suppose, but I dinna feel the air getting any warmer. What was yer weather in the east?"

"The same."

"So the roads were wet."

"Wet, but passable."

"It made travel slow."

"Yes."

"Ye had a lot of time together. Alone."

Ellen nodded. It was as she'd thought. Mairi had not brought her here to see the view. "We did."

"I'm told that everaone thought Jamie was Neil at Dunfallandy."

"Yes."

"It must ha' been easy to fall in love with the Earl of Torridon."

Ellen bristled. "I suspected, long before he told me, that he was James and not Neil. Ask him; he'll tell you. I heard Duncan call him Jamie."

"But ye did fall in love wi' him?"

Ellen took a deep breath and looked into Mairi's eyes. "James has saved my life over and over. He is the most splendid man in the world. He's wonderful. But you know that."

The older woman chuckled. "Aye, I do. He's verra important to this family. Ye do ken he'll no' be laird of Torridon?"

"I am aware of that."

"He's no' as wealthy as Neil, nor will he ever be. Second sons rarely are."

Ellen paused, warning herself to speak carefully. "Madam, if you are telling me that Neil is the one to set my cap for, you are mistaken in my intentions. I feel gratitude toward your grandson, not avarice. James saved my life, more than once. He brought me here to protect me, yes, but also because he wanted to hurry home to be with Neil. I had intended to go to Glengarry, and I will go there. In fact, I can leave with the runner if you wish me to."

"I wish nothing of the kind, lassie. I'm merely trying to find out who ye are and why ye're here."

"I am here because your grandson brought me here." Ellen looked at her hands, trying to control her anger. When she was calmer, she turned to Mairi again. "If I had been seeking a man with a title and wealth, I could have found one far closer to home, with far less danger involved in the selection. I did not set out for Dunfallandy to fall in love, but to warn my cousin. Making sure John knew of his danger was my goal, not a ring on my finger. We do have men in Dundee."

Mairi watched Ellen for a moment, then chuckled. "Well said, lassie."

"Well meant, madam," Ellen said, rising to her feet.

"I didna mean to insult ye, lassie. I apologize if I ha'. As I've said, Jamie is verra important to this family."

"And Neil has plans for James to marry elsewhere."

"Jamie will marry where both duty and inclination lead him. He isna free to decide without considering all factors. Many people will be affected by who he marries. I'm sure ye can understand."

"I do."

"Good." Mairi smiled then. "I ken ye care a great deal for our Jamie, Ellen, and he for ye. We've all seen that. But I dinna ken what the future will bring for ye. Guard yer heart, lassie. Now, come, ye've letters to write."

Ellen's letters were difficult to write, even though she'd been composing them in her mind for days. What would her mother think when she discovered Ellen was not safely at home caring for Bea, but at Torridon? That Pitney had harbored those who would kill John, that he might even be part of the plot?

Bea would not be surprised, for Bea had often pointed out that Pitney kept company with unsavory people. Ellen added a line to her great-aunt's letter, cautioning her to do nothing, hearing even as she wrote Bea's snort of derision. Bea would do exactly what she chose to do. Ellen folded her letters and sealed them, rising to her feet.

The hall was full of people receiving instruction. Duncan stood in the middle of a group of men, rearranging tables; Anne spoke to several women in a corner, and Neil and James looked at maps with others. She passed James's grandmother on her way to the runner. The older woman put a thin hand on Ellen's arm.

"Lassie," Mairi said, her tone quiet. "I want my grandsons to marry happily. I ha' no other plans for them but that. Whatever Jamie decides will ha' my blessing."

Ellen nodded. She would not discuss this further with anyone but James.

James saw her the minute she came into the hall. She held two letters in her hand, which she gave to the runner. He'd forgotten she wanted to write to her mother and great-aunt. So that's where she'd been.

"I'll be back in an hour," he said to the men as he walked away from the table, leaving Neil staring after him. The talk of war and preparation was endless. He needed a few moments with Ellen.

"Shall we take our walk now?" he asked her, offering her his arm.

"Aren't you talking with Neil?"

"I'd rather talk with ye, lass. The rain is gone. Let's go out."

"I'd like that."

He led her across the courtyard and down the path to the village in the strengthening sunlight, telling her when the different structures had been added, and by whom.

"Neil wants to build an addition to the west, a new wing where the family will live. We've been talking about it for years."

"Is there enough room on the headland?"

"Aye. It'll be attached, of course, but there's already a curtain wall there. It'll actually be quite simple. We've only to extend the outer wall." He gave her a sharp glance. "He'll start when we come home."

"From the war."

"Aye." He smiled. "I havena seen much of ye since we got here."

"No."

"We'll ha' to correct that."

"How?"

"By doing what we're doing." He waved at the guards as they approached the inner gatehouse. "I thought I'd start by showin' ye the oak tree."

He took her elbow and turned her as they came through the gate to a small square of land. He led her closer to the tree. It never failed to stir him, this huge ancient tree that represented so much to his clan, to him. As long as anyone could remember, there had a been a tree here. MacCurries wore a sprig of oak in their bonnets; their clan shield and badge showed an oak tree silhouetted against the sea.

This tree had been whole twenty-nine years ago, then split, just as the Brahan Seer had foretold. It was amazing to him. How could the Seer have kent? James ran his hand along the cleft, healed now, but still bearing the scar of the lightning strike. He felt the familiar emotions that the tree always evoked, the awe and sense of destiny, mixed now with bittersweet memories of his father.

"I didn't think it would be so big," she said. "It must

have been quite a sight, to see it whole." She looked at him. "Do you truly not believe the legend?"

"I do believe it, lassie."

"But you told Janet it was superstition."

"Aye, it is. But I believe it. Well, some of it."

"What parts?"

"That my da and grandfather and great-grandfather will be born and die on the same day."

"Which they did. What else?"

"That the tree will be split the night Neil and I are conceived."

"That happened as well. What else?"

His tone deepened. "That we'll lead the clan to war."

"I think you will."

She sighed. It was difficult to stand here in this beautiful place and think of war. Long streaks of clouds stretched across the sky, stopping to pause at the peaks of the mountains across the water. The scene was lovely, peaceful, if one did not look closely. Even now men on the ships below them were hauling cannons to the middle of decks. She glanced at James, memorizing his profile, the way his hair fell across the corner of his forehead, the scar on his hand from the fight at Dunfallandy with the MacLeod.

When she was with him, she felt safe, protected, and more alive than at any other time in her life. It was easy to forget that Scotland was about to go to war, that his brother wished her gone, that his grandmother had just warned her not to fall in love with him, that her cousin was raising troops to fight for a king who had lost heart, and that her well-loved maid was missing. Soon they'd go back to the castle and face the future, but for now she was content just to be with James.

James took a deep breath and gazed into Ellen's lovely

eyes, watching as she brushed back the hair that blew across her cheek. He wanted to throw her across his shoulder and carry her to his ship, to sail from all his responsibilities and just be with Ellen. But he could not. Yet.

"There are parts of the legend I do believe, but other parts I dinna want to," he said. "The Seer also said that we will each rule, but never will both rule, which would mean that Neil would die without fathering a child, and I would succeed."

"Perhaps there is another way that could happen without Neil dying. Or perhaps the prophecy has changed as people retold it over the years. Perhaps it isn't what the Seer originally said."

"Aye, perhaps. If it's fate, lass, I canna change it. If it isna, I'll discover that in time."

She nodded. He took her hand in his and led her to the other side of the tree, where the lochs spread below them and the mountains on the far side of the water stood rosy gray against the clearing sky. The islands that dotted the loch on its way to the sea melded together, crisscrossing the deeper blue of the water.

"So beautiful," she said.

"Aye. So beautiful. A verra beautiful woman." He lifted her hand to his mouth and kissed her fingers one by one. "Verra bonnie," he said, leaning to kiss her.

She raised her mouth to meet him without hesitation, the touch of her lips on his making him want to tear their clothes off and hold her to his naked body, to explore her again. Instead he kissed her, slowly, deeply, mindful of those who passed on the path behind them. There would be talk about them later, he knew. Let them talk, he thought, and brushed his lips against hers one last time.

"Come, lassie, I'll show ye my ships," he said.

She smiled up at him, and he laughed, his mood lightening. Who kent what was to come? They had today; it would have to be enough.

James pointed out his ships from the shore, then rowed Ellen out to the closest, helping her aboard with a surge of pride. He loved this ship; since the day she was built, he had cared for her, made sure she had the best of everything. He wanted Ellen to love her as he did. He showed her everything, letting the crew join in with comments as they walked through the decks.

He talked about the ship's speed, her grace through the heavy seas that winter brought and in the light winds of summer. He had no castle of his own to show her, no jewels, no title. But he had his ships and his land. He'd show her both. Ellen was properly enthusiastic, although she confided that she'd been on a ship only a few times in her life.

"We'll change that," he told her.

Ellen walked to the railing, gazing up at the castle. "It looks even bigger from here than from on land," she said.

"It was meant to. It was supposed to strike terror in the hearts of those who would attack us."

"How long have the MacCurries been here?"

He shrugged. "Centuries. We've held this land through many years, many kings. And we'll weather this storm as well."

"Do you think King James can win?"

"Aye. Yer cousin is leading the army, Ellen. How can he not?"

She was silent for a moment, then sighed. "A month ago my life was simple. Tell me it will be simple again."

"I canna, Ellen. I suspect life willna be simple for any of us for a long time."

"No."

"Did ye write to yer mother?"

"And to my Aunt Bea."

"Good. That should make ye feel better."

"How often do you get news of the outside?"

"D'ye mean Scotland, or the rest of the world?"

"Scotland."

"Verra often." He gestured to the water before them. "This is our highway, lass. Ye'll see ships comin' in and out of here all day, bringing goods and news. We may seem isolated when ye come by land, but we're no'. We hear most of the news in short order. We'll hear as soon as yer cousin calls for us to join him."

"And then you'll all go to war."

"And then we'll go to war." He looked up at the castle, then at her. "I would ha' ye stay here, Ellen, safe with my family, during the war. Will ye consider it?"

She met his gaze, her eyes shadowed. "I will consider it."

Neil was waiting for her when she opened her door to go down to dinner. Her heart had leapt at first, thinking it was James who leaned against the wall, his long legs lean under his kilt, his handsome face turned to the side. But when he turned to her, she knew it was Neil.

"Miss Graham," he said, stepping away from the wall.

"Lord Torridon."

"Please call me Neil."

"Please call me Ellen."

"May I escort you down to the meal?"

"Of course," she said as he fell into step beside her.

They talked of the day, of the lovely sunset. She waited

for him to reach the end of his small talk, which he did as they paused at the top of the stairs.

"Do you have property of yer own, Ellen?" he asked.

"No. I have a small income from my grandmother, but no property."

"So you must marry well." His tone was mild, but his gaze intent.

"I have been told that I will always have a home with my Aunt Bea. My needs are simple. I do not need to marry at all."

Neil raised an eyebrow. "An independent woman."

"If need be." She walked down four steps; he followed.

"How interesting."

"I will marry when and if I choose," Ellen said, continuing down the stairs. "I am looking for neither fortune or a title; I've met men with titles and no courtesy. Who would want one of those? Life would be an endless round of sparring."

Neil gave a bark of laughter. "Point noted, madam."

She looked into James's brother's eyes. "I will not marry where I do not love."

"A noble sentiment. Not practical for everyone. Take Jamie, for example. If he were to marry one of the MacLeod lasses, it would help the struggles we've had between the clans. If he were to marry a MacKenzie, it would strengthen our alliance with them."

"You are planning to marry a MacKenzie, which should strengthen your alliance considerably. Surely you would want your brother to marry where he wishes. It would be a luxury you will not have."

Neil smiled sardonically.

"Have you considered," she asked, "that perhaps you are

overstepping yourself in protecting James from me? Perhaps he neither desires nor needs your protection."

Neil gave her a cold stare.

"Perhaps you want his attention for yourself. Perhaps you simply don't know how to share James with anyone but Duncan."

"Perhaps I dinna choose to share James with a woman who doesna have his best interests in mind."

"If that were the case, then you would be correct to distrust me. But it is not." She stopped on the step above him, her eyes level with his. "I care for your brother very much. He's been courageous and kind, and I think he is wonderful. I want only the best for him. But he should choose what that will be, not you. You will someday have to face that James will have his own life, which may include his marrying, may even include his marrying someone you haven't chosen. Wouldn't it be nice if his brother, the man he's closest to on earth, could be happy for him in whatever or whomever he chooses?"

"Marriage is a practical matter, Miss Graham."

"I pity the woman who will share your life. Marriage can be much more than that. It was for your parents. I'm told they were quite happy, that your youth was richer for that." She watched his expression change. That barb had hit home. "Think carefully before making an enemy out of me, Neil. You may be twins, but you are not identical. Your brother has a heart." She brushed past him and continued down the steps.

"So do I, Ellen," Neil said, his voice low and angry. "And I will destroy anyone who tries to harm my brother."

"I will help you," she said.

* * *

The next three days were clear and sunny. The fourth brought visitors. The MacLeod laird did not come himself, but sent an emissary—his nephew, who brought enough men with him to start a small war. Neil sat with James and Duncan at a long table in the hall, trying to keep his expression solemn as the MacLeod's nephew and his men talked among themselves, obviously at sea. He'd not seen a less likely diplomat.

At last MacLeod marched up to the table, took a deep breath, puffed out his chest, and said his laird was too busy to deal with this matter, that he had come to speak to Neil in his stead. Neil looked the man over, then raised one eyebrow.

"I willna talk with ye," Neil said. "Tell yer laird he needs to come and speak to me himself. And bring money. He has debts to pay to my clansmen."

The emissary folded his hands in front of him. "My laird says ye owe him for the five farms ye've burnt and all the cattle ye took."

Neil leaned back and crossed his arms. "Yer people attacked three of my crofters' homes and killed three men. I havena killed anyone. I'm keepin' the cattle. And the prisoners, for now."

"My laird says yer brother murdered one of our men at Dunfallandy, and that he should be turned over to us for punishment."

Neil smiled slowly. "Yer kinsmen tried to kill my brother on his way here. Ask yer laird if he wants war. Tell him that if he does, I will be happy to oblige. Tell him my men need to practice running people through and I canna think of a group of men I'd be more pleased to lose. Tell him that he needs to think about what he does now verra carefully, for we are prepared and willing. Now get out."

Neil waited until the emissary and his men were gone, then he rose to his feet and gestured for James and Duncan to follow him. If the MacLeods wanted war, he was just in the mood to give it to them.

Chapter Thirteen

Ellen watched James stride across the room, deep in conversation with his brother. He'd forgotten her already, she thought, and tried to press down the panic she was feeling. She was being ridiculous. Of course Neil would want to discuss the situation with the MacLeods. Why did she feel so abandoned?

She knew why. She'd underestimated the bond between the brothers. Since her conversation with Neil, he'd been charming to her, but he'd kept James so busy that they'd hardly had a moment to speak, let alone spend any time together. She missed James, missed his touch, his kisses, his attention. She doubted James even realized that Neil was purposefully keeping them apart.

She'd been a fool to show her hand. If she'd thought to intimidate Neil MacCurrie, she'd been very wrong. He held all the cards. He was James's brother, and his chief. It was reasonable, with war on the horizon, to need James's complete attention; everyone was working long hours to prepare for the future.

She asked Anne and Mairi if she could help and was immediately put to work, which helped to pass the time. She did needlework, repairing clothing that the men would need when they went to war, and oversaw the household staff as they stored food in case of siege. The work was interesting, and she heard many stories of when James, Neil, and Duncan were young.

In the middle of a lovely spring day when the air was warm and many of the clan lingered outside to enjoy it, the MacLeod laird was announced. She'd almost forgotten that the prisoners still waited in the cell in the stables. The family had been at their midday meal, which was hastily cleared as the tacksman came in. MacLeod was no longer young; he moved stiffly, his heavy body swinging from side to side as he approached the table.

The negotiations were swift. MacLeod pretended that his clansmen acted without his knowledge or approval, and Neil pretended that he believed him. Neil agreed to let most of the prisoners leave; MacLeod would pay no reparations. Neil would keep the cattle he'd taken, which would be returned to the crofters who had owned them. And he'd keep one of the prisoners as well. MacLeod's grandson would stay at Castle Currie as a guarantee of the MacLeods' continued good behavior.

Neil sat back then, while James told MacLeod that should a repeat of the attempted ambush happen, he himself would bring the entire might of Torridon's forces down upon their villages. The MacLeod tried to pretend he was not shaken, but he hurried from the hall, his face pale.

Ellen went to the courtyard with everyone to see the MacLeods leave. The boy who would stay with them waved to his grandfather, then turned to face Neil, his eyes defiant.

"Do ye recognize that ye're here to keep the peace between us?" Neil asked.

The boy nodded.

"Then let's do that, laddie. Let's keep the peace for a change. We've had enough bloodshed." He glanced at James. "And near bloodshed. Ye do ken that if my brother had been injured, ye'd all be dead?"

The boy nodded again.

"Good. Then let's hope for yer sake that yer kinsmen behave. Come, laddie, let's find ye a whisky. It's been a long day, aye?"

Neil led the way inside and everyone followed except James and Ellen.

"That was simple," she said.

"Aye. If ye pretend they didna mean to kill us at the ambush."

"Why settle so quickly then?"

"We dinna need two wars at the same time, and obviously they dinna either." He paused, looking over the battlements, then into her eyes. "There's to be a gathering in Inverness of the northern clans. Yer cousin John will be there."

"Who will go?"

"Duncan and I."

Ellen stared at him for a moment, trying to control the sudden wave of fear that washed over her. "When is it?"

"A week tomorrow."

"How long will you be gone?"

"About five days, maybe more if it rains and the roads are bad." He grinned suddenly. "I'm no' expecting the same excitement I had at the last gathering."

She hugged her arms. "Do you think Fraser will be there?"

"He'll no' risk it, Ellen. Too many people ken who he is

and what he tried to do. No, he's gone back to Dundee or Edinburgh, or wherever he's from."

"Perhaps he's sent someone else."

"Yer cousin is aware how much danger he's in. He'll be well guarded."

"Can I come with you?"

"I'd love yer company, but it's better if ye stay here. It'll be some hard riding and then home again." He leaned to kiss her forehead. "Dinna fret, Ellen. Yer cousin will be safe."

"And what about you and Duncan?"

"We'll be safe as well, lassie. Dinna look so frightened, Ellen. This is only a gathering. We'll all be fine. And ye'll be safe here."

She nodded, unconvinced.

A ship arrived the next day from Kilgannon, bearing letters from Lochiel and Alexander MacGannon for Neil. And one for Ellen from her mother. The captain of the ship delivered the letters personally, then joined the family for their meal. Ellen tried to concentrate as the captain told them that the clans around Kilgannon were all preparing for war, but she heard little of what he said, her mind on what her mother might have written.

The man left at last, heading north to bring more news. The three cousins retreated to discuss their letters, and Ellen, to her room, tearing her mother's letter open as the door swung shut behind her.

"My darling Ellen," her mother had written.

Ellen's eyes filled with tears. It was all right. Her mother still loved her, even after all that had happened. She sank onto the bed and read more.

Rose wrote that she had been horrified by all that had happened. She was not pleased that Ellen had gone to Dunfallandy, although she understood why Ellen had done so, and she praised Ellen for her courage. She was grateful to James for saving her, asking Ellen to thank him for her. She was comforting herself that Hugh had only good things to say about the MacCurries.

Ellen was also to thank Neil for his lovely letter offering his hospitality to her daughter for as long as she needed it; Rose extended her greetings to all at Torridon. Ellen paused to look across the room. Neil had never mentioned that he'd written to her mother. But then, he wouldn't, would he?

As for Pitney, Rose was shocked beyond words. "I knew he was keeping company with unpleasant men," she wrote, "but I had no idea what they were planning. I would have tossed him out on his ear if I had. Things will change when I get home, believe me. I had already made some inquiries with Bea's solicitor before I left. I will make more upon my return."

All was well at Glengarry, even with all the turmoil in the rest of the country. Margaret had had a big, healthy son with no complications. Hugh was thrilled, strutting around as though he was the first man to produce a son. They had named the baby Richard after Margaret and Ellen's father, which had pleased Rose very much. Flora was still with them, but Tom had left to join John, and Rose was fearful of what war would bring.

Rose also worried about Aunt Bea, with Pitney still at Netherby. As soon as things were a bit more settled, she would be on her way to Torridon to collect Ellen. In the meantime, she sent her love. And her admonitions to be careful and to stay where she was safe.

Ellen read the letter three times. Her mother wrote as she spoke, and Ellen realized yet again how much she missed her family. If only they could be safely at home at Netherby.

But Pitney was there, she thought with a wave of anger. He was the cause of so much ill. If he had not let murderers use his house to plot John's death, Evan would be alive today. And John's men. And Britta and Ned would be safe at home, not missing.

She smiled at the vision of her mother marching back to Netherby to throw Pitney out. She had no doubt that Rose would win the day. If Bea backed her, perhaps the marriage could even be annulled; stranger things had happened.

Ellen folded the letter carefully, then lay back on the bed and stared at the bed hangings above her, missing her mother, her sisters, and Bea. To go to Netherby was impossible just now, but perhaps it was time to make plans to go to Glengarry. It was time to face the future.

She knew James cared for her, could see his eyes light when he saw her, felt his ardor when he held her close. But there was a reserve, a withholding, in him that she might never break through. Why did she stay? To wage war with his brother and catch stolen kisses from James in the hallway? She shook her head. Eventually she'd find herself in his bed, with no promise, no ring, no plan for the future. If a break between them were to come, let it be now. But how?

Lochiel had written that he was gathering men and was planning on Neil's support; Kilgannon had written much the same. Both asked for a report from the gathering at Inverness from James. The cousins talked about little else throughout the evening meal. His grandmother joined the discussion, but Ellen was quiet, his mother the same except when she said that she did not want to lose another man she loved. There was silence, then James leaned forward with a smile.

"Ye willna, Mother. Remember, the legend says we'll

lead the clan to fifty years of peace. We have to be here to do that."

"And Duncan?" Anne asked him. "Can you guarantee Duncan's safety?"

"He canna, Anne," Duncan replied. "But I can. I'll come home."

Anne gave him a sad smile. "I will hold you to that."

"And I as well," Mairi said.

"It all depends on whether France and Ireland send troops, Mother," Neil said. "If they do, we'll win the day quickly."

"And if they don't?"

Neil laughed. "We'll win the day slowly."

Anne looked at her sons and nephew for a moment, then nodded before turning to Ellen. "How is your family?"

"All are well, thank you. My sister had a son, and my mother sends her greetings to you all. Neil, she sends her thanks for your letter."

Neil's cheeks reddened. "My pleasure. It was my grandmother's idea, but I was pleased to do it." He paused, then gave her a wide smile. "I am not the ogre you think."

"No," Ellen said, her own cheeks flushing. "Thank you again."

Neil inclined his head gracefully. James reached for Ellen's hand under the table, surprised when her response was lukewarm.

James and Duncan left at daybreak two days later, taking with them Ellen's letters to her cousin and brother-in-law, six men, and eighteen bandoliers of gunpowder. She had risen early to see them off, standing in the courtyard with Neil in the misty light as they mounted their horses and turned for final farewells.

Duncan told her they expected a much calmer time at this gathering, since she would not be along. She laughed with him and told him to have a safe journey. James, who had watched her with an unreadable expression, brought his stallion next to her and leaned low.

"Will ye miss me, lassie?" he asked quietly.

She put her hand on his cheek. "More than you know. Please be careful."

"I will. I'll burn the road between here and Inverness to get back to ye." He bent lower and kissed her forehead. "I'll miss ye, Ellen. Keep yerself safe until I come back."

She nodded. "I will," she said. "You as well."

"I will." He stroked her cheek again, then straightened and nodded to his brother, giving the signal for his small troop to leave.

"Godspeed," she called.

James waved before he went through the first gatehouse. Neil gave her a glance, then strode away, leaving her alone in the courtyard. She folded her hands together at her throat, saying a prayer for their safety and ignoring the wave of loss that overwhelmed her.

James had been gone six days when Ellen got the letters. At first she was very pleased. Two letters, she thought, as she walked back to her room, delighted. She'd never gotten two letters at once. One was from her mother, the other from Aunt Bea. She smiled to herself as she unfolded her mother's letter first.

All was well at Glengarry, although Hugh would not even discuss a trip to Torridon just now. Rose reluctantly agreed that traveling these days would not be wise. The MacDonnells were preparing for war, and she was sure the MacCurries were doing the same, as was most of Scotland.

She knew it was unlikely, but she longed for the day they would all be together. If there were any way that Ellen could come to them, her mother would be delighted.

Ellen was still smiling as she opened Bea's letter, but her smile faded as she read Bea's opening words.

My solicitor is dead, and I must tell you what I have done. You are now my heir.

I changed my will shortly after you left. When I read your letter telling me that Pitney had those vile men in your mother's house, I knew I had to change everything. I could not bear to leave my property in Pitney's control, which is what would happen if my will had stayed as it was.

Until the day married women can legally control their own property, men like Pitney will destroy fortunes. I did not want that to happen to your mother. I know you will care for her always, which was my original intent. Your sisters will each receive a sizable amount of money, but you will inherit my home and all my personal property and land.

I had my solicitor draw up the papers at once, keeping them in his office. The documents concerning these changes are all missing now, and he is dead. I do not know what to think. His office was ransacked, then set afire. The smoke brought the neighbors, and they found the poor soul tied to his chair with his throat slit. I can only imagine the horror of his last moments.

Ellen, Pitney is the only one who would profit from this change. Could he have done this horrible thing? I don't know how he learned that I'd changed everything, but he confronted me about it only a few days ago, completely enraged. I had told only my lawyer and David, who despises your stepfather.

David, by the way, is not himself. He thought you were dead and is trying to understand that you are alive and safe at Torridon. He has always loved you, you know. I had hoped that you two would marry, and perhaps you can now. The money I had planned to give you as a wedding gift will still be yours if you do. David knows the details.

Take care, my dear child. I am writing not to alarm you, but to inform you. My property will be yours, and you need to know this if anything happens to me. Keep this letter safe. My lawyer's partner has agreed to honor my wishes and is drawing up new papers, but one never knows what may happen. Stay where you are. I have taken precautions to keep myself safe here.

My love, Bea.

Ellen read the letter again. She looked into the distance, trying to convince herself that this was real.

She found Neil in the hall and pulled him away from the men he was talking with, saying she must speak to him. His eyes narrowed, but he came with her to a corner of the hall, crossing his arms over his chest just as James always did. She stared at him for a moment, trying to find words. In the end, she let him read Bea's letter. He looked up at her with a worried frown, all impatience gone.

"I must leave at once," she said.

"How will it help to go to Netherby?"

"I'm not going to Netherby; I'm going to Glengarry. My

mother needs to know what has happened. We'll decide what to do together."

"Won't Bea have written your mother as well?"

"Perhaps. Probably. But Hugh won't let her come here."

Neil watched her for a moment, his expression concerned. Then he nodded. "What do you want me to do, Ellen?"

"Send men with me to Glengarry. I will ride as quickly as I can, and then they can come back to you."

Neil shook his head, and Ellen's heart sank.

"No," he said. "I can sail ye to Kintail, and ye can ride from there. It'll be much faster."

She let out the breath she'd not even realized she was holding, then stretched to kiss his cheek. "Thank you," she said. "Thank you, Neil."

He looked embarrassed. "If there is anything else ye need, ye'll tell me, aye?"

"I will. When can we leave?"

"With the tide. I'll tell the men. Go and pack, lass."

They left within hours. She'd thrown her meager possessions together, glad for once that she had so little with her, then wrote a letter to James in which she thanked him for rescuing her, for bringing her home, and for his many kindnesses. She dared not tell him that she would remember him forever. She signed the letter with her name, nothing more, and slipped it under his bedroom door.

Downstairs she bade a hasty farewell to Anne and Mairi, thanking them. They clasped her hands and embraced her, asking her to stay, saying they were afraid for her. She shook her head and said she must go. They agreed at last, Anne wiping a tear away as she said farewell, Mairi giving her a brave smile.

Neil accompanied her to the ship and saw her aboard. He gave her letters that he said would introduce her to the men whose lands she would ride through, and then he offered to go with her. She was tempted for a moment to accept his offer, but she knew he should stay at Torridon, and she thanked him for the use of his ship and the ten men he was sending.

"You are needed here, Neil. It's best you stay at Torridon. But I thank you for everything."

He took her hand in both of his. "I wish ye safe journey, Ellen Graham."

Her eyes filling with tears again, she thanked him again. He climbed back into the boat and waved as he was rowed to shore. And then she was off.

James frowned. The message from Neil was garbled. Not danger, not fear. An apology. For what? What had happened? He rose to his feet and stepped past the bench full of Highlanders, going to the side of the crowded hall where the press of men was less. Duncan followed him, but James only shook his head. He didn't know what Neil was feeling, but it was powerful. Satisfaction mixed with regret? An apology? It made no sense.

Ellen. It could only be Ellen. He felt his heart leap. The message was not to come home, but to be prepared. But for what?

He'd been a fool. He should have told her he loved her, should have asked her to marry him, should have told her he could not live without her. He'd been gone for only a few days, and he ached for her. No more. When he returned to Torridon, he'd ask her to be his wife. Damn the consequences. He was going to war; he should at least be able to wed the woman he loved beforehand.

They'd work out the details somehow. He knew everything that should separate them, but none of that seemed very important now. He loved her. And whatever was happening with Neil would not affect that. Nor with the world.

A roar of approval from the Highlanders brought him back to the present. The clan chiefs were on their feet now, cheering wildly, Dundee standing on the table at the front of the room with his arms raised. James had no idea what he'd said, but it didn't matter. These men would follow Dundee to hell and back, that much was obvious.

When Duncan leaned over to ask if he was all right, James nodded. He was fine. He was going to marry Dundee's cousin, and then he was going to war with the man. Life was simple again.

That evening, James and Duncan sat with Dundee and Tom Stuart, Ellen's brother-in-law, in the small room Dundee had claimed as his own. Both men listened with stony expressions as James told them what had happened after they'd parted near Dunfallandy. Tom was visibly angry as he talked about Pitney Malden and what he'd like to do to him. He shook his head when James asked if he'd heard of Cecil Fraser, but said he would make inquiries.

James gave them the letters from Ellen, watching their expressions soften as they read them. These men loved the same woman he did, he realized, and felt a bond he'd never expected. Soon they would be family.

"She's quite a woman, our little Ellen," Dundee said. "She was always brave, but I had no idea just how courageous she could be. She's very dear to me."

James nodded. "And to me."

"Ah. I did think that."

Tom's eyes narrowed. "How dear?"

James laughed. "I havena harmed her, Stuart. She's safe and well protected at Torridon."

"How long will you keep her there?" Tom asked.

"I'm going to marry her."

Duncan gave him a sharp glance, and Tom leaned back, crossing his arms.

Dundee smiled. "I'm hardly surprised, MacCurrie. It is James and not Neil?"

"James, sir. From the first."

"I thought as much. You have my blessing. May your life together be long and happy. May all our lives be long and happy." He called for whisky. "We have something to celebrate at last, gentlemen." He waited while glasses were poured, then raised his high. "To love, and happiness, and cheating death."

And cheating death, James thought, the words ringing in his head. He felt the hair rise on the back of his neck.

Ellen frowned at the sky. Surely there was another hour of daylight left. But no, she realized, it was so dark already that she could hardly make out the crofthouse just ahead. She bit her lip, telling herself to be patient. Their progress seemed so slow, but it had only been a few days since she'd been at Torridon, reading Bea's letter in horror.

Neil's ship had brought her to Kintail, and his letter had introduced her to the MacRaes, who had been very welcoming. She spent a comfortable night at Eilean Donan, but she hardly noticed the lovely castle. Nor, the next day, did she give more than a glance to the Five Sisters, the mountains that guarded the road east. She counted the miles to Glengarry. And the hours she'd been parted from James.

The talk everywhere had been of war, of the gathering at Inverness, which was said to be the last one before the call came to join John's army. Who had time for love? Why then, if her mind could understand that, did her heart ache at the thought of James returning to Torridon to find her gone?

She'd probably never see him again. She'd hear of him in the years to come, that he had married the MacLeod or the MacKenzie girl, that Neil had married as well, that the MacCurrie brothers were populating the world with dark-haired sons who had their father's blue, blue eyes. It would be unbearable. Or would the pain fade with the years, as Bea's had?

And what would she do? Probably never marry. She'd live with Bea, and perhaps her mother as well—three women who had all been unlucky in love. Bea, of course, would want her to marry David, but that would end as soon as Ellen told her what had actually happened. How shameless he was, to return home, to tell Bea he was sure Ellen was dead. What story had he concocted to explain how he'd survived and she had not? Catherine was welcome to him.

Glengarry at last. The guards refused to let her pass through their station. They would, they said, send a message to Lord Hugh that a woman claiming to be his sister-in-law was arriving from the west. She nodded, too miserable to argue, and waited in the damp while they sent for him. At least it had stopped raining.

A few minutes later a large man dressed in black, his hair streaming behind him, raced down the road from the castle. Neil's men, their faces grim, muttered among themselves and drew their weapons. Hugh's men did the same, facing the strangers with wary eyes.

Ellen ignored them all. The man who pounded toward her was her brother-in-law. She raised her arm to wave to him. He did not wave back, but skidded to a halt before her, his horse breathing heavily.

"It is ye! Ellen, lassie, why ha' ye come?"

"I got a letter from Bea, Hugh. I came to see my mother. Is everyone well? Is Margaret—"

"Margaret and the bairn are fine. We're all well here. But yer mother's gone. She left for Netherby three days ago."

"Gone. How can she be gone?" James stared at his brother.

Neil told him about Bea's letter again, explained how insistent Ellen had been that she leave at once. James didn't understand it. All he could understand was that she was gone. Why had she not waited for him? A few more days, and he would have gone with her. She'd kent his schedule, but she'd chosen not to wait.

"How could ye let her go?" he demanded of Neil.

"I couldna stop her, Jamie."

"One lass, one mere slip of a lass, and ye couldna stop her?"

"Ellen insisted."

"Ye didna try to stop her," James said. "Ye helped her leave. Ye gave her a damned ship and escorted her away."

"It wasna like that!" Neil said. "I did help, but it was what she wanted. I was trying to help."

"Ye didna want her here."

"No' at first."

"No' at ever. Ye did everything ye could to make her want to leave. Ye could ha' gone to Inverness, but ye wanted me to go. Ye kept us apart, dinna think I didna see it."

"I dinna do that, Jamie."

The brothers stared into each other's eyes, then Jamie made a disgusted sound.

"Och, I ken all that," he said. "Ye've told me ye couldna stop her. Truth is, ye didna try."

"No," Neil said.

"I'm going to marry her, Neil."

"Ye need to think on it more. She's a Lowlander."

"She's Dundee's cousin. That should be recommendation enough."

"She has no money."

"And I ha' no need for it."

"What about the alliances?"

"Ye're marrying a MacKenzie. That should be enough."

"There's still the MacLeods."

"Ye scared them enough last time. Do it again. I'm marrying Ellen, if she'll ha' me."

"She'll ha' ye, Jamie. Dinna fear that."

"Then why did she leave?"

"She was afraid for someone she loves. Her great-aunt is the same age as Grandmother. If Grandmother had written a letter like that, what would we do?"

"Go to her."

"Aye. And that's what Ellen did."

"So now ye're defending her?"

"I'm explaining what she did."

"Ye used to think she was after my money."

Neil looked uncomfortable. "Aye."

"And now?"

"No."

"Even though she left when she discovered she would inherit? Doesna that make ye wonder if she was in a hurry to go because she no longer needed me?"

"Are ye daft? She's no' like that."

James smiled. "No, she's not."

Neil watched him with narrowed eyes. "Was that a test?"

"Aye."

"How did I do?"

"Ye passed."

Neil leaned back against the wall and grinned. "Ye bastard."

"If I'm one, so are ye."

"Are ye really going after her?"

"Aye."

"Ye'll take some men."

James nodded.

"What else d'ye need?"

"Yer blessing."

Neil extended his hand. "Ye have it, Jamie. Go and bring her home."

Chapter Fourteen

Ellen felt ill. She'd so wanted to see her mother. It was impossible that Rose was gone.

"She wrote to you before she left," Hugh said, his tone gentle.

"I didn't get her letter," Ellen said.

"No. Come, lassie, Margaret wants to see ye, and Flora as well."

He gestured to her men to follow them. Ellen let him lead her up the hill.

Her sisters welcomed her with cries of joy and warm embraces. Margaret, after scolding her for not staying safely at Torridon, led Ellen to the cradle where her son slept. Flora wrapped her arm in Ellen's as they bent to watch their nephew.

"He's beautiful," Ellen said.

Margaret beamed. Hugh bristled. Flora laughed.

"Bonnie, Ellen. Braw. My son isna beautiful, lass."

Ellen smiled at her brother-in-law. "He's beautiful, Hugh."

"Yes, isn't he?" Margaret put a gentle finger on

Richard's cheek. The babe turned at her touch. "Not yet, little one. Sleep now. I need to talk to your Aunt Ellen."

"Aunt Ellen! Isn't that lovely to say?" Flora cried.

Ellen nodded. "And Aunt Flora."

"I want a babe," Flora said.

Ellen laughed with the others. "Goodness sake, Flora, you've only been married a few weeks!"

Flora's expression grew serious. "What if Tom doesn't come back? I hope I'm already with child. Otherwise I might never have one!"

Ellen watched Flora, shocked by her own thoughtlessness. She'd been so caught up in worrying about John—and James—that she'd not even thought of the danger to Tom and Hugh, of the fears that Margaret and Flora were facing. Flora's new husband had already left for war. Margaret's child was only a few weeks old, but his father would soon leave as well. She was not the only one worrying about a man she loved.

"Tom will come home," Hugh said. "Dinna fash yerself. He'll come home."

Margaret nodded. "We'll win, and King James will be restored, and all will be well with the world."

Flora looked at them with tears in her eyes. "I pray you're right."

"I am," Margaret said, her old forcefulness reappearing. "Come now, Elle, change out of those wet things. We'll get you something to eat, then we'll talk."

"I know you wonder why we let Mother go home," Flora said. "But we couldn't stop her. You know how she is when she's determined. And she wouldn't let me go with her. She said I might be in danger, since Tom is with John, and that I needed to stay here to take care of Margaret. I did try, Ellen."

"Hugh sent as many men with her as he could," Margaret said, with a glance at her husband. "He couldn't go himself, since Glengarry needs him here. They are all in the midst of preparations to join John. The men who went with her had orders to be sure both Mother and Bea were safe before they left them there."

"And if they were not?" Ellen asked.

"Then they would bring them home."

"Home? Here?"

Margaret smiled. "Here, Ellen. This is home to me now."

"You look so pale, Ellen," Flora said.

"I've been worried about Bea, and now Mother."

"Hugh's men will take care of both of them," Margaret said. "I want them to bring Bea back here with Mother. At least you're here now."

"I'm going to Netherby."

Margaret exchanged another look with Hugh. "I do not think so. Change your clothes. Then we'll talk."

They did talk, long into the night. Ellen told them everything that had happened to her since Flora's wedding, sparing no detail except for what had happened in the cave. And that she loved James. Flora told her of her wedding trip, cut short by the talk of war. And Margaret talked of her life at Glengarry, of her husband and now her son, of her fears for the future.

Ellen watched her sister hold her baby with a sense of wonderment. Her sister had changed. She'd softened, her moods not as brittle. When Ellen asked her if she was happy, Margaret laughed.

"Very. Love changes everything," she said, then looked at Ellen speculatively. "And what about you? Who will you marry?"

"Bea wants her to marry David," said Flora. "But that was before."

"I think she's chosen someone else," Margaret said. "Am I right?"

Ellen blushed.

Flora and Margaret exchanged a look. "James MacCurrie," they said in unison and laughed.

"Are we right?" Flora asked, leaning forward eagerly.

Ellen nodded. "But I'm not sure my feelings are returned."

Flora shook her head. "Oh, no, he took you home because he couldn't think of what else to do with you. Ellen in love. Who would have thought I'd see the day? Mother will want to meet him."

"I don't think she will get the chance," Ellen said.

"Which brings us to the next topic," Margaret said. "Elle, you are not going to go to Netherby."

"Margaret, I am."

Hugh MacDonnell's home was a fortress, set on a black rock that rose steeply from the hills around it. It was well guarded, and the guards were wary of the strangers who had arrived just as the sun was setting. James gave his name, then waited while a runner was sent to the house. A few moments later the runner returned, saying James was welcome.

Ellen, he thought, I'm here.

His men were sent to the hall, but he was shown into a sunny parlor. Two women sat on a couch, side by side, while behind them a tall Highlander stood, legs wide apart and arms folded. He must be Hugh, James thought, and they must be Ellen's sisters. One looked much like Ellen, quite beautiful, but older and with darker hair. The other was fairer and very pretty. And very curious.

"MacCurrie," the man said, extending his hand. "Welcome. I am Hugh MacDonnell. This is my wife Margaret and sister-in-law Flora Stuart."

James removed his bonnet and bowed slightly. "Sir. Madam. Madam. Thank you for your hospitality."

"Ye are welcome," Hugh said. "How was yer trip from Torridon?"

"Uneventful."

"And ye are on yer way to—"

"I have come seeking Miss Graham."

Hugh exchanged a look with his wife, then met James's gaze. "Why?"

"I must talk with her."

"Why?"

James lifted his chin. "That is between Ellen and me."

Hugh gave him a sharp glance, then crossed to a table and poured two glasses of whisky, handing one to James.

"Sit, if ye will," Hugh said. "We're strangers. We'll talk for a bit. How is it ye ken Ellen?"

"We were both at Dunfallandy," James said, keeping his tone mild.

"So I've heard. All of the Highlands ha' heard the story."

"Ask Glengarry if ye wish someone to vouch for me, MacDonnell. He kens me. He kens Ellen as well. He spent a bit of time talking wi' her." He felt his eyes narrow. "Has she gone to see Glengarry?"

Margaret exchanged a glance with Flora.

"No," Hugh said.

"Madam," James said to Margaret. "I need to talk wi' yer sister. Is she here? Will ye no' bring her to me?"

Hugh sipped his whisky. "How do we ken ye dinna wish her ill?"

"Ask her. Ask Ellen," James said. He sat down on the chair behind him. "I'll wait. Ask her and see what she says."

"We cannot," Margaret said.

"Margaret!" Hugh cried.

Margaret frowned at her husband. "For heaven's sake, Hugh, let's not pretend. Mr. MacCurrie, why do you need to talk to my sister?"

"She left Torridon while I was at Inverness, madam, to come here to see yer mother. There were things left unsaid between us."

"Will she want to hear them?" Flora asked.

"I hope so. I think she will. But she'll decide, madam."

Margaret leaned back, studying him for a moment, then exchanging a look with Flora. "My sister has sent your brother's men back, and she has gone to Netherby."

James stared at her. "With her mother? Yer mother?"

"Our mother left earlier."

"Did something else happen with yer Aunt Bea?"

"No. But Mother insisted on going home. Ellen insisted on following her."

James leapt to his feet, handing the whisky to Hugh. "Thank ye. I'll go now."

"Stay, Mr. MacCurrie," Flora said. "It's already dark. Spend the night, and we can tell you her probable route. You can find her more easily in the morning."

"He's done it!" Her host burst through the door, into the small room where Ellen ate her dinner alone. "He's done it! Yer cousin, Miss Graham! He's raised the royal standard for King James. I've just heard the news!"

Ellen's lips were suddenly dry. "When?"

"April 16th. Four days ago, in front of fifty of his men, on the verra top of Dundee Law. Then he went to

Glenogilvie, to see his wife. She told him to 'go where the honor of his king commanded.' What a lass! Are ye no' proud?"

Ellen nodded. "Of course," she said woodenly. "Very proud."

"We'll get King Jamie back on the throne, lassie! Then those Williamites will be singing a different tune, aye? And I'll tell the tale that Dundee's cousin stayed in my home the night I heard the news! I must tell my wife!"

He went out with as much noise as he'd entered, leaving Ellen staring at the still-swinging door. John had issued his war cry. The call to arms was next. Dear God, she prayed, protect my family, protect those I love. Protect James. Protect my country. And my king, she added belatedly.

James heard the news the night after he left Glengarry, sitting with his men in an inn on the River Spean. Dundee had raised the standard. They were going to war. He should be pleased, he thought, and he supposed he was, but he sat back in his chair and looked across the small room full of cheering men. Did they ken what war was? Were they ready?

Neil, he thought, it's coming. Be ready.

Before he'd left, he and Neil had talked about what they'd do if the call to arms came during James's absence. They'd decided to meet wherever and whenever Dundee had asked the clans to gather. Neil would bring James's things if necessary. Now that the standard had been raised, would the wait for the call be much longer? How would he get Ellen to Torridon and still join Dundee?

He spent the next two days going as quickly as he could, eating meals on horseback and letting no one rest for long. The third day he stopped to ask about Ellen at an inn on

Hugh's list, and was rewarded with the news that she'd spent the previous night there. He was getting closer. If she followed Hugh's instructions, he'd find her tonight. He leapt on his horse and waved for his men to follow.

It was late when they arrived at the tacksman's home. The house, on a rise above the river, was large and well kept, built of the local stone, two long wings spreading from the center door. The tacksman looked harried and weary, but he nodded when James asked him about Miss Graham.

"She's here, sir," the man said. "But my children are both ill, and we haven't done more than show her a room. I put her in the wing overlooking the river, with her men. Shall I send for her?"

"No, ye ha' enough to do, sir. I ken ye ha' MacDonnell's men here, and now I'm adding mine. If ye would tell me where she is, I'll find her." He handed the man coins to feed his men.

The tacksman seemed relieved and pointed out the hallway for James to follow. "Her men will tell ye which room she's in, sir. She's the only guest tonight."

James thanked him, then walked slowly down the hall, his heart in his throat. In a few minutes he'd be with her again. Would she want to see him? Or had she left as much to leave him as to help her Aunt Bea? Whichever it was, he'd soon find out.

The hallway turned, then led into a dimly lit foyer where four men played dice on the rug in the middle of the hall. They scrambled to their feet, hands on the handles of their pistols. He held up both hands to show he carried no weapon.

"I ha' come to see Miss Graham," he said. "Where is she?"

"Who are ye, sir?" one of the men asked.

"MacCurrie of Torridon. Who are ye?"

"We're not to let anyone talk with Miss Graham, sir."

"Let her decide. Tell her James MacCurrie is here."

The men exchanged glances, then one shrugged and climbed the stairs at the other side of the foyer that ended in an open hallway above. Through the wooden railing James saw the man walk a few feet, then disappear around a corner. A moment later he reappeared.

"She's on her way, Mr. MacCurrie," the man said, his tone disapproving.

James nodded.

Her face was pale, her hair loose, her cloak wrapped around her shoulders. She leaned over the railing, her hands white against the dark wood.

"James?"

He stepped forward into the light. "I'm here, Ellen."

"Oh." Her eyes grew wide.

"I'd like to talk with ye."

"Yes," she said, her tone hushed. "Yes."

James turned to the men who watched them. "Leave us."

"We canna, sir. Lord MacDonnell told us—"

"Leave us."

The men exchanged glances, then glanced at Ellen. "Miss?"

She took a deep breath. "Yes, you may leave. I will be quite safe with Mr. MacCurrie."

When they were alone, James stepped forward.

"Ellen, lassie, why did ye leave?"

"Did you not get my letter?"

"Yer letter said ye were worried about yer Aunt Bea."

"Yes. I was. I am."

Her letter had been quickly written, he knew, but there had been no warmth to it, no recognition of what they'd become to each other. Or had he read too much into a few kisses? He felt suddenly weary, as though he'd invented something that did not actually exist.

Her voice was low, tentative. "James, why are you here?"

"I couldna let ye leave like that, wi' so much unsaid between us."

"What was unsaid, James?" She almost whispered now.

"Ellen, why did ye leave?"

"I got Bea's letter. I had to come."

"I went to Glengarry."

"You did?"

"Yer family is quite protective."

She smiled softly. "Yes. Yes, they would be."

"Dundee has raised the standard."

"I heard."

"He'll be calling the clans soon."

"James, have you come to tell me that John is going to war?"

"No." He crossed to the foot of the stairs. "I came to tell you I love ye."

She stared at him.

"Ellen, did ye hear me?"

"Yes," she said, her voice so low he had to strain to hear her.

He took the stairs three at a time, stopping a few feet from her. She stared at him with wide eyes.

"I love ye, lass. I ha' loved ye since the first day I kent ye. I should ha' told ye long before this." He took a step toward her. "Ellen? Ha' ye nothing to say?"

She was crying silently, tears streaming down her cheeks. He moved to stand before her.

"Dinna cry, lassie, dinna cry. I came to tell ye I love ye, no' to distress ye."

"Oh, James," she said, half laughing, half crying. "You are not distressing me. Tell me again."

"I love ye, Ellen Graham." He opened his arms, and she flew into them.

At first she thought she was dreaming. She'd done that so often, pretending to herself when she lay in some hideous strange bed full of lice and God only knew what else, that James would come through the door, telling her he loved her, asking if she loved him.

There had been a moment, when she stood peering down into the dim foyer, that she thought she'd dreamed him, had wished so hard for him that some sort of vision was appearing to her. But he was real, this big man in her arms. She clung to him, wrapping her arms around his shoulders.

"James," she said. "James. You came for me."

"How could I not?" he murmured against her hair.

She raised her face to his, his mouth immediately on hers. How she had longed for this, the pleasure of his touch. He groaned as she opened her lips and offered herself to him. He was real, warm beneath her fingers. She caressed his back and sides, bringing her hand forward to stroke his cheek.

"James," she said, leaning closer.

He groaned and lifted his head at last. "Ellen, do ye love me?"

"Do I love you?" She laughed softly. "I think I have loved you from the first moment I saw you, James MacCurrie. How could I not?"

His mouth claimed hers again, his lips insistent, pressing hers open, then teasing her to join him in the dance that lovers played, the thrust and parry of a real kiss. She arched against him, trying to get closer, then leaned away.

"Come," she said, taking his hand and leading him down the hall.

She was alone in this wing. Some of Hugh's men had planned to sleep in the foyer below, but there was no one else on this floor. Her bedroom was large, paneled with a dark wood that gleamed in the light from the fire. She led James inside, then released his hand and closed the door, leaning against it, drinking in the sight of him.

He was dressed for travel, in tartan trews that hugged the muscles of his legs, his thighs solid beneath the plaid draped around his shoulders. His jacket was a blue that matched his eyes, his shirt a saffron that made his hair look even blacker. His eyes were dark, his hair torn from its binding by her hands.

"I cannot believe you're here. Talk to me," she said. "Prove you are not a vision I have conjured."

He tossed his bonnet onto the chest in the corner, then unbuckled his bandolier and baldrick, placing them on the floor next to the chest, his pistol atop the pile.

"Ellen," he said, turning to face her, "I ha' missed ye, lassie."

"And I you."

He laughed softly, touching his lips. "Aye. I can tell."

"I love you, James."

He took a step toward her.

"I love you," she said again and threw her arms wide. "I love you, James MacCurrie!"

He was in front of her before she saw him move, pulling her into his arms as he bent his head to hers. He traced a line of kisses across her forehead, then down her cheek, to lavish attention on her jaw, then her neck. He peeled the cloak from her shoulders, tossing it on the floor, and then he stepped back to look at her from head to toe, his hand smoothing her hair and lifting her chin for his kiss.

"Ye are so beautiful, Ellen," he said reverently. "So beautiful. Marry me." His hands circled her neck, then slid lower to her collarbone, pushing the neckline of her nightgown apart. "Marry me. Be my wife. I canna live without ye, Ellen. Say ye will."

She smiled slowly, wrapping first one arm around his neck, then the other. She leaned back to look into his eyes. "Yes! Yes and yes and yes!"

He bent to kiss her again, his ardor matched by her abandon. He ran his hands through her hair, circled her neck, and leaned against her.

"Ye are mine, Ellen Graham. Swear it."

"I swear it," she said.

Grabbing her discarded cloak, he led her to stand before the fire, pulling the ring off his finger while he watched her. "We'll handfast now and marry when we can. D'ye ken what it means?"

"Handfasting? That we promise to live as man and wife for a year. At the end of the year, if either of us wants to leave, we dissolve the handfasting. If we want to stay together, then we're married."

"Aye. Do ye consent?"

She brushed a dark lock of hair from his temple. "No. I will handfast tonight, James, but I will consider us wed. We'll have the ceremony later, but you will be mine tonight."

"Aye," he said, his voice rough with emotion. "Aye. I will be. I ha' been from the first, lassie."

"I love you, James."

"And I ye, Ellen."

She watched through a blur of tears as he put his ring on her finger and closed his hand around hers, pulling her cloak around their joined hands. He looked into her eyes.

"I, James MacCurrie, pledge my love and faithfulness, my body and my heart, to ye, Ellen Graham."

She took a deep breath. "I, Ellen Graham, pledge my love and faithfulness, my body and my heart, to you, James MacCurrie."

He kissed her until she had to gasp for air. "It is done, Ellen. Ye are mine."

"And you mine."

He tossed the cloak aside, then pulled her back into his arms, claiming her mouth with a ferocity that left her breathless. He tasted like whisky, like nectar. Like heaven.

"Now, teach me the rest of it," she said. "I am eager—"

His mouth covered hers before she could finish her sentence, his hand reaching under her nightgown, stroking up her leg. He put a hand on either side of her, lifting the material slowly in his hands until it bunched around her waist. He stroked his hand down her leg and leaned against her.

She moaned when his hand touched her, then again as he separated her thighs with his leg, moving closer until his thigh rested against her flesh, the wool of his trews soft against her leg. His fingers slid along her skin, leaving a trail of sensations that warmed her, soon forgotten when he replaced his leg with his fingers, cupping her softly.

His mouth found hers as his fingers began to move, parting her lips with his tongue and her folds with his fingers. Ellen gasped as he slipped inside her. His breathing grew more rapid as he moved his finger slowly deeper into her. He kissed her cheek, her jaw, her neck.

She put her hands on his chest. "I can feel the warmth of your skin through the shirt."

He leaned back from her, and with a few swift movements shrugged out of his jacket, lifting his shirt over his head and throwing it behind him.

"Now feel the warmth, Ellen," he said, guiding her hands to his chest again.

He was beautiful, she decided, his upper body muscled and smooth, his eyes a deep blue as they watched her study him. She smiled and put a hand on each of his wide shoulders, letting her fingers glide down his chest, tangling her fingers in the dark hair there, then stroking lower. She followed the line of hair to his waist, tracing the contours of his stomach, stopped by the waist of his trews.

His skin felt like silk. She lowered her fingers, dipping them under the trews, to the softer skin of his buttocks. She explored farther, her hands between their bodies now. He leaned back to allow her access, then moaned as her fingers closed around him. She looked into his eyes and laughed with triumph. How wonderful he felt, how male, how perfect.

He lifted her nightgown over her head, pulling her against his chest, the feel of his skin on hers amazing. He stepped back from her and smiled, then pulled the trews from him, standing before her naked and ready, his body glowing in the firelight. She smiled. Hers. He was hers.

He tilted his head and studied her. "Ye are magnificent, Ellen. Let me look at ye."

Ellen did the same, letting her gaze slowly lower from his lean face, shadowed now on one side, the other lustrous in the light from the flames, to his shoulders, straight and strong, past his stomach. She traced her hand down from his waist to circle him again.

"Ye are driving me mad," he murmured.

"Then let's go to the madhouse together."

He kissed her throat and her shoulder, then cupped her breasts, holding them in his hands, smiling, then bending to claim her nipple, drawing her into his mouth. She gasped, raking her hands through his hair.

"James," she said, stroking his back as he moved to her other breast. She closed her eyes, concentrating on the sensations he was causing, hardly noticing when he lifted her against him.

She clasped his shoulders as he slid his arm beneath her legs and carried her to the bed, throwing the covers aside and laying her on the cool linen. He stretched out next to her and bent to her breast again.

She moaned as his finger slipped inside her, moving quickly this time, and wrapped her fingers around him, tightening her hand until he groaned with pleasure.

"Ellen," he said, pushing into her touch, moving his hand and hips in the same rhythm. "Are ye ready?"

When she nodded, he slid on top of her, parting her thighs with his legs. He linked their fingers and pulled them over her head.

"I love ye, Ellen," he said. "Lassie mine, I do love ye."

She arched to meet him as he slowly entered her. He moved forward, then paused, looking down at her with dark eyes.

"Are ye a'right?"

"Yes. Oh, James, I had no idea—"

"Does this please ye? Or do ye want me to stop?"

"Don't stop." She gasped then as he moved deeper.

He froze, leaning back to look at her. "Are ye still a'right?"

"Oh, yes." She took a deep breath and shifted below him. "I'd heard about this, but could not imagine what it would feel like. I feared all the songs and stories were exaggerations."

"And what d'ye think now?"

"That they didn't tell the half of it. Show me more."

He laughed and thrust into her. "I'll try to educate ye well, my love."

Chapter Fifteen

Neil examined the swords on the table before him, trying to see them as weapons, not the fulfillment of a prophecy. If Jamie was here, they would have made jokes, would have made the task seem commonplace, not fraught with meaning. But Jamie was on the other side of Scotland. And, from the feelings Neil was receiving, very busy.

The bond had been very strong just after Jamie left, then broken in the last day, which could only mean one thing. He'd found Ellen. Neil was no longer sure what he felt about it. Jealousy? Or was he pleased that his brother was so in love with the lass that she eclipsed all else, including him? It was time for each of them to marry and start a new phase of their lives, but somehow he'd always thought he'd be first. It was a strange feeling to be left behind.

Marriage was a practical matter, he'd told Ellen. She'd been contemptuous, all but laughing at him. Was she correct? Could one love within the bounds of marriage? It seemed unlikely, but she was right that his parents had done just that. He shook his head. It was so much easier to consider the political gain alone. Would whatever it was between Jamie and Ellen last? Or would his brother return, sadder but wiser, and things return to what they'd been?

But no, nothing could be as it was. They were going to war.

His grandmother moved through the hall now with several young girls who carried the breastplate armor he, Jamie, and Duncan would wear, their father's armor. Upstairs his mother directed her women who sewed new shirts for them. In the harbor below, men pulled the fishing boats to form a barrier across the entrance to the Upper Loch. And in the fields, crops were being sown even though the men would not be here to tend them.

Neil looked out the window at an oak tree, split into two, and he thought of a tale of twins who took their clan to war. War, then fifty years of peace, the Brahan Seer had promised. God willing, that much would be true.

Jamie, he spoke silently. I need ye. Come back.

"Lord Neil?"

Neil came back to the present, turning to the lad.

"Duncan has returned."

Neil strode across the hall of the old keep to meet his cousin. Rain, driven horizontal by the wind, followed Duncan into the building as he struggled to get the door closed before the whole hall was flooded.

"Tell me again why we live here," Duncan said as he shrugged off his wet jacket. "At least the storms will keep the MacLeods at home. I thought ye were going to let old MacLeod's grandson go. I just saw him in the stables."

Neil grinned. "I did release him, but the lad wants to go to war with us. He's written to his grandfather for permission."

Duncan snorted and followed Neil through the corridor to the fire in the hall, taking the offered chair and settling to face his cousin. "Clanranald. Glengarry. Keppoch. Lochiel. Glencoe. Glenmoriston. Sleat. All going. Hear anything from Jamie? I mean actual news, no' one of yer 'feelings'?"

Neil shook his head. "What of Mackay's numbers?"

"Not sure. I've heard he has twice as many as we do."

"Aye, well, they're only Lowlanders," Neil said, and the cousins laughed.

Ellen stretched her arms above her head, then froze when she touched him. She looked to her right. James. She sat up and stared at him. It had not been a dream. His ring was on her finger, and he was in her bed. Naked. And smiling at her. She swallowed.

"Good morning, love," he said.

"James," she whispered, clutching the covers over her breasts. She was naked as well, her body sore from the night's activities. What had she done? He leaned to kiss her side, and she jumped, staring down at him. He laughed.

"Dinna tell me ye've forgotten me already?"

"No," she whispered.

His expression sobered. He reached to pull her hand away from the blanket, holding it up between them. "Ellen. Look at the ring, lassie. We've handfasted. It's aright. Ye dinna ha' to look at me like I ravaged ye." He sat up and gave her a sharp look. "D'ye regret it?"

She shook her head. He'd not forced her; he'd not had to. She'd willingly gone into his embrace, had participated as much as he, with abandon, as he had. And how did she feel now?

Loved.

She smiled slowly. It was all right. She held her hand higher and wiggled the finger that wore his ring.

"I'm married," she said.

He nodded. "So am I."

"I'm married," she said in wonderment.

"Handfasted, to be exact. No' married yet." He yawned. "But ye're still mine, lassie. Handfasting is legal where I come from."

She leaned forward to kiss his chest. "You'll have to tell my mother that," she said, trying to keep her tone light.

"I will, assuming we're still goin' to Netherby?"

"Yes."

"We'd best get out of bed then, aye?"

She smiled again as she ran a hand down his chest to where the cover stretched across his stomach, then slid her fingers under the blankets. He grinned and rolled over on top of her, tracing a line of kisses down her cheek and neck.

"We'll leave later, I'm thinking."

"What will everyone say?"

"That I'm a lucky man."

The weather was clear, and they made good time. James shared her bed, their nights filled with passion, with humor. They talked until the wee hours, learning each other's histories, each other's fears and goals. The more he talked, the more she loved him, this splendid man who was hers.

If he'd ever spoken of it to his men, he'd not told her, and she'd not asked. Nor had the men behaved as though anything had changed. Perhaps she was the only one who felt different, as though she saw the whole world through new eyes.

She was loved. She loved in return. Even the dreary landscape seemed beautiful to her. She saw new growth on the trees, saw the bees beginning to make their rounds. It was the end of April, and winter was at last leaving Scotland. She smiled and raised her face to the sun.

They stayed at the places on Hugh's list, and although they heard that her mother had been there earlier, they did not catch her. When they passed the turn to Dunfallandy, James asked her if she'd like to stop and pay Fergusson a visit. Ellen shook her head and laughed.

The innocent girl who had ridden that road just a few weeks ago no longer existed, and the woman she was now had no desire to see Dunfallandy, or Fergusson, again. That shrewd man would know with one glance what had happened between them.

She tried to ignore the signs of war, to forget that in a few weeks, or even sooner, James would be leaving her and joining John's army, but the signs were everywhere. Men filled the roads, and the villages and towns they passed were humming with activity. People could talk of little else.

James and Ellen had kept their views to themselves, not discussing their loyalty to the Jacobite cause with those they encountered. But James wore Highland dress, and it was often assumed that he would join Dundee. When they were sure of their welcome, as they were with those on Hugh's list, she and James would talk with their hosts, asking the latest news.

The countryside was teeming with rumors, with tales of troops being massed on both sides. As they went east, they heard stories that Mackay had captured John, that John had captured Mackay, that Highlanders were marching toward the capital, eating the young of those who opposed them. People came out of houses to stare with fear in their eyes as the Highlanders passed.

James had laughed at the stories at first, but as the fear of the people they passed grew in intensity, he became silent. He ignored the stares, but he had Ellen keep her father's pistol loaded and handy, and he rode at her side. At night they slept with their door locked and barred, his sword handy. At daylight they rode even faster.

It was in Perth, almost home, that they heard that John had asked the clans to meet him at Lochaber on May 18. Their host, a burly man with eyes that missed nothing, told them quietly that the word was being spread about the date of the rising. The reward on John's head had been increased, and he was now officially considered a traitor to the court of King William, but the clans and many Lowlanders were making their final preparations to join him.

Ellen listened without comment. Another day and a little more would bring her home, and that was all she could think about. Once there, after they'd discovered how her mother and Bea were, after they'd confronted Pitney, she'd decide what to do next. She knew what James wanted. He wanted to collect Rose and Bea and head west, to leave them at Glengarry, or to travel on to Torridon if there was time, where they would be safe for the duration of the war.

She refused to discuss leaving Netherby again. No matter what they found at home, there were more than three people to consider, she told him. The household staff, the tenants, the farmers who tilled their ground—all would need to be cared for. She would not leave until she was sure that they'd be all right. Or that all was lost.

She knew what war could mean to Netherby. She was the cousin of the leader of the army trying to oust the current king, and Dundee was not only within striking distance of Edinburgh, the city itself was a symbol of John's defiance. Netherby, owned by his cousins, would be an easy target for vengeance. Ellen would not leave its people to their own defenses.

She and James argued about it, their inability to convince each other frustrating. And that each could see the other's position only made it worse. At last they stopped trying, concentrating on the last few miles that they must travel.

Netherby. Ellen stopped at the turn to the house, although she and James had already decided that they'd go farther, to Bea's house, assuming that Rose would be there with Bea. Ellen was pale but calm, and turned to meet James's gaze.

"If ye'd like, lassie, I'll ride with the men and kill the bastard. Then it'll all be over, and yer mother can go home."

Ellen shook her head slightly. "I would like nothing more, but we cannot do that."

"No' yet. Let's find yer mother and Bea and see what they want me to do. It could be arranged at verra short notice."

James watched as she took one last moment to look down the drive to Netherby before lifting her reins and continuing on. She'd been quiet all morning, distant, her thoughts preoccupied. She was withdrawing from him, not relying on him at all.

She'd been passionate in bed at first, but each mile that brought her closer to home took her further from him. Last night she'd lain silent in his arms, keeping her thoughts to herself. He did not ken what to think. Was she reconsidering their handfasting? Had he won her at last, only to lose her to Netherby? Was she thinking about her mother and Bea? Or Grant?

The thought of David Grant made his blood boil. He was afraid that he'd not be able to control his contempt if he saw the man again. How could Grant have returned to Dundee after what he'd done, and to continue to woo Ellen through her great-aunt? He was convinced Bea had told Grant her plan to make Ellen her heir, and that Grant had told Pitney

Malden. He'd like a moment or two alone with the man to discover if he was correct. And then to put Grant's teeth down his throat.

Bea's house was a handsome structure that stood on a rise above the glen, its gray stone front symmetrical and well tended. As they arrived, their twenty men kicking up the dust of the drive, the front door opened. A footman gaped at them, then slammed the door with a horrified expression.

Ellen laughed, the first time today. "He probably thinks the Highland hordes have come to pillage."

James grinned. "Well, what does yer Aunt Bea have? We might be tempted."

"A wonderful cellar."

"That's a start," he said, sliding off his horse and reaching for her.

Ellen put her hands on James's shoulders and slipped off her horse as the front door opened again, this time wide, filled with two figures. Ellen gave a hoarse cry, and James turned to see what she was looking at.

Britta charged down the stairs, her hair and skirts flying, her face lit with delight, Ned at her heels. James stared in disbelief.

"Miss Ellen! Miss Ellen! You're home! You're safe!"

"Britta! Ned! You're alive! God be praised!" Ellen cried, opening her arms.

The maid threw herself into Ellen's embrace; Ned stopped at James's side and they both watched the women laughing and crying.

"Ye're alive," James said, clapping the lad on the shoulder. "I'm verra glad of it, laddie. I ne'er thought to see ye again. I'm verra glad to see ye."

Ned grinned. "Yes, sir. I have a few scars, but we're here."

Britta stepped back from Ellen at last. "Welcome, Mr. MacCurrie."

James smiled. "I'm verra glad to see ye well, Britta. Ellen's been praying every day for yer safety. And I ha' as well. I didna think to see ye again, lassie."

Britta exchanged a glance with Ned. "We weren't sure we'd make it home, but we did. We'll tell you all about it. Miss Ellen, your mother will be so pleased to have you here."

Ellen looked up at the house. "She's here?"

"At Netherby," Britta said. "Everyone's at Netherby. I just came here to get more clothes for your aunt."

"How is Aunt Bea? Is she safe?"

"Oh yes, miss. She's staying with your mother. The funeral is in the morning."

"Funeral? Whose funeral?"

Britta looked surprised, then recovered. "Your mother wrote to you, but of course you won't have gotten the letter yet. Your stepfather, Miss Ellen. Mr. Malden. He's dead."

Netherby Hall looked the same as when she'd left, the windows glowing with light that was diffused through the sheer curtains her mother always had pulled at sunset. James helped Ellen to the ground, and she paused, saying a prayer of thanks that her mother and Bea were safely inside. She had questions, and much to say, but all that could wait. Home, she thought. I'm home.

The door opened, and a footman appeared, calling over his shoulder. A moment later Ellen's mother brushed past the man. With a cry, she ran down the steps, her arms outstretched.

"Ellen! Oh, my sweet girl! How did you come so quickly?"

"Mother!" Ellen ran to meet her mother's embrace.

Rose was pale, her eyes red, but calm. "I am so glad you are here, my darling girl."

"Mother," Ellen said, "is it true? Is Pitney dead?"

Rose nodded. "Yes. Two days ago." She looked from Ellen to James. "And this is—"

Ellen took James's hand in hers. "Mother, this is James MacCurrie. James, my mother."

James bowed. "Madam."

"Mother, what happened to Pitney?"

"He was murdered. On the road just outside our drive." She glanced at James's men, who watched them curiously. "Come inside, and we'll talk. Mr. MacCurrie, have your men go to the kitchens." She took Ellen's arm and led her up the stairs to the house.

"How is Aunt Bea?" Ellen asked.

"She is well. Resting just now, but we'll have someone fetch her. She'll be so relieved to see you." She put a hand to Ellen's cheek. "My dear daughter. I cannot tell you how happy I am to have you home."

"I cannot tell you how happy I am to be home," Ellen said, and saw James give her a sharp glance.

Ellen could not believe that Pitney was dead. He'd been found dead in the middle of the road, his hands tied to his horse's reins. He'd been stabbed, many times, and left to die in the dark. A footman, returning from an evening out, had come upon him and raised the household. Bea had been summoned from her home, had left her bed in the cold of the night to see Pitney's body. She'd sent a footman for the magistrate, then waited for the hours it took for him to arrive.

James listened quietly while Rose told them the story, standing when the door swung open and Bea came in, calling Ellen's name. Their reunion was joyous. Bea seemed to have no sadness about Pitney's death, only relief. Bea had given James a thorough scrutiny when they were introduced, taking in his travel-worn clothes and Highland dress. She welcomed him with a broad smile.

When Ellen raised the subject of who had killed Pitney, her mother and Bea exchanged a glance. "What?" Ellen asked. "What do you know?"

"Precious little, child." Bea said. "I am convinced that Pitney killed my lawyer. But who killed Pitney? And why? I don't know." She shook her head. "He had some unsavory characters here. It must have been one of them. He owed money everywhere. He left a staggering number of debts."

Rose nodded. "He did. I will have to sell land to pay them all. But no matter."

"No matter!" Bea snorted. "You are kinder than I am, Rose. The man stole your money and has left you in debt. I, for one, will not miss him."

"No matter what one thought of him," Rose said, "he did not deserve this."

"Someone thought he did," Ellen said.

Rose shook her head and sighed.

"Mother," Ellen said, leaning forward, "someone killed Pitney. Someone killed Bea's lawyer. I think I know who it is."

"That Fraser man," Bea said. "Britta and Ned think so too. The man is a beast. He was here not too long ago."

"Here?" Ellen stared at Bea. "Here? Fraser was at Netherby?"

"About a fortnight ago. I didn't see him. I didn't come here while you were gone. But Ned saw him. He followed him to Dundee, in fact."

Ellen thought of Fraser's cold stare, of his cruel acts, and shivered. Fraser, here. The thought terrified her; she reached for James's hand. Her mother and Bea both noticed, but neither mentioned it.

James broke the silence. "I am sorry for your loss, madam," he said.

"Thank you, Mr. MacCurrie," Rose said. "I will survive. What I've learned about Pitney has destroyed any feeling I'd had for him earlier."

"I understand," James said with a glance at Ellen. "I canna forgive the man for what he put yer daughter through. She might have been killed."

"But for you," Rose said.

Ellen smiled and tightened her hand on his. "He was so wonderful, Mother."

James then looked at Rose. "I was in the right spot, madam, for which I will be forever grateful."

"We thank you for your courage, Mr. MacCurrie," Rose said. "And for bringing my daughter safely home to me. Please do stay with us while you rest from your travels."

Your travels, he thought. What did the woman think he was, a mere escort? Could she not see Ellen clasping his hand, his ring large on her finger? He knew Bea had noted it, had watched her look from the ring to his face. Perhaps Ellen's mother was too caught up in her shock and grief to realize what they were to each other.

He suspected Rose wanted no part of him. It was too early to speak of marriage, with a funeral on the morrow, but the discussion would have to come, and soon. He would have to be at Lochaber by the eighteenth of May, and he'd have Ellen as his wife before that if he had any say.

He kept his tone mild. "What did the magistrate do?"

"Very little," Bea said. "Said Pitney was dead, that he'd been murdered by unknown persons. As if we hadn't realized that. He'll do nothing. He kept a man here for a day, then ordered him away. We're quite on our own."

"No' anymore, Miss Graham. I ha' twenty men with me."

"Good. Call me Bea, sir." Bea smiled and gave a pointed look at James and Ellen's joined hands. "I suspect it's a bit late to be formal, James."

James felt a knot of tension relax. Ellen's great-aunt would not oppose his suit. But her mother? He'd ken soon enough.

Rose called Britta and Ned in to tell their story. Ellen listened with a horrified expression and James with growing anger as Britta told of seeing Ned wounded and fall. Fraser's man had ignored Britta's screams and futile attempts to hold him off, turning the unconscious Ned over, then leaving him for dead, joining the others when James had attacked Fraser.

She'd pulled Ned into the undergrowth, hiding them both. When the fighting moved toward the road, she'd dragged Ned down to the river and to the other side. By the time James and Ellen had been searching for them, Britta had half carried, half dragged Ned away. They'd been taken in by a crofter who had hid them well.

"We looked everywhere," Ellen said.

"I was terrified Fraser would kill us," Britta said.

Eventually the two made their way back to Dunfallandy, where Fergusson had offered them shelter. When Britta said they must go home, he'd supplied them a few coins but no protection. They'd headed east and, afraid to go back to Netherby, had at last arrived at Bea's house, where Bea had welcomed and sheltered them.

Rose dismissed Britta and Ned, and led Ellen and James in to dinner. James's anger grew even more when Bea spoke of sleeping with Ned outside her door and Britta in the room with her, of living in fear of attack any moment, of the ugly argument with Pitney about her plans to leave her lands to Ellen.

"I still don't know how he knew," Bea said.

"Grant," James said with disgust. "Ye wrote that ye told Grant. He must ha' told Malden."

"But why?"

James shrugged. "I dinna ken why he would, or if he did. But someone did, and Grant was one of the few that kent yer plans."

"David ran," Ellen said, and told the story.

Bea stared at her with wide eyes. "That's not at all what he told me."

"No, it wouldn't be, would it?" Ellen said.

"He wants to marry you," Bea said.

"He won't," Ellen said firmly. "I'm going to marry James."

Rose gave a cry of protest, quickly smothered. James looked into her eyes, seeing her resistance. He'd been right; she would oppose them.

"What are your politics, James?" Bea asked.

"The same as yers, madam. The MacCurries are preparing to join Dundee's troops. We'll fight for King James."

"A dangerous position these days."

"And the only correct one."

Bea nodded. "I agree. But that means you'll be at Lochaber on May eighteenth."

"Aye." He glanced at Ellen. "I'll hate to leave her."

Ellen smiled at him. "We have handfasted. We're going to marry."

"I will be asking for yer daughter's hand in marriage, Mistress Malden," James said. "Not the now, when ye've just had a death. But ye should ken what's in my mind."

Rose looked from James to Ellen. "I cannot discuss this now."

"I love yer daughter. I want to spend my life with her. I will spend my life with her."

There was a silence, then Rose nodded at last. "We will discuss it, Mr. MacCurrie, but not now."

"As ye wish, madam."

"Thank you. And now," Rose said, rising from the table, "it is late."

"Where should my men and I sleep, madam?" James asked.

"You may use my house," Bea said. "It's empty. I've been staying here."

"I thank ye, madam, but it's too far. I canna be that far from Ellen."

"You are not married yet," Rose snapped.

"I ken that." He looked from Bea to Rose to Ellen. "I dinna mean to frighten ye, but someone killed Malden, someone killed yer lawyer. I'll no' be at a house five minutes away. I'll be here."

Rose studied at him for a long while, then relented. "I agree. You may sleep in Margaret's room. We will find places for your men."

Ellen stood with her back to her bedroom window, facing her mother. She was beginning to recover from the shock of Pitney's death, beginning to think of where life would go from here. She was not alone in that; her mother had come to talk about Ellen's plans with James.

Rose had been candid, telling Ellen she understood what handfasting meant, all that it entailed. Ellen saw no condemnation in her mother's eyes, only concern, which had disarmed much of her anger.

"Give me time," Rose said with a shaking voice. "I will bury my husband tomorrow. It's too soon to think about you marrying. I cannot bear it all at once."

Ellen felt selfish for adding to her mother's cares. "I'm sorry, Mother. It's difficult for me to mourn for Pitney, but I know you are."

"I'm not sure I am," Rose said. "I'm not sure of what I feel. Let us get through tomorrow and then face what's next. If he truly loves you, and if you truly love him, I will consider this marriage, but not now. We will wait the year of mourning. If he is not genuine, that will give us time to discover it."

"A year! Mother, we cannot wait a year! I love him! How can you even think that he is not genuine? What would he have to gain?" She laughed ruefully, thinking of Neil's worries. "James's brother was worried that I was after his money. Why is everyone so difficult?"

"It is very sudden," Rose said.

"I love him, Mother."

Rose sat on the bed with a weary sigh. "He is very handsome. I know you are grateful to him—"

"Grateful! Yes, but it's more than that! I love him!"

"You think you do. Of course you would feel a strong emotion for someone who has saved your life—"

"More than once."

"More than once."

"I love him, Mother."

Rose sighed again. "Hear me out, child. You do not know this man. No one is doubting that he is brave and has been kind to you. No one is doubting that you both are caught up in strong emotions. There will be war soon. We are all affected by that. Don't confuse attraction and sentimentality for love."

"Mother—"

"Ellen, listen to me, please! I have been married twice. Once to your father, a man I had known all my life. And then to Pitney, a man I knew for only a few months. You see what a disaster that was. I was lonely, Ellen, and I made a terrible mistake. There is no need to rush into this marriage."

"Yes, there is, Mother. He's leaving. James loves me. I love him."

"You hardly know him."

"I know all that is important to know about him. He protects me and cares for me and tries to make me happy."

"A good start, but there is much more in a marriage. You need time to get to know each other."

"We don't have that luxury. He is going to war."

"All the more reason you should wait."

"All the more reason we should marry. Mother, I beg you for your blessing."

"I cannot give it."

"Why? I have handfasted with him. I would think that would make you insist we marry. No one else will have me now."

"I want you happy, not wed to a stranger! Marriage is a legal matter, not merely an emotional attachment. Bea has made you her heir; you will be a wealthy woman someday."

"Bea can change her will now. With Pitney gone, everything has changed."

"Ellen, when all of this settles down, you may find that

you were in love with an ideal, not whomever MacCurrie actually is."

Ellen pressed her lips together, trying not to cry. "I don't understand. I have finally found someone to love who loves me in return. No man has ever affected me like this. No one else has ever made me feel so cherished."

Rose nodded slowly. "I can see that. But, Ellen, there is much more to a marriage than the physical part of it. You have discovered how lovely it can be to be a woman, but you have no idea what it is to be a wife."

"That's exactly what I am trying to be."

"Perhaps you will be. But it will not be now. Handsome as he is, tender as he is, he is a stranger."

"I don't understand. When Margaret came here with Hugh, you welcomed both of them."

"We were not on the brink of war. Now we are. What if the Jacobites lose?"

"Then we all lose. Our cousin leads their forces."

"No one will pay attention to three women living quietly in their homes. But James MacCurrie might lose everything. No, Ellen, we will wait. The year of mourning is the perfect excuse."

"I will not mourn Pitney for one minute, let alone a year, Mother!"

Rose held up her hand. "Hush, Ellen. I have nothing else to say on this. You must get to know the man before you take such an irrevocable step." She started away. "When he's gone, you may find you don't even miss him."

"That won't happen," Ellen said.

The door closed softly behind her mother. Ellen walked to the window and stared out at the dark. She was no longer the girl who had grown up in this room, the girl who had dreamed of finding a man worthy of her love. She had found him.

James pulled the cover over his shoulder and stared at the ceiling. He would be on good behavior. For a while. Rose Malden had made her lack of enthusiasm quite plain. He knew she was only trying to protect her daughter, but it was just as well that they'd not been able to read his mind.

All through their meal, he had watched Ellen and thought of her in bed, of her under him, arching her back to receive him, of the humming moan she made when he'd pleased her and how he loved to hear that, to make her moan again and again, to listen to her whisper his name.

This wasn't helping at all.

He'd written to Neil this evening, telling him what they'd found at Netherby, assuring him that he'd be at Lochaber on the eighteenth. In the morning half of his men would leave for Torridon with his letter. He wished he was leaving as well, and taking Ellen with him. But would she go?

This situation could not stand. Either Ellen would marry him, with or without her mother's approval, or he'd leave. And the decision would be soon.

Chapter Sixteen

Pitney's funeral was sparsely attended. Ellen could not believe it was real, especially when David arrived in the chapel with Catherine. David nodded to her, as though he hadn't run from danger, leaving her to die, the last time they'd been together. But he didn't come close, didn't speak to her.

It was as well, she thought, giving James a glance. She wondered what James would do, but he merely glared at David, who pretended not to see. Her mother greeted David coolly, Bea not at all.

Some of their friends and neighbors stood with Ellen's family in the chapel as the words were said over Pitney's body. Few of them went to the graveside where Pitney Malden was lowered to his final resting site in the rain; fewer still accompanied them home. David and Catherine were not among them.

James stood next to her through it all, his hand often in hers. She introduced him to everyone, knowing that he and their relationship would be fodder for the gossip mill for days. No matter, she thought. In years to come they could talk of having met Ellen's husband for the first time at her stepfather's funeral.

They spent the next day sorting through Pitney's papers. It was Bea who found the documents, rolled in a square of oiled cloth, stuck up under Pitney's desk. She gasped.

"My will," Bea said, her voice a croak. "My will. Hidden in Pitney's desk."

Rose exclaimed and went to stand next to Bea. James strode across the room and looked over Rose's shoulder, reading the will.

"If Malden didna kill yer lawyer," he said to Bea, "then he kent who did."

Ellen knew his thoughts as though he had spoken them aloud. Pitney could have killed the lawyer. Or Fraser could have. And then killed Pitney as well. But why?

Ellen and her mother began questioning the staff that afternoon. James sat silently in the room with them, watching the procedure. The maids were quite forthcoming. Pitney had not been well liked. They had many stories, including tales of frequent visits by Cecil Fraser, late at night or when Rose and Ellen and Bea were off at a party or dinner. He had been at Netherby two nights before Pitney was killed. When Fraser finally left, Pitney drank heavily, cursing at everyone in sight before falling into a stupor on the parlor floor.

He'd done the same, they said, after John's soldiers visited. He'd ranted at them when they first arrived, but soon he'd been a quivering mass, begging them not to hurt him. He'd not had a mark on him, but when they left he drank himself into oblivion.

The footmen had stories as well, of being ordered to lie to Rose, of taking Pitney to seamy places in Dundee and spiriting women into the house when Ellen's mother was gone. Rose had stopped the questioning then, her face ashen. They had, she said, all heard enough.

James agreed. The portrait of Ellen's stepfather was consistent—the man was a reprobate, now a dead reprobate. He sent several of his men, dressed in Lowland clothing, to see what information could be found in Dundee and Perth about Cecil Fraser. They brought back little.

One man claimed to have worked for Fraser once, although not in the last few years. He'd heard that Fraser was working for a nobleman now; another said that Fraser had joined Mackay's troops. A third said he'd heard Fraser was dead. James sent his men back out for more. If there was anything to discover, he would. And then he'd go to war, leaving Ellen here with her family. But first, God willing, he'd marry her.

For days he'd been well behaved. For the most part. There was the morning when he and Bea had been downstairs before everyone else. He'd been standing outside on the drive, looking over the lawns at the green glen below, remembering Ellen's description of her home, when Bea had come to his side.

"I have made a decision," she said, looking up at him, her eyes merry.

"Aye?"

"Yes." Bea sighed dramatically. "I am changing my will."

"Ye are?"

"Yes. Originally I left my property to Ellen instead of Rose so that Pitney would not have control over it. And now that is no longer a concern."

James met her gaze then. "Miss Graham, do what ye wish with yer house and property. Ellen won't need it; I dinna want it. I would take her as my wife if she came naked and penniless."

Bea's smile was wide. "You might prefer her that way, I suspect."

He laughed then. "I might, at that."

She left him, her laughter drifting back to him as she walked away. He quite liked Ellen's Aunt Bea, and he suspected it was mutual, which pleased him.

Less satisfactory was that he seemed to have hit the limit of information about Malden and Fraser, and at last he gave up. He kept himself busy teaching Ned more swordsmanship. The lad was an eager student, and James found himself enjoying their time together. By the third lesson they gained an audience, as many of the staff—and Ellen—watched. James turned from shedding his shirt to find Ellen watching him with an expression he'd only seen in bed.

He threw her a kiss, watching her cheeks grow red, and then gave Ned a lesson the lad would not soon forget. He knew he was showing off, but damn, it felt good.

Rose cornered him as he went up the stairs to his room to change clothes before dinner, her eyes narrowed.

"I was not pleased by your demonstration this afternoon, Mr. MacCurrie," she said, her tone glacial. "In the future, you will restrain yourself."

"What did I do?"

"You threw my daughter a kiss in front of the staff."

James clenched his fists. "Madam, I ha' handfasted with yer daughter. Ye ken what that means, all that it means. I ha' been patient, waiting for ye to agree to let us marry, letting ye and Ellen find a way through this. But time grows short.

Ellen and I will marry, with or without yer permission. And I wilna wait a year."

Rose glared at him. "That sounds like a threat, sir."

"I would like to have yer blessing, but Ellen and I will be together, whether ye give it or no'."

"A bold statement, Mr. MacCurrie," Rose said, her cheeks flaming.

"I mean no discourtesy to ye, madam, but I mean to let ye ken my intent. I love Ellen; she loves me. War is comin'. Will ye no' let us be together as man and wife before I must leave?"

"No."

"Why? Is it because I am a Highlander? Is it because ye find me personally objectionable? I love yer daughter, Mistress Malden, with all my heart. I promise ye that as long as I live, I will care for her. I ken ye dinna believe that love like this can grow in such short a time, but I'm tellin' ye it can. It did. What do ye need from me that will convince ye to let us wed?"

Rose glared at him. "Something you cannot give, Mr. MacCurrie."

"Which is?"

"The assurance that you are the man my daughter thinks you are."

"I dinna ken what ye mean."

"Ellen's head has been quite turned by you, Mr. MacCurrie. She fancies herself in love with you."

"Perhaps it's more than a fancy."

"Young women often fall in love with a handsome face. It remains to be seen if there is anything behind the face."

He took a deep breath, telling himself to curb his anger. "Surely ye dinna mean that as insulting as it sounds."

"Mother! James! Stop this! Please! I cannot bear it!"

Ellen stood in the hallway above them, her eyes wide with horror. Rose flushed and closed her eyes. James lifted his chin.

"Ellen," he said, "yer mother doubts who I am. Ye'll ha' to decide. Will ye marry me, or no?"

Rose opened her eyes. "It is too soon, Ellen. I beg you to wait."

"We dinna have time to wait," James said. "I ha' to leave in ten days. What's it to be, lass?"

Ellen opened her mouth but couldn't answer. James looked at her for a moment, then at Rose, then came quickly up the stairs, brushing past Ellen. He slammed the door to his room behind him. Ellen stared at her mother. Rose turned and went down the stairs, leaving Ellen staring into space.

He did not answer when she knocked, nor when she called. "James, please," she said, leaning against the door to his room. "James."

She tried the latch; it was unlocked, and she let the door swing open. He stood before the window, staring into the distance.

"James. Talk to me."

He swung to face her, his cheeks scarlet, his eyes flashing.

"I do love you," she said.

"But no' enough to say so in front of yer mother."

"I have told her that I love you."

"I ha' been patient, Ellen."

"It's only been a few days."

"We only have a few days, lass."

"Let her get used to the idea. She's just buried her husband."

"A man she didna love."

"She did once. That's why she wants us to wait, James."

"Aye, so ye can see the error of yer thinking. So ye can see me for the bastard I am."

"That's not what she means!"

"That's exactly what she means! I'm no Pitney Malden, Ellen, and ye ken it. Why should we wait because yer mother made a mistake? It makes no sense."

"She just needs a little more time."

"I'm no' marryin' yer mother. We dinna need her approval. Ye are of age. Ye can marry where ye wish."

"I would like her approval."

"And I would like the lass I love to love me enough to marry me."

"I do love you!"

He shook his head. "No' enough, it seems. No' enough." He took a step toward her. "I dinna understand ye. How can ye play me false like this?"

"How am I playing you false?"

"Ye make me think you love me, but ye dinna want to prove it."

"I have proved it, James! We shared a bed, if you remember."

"I remember. When ye needed me, ye took yer solace wi' me. Now ye're home, and ye dinna seem to need me so much."

"You cannot expect that we would share a bed in my mother's home before we're married!"

"We've handfasted, or d'ye no' remember? If we were at Torridon, we'd share a bed. Look at the ring on yer finger, Ellen. Does it no' mean anything to ye?"

"It means everything."

"Then prove it. Marry me. Tonight. We'll find someone

who will marry us somewhere in Dundee. Or we'll go to Edinburgh."

"James! I cannot!"

"I see."

"No, you don't. I do want to marry you. But I want my mother's blessing, and I want to get married in the chapel here at Netherby, not in someone's office in the middle of the night! I want it to be a celebration, not a furtive rush."

"I ha' ten days before I ha' to leave, Ellen."

"I will talk to my mother again."

"It's no' her decision. It's yers."

"And when Neil disapproved, what did you say to him?"

"He did not disapprove."

She laughed derisively. "Of course he disapproved! He did everything he could to keep us apart. He could not bear for me to be important to you. He was afraid—"

"My brother is no' afraid of ye, Ellen."

"Yes, he is, James!" She shook her head, trying to calm herself. "I hated Hugh MacDonnell at first. I could not bear that my sister went on a trip to visit a friend and fell in love with him and never came home. I felt he'd stolen my sister." She sighed at the memory. "It took months for me to forgive her. And longer to forgive Hugh for stealing her away. I'm sure Neil is afraid of just that happening with you. I'm sure he feels deserted. If I could feel so lost with a sister, what must it be like with a twin? How lonely Neil must feel right now."

"Ye're right, Ellen, he didna want us to be together. And I'm sure ye're correct that he's feeling lonely. The difference between ye and me is that I didna let anyone's disapproval keep us apart. Right now I'm wonderin' why." He stared at her for a moment, then turned to look out the window.

Ellen came to stand behind him. "James, I do love you."

"So ye say, Ellen. Talk to yer mother. I'm weary of words."

She leaned her head against his shoulder. "I do love you, James."

He was silent, and at last she left.

Dinner was solemn. Bea chattered most of the time, but Ellen and James hardly spoke, and Rose said as little as possible. Ellen was miserable. How could her mother not see in James what she did? How could she not see how wonderful he was, how courageous, how honest? She could not eat her meal, and at last she put her fork down and looked at her mother.

"I love James," she said.

James lifted his head and watched her. Rose stared at her with a stunned expression. Bea looked from Ellen to Rose. The girl serving the meal stopped moving.

"Mother, I love James. With all my heart. I'm going to marry him. I'm going to spend my life with him."

"This is not the place nor the time to discuss this, Ellen," Rose said. "You may go now," she said to the girl.

"We have to talk about it."

"Not now."

"When?"

Rose shook her head, her eyes filling with tears. She put her fork down and pushed back her chair. "I cannot lose you as well! I cannot bear to talk about this now. You don't know him! You don't know whether he'll turn out to be a liar, or if he'll spend your money on other women."

"James is not Pitney, Mother!"

Rose stood. "You don't know that!"

She ran from the room. Ellen, James, and Bea stared after her.

"You have my blessing," Bea said to James.

"Thank ye," he said.

"Rose is not herself just now," Bea said. "She did love him. That's the worst of it. She pretends that she didn't, but she did. She's heartbroken. She didn't know what he was until it was too late, but part of her still loved him."

Ellen nodded, but James neither spoke nor agreed. A few moments later Bea went to bed, saying she was exhausted and far too old for this much emotion. James and Ellen walked out to the edge of the lawns. James stood looking over the valley, then turned to Ellen, his expression bleak.

"I'll no' fight her, lass," he said, his voice low. "I'll no' fight her. I canna prove to her that I am a decent man before I go to Lochaber. We'll wait."

"I love you, James."

"And I ye, Ellen. But perhaps yer mother is correct. Perhaps we need to wait and learn more about each other."

"I don't need to know more. I know who you are."

"Perhaps ye think ye do, lass. Perhaps we did rush things."

"James, what are you saying?"

"That the world's gone a bit mad. Perhaps we have too."

"Then I am quite content to be mad."

"How can we marry if yer mother is going to weep and wail? I canna do it. After the war . . . perhaps then."

He put a hand on her cheek, and she leaned against it, watching his eyes. She lifted her mouth to his when he bent to kiss her, wrapping her arm around his neck, savoring the feel of his lips on hers.

"James, let's marry tonight. We'll go to Dundee, or Edinburgh if we need to."

He kissed her again, this time with more passion, his tongue pressing between her lips until she opened to him. She leaned against his chest, felt his breathing grow more rapid, his body respond to her touch. She slid an arm around his waist, and he wrapped his around her, holding her tight against his chest.

"No, lassie, we'll wait."

"I love you."

"And I ye. It'll ha' to do for now."

It was daybreak. He was going to war. Neil said his farewells to the castle and loch, standing on the parapet looking out over the water of Loch Torridon, wondering if this was the last time in his life that he would do so.

He'd made list after list of instructions, had drilled those staying behind in what their responsibilities were. He'd talked with his mother and grandmother. Now it was time to go. Duncan was below with the men, waiting for him. He took a last deep breath of the sea air. He wouldn't get air like this until he came home.

If he came home.

Where was James? Still at Netherby with Ellen? He'd gotten just the one letter from James, in which he had written that he would join Neil and Duncan at Lochaber. And telling of Malden's death. Neil had had no sense of danger for James, rather an unsettled feeling, an uneasiness that something was being left undone. Maybe James had tired of Ellen Graham. Maybe he'd married her.

Neil closed his eyes, raised his arm, and asked his father to guard Torridon and his family in his absence. Then he turned away from the water. It was time to go. He'd touch the oak tree for luck, then join his brother to lead the clan to war, just as the Seer had prophesied.

The days passed much too quickly. James would leave soon, to be in Lochaber to meet John. Mackay's army was roaming the countryside hunting her cousin and his troops, so far unsuccessfully. Rumors had John in Inverness, in Dundee, and in the Borders at the same time. But Ellen knew where he was, and her brother-in-law Tom: in the Highlands, gathering support from the most influential clans.

Mackay was gathering recruits as well, and the clash between factions came even to Dundee, where brawls broke out among men who had formerly shared their evenings, and the same king. James listened to the news without comment, but more than once she caught him gazing into the distance and knew he was thinking of the war ahead. Of his brother. Not of her and their future together.

Rose thawed somewhat, had several amiable conversations with James. He was polite, but Ellen could see how unhappy he was; she was, too.

She continued to help her mother sort through Pitney's papers, although there seemed little left to discover. Pitney had left debts, many of them, and letters that made even Bea blush, with stories of squalid evenings spent with friends and other women. It helped to explain Rose's opposition to her marriage, but surely even her mother could see that James was as far removed from Pitney as it was possible for a man to be.

Two days before he would leave.

She found him in the barn, sharpening his sword, holding the blade up to the light to examine it, and she shivered, thinking of the steel plunging into flesh. She sat down to watch, wrapping her arms around herself. James laid the sword down and looked at her.

"I canna bear this, lassie. We ha' to talk. I canna leave like this."

She did not trust herself to speak.

"Do ye love me, Ellen? Did ye ever love me?"

"I have loved you from the first moment I saw you, James MacCurrie."

"And now?"

"Never more."

"Do ye think I am like—"

"Do I think you're like Pitney? No. Never." She came to stand before him and raised her hand to his cheek. "Never."

He caught her hand and drew it to his mouth, kissing each finger. Her body started a humming that she recognized, a need that only he could fill.

"James," she said. "Kiss me."

He was not gentle as he pulled her into his arms. His mouth pressed against hers, probing and teasing. She met him in kind, leaning into his kiss, parrying and exploring his mouth as he did hers. She drew back and looked into his eyes.

"James," she said. "Close the door. Lock it, love."

His eyes were dark. "Here, Ellen? What if someone comes lookin' for ye?"

"Then they'll have to break down the door. We'll be well warned by then."

She pulled his clothes from him; he did the same to her, and at last they stood naked before each other. He stroked a finger from her collarbone to the tip of her breast, then followed the path with his lips, until she strained against him, one hand around his back, holding him tight against her, the other wrapped around his readiness.

He lowered her to his discarded plaid, kissing his way slowly down her body, from her cheek to her thighs, until she begged him to come to her. Even then he moved slowly atop her, kissing her deeply as he filled her. She sighed with contentment and smiled against his shoulder. He was hers again at last, if only for a few more moments.

When at last they lay quietly wrapped in each other's arms, Ellen could not control her tears. She wiped them away with a shaking hand, trying to calm herself. She'd not expected to be so overcome, but she could not think of anything except this might never happen again. James stroked her hair.

"I love ye, Ellen Graham," he said. "And I ha' considered that we are man and wife since we handfasted. Nothing since has changed that, nothing will. Come with me to the chapel, and we'll pledge again."

She looked into his eyes, then nodded. He rose first, dressing quickly and helping her. She held his hand as they walked down the short path to Netherby's stone chapel, then stood with him before the altar and said a prayer.

The long rays of the afternoon sun came through the stained glass, drenching them in blue light as they knelt to face each other. James's hands were warm and strong; the smell of the beeswax and flowers filled the air. She was in the place she loved most on earth, with the man she loved. Ellen looked down at their joined hands, his large, hers pale, and tried not to weep.

His voice was hoarse with emotion. "I, James MacCurrie, pledge my love and faithfulness, my body and my heart, to ye, Ellen Graham, for now and forever."

She raised her chin and gazed into his eyes. "I, Ellen Graham, pledge my love and faithfulness, my body and my heart, to you, James MacCurrie, for now and forever."

He kissed her softly, then lifted her to her feet and kissed her again. "It is done, Ellen. We ha' married at Netherby, as ye wished. It matters to no one else on earth whether the words ha' been said by a priest. We have said them ourselves. We are one."

"We are one," she said. "Forever."

"Aye, love. Forever."

James left at dawn. Ellen wrapped her cloak around her, following him to the yard, her eyes red from weeping. His men waited while he talked to her in low tones, telling her he loved her, that she was to keep herself safe. Then he climbed into the saddle, his heart tight in his chest.

Bea and Rose came to the doorway wrapped warmly against the chill morning. They wished him well, and he thanked them, his nod curt. Britta and Ned arrived, Britta's eyes fearful as Ned asked yet again to come with James.

"Nay, laddie, I need ye here, keeping Ellen safe for me."

"But, sir," Ned pleaded, "let me come. You've trained me well. I could guard your back."

"Ned," James said, "I need ye here, guarding my heart."

The lad gulped and nodded, then tried to smile as Britta thanked James over and over. He patted Britta's shoulder, then turned to Ellen again. She held her hand to her lips, her eyes filled with tears, and he clenched his jaw. If he looked too long at her, he'd never leave.

"I will come back for ye, Ellen," he said quietly. He raised his voice so everyone in the yard could hear him. "I will come back for her," he said to Rose.

Ellen's mother put her hand to her throat and nodded. James bent low, pulling Ellen to him for one last kiss, one last touch of her soft lips on his.

"I will come back," he whispered.

"I will be waiting," Ellen said.

He straightened in the saddle and nodded to his men, then lifted the reins.

Chapter Seventeen

Neil was already there. He could feel it. James rode slowly into the camp, looking for his brother and cousin, for the MacCurrie banner. It would not be easy to find them in the crush. Lochaber was crowded with clans from all over the Highlands. James rode slowly down the center path of the camp. Pipers practiced in a group to the side, their skirls lifting high above the throngs. Men played dice on the new grass; others stood in tight groups talking. Friends slapped each other on the back as they greeted, or spoke in low tones, heads together.

The MacDonalds of Sleat waved when James passed, calling their welcome and pointing farther into the encampment. The MacKenzies stopped him to talk for a bit, asking how the east was. Apparently everyone knew where he'd been.

"Jamie! Over here!"

Duncan's cry came from his right, and James turned in the saddle to look for his cousin, seeing him at once. Neil and Duncan waved as they walked quickly toward him, the MacLeod lad right behind them. James slipped from his horse to the ground. Neil wrapped him in an embrace, pounding him on the back, then Duncan did the same.

"Ye dinna look different. No ring through yer nose yet," Neil said.

"Still in love?" Duncan asked.

James nodded. "We've handfasted. Said our vows in her church."

"I am happy for ye, Jamie," Neil said quietly.

"Thank ye," James said, feeling the knot of worry that had plagued him all across Scotland slip away. It would be all right between them.

Duncan led the way to their camp. "We're over here. Neil should be meeting with the other chiefs, but he kent ye were coming, so we waited. Nice to ken when ye're having company, aye?"

James grinned. "Who is here?"

"Glengarry, Keppoch, Kilgannon," Neil said. "Grant."

"Grant?"

"Aye," Duncan said. "Perhaps yer friend David is among us as well. Havena seen him, but havena looked."

James laughed. "I left him with the other women." He waved at the clansmen who were coming to meet him. "So when do we ride?"

Duncan rolled his eyes. "No' yet. First we talk."

"And talk," said Neil. "Getting these clans together wasna easy; keepin' them together will be a feat worth watching."

"If anyone can do it, Dundee can," James said.

Neil and Duncan exchanged a glance.

"He's gone over to the Grahams a'ready," Duncan said with a smile.

Neil nodded, his expression thoughtful.

* * *

The camp had an almost festive air. Each clan held its own territory, but the clansmen mixed freely. Traditional enemies ate meals together, told jokes, and made disparaging remarks about one another's abilities. There were the predictable disagreements as well, the jealousies over which clan would have what spot, who would have Dundee's ear.

James had no problem getting access to Dundee. The first time Ellen's cousin saw James, he paused for a moment, then asked if he was James or Neil. When he was assured it was James, Dundee welcomed him to Lochaber, asking how Ellen did. James told Dundee he'd left Ellen well, and Rose and Bea with her, then told him of Malden's death. Dundee was shocked, and asked for the story, which James told him in full detail, including his suspicions of Fraser's part in it. Dundee listened, then offered his help to find Fraser when the war was over. James accepted with grim pleasure.

Ellen's cousin was everywhere, greeting new arrivals, meeting until the wee hours with the clan chiefs. He listened as much as he talked, and chose his words carefully. Many were pleased with Dundee's willingness to be guided by the Highlanders, not to take charge without considering their suggestions.

He rallied the men with stirring speeches, assured the clan chiefs that they would receive military commissions from King James, and promised that their expenses would be paid. But James saw the worry in Dundee's eyes.

And in Neil's. Neil was often preoccupied. James watched his brother changing, growing into the leader James had always known he could be. It was gratifying, but a loss as well. Neil was moving to a place James would not go. He was the chief of the clan now, in action as well as name. Once again the twins' lives were separating. It was natural,

James told himself, thinking of Ellen; it was time. But it was also the end of something he'd assumed would always be there.

James had changed. There was a shadow behind his eyes that had never been there before, a reserve in the thoughts that flew from him to Neil. James was forthright about his plans, that after the war he would return to Netherby and marry Ellen, whether her mother wished it or not. Neil listened but did not comment.

Before he'd left Torridon, his grandmother had told him and Duncan more details of the legend. The Seer had said the twins would go to war with a red-haired kinsman who would return to Torridon with the eldest son, then would roam the seas, eventually bringing home a foreign wife. The eldest son would rule Torridon alone; the second son would not return with his brother. Neil had met his grandmother's gaze, had seen the fear in her eyes.

She'd shaken her head. "I dinna ken whether it means that he'll marry Ellen and stay at Netherby, or . . ." She'd let her words trail off, but there was no need to finish the thought. "Ye need to ken if he's married her yet. The legend says he'll marry a lass from the east. If they've no' married, then at least ye ken he'll live through the war."

"What about the fifty years of peace?" Neil had asked.

"I ken no more than what I've told ye. Well, only that the twins are to marry lasses wi' the same name." His grandmother had put her hand on his arm, her eyes filling with tears. "Guard Jamie well, Neil. Bring him home to us and prove the Seer wrong. We canna bear another loss. Guard him well."

Neil had nodded, wondering how he was to protect his brother from a force larger than all of them.

* * *

On May 28 Dundee led the clans from Lochaber, marching out to the sounds of pipes and bugles. The MacCurries were not far behind him. James stood in the saddle, trying to memorize the moment as he waited for their turn to join the march. He'd never seen the like of this gathering, and he felt his blood rise.

Each clan had brought its own pipers, and the air was alive with the music. And with color. Dundee's regiment wore their red uniforms, laced and faced with yellow, at the head of the procession, followed by clan after clan of Highlanders, dressed in their bright plaids. Some chiefs had dressed their men in similar patterns or colors in their plaids to show their allegiance.

Most clansmen wore clan badges of bog myrtle or holly visible on their bonnets, saffron shirts tucked beneath belts holding dirks on the right hip, basket-hilted swords on the left. They were armed with many kinds of weapons, the more wealthy clans with pistols and flintlock muskets, the less with old matchlocks. Many carried axes or javelins as well, and most had targes, shields of leather, many decorated with Celtic designs.

MacDonald of Keppoch wore a helmet and carried an old-fashioned claymore, the huge two-handed sword that few used these days. Lochiel, well over sixty now, wore gleaming armor, his expression so fierce that James had to smile. Alasdair MacIain, the chief of the MacDonalds of Glencoe, wore his long beard twisted and curled backward.

The MacCurries were no less colorful. James, Neil, and Duncan wore breastplates that had been Alistair's, polished and gleaming, the MacCurrie crest in the center of each gilded with gold. Their bonnets were adorned with eagle feathers and sprigs of oak, their targes oiled and studded with metal. Their men were well armed and ready to go, their eagerness apparent in their steps.

The army marched through the mountains of Garvamore, crossed the Spey, and reached Raitts Castle, the ancient stronghold of the Comyns, where they celebrated the anniversary of King Charles II's restoration. Lit by the flames of the blazing bonfire he'd ordered, Dundee addressed his army, toasting the health of King James and his triumphant return to Scotland, assuring his men that they would defeat the enemy, that order would be returned to their country and they to their homes. The trees shook with the sound of cheers.

Dundee and Mackay chased each other through the Eastern Highlands for six weeks. Small parties from each side met in skirmishes that were becoming more frequent. And larger. June passed, and much of July, and still who would be king had not been settled. Dundee waited for reinforcements and King James to arrive from Ireland.

Mackay waited for more troops from Holland, for Huguenots and Spanish mercenaries, most of whom did not come. Mackay's men were openly rebelling, many of the officers making no secret of their plans to desert and join Dundee at the first opportunity. Mackay pressed William's supporters for more money, more equipment, more men.

And still the armies had not met.

The rest of the country waited. Catherine visited often despite Ellen's lukewarm welcomes, bringing news from the outside and, on a warm sunny afternoon, the word that David had left the evening before, gone to join Dundee.

Catherine wept as she told the story. Ellen listened without comment, thinking of when Fraser had attacked them in the clearing, of David's face just before he'd bolted. Gone to war? Why?

"I still cannot believe it!" Catherine wailed. "He's not like that, not like the Highlanders. Not that all Highlanders are bloodthirsty savages, but the stories— At least David is civilized."

Civilized indeed, Ellen thought derisively.

"Catherine," she said, "we can know someone for years and not know him. Have I told you what happened after we left Dunfallandy? David was with us, you remember, when we left for Glengarry. . . ."

Catherine listened with her hands wrapped in each other, her mouth open. When she left, pale and shaken, Ellen stared after her, wondering if she had saved a friend from a dreadful mistake, or if she'd destroyed something Catherine had treasured. If this was revenge, it was not sweet.

James was outside the MacCurrie camp, talking with Duncan and Hugh MacDonnell, when he saw David Grant arrive. Grant did not see him, the dark easterner deep in conversation with a clansman. He was armed with sword and pistol, a targe tied to his horse's neck. He'd use the targe, James thought with contempt. The weapons probably would stay clean.

"Jamie, who the hell are ye sneerin' at?" Duncan asked, turning to follow James's gaze. "Ah, David Grant."

He told Grant's story to Hugh, who turned to look as well.

"Why is he here, d'ye suppose?" Hugh asked.

Duncan shrugged. "Perhaps he needs to prove something to himself."

"Perhaps he's a spy for Mackay," James said.

Duncan looked at him with narrowed eyes. "Ye dinna believe that."

"He ran away once. Why would a man like that join an army?"

"He was at Dunfallandy."

"Only because he went there to find Ellen. As far as I ken, she's no' here." James felt his brother's approach. "Neil's comin'. The war council must be over."

Duncan laughed as Hugh looked around him. "Ye'll no' see him yet, MacDonnell. James and Neil ha' their own way of communicating. Just wait a minute."

In moments Neil and Glengarry, the MacDonnell chief, came into view.

Duncan grinned at Hugh. "Told ye."

"How d'ye do that?" Hugh asked James.

James shrugged. "Be born a twin, I think."

Hugh laughed and waited with the cousins as Neil and Glengarry approached.

"What's the news?" Duncan asked.

Neil answered. "D'ye remember when we went to Blair Castle to try to convince Lord Murray to join us?"

"And he wouldna even talk wi' us?" Glengarry added.

The other three nodded.

"Murray went to Edinburgh to meet with William's advisers," Neil said. "And in his absence his factor, Patrick Stuart, took over Blair Castle and is holding it, waiting for us to join him."

"Now Murray's on his way from Edinburgh to take his own castle," Glengarry said. "He'll have to lay siege to his own home."

"We have to hold Blair," James said. "It's the gateway to the west, into Lochaber. If Murray retakes it, we'll be cut off. Any men King James sends would have to travel twice as far."

"And we would be cut off from supplies and news of home," Duncan said.

Neil nodded. "Aye. Whoever has Blair has the advantage. Ye ken Mackay will be on his way there as well. He willna leave Murray laying siege to his own castle. He kens as much as we do how important Blair is."

"How many men does Murray have?"

"A few hundred, but he's collecting his tenants as he comes north."

"And Mackay?"

"I've heard three to five thousand," Neil said.

"How many do we have?" James asked.

"Less than two thousand."

"Are we going to wait for more troops from the king?" Hugh asked.

"Who kens when they'll be here?" Glengarry said. "We were expecting thousands last week and only got three hundred."

"We're not going to wait," Neil said. "We're going to Blair. We leave in three days."

Dundee's army rode out on July 22 with eighteen hundred Highlanders. Mackay marched west from Edinburgh with four thousand men. The race was on.

On July 24, Mackay was in Stirling. On the twenty-fifth, he was in Perth. On July 26 Dundee's army camped three miles from Blair Castle, its arrival uncontested.

John Graham had won the race to Blair. Murray retreated that afternoon to the pass of Killiecrankie, to wait for Mackay to join him. Dundee moved his men into the castle and waited.

* * *

James stared up at the hammered ceiling of the hall of Blair Castle, then lowered his gaze to Dundee, watching Ellen's cousin listen to the clan chiefs. It was time to make a decision. Everyone had an opinion, and Dundee was willing to listen to each one.

James had attended this war council at John Graham's personal request and now sat next to Neil just few feet from Dundee. What they decided here would affect the coming battle, Dundee told them all, perhaps the entire war. Perhaps the very future of the country.

Mackay outnumbered them almost two to one, despite the recent additions to their ranks, and his army was nearing. Soon he'd meet up with Murray's men, said to be a thousand strong. Even more men were on their way, from England and the Continent. Within a few days, Mackay's numbers could be expected to swell to eight thousand.

The Jacobites were tired and hungry from their swift march to Blair. The reinforcements promised by the king had yet to appear. More clans were set to arrive, but not until the twenty-ninth, the original date for the gathering at Blair. If they fought now and held off Mackay, they would keep Blair Castle and the road to the Highlands—and their cause—alive. If they waited, the Williamites would have gained a foothold in the west.

Alexander Cannon, the man who had brought the last reinforcements from King James, was adamant. They should wait. The Highlanders, he said, were untested. Dundee should wait until more seasoned troops arrived from the king.

"How can we wait?" Kilgannon asked. "That gives Mackay two days to get here, to rest and prepare. And two days for more men to join him. We'll lose Blair. We could be facing a much larger army. We canna wait for the others to join us."

"We should wait for the others," Cannon said.

Glengarry shook his head. "We dinna need them."

"We should not risk an engagement now," Cannon argued.

James looked at Cannon with distaste. This was the man who was supposed to arrive with well-fed men to aid Dundee. Instead, he'd lost his men's provisions on the trip to Blair and had arrived hungry and exhausted, with one-tenth the men promised.

"Mackay's men are trained and experienced," Cannon said. "We cannot rely only on the Highlanders."

The rumble of murmurs through the gathering was loud. Cannon was a fool, James thought. This was hardly the time to insult most of the men in Dundee's army. He exchanged a look with Neil; his brother was in agreement.

"Why wait for Mackay to get stronger? Every day brings him more men," James said. "We're ready to fight now."

"I agree," said Kilgannon. "We dinna need the others. We're ready."

Dundee nodded, then looked at Neil. "Torridon?"

"We're ready," Neil said.

Dundee went through the ranks, asking one chief after another. Almost to a man, the Highlanders wanted to fight now, not wait. At last Dundee looked across the gathering to the gray-haired chief of the Camerons, Lochiel, one of the most powerful men in Scotland. Whatever Lochiel said would carry the day, and they all knew it.

Lochiel did not hesitate. "We fight. Our men are in heart. They are eager to engage the enemy. I can assure you not one of them will fail you, Dundee."

Dundee nodded. "Then fight it is. Prepare, gentleman, we go to battle."

The cheers from the clan chiefs were deafening, echoed moments later by the cheers from the troops waiting outside. Word had spread quickly, and the decision was popular.

James and Neil were satisfied. They'd polled their men the night before, and to a man the MacCurries were weary of waiting for the enemy to gain strength. They were ready to fight. They moved next to Ellen's cousin to say so.

"One more thing," Lochiel called to Dundee.

The room quieted.

"I beg you, sir," Lochiel said to Dundee, "to hold back from the battle yourself. On your Lordship depends the fate not only of this army but also of our king and country."

Several nodded or called out their agreement, Neil among them. Dundee looked around the room, then met James's gaze. "To cheating death," they'd said at Dunfallandy, James thought, hearing their voices lifted with their glasses. Was Dundee remembering the same night?

"MacCurrie?" Dundee asked quietly.

"Stay back, sir," James said, keeping his tone so low that only Dundee could hear him. "For Ellen, John. Stay back."

"I cannot," Dundee said, then raised his arms for quiet. When he had everyone's attention, he addressed the room. "Lochiel, I thank you for your concern. I am sensible that I may be killed. But, sir, do not deny me this. I will fight alongside your brave Highlanders for our king. I cannot ask them to risk their lives while I sit back and watch them. I will be in the field."

James felt a wave of cold; at his side Neil stiffened. He did not need to meet his brother's gaze to know he had felt the same thing. Death was stalking Dundee.

* * *

Ellen leaned against the side of the window and sighed as she looked out through the twilight to the valley below. They'd had little news other than that Mackay's army was marching west to meet Dundee's near Blair. Near Killiecrankie, the pass through which she'd ridden with James after they'd left Dunfallandy.

They'd talked that day of what the pass would look like in summer. She tried to imagine it now—the rowan and beech trees displaying their leafy finery, the wind rustling through the branches of the pines and rising high to soar out over the meadow to the north, the river full and musical as it wound below the steep sides of the pass. Killiecrankie must be beautiful now.

She traced a finger along the edge of the window pane, thinking she'd been such a fool not to marry him immediately, to let her mother's tears and worries affect her. In the last few weeks Rose had been calm, sure that she was right, confident that Ellen and James would have a long courtship, even though Ellen had said clearly that she and James would wed as soon as he returned.

If he returned. She had been tormented by nightmares, by dreams of fallen soldiers, of a man on his back, his long dark hair streaming out behind him. Dying. She woke each time, drenched in dread, to stare into the darkness and tell herself that the dream was not a vision, only a manifestation of her worst fears.

James, she said to the first star to appear in the sky. Keep safe, my love. Come home to me. I'll be waiting, no matter how long it takes.

Then she prayed.

Saturday, July 27. It had rained for two nights, but this day had dawned dry and warm, the sun rising in a clear sky.

James stretched and looked at the wall of trees that surrounded Blair Castle, the pine and birch that blocked the mountains behind them. Mackay had spent the night in Dunkeld. And today they would engage his army.

The Jacobite camp was busy already. He could hear the jingle of horses' bridles as the cavalry prepared, the sound of men talking in excited tones, spreading the news he'd just heard himself. Lord Murray's men had faded away; he waited in Killiecrankie with only three hundred of his original thousand. Mackay's extensive troops and four light cannons were struggling on the steep sides of the pass. He had sent to Perth for more cavalry, which would need to be in place before he could get his men out on open ground.

Field position might well determine the day, and that was what this morning's war council had discussed. James was not attending, preferring to stay with Duncan and help their men with the last-minute preparations. He had talked with Dundee last evening, saying all he'd had to say about today's battle, and then Dundee speaking for a few moments of the future. He talked of his wife Jean, of having other children, of the joys of marriage, wishing James and Ellen the same happiness he'd found. James looked into Dundee's eyes and promised he'd care for Ellen, vowing silently to protect Ellen's cousin as well.

Now the war council ended, and Neil relayed what had had been said. Dundee had refused to try to stop Mackay's army in the pass. He did not want them slowed or stopped, hunkering down to wait for reinforcements from Perth or Edinburgh. He wanted Mackay's army to come through the pass, weary and wary. And be annihilated.

Midday came and went. Scouts returned with more news—that Mackay was through the pass, had met Murray's scanty troops, and was now at the base of the ridge, waiting for his baggage to join him. They held the low ground. The reinforcements had not arrived.

Perfect, James thought. Mackay could not lead a charge uphill. Dundee obviously agreed, for he gave the order to march. The Highlanders moved east from Blair at a run. They crossed the River Tilt, then headed south, coming at last to stand on the summit of the ridge above the enemy.

Below them, Mackay's army scrambled to its feet. Dundee had secured the high ground. The Jacobites filed into place as noisily as they could, the pipers from each clan playing loudly, the drums beating in a deafening rhythm, the men roaring.

"We'll stop their hearts!" Duncan shouted over his shoulder.

James laughed. That was the idea. Mackay's troops were rapidly getting into position now. The MacCurries crossed to their station, on the right side of Dundee's troops, next to the MacDonalds of Glencoe. James gave Hugh a wave as they passed the MacDonnells, laughing again when Hugh made an obscene gesture at Mackay's troops.

The Grants were between the MacCurries and the center of the line. James looked through their line for David, finding him at last. The easterner was adjusting his musket, his lean face intent on his task. No one spoke to him; he stood alone.

"So he is going to fight," Duncan said to James.

"Dinna ken that, laddie. He's here, is all we ken," James said as David Grant looked up and saw him. Grant went rigid, his face set in stiff lines. For a moment the noise around them seemed to quiet, then Grant flushed and turned his back.

"Dinna let him be behind ye, Jamie," Duncan said. "I suspect he's no' going to be invitin' ye to drink wi' him."

James snorted. "I still dinna ken why he's here."

Dundee's men were ready for battle. Dundee would be in the middle with his cavalry, the clans spread out on either side of the center. Mackay's army was twice as large, his line extending well beyond both ends of the Jacobites. Kenmure's men were opposite on one side of Mackay's cannon, Leven's regiment on the other.

Neil leaned over to James and Duncan. "We'll go straight down the hill. We'll drive them into the river." He grinned, his eyes bright. "The first one to the water wins."

James and Duncan laughed. When they'd been lads, the three had played the game constantly. They'd start at the top of the battlements of Castle Currie and sprint down the stairs and through the hall, rushing down the hill, arriving at the shore of the loch breathless and laughing. The first one to the water won, the prize to be determined by the victor.

"I'll take yer chestnut stallion," James said to Neil. "And yer newest ship," he told his cousin.

Duncan gave him a fierce grin. "We'll see, laddie, we'll see."

They waited through the long afternoon, while Mackay fired his guns ineffectively, filling the center of the battlefield with large clouds of smoke and terrible noise but doing little damage. One of his leather-covered cannon disintegrated under the strain after only a few rounds, and the Highlanders jeered as the pieces were dragged from the field.

Both armies waited. Mackay had no choice. He could not charge uphill and hope to be successful; he could not lead his men from the field without exposing them to Dundee's left flank. So he waited for the Jacobites to make the first move.

At six the sun was in their eyes, and they knew why Dundee had waited. If they charged now, the Highlanders would be blinded as they ran downhill, the advantage all on Mackay's side. At seven it was little better, and the cousins speculated whether Dundee would wait for nightfall, to add the terror of darkness to that of the Highland charge.

At almost eight, the sun moved behind the ridge on the other side of the glen, and as the light dimmed, Dundee moved before his now-cheering army. He raised his arms, and the Highlanders quieted.

"Gentlemen," Dundee shouted, "you are come this day to fight for the most noble of causes, for king and country, against usurpation and rebellion. Behave yourselves, therefore, like true Scotsmen. Let us, by this action, redeem the credit of this nation, which is laid low by the treacheries and cowardice of some of our countrymen.

"I ask nothing of you that you shall not see me do before you. And if any of us fall upon this occasion, we shall have the honor of dying in our duty, as becomes true men of valor and conscience!"

The answering cheer was deafening. Dundee turned to face the enemy.

Chapter Eighteen

Neil raised his targe, and the MacCurries joined the roar of defiance that swelled from the army around them. James said a prayer for his soul, another for the protection of his family and Ellen. He could not think of her now, could not remember the feel of her under him, of her lips on his, of her eyes lighting when he touched her.

He drove all thoughts of her from his mind as the shouts around him intensified, then joined his voice to theirs, the sound echoing off the ridge, tumbling down the slope to envelop Mackay's army. The very ground seemed to shake with the noise.

Dundee raised his arm. The battle had begun.

James followed Neil down the hill, Duncan on his right as they raced toward Mackay's men. The savage roar grew louder as the Highlanders closed in. James could see the terror in the faces of Kenmure's men, could see their guns aimed at him. He lifted his musket; Neil did the same, the others joining them. The volley was deadening and effective, but there was no time to reload and fire again. He dropped his musket and drew his sword as he leapt forward.

The left flank had engaged already. Mackay's men on that side were falling back, fleeing, many without firing a shot. In front of them, Kenmure's men released a burst of fire. Glengarry's men took the brunt of the volley, falling by the score, while the MacCurries thundered through the first ranks of the enemy's line, knocking aside muskets with their targes.

Mackay's men, struggling to insert bayonets into the muzzle of their fired muskets, were caught defenseless, many dying in the first moments, many more running. James swung away from the man he'd just dispatched, looking for Neil, who was ordering men down the hill after the fleeing enemy.

Kenmure's was not the only regiment to retreat; all along the line, regiments were folding. The far left had all but disappeared, and on the right, Mackay's own regiment was fleeing down the hill, their red coats bright in the twilight.

Neil was handling the last of Kenmure's troops, Duncan closing in with him, while most of the MacCurries chased the Williamites down the slope. All was under control here. James charged back up the hill to see if Hugh MacDonnell was among the Glengarry men who had fallen in the musket volley. He climbed through the dying men but did not see Hugh. Instead, he saw Dundee, alone in the middle of the field.

Ellen's cousin stood high in his stirrups, his arm raised, his white helmet shining. He gestured for his cavalry to follow him, then plunged into the cloud of smoke before him. A volley of shots came from James's right, cutting across the field and into the cloud, and a moment later a riderless horse bolted from the smoke. Dundee's horse.

James shouted for help as he ran uphill. He dove into the smoke at the center of the field. From behind him came a volley of shots, plunking into the ground at his heels. He whirled to his right, waving his arms to clear the smoke, calling for Dundee.

There was a man in front of him, a dark-haired man, lifting a sword to fight off three of Mackay's men. James ran forward with a roar to help. But it was not Ellen's cousin who fought to parry the blows; it was David Grant.

The easterner fought like a raw recruit; he wouldn't last long. James plowed into the knot, quickly felling one of the attackers. He and Grant together dispatched the second almost as quickly. The third man stepped back, gave James a terrified look, spun around, and ran down the hill.

Grant stared at James wildly.

"Thank you," he gasped.

"Dundee's down. In the center," James shouted. He raced uphill again, not looking to see if Grant followed.

From behind him came another burst of gunfire. He felt a thud against his shoulder, the breastplate swinging across his chest with the force of it. Then a blow to the back of his head, knocking his helmet off. He fell to his knees, staring into the smoke. There was no pain, but something was seeping down his neck.

Ellen, he thought. And then there was only darkness.

At the top of a cluster of rocks above the river, Neil stopped, looking back at the battlefield in surprise. Jamie was in danger. He'd been at Neil's side when they started down the hill; he could swear it.

There had been a short burst of gunfire from above a moment before, but all was silent now. The last of the enemy were fleeing. Mackay's men had run two ways, down the road to the baggage train, where the Highlanders chased them easily, and down the steep sides of the glen to the river, where many were slaughtered on the gray rocks overlooking the River Garry.

Many had tried to leap into the water, others across. Broken bodies were strewn across the rocks that dotted the river. Some of Mackay's men had been swept downstream alive; some had made it to the opposite bank, scrambling up the steep side of the pass, their scarlet coats bright through the greenery of the trees. The Highlanders were still in pursuit.

Below Neil a group of his men stood at the edge of an outcropping, leaning down to look at the river below, Duncan among them. Neil called to his cousin, who climbed up the steep incline, at last reaching Neil.

Duncan's grin was wide. "We have taken the day!"

"Aye. We have. Where's Jamie?"

"I thought he was wi' ye."

Neil shook his head slowly, a knot of dread forming in his stomach.

The dead and injured lay everywhere, Highlanders in their plaids and saffron shirts mixed with Mackay's regimental uniforms. Some were being tended, others dying alone. Neil and Duncan stared up the ridge from the bottom. From down the road, on their right, came sounds of battle, but here, on this smoke-filled ridge, silence washed over them, broken only by moans.

The Highlanders may have won the day, Neil thought, but death was the real victor. He skirted a lifeless horse, then sidestepped around a fallen man, swearing as he recognized him. Just this morning, he and Jamie had laughed with the MacDonnell; now he was gone.

Duncan paused beside another Glengarry man, this one

still alive but barely so. Neil knelt next to his cousin, bending low to hear the Highlander's last words; a moment later they bowed their heads to say a prayer for the man's soul.

Neil rose to his feet, looking through the dimming light at the hill above him. Jamie could not be here in this mayhem. He must have run by Neil in the smoke and confusion. He must be down by the river. He must be.

Neil started down the hill again, the lump of dread in his gut growing larger.

It was dark by the time Neil and Duncan got back to the ridge with their men. Jamie had not been on the road, nor down by the river. No one had seen him since their charge down the hill.

"Take some of the men to Blair," Neil said to Duncan. "See if Jamie's there."

"I'll stay wi' ye," Duncan said quietly. "We'll tell them to bring back torches."

Neil nodded and fought his panic. Jamie must be at Blair. Or here, on this hill. Dim figures moved among the fallen, barely visible in the summer darkness, carrying away the wounded and the dead.

Jamie, where are ye?

Neil stood silently, trying to catch something of his brother, but there was no answer, only the soft moan of the summer wind. The men who stayed with him and Duncan fanned out, moving slowly up the hill, turning bodies over and leaning over dying men, giving comfort where they could.

There were hundreds of dead here in the center where the cannons had been, where Mackay's cavalry had whirled into its own army and killed many. It was here that the gunfire had been the heaviest, and here where the dead lay piled atop one another.

When it was too dark to see anything, Neil stationed himself in the center of the ridge. He leaned forward, listening. There, faintly, he felt it. Then it was gone. He turned, trying to see. Jamie was out there.

"Jamie!" He listened, then called again. "Jamie!"

"Did ye hear something?" Duncan whispered.

"No, but he's here. I can feel it."

Duncan put a hand on Neil's shoulder and stared into the darkness. Neil strained to hear even the faintest of sounds, then he closed his eyes and prayed. The MacCurrie men returned with the report that torches were coming, that Blair Castle was in an uproar. Dundee was missing.

They found Jamie just before daybreak, when the first of the light touched the sky. He lay on his back, his helmet gone, his eyes closed, his hair streaming out behind him, damp with his blood. Neil let out a low cry as he bent over his brother.

"Jamie!"

Duncan put a hand on Jamie's neck, then looked up at Neil. "He's alive."

Dundee had fought his last battle, as had many others. The Jacobites had lost six hundred men, Mackay twelve hundred, four hundred more taken prisoner. The Camerons, Macleans and MacDonalds of the Isles had suffered heavy casualties; Glengarry had lost a third of his men, including his brother.

In comparison, Neil told himself, the MacCurries had lost few. It was small comfort. His brother lay in the hall at Blair, unmoving, his face gray, and Neil thought of little else. He did not attend the war councils, did not walk among the clans and discover who had lived, who had died.

The bleeding had stopped, but Jamie was still unconscious. The helmet had saved his life, the dent in the metal proof of what would have happened had he not worn it. For now, Jamie was alive, praise God—but only just.

Neil looked up at the sky. It would be a beautiful summer day, but he did not see the blue sky, nor the pines' green branches, dark against the clouds overhead. He saw his grandmother's face, her eyes full of tears as she told him to guard his brother well.

News of the Jacobite victory at Killiecrankie spread quickly across Scotland. Ned brought the word to Ellen and her family before midday on the Sunday that Mackay's army had broken and run before the Highlanders. Ellen closed her eyes and breathed a prayer of thanks. The Jacobite cause was still alive. But what of James? And John? And Hugh and Tom? And Duncan and Neil? So many men to fear for.

"This is wonderful news!" Rose cried.

Bea echoed the thought, smiling at Ellen. "Had you any doubt?"

James, Ellen thought. She had to know. She looked across the room to meet Britta's gaze. The maid nodded; she'd talked to Ned, as Ellen had asked her to.

"Mother," Ellen said, "I'd like to send Ned to Killiecrankie. I need to know that James is alive. And John. And Hugh and Tom, of course. Please."

Rose looked at her daughter doubtfully. "It might be dangerous for the boy."

"May I ask him if he's willing?"

Bea snorted. "Willing? He'll kiss Britta and be gone in ten minutes."

"Mother?"

"Yes," Rose said. "If Ned is willing, let him go at once."

Ned left at daybreak, armed with two pistols and letters for James and Ellen's brothers-in-law. The boy's face was lit with determination. He'd leapt at the challenge, saying he was delighted to at last have something important to do, promising to hurry back with the news. Britta waved until he was out of sight, her expression fearful but proud. Ellen fought her misgivings. She'd sent the boy with several men. Would it be enough?

Godspeed, she thought. Travel safely, Ned, and bring me word of my love.

Details of the battle and the Jacobite victory filtered in all day. Catherine arrived at noon, crowing, declaring that she'd known all along that John's forces would win. Ellen listened to her friend's excitement, her own tempered by her worry for James and by the realization that this had been only one battle. The war was far from over.

She said as much, but Catherine would not be contained, babbling on about David's heroism for joining the army, about the parties they'd hold when King James was reinstated. When at last Catherine left, Ellen walked across Netherby's lawns, picturing the Jacobite army celebrating, John in the middle of them, lifting his glass high in a toast. "To cheating death." The words came unbidden, and she caught her breath as a wave of fear washed over her.

Ned, she thought, ride swiftly. Ride safely. Bring me word that my cousin lives, that my love is celebrating victory today.

* * *

Dundee was buried at Blair Castle. Neil bowed his head as the prayers were said in the tiny stone chapel, his heart leaden as he sat among the Highland chiefs. The pipers played the funeral dirge, and more than one man wiped tears from his eyes. They mourned a hero today, Neil thought. History would remember him well.

News had come that Edinburgh was in turmoil. The Duke of Hamilton was reported to have written that Dundee was master of all on the other side of the Firth of Forth. The Jacobites at Blair cheered, pretending to be pleased with the news, but among the chiefs the mood was sober. Dundee was dead, and no one knew what the future would hold.

Neil and Duncan kept a vigil at Jamie's bedside. His brother had neither moved nor spoken for two days. When the healers came to tend his wound, they'd shaken their heads, saying his recovery was in God's hands. Neil prayed, his hope dying as the hours passed.

Duncan prayed as well, going to the stone chapel where Dundee had been mourned, returning to Jamie's bed to let Neil do the same. In the tiny church, Neil bent his head and wept, praying through his tears. Outside he lifted his face to the sky and begged once again, praying to any god who would listen, then closed his eyes and listened.

He felt the wave of thoughts, faint at first, then louder, and lifted his head, staring at the hall where Jamie lay. As he watched, Duncan burst through the door, waving to Neil.

"He's back!" Duncan shouted with a fierce joy. "Praise God, Neil, he's back!"

Jamie opened his eyes as Neil bent over him. He smiled weakly at his brother. "I lost the race to the water. Can we do another?"

Neil stared at him while he controlled his emotions, then shook his head. "Hell no, Jamie. Ye should ha' run faster."

James closed his eyes. "Run faster. Next time."

Neil wiped tears from his cheek while Duncan slapped him on the shoulder.

"I'm thinking whisky, aye?" Duncan asked.

"Several," Neil said.

Britta was crying when she came to tell Ellen and Bea that Ned had returned. Ellen rose to her feet, her hand to her throat.

"Britta! What does he say?"

"Oh, Miss Ellen!" the girl wailed.

Ellen pushed past her, running from the room, Bea at her heels. Ned stood in the foyer talking with her mother, who was wiping a tear from her eye. Ned turned to Ellen, his face pale. Ellen stopped moving, her heart beginning a slow pounding.

"How did you get back so quickly, Ned?" Bea asked.

"I only got as far as Perth when I heard. I came back to tell you."

"James?" Ellen asked. "Is it James? Oh, dear God, what has happened?"

Ned shook his head. "No, miss. It's your cousin."

"John?" She could hear her voice growing shrill. "How badly is he hurt?"

Ned looked from Ellen to Bea while Rose began to sob. "He's dead, miss."

"No!" Ellen shouted. "It's not true. It cannot be true. They won the battle. Everyone was celebrating."

She'd braced herself to hear that James had been wounded, or worse, but she'd not anticipated this. John dead. How could that be? How could his vigor and strength be gone? She would never laugh with him again, never seek his counsel, feel his embrace.

And what of Jean and his newborn son? Jean would be devastated. Her son would grow up without his father, never knowing the man who had loved him so. John was dead. The words were hateful. How could this be?

What would happen to Scotland without him? To the Jacobites? It had been John, by the force of his will and spirit, who had raised that army, John who had kept it together. It was to John that the clan chiefs had pledged their support. He was the one they trusted. What now for the Jacobite cause?

And what of James? And Tom and Hugh? Ellen put her hands over her face and let her tears fall.

James looked down the hill. He'd come to the top of the ridge with Neil and Duncan to look at the spot where Dundee had been cut down, where he had fallen. To cheating death, they'd toasted at Dunfallandy. James had lived; Dundee had died. Death had successfully stalked Ellen's cousin. Knowing he'd sensed it beforehand was no solace.

What now?

Both armies were regrouping. Mackay had retreated again, supposedly all the way to Stirling. His troops had been cut in half; he'd not be advancing soon, which was good, for Cannon had been placed in command of the Jacobite army.

The other clans had arrived; the Jacobite army had swelled to five thousand men. Some who had survived Killiecrankie had left when the reinforcements arrived, David Grant among them. James had smiled grimly at the news. Last to arrive, first to leave. He should have expected it.

No doubt Grant had run all the way back to Netherby. He probably had been the one to tell Ellen of their victory, exaggerating his part in it. Ellen. It hurt to think of her, to imagine her face when she heard of the loss of her cousin. She would mourn him as a loved one, but she also, as much as anyone in Scotland, would know just what Dundee's death would mean to their cause.

Ellen.

"I suppose Ellen's heard about Dundee," Neil said.

James nodded. "Probably by now, aye."

"Are ye going to marry her?"

"Aye."

Neil stared out over the battlefield, then back at his brother. He put a hand on James's shoulder. "Good," he said.

"Thank ye."

"I am bowing to the inevitable," Neil said.

"So am I," Duncan agreed. "It's time to go home."

Both brothers looked at him in surprise.

"Ye led the clan to war. Now it's time to go home and start the fifty years of peace. The war's over now that Dundee's dead. I'll no' follow Cannon."

"Let's see what the next month brings," Neil said. "But first, we ha' to get James to Netherby to marry the lass. As I said, I'm bowing to the inevitable."

James gave him a grin.

Ellen let the curtain fall and ran across the room. David Grant had just ridden into the yard. She didn't want to talk to him, but he might have news of James. She took the stairs quickly, crossing the foyer and flinging open the door. David, still holding his horse's reins, was talking to her mother.

"David!" Ellen called, hurrying down the steps.

David's expression was grim as she came to stand before him. "Your mother has told me you've heard about John. I'm so sorry, Ellen."

Ellen nodded, not trusting her voice.

"He was a great man, and well loved by his soldiers."

"That's what we've heard," Ellen said. "We will all miss him greatly."

"It was a sad day for Scotland," Rose said. "A sad day for our family."

"Yes," David said. "And I have more sad news. Ellen . . . James MacCurrie is dead. I'm sorry."

Ellen took a step back. "No."

Her mother gasped. "What happened?"

"The last time I saw him, he was running into a cloud of smoke in the center of the battlefield, looking for Dundee. I followed, but we were fired upon again, and I was drawn away. I was told that he died quite close to John."

"No!" Ellen shouted. "No! You are mistaken, David. It cannot be! James cannot be . . ."

She sank to the ground, her mother bending over her, holding Ellen to her.

"No," Ellen whispered to her mother. "No."

"My darling girl," Rose cried. "I am so sorry!"

Midnight. Ellen walked across the foyer, shielding the candle flame with her hand. Her letter was ready. She did not want Ned to forget it when he left in the morning for Killiecrankie. She placed it on the table next to the door.

David had stayed for dinner, telling Rose and Bea about the battle, about John's death and funeral. And about James. Ellen had not joined them. She'd gone to sit silently in the chapel, staring at the stones behind the altar, thinking of kneeling here with James just before he'd left, remembering their vows to each other.

"My love," she said, but that frightened voice could not be hers. It was someone else who whispered in the silence of the church. This was not real.

She had no more tears. Part of her still worked rationally. She'd sounded calm when she'd asked Ned to go to Killiecrankie, telling him, and then her mother and Bea, that she wanted to know if James would be buried there, or at Torridon; she wanted to know everything Neil and Duncan could tell her of James's last days.

And then she wrote to Neil, saying that she had heard the news and acknowledging their loss. Their loss, she'd thought as she'd folded the letter. What a strange way to think about it. Their loss, as though they'd misplaced a piece of clothing. Their loss. And what was it to her?

She put the candle on the floor and opened the front door, looking out into the yard, thinking of the last time she'd seen James, of waving as he left, of him leaning low to kiss her, then telling her mother he would come back, his eyes dark blue and defiant. James.

The summer wind was soft tonight, curling around the trees and up the steps to brush past her ankles like a cat. The candle flickered. She stared in horror as the flame bent sideways and then went out. James was dead. Her vision was blurred by tears.

Four days passed. Ellen had discussed James's death with no one. What was there to say? Her mother hovered near her, but Ellen only shook her head when Rose asked how she was. She avoided Bea and Britta as well, seeing sympathy in their eyes; she wanted no sympathy. She was either numb or angry most of the time, and she wanted to stay that way.

If her mother had let them marry, they would have had a few days together. If she'd been strong enough to defy her mother, they would have spent their last nights together locked in each other's arms.

If William of Orange had stayed home and been content to rule his Dutchmen, if King James had been a fit ruler, none of this would have happened.

If, if, if. It was no consolation. She hugged her arms and walked to Bea's alone.

Her great-aunt's house was quiet and clean, but had the look of abandon that unused spaces acquire, and the smell that accompanies it. She left the door open to let the afternoon air in while she roamed through the upper floors.

All was in order upstairs, and she paused before descending, looking out over the valley, watching the play of the light through the luxurious emerald leaves of midsummer. They'd turn crimson and chestnut as autumn came, then fall to lie under winter's snows.

And her heart would still be broken. Season after season would come, year after year, before she would heal from the loss of James MacCurrie. She would never forget him.

Ellen went slowly down the stairs, letting her hand drift behind her on the railing. She was in no hurry to go home; she'd go to the chapel instead. It was there that she felt closest to James, in the quiet peace of the stone church where she could hear the echoes of their pledges to each other. Forever, they'd said.

She frowned as she came down to the ground floor. She was sure she'd left the front door open; it must have blown closed. Her hand closed around the knob, tightening as another hand was laid atop hers. A male hand, large and square, with blond hair on the back of it. Ellen held her breath, feeling the heat of his skin on hers. Then she turned and stared into Cecil Fraser's blue eyes.

"Remember me?" he asked.

Chapter Nineteen

Fraser turned her easily to face him, holding her against the door, leaning over her with a smirk. He bent his head low, and she thought for one horrible moment that he would kiss her, but he whispered in her ear instead.

"Remember me, Miss Graham?" His voice was low and taunting. "I think you do."

He grasped both of her wrists, holding them high above her head while he pressed against her, staring into her eyes.

"I hear you've been lonely," he said.

"What do you want, Fraser?" She saw the flicker of his eyes as he heard the tremble in her voice, saw his pleasure in her fear. She tried to twist away. "My cousin John is dead. What do you want now?"

He laughed in her face, then released her and stepped back, watching while she shrank against the door. Still smiling, he struck her across the face, then again with the back of his hand, slamming her head against the wood. Ellen stared at him, unbelieving, as the pain hit her. She raised her hand to her mouth and felt blood. He hit her again, then again. She slid down the door. And remembered nothing else.

She woke in the dark, lying on her back, on a thin mattress. She could not move. Her arms were tied behind her back, her feet bound at the ankles. Her mouth was filled with a foul-tasting wad of material, another wrapped around her head to keep it in place. She fought a wave of nausea, then counted to one hundred, fighting her fear. It did not help. She strained to see, listened for any sign that she was not alone. Except for the skittering sound of a mouse running across the wooden floor, there was silence. She must still be at Bea's, probably in one of the attic rooms, where the beds were small.

Why was Fraser doing this? He'd not been surprised when she'd said that John was dead; he'd already known it. Was he planning to hold her for ransom? If so, he'd be disappointed; there was no one to pay except her mother, and Rose had no money left. Bea might have, but how could he know that?

If he were not holding her for ransom, then why was he here? She shivered at the memory of his blows. Was this his revenge for her thwarting his attempt to kill John at Dunfallandy? This man murdered without compunction. What did he have planned? And if he meant to kill her, why had he not done so when she was unconscious? That was even more chilling.

There was no one to help. Her mother and Bea were no match for Fraser. James was dead. John was dead. Ned was gone. David would be with Catherine. No one but Britta even knew she had gone to Bea's, and she was not even sure if that was where she still was. She was alone, at Fraser's mercy.

* * *

Neil looked at the lad standing before him and rubbed his chin. The lad was blathering something about Ellen Graham and holding out a letter, saying he was sorry. Neil didn't listen as he took the letter with misgivings. Why would Ellen write to him and not his brother? The damned woman had better not have changed her mind about marrying Jamie. He looked up at the lad with the thick unruly hair and the wide eyes full of apprehension. And intelligence.

"Tell me again—who are ye?" Neil asked.

"Ned, sir, from Netherby. Miss Graham sent me to you, to find out . . . She sent the letter, sir. I'm sorry for your loss."

"My loss."

"Please read the letter, Lord Torridon. I . . . You look just like your brother, sir. I thought you were James at first."

"Aye, we're twins," Neil said gruffly as he unfolded Ellen's letter. He read it in stunned silence, then looked up at the lad. "Who told her Jamie was dead?"

"Mr. Grant. He said he saw your brother fall, sir, in the battle."

"Grant? David Grant?"

Ned nodded.

Neil swore and read the letter a second time, then looked up at the lad. "Ned, my brother is alive, verra much so. Come with me."

He led the way around Blair Castle, to the field where the clans were training the new reinforcements. The field was crowded, and Neil wound through the knots of men, to the spot where he knew he'd find Jamie and Duncan. His brother and cousin stood to one side, watching a pair of men practice thrusting and parrying, their faces intent on the exercise.

"Jamie," Neil called, then turned to Ned. "See?"

As James joined them, Ned watched with wide eyes and an open mouth, looking from one brother to the other.

"Ned!" James cried with a grin. He slapped the lad on the shoulder. "So ye couldna stay away. Glad ye've come to join us." His expression suddenly sobered. "Is everything a'right at Netherby? How is Ellen? Has she heard about Dundee?"

"Yes, sir," Ned said. "And she thinks you're dead too."

James handed Ned more charges of gunpowder and a bandolier. Crossing Scotland just now could be dangerous, and he wanted to be prepared. They were leaving at once. Neil was off now, telling Cannon that he was leaving for a few days. Duncan was helping to pack. They'd be on their way with the daylight. There would be four of them. James had intended to go with Ned by himself, but Neil and Duncan had refused to stay behind.

James had read Ellen's letter several times, then folded it and put it in his shirt, next to his heart. She'd told Neil that she would love James until the day she died. Forever, she'd said.

I'm coming, Ellen, he thought. I'm coming.

Morning came at last, the light slowly filtering through the lace curtain on the window across the room. Ellen lay on a small and very hard bed in an upper room, just below the sloping roof. Through the curtain she could see the top of a rowan tree. She was where she'd thought, in the attic room where she had played as a child.

She tested her bonds again but could not shift them, and she fought the urge to scream as panic flooded her. It would do no good—she'd not get any sound past the wad of material in her mouth, and even if she could, there was no one at Bea's. No one came here but her now.

She marked the hours that passed by watching the sunlight on the tree branches brighten, then dim, drifting between sleep and a dazed wakefulness, starting with a jolt of fear when she heard boots on the stairs. As terrifying as it had been to wait, it was worse now that he'd come. She tried to control her panic as the door was unlocked and swung open. Fraser leaned against the doorjamb, smiling at her, a bottle dangling from one hand.

"Enjoy your day?" he asked. He moved into the room and leaned over her, his hand on her chin, moving her face back and forth as he examined her. "Oh, you're swollen now. Why did you make me do that, Ellen?"

Fraser lingered over her name, as though savoring it, which frightened her more than his blows. He reached behind her head and undid the knot that held her gag, removing it and watching as she pushed the wad of cloth out of her mouth. Ellen tried to curse at him, but her mouth wouldn't work.

"Thirsty?" he asked, then laughed softly when she didn't answer.

He tipped the bottle to her mouth and forced it between her lips. She drank the water quickly, ignoring the liquid pouring onto her neck and down her bodice. Fraser then took the bottle away, putting the stopper into it, his face emotionless.

He reached to the back of her head and grabbed a fistful of her hair, then pulled a knife from his belt. Ellen turned her head as a jolt of terror gripped her; she wouldn't let those cold amused eyes be her last sight on earth.

Fraser chuckled and sliced at her hair, then stepped back

with a grunt. "I'll be back later," he said. "Don't go anywhere."

"Fraser!" Her voice was a croak.

He turned.

"Why are you doing this? Why?"

He smiled and stepped through the door and locked it behind him.

The second dawn. Or was it the third? She'd lost track of time, had spent the hours in a haze of emotion and hunger. She'd screamed, called, cried. No one had come. It was as she'd thought. Bea's house was empty except for her.

Her mother and Bea must be frantic by now. And Britta. The girl had been worried enough before; after two nights she would be sure something dreadful had happened. Ellen laughed scornfully. Something dreadful *had* happened. And, if she was right, it was only the beginning. Fraser had a plan; that much was obvious. He was using her hair to show someone, to prove he had her in his control. To whom? Only her mother and Bea would care if she were missing. What could he want from them?

Sometime later—midmorning, she thought—the door burst open. Fraser stood in the doorway with a bundle under his arm, studying her with a mocking smile. He came to sit beside her on the bed, turning her face and studying it.

"You're a mess," he said at last. "But at least the swelling is gone."

He untied the bonds on her feet and slipped his hands up to her ankles. She tried to kick him, but her legs would not move quickly enough. She expected him to attack her, but he surprised her by rubbing her ankles between his hands, driving the blood back into her feet, his expression intent as he worked.

"Fraser?"

He glanced up at her, moving his hands up to her knee, rubbing it briskly as he had her ankle.

"Why are you doing this? What do you want? Why did you take my hair? Why did you try to kill my cousin?" Instead of the contempt she'd intended, she sounded fearful, her voice rising as she spoke, shaking with emotion and weariness.

He looked up from rubbing her knee. "Have you heard of Sir John Dalkey?"

"Dalkey!"

Who hadn't heard of the wealthy nobleman who had opposed John a decade ago, when John had kept the peace in the southwest? It had been the talk of Scotland when Dalkey, a petty tyrant, had broken the law once too often, and John had thrown him into jail with a hefty fine. John had laughed at Dalkey's outrage, and Dalkey had sworn revenge. It had been a long time coming. She'd gone over and over the list of all the people who might wish her cousin ill, but she never would have thought of Dalkey.

"That was years ago!"

Fraser shrugged. "He still hates Dundee. Hated. Wanted him dead."

Ellen swallowed, remembering the conversation she'd overheard all those months ago. It was Dalkey whom Fraser had spoken to, Dalkey who was the money behind it. Fraser dropped her left leg and started to work on her right.

"Revenge," she said softly. "He wanted revenge for being punished for breaking the law."

Fraser looked into her eyes with a horrifying calmness. "And he had a vague promise from King William to be rewarded for anything that would defeat James Stuart. And obviously, Dundee's death has dealt a serious blow to the Jacobites. As I knew it would."

"It was your idea to kill John."

He shrugged. "I know you heard us. Why do you think I went after you?"

"For money," she said with a sneer. "Dalkey paid you."

Fraser shook his head. "He would have," he said without heat. "I didn't get Dundee—thanks to you—so he didn't pay. You were responsible for me not receiving a great deal of money, Miss Graham. It's time to correct that."

He smiled, his eyes almost merry. If she didn't know what a monster Cecil Fraser was, she'd find him almost attractive, handsome, his eyes a clear sparkling blue, his hair shining in the slanted sunbeams. Ellen shivered. She'd always thought of him as a thug, but he spoke like a gentleman, as though he'd been educated.

"Who are you?" she whispered.

His smile faded. "The son of a man who would not recognize me. Life is far different for those of us born on the wrong side of the blanket, Ellen."

He looked down at her feet and sighed, then held her ankles together, retying them with a few swift motions. He untied her hands then, watching without touching her while she struggled to sit up. Her body ached from its confinement, the muscles taking a long time to work correctly.

"Whose son are you?"

"Does that really matter? You need to eat."

He leaned down to open the bundle he'd brought, producing another bottle and some bread and cheese. He handed her all of it. When she held the bottle to her nose and sniffed, he chuckled.

"Water," he said.

She ate everything, inhaled it, then drank all the water,

wiping her mouth with her hand like a child. "Why are you holding me prisoner?"

"Your stepfather promised me property in exchange for some things I did for him. I recently discovered the property was not his to deliver, that it belonged to your Aunt Bea. He's dead now, as you know."

"Did you kill Pitney?"

Fraser smiled enigmatically. "I had intended to use you to force your great-aunt to sign her property over to me, but that will no longer be possible. It seems that your Aunt Bea has already deeded over her property to you." He watched her reaction. "Ah, you did not know."

"Why do you want the property? Why her property?"

He shrugged. "Why not? It produces income. There is no one to contest me. It will provide me with income for years. Why not?"

"I will deed it to you."

He nodded slowly. "Ah, yes, Ellen, I believe that. No, you'd run off to one of your brothers-in-law as soon as the ink was dry, and they'd be on my doorstep within days. The only thing you'll sign is our marriage license."

"Marry you?" She stared at him, her heart beginning to pound wildly. "I cannot marry you, Fraser! I will not!"

"You will. The marriage will be legal, and the lands mine. After that you may do as you like."

"Never! I will never marry you!"

He shook his head sadly. "How predictable of you, Ellen. I was prepared for that. I would prefer that you were willing, but . . . Let me put it another way. If you marry me willingly, I will do no harm."

"And if not?"

"And if not, then I will murder your Aunt Bea and your mother."

Ellen stared at him with her mouth open. "You cannot be serious!"

"I am. Your mother and great-aunt will die if you do not agree to marry me. It's that simple. There are stipulations, of course. Our wedding will be witnessed and legal; I want some of your household there, so they can swear later that they were witnesses."

"No one would believe that I would willingly marry you!"

"They will if you tell them you're willing. Which you will."

"You cannot be serious!"

"Ah, but I am. I have purchased the special license for the waiving of the banns. You will tell the priest that you are marrying of your own free will. No one must suspect that you are not."

She stared at him, horrified. "I cannot do it."

"Yes, you can. And you will, if I know anything of you. I'm sure you would not want your mother's death on your head. Or your Aunt Bea's."

"What have you done to them?"

"Nothing yet. Showed them your hair. They had already noticed that you were missing. What happens now is up to you. After we marry, they'll live to an old age."

"And if I refuse?"

He reached into his jacket, pulling out a velvet bag. "I thought you might protest. Let me help you decide." He opened the bag and dropped its contents on her lap. "Your mother's wedding ring. Her finger is currently still attached to her hand, but I can have it brought to you. You decide."

Ellen stared at the ring. Mother's wedding ring, the ring she never removed.

"It is a symbol of my determination," Fraser said. "Make

no mistake, Ellen, we will marry one way or another. Or must I bring you pieces of your mother until you agree?"

"What is to prevent me from annulling the marriage afterward? Or from going to the authorities?"

"With what? Some wild tale that I forced you to marry me? No one will believe you. We are in the middle of a war; the entire country is concentrating on that. Your brothers-in-law, if they are still alive, are with what is left of Dundee's army. Your cousin is dead. Your lover is dead. You have no choice.

"Our marriage will be legal, if not happy. And before you consider complaining to your brothers-in-law at a later date, remember that I can still harm your mother and great-aunt at any time after the marriage. As far as the rest of world is concerned, I will be your legal husband. Your property will be mine. And under Scottish law, you cannot testify against me. But you will be alive, and so will your mother and Bea."

"No one will believe I willingly married you."

"What does it matter what they think? Why do you imagine anyone will care? The world does not care what happens at Netherby. Scotland's at war; King James is losing his crown to his son-in-law. No one is watching us." He sighed. "It's in your hands, Ellen. What is it to be?"

"This is madness."

"Yes or no?"

"No one will perform the ceremony."

"I have found a priest who will. Tomorrow."

Ellen stared at him. "Tomorrow!"

"Did you think I'd give you time to come up with a plan to thwart me?" His tone hardened. "Make your decision. Does your mother need all of her fingers?"

"You are a monster!"

He shook his head. "Far from it. I am simply taking what

was promised to me." He touched her cheek. "And a little more."

"Why don't you go to Dalkey and see if he has any more murders he'd like you to commit? You're good at it. You could make a lot of money."

"I am weary of working for others, Ellen. From now on, I will direct my own fate."

Her laugh was almost hysterical. "You cannot be serious! This is all so that you can be a gentleman farmer, so that you don't have to work for someone else?"

"Ellen, be sensible. There are times in everyone's life when he must do things that are . . . unexpected." He ran a hand from her shoulder to her breast. "Now, your answer, please."

Ellen swallowed. "If I marry, you will leave us alone? Will you leave me alone?"

"After we marry, you and I will live here, in this house, as man and wife."

"We will never live as man and wife, Fraser."

"We'll see, Ellen. You might not find it as unpleasant as you think; you may find you like it."

"Never." She looked into his eyes. "You will have to sleep sometime."

He smiled slowly, lifting a lock of her hair. "I must guard only myself, Ellen. You must guard yourself, your mother, your great-aunt and that maid you care about. I have people already within your household, who will continue there." He rose to his feet, his patience clearly at an end. "Enough talk. Shall I go and cut off one of your mother's fingers? Or will you marry me?"

Ellen nodded.

He watched her for a moment, then leaned down to glare into her face. "Say it," he said savagely. "Say it!"

"I'll marry you," she whispered.

"Good." He checked the bonds that held her once again, then left without a backward glance.

Fraser returned in the morning, just after dawn, bringing clothing for her, her favorite blue dress, shoes that matched, earrings that had been her grandmother's. Someone who knew her had chosen these. He also brought a mirror, a basin, and soap as well as food, leaving her alone to bathe and dress herself.

He was polite, explaining to her that her mother would be brought to the chapel and would witness the ceremony, but that Bea would wait at an undisclosed location until they were wed. If Ellen misbehaved, or for any reason the marriage was not performed, Bea would die. It was, he said in that cool voice, quite simple.

She told him that if both Bea and her mother were not at the chapel, Ellen would refuse to marry him. He laughed.

"Bea will wait elsewhere. Your mother will watch you marry me. If you balk, if there are any problems, if I do not countermand the order, Bea will die one hour after I leave my man. If I am dead, so will she be. You need to understand that."

She stared at him, believing him. He touched her cheek again and then left her. As soon as the door closed behind him, she ran to the window. There was no easy way down to the ground. And below, in Netherby livery, a footman paced. Fraser had people in the household, he'd said.

She turned from the window. There was no escape. She moved slowly, sinking to the bed, looking at herself in the mirror. She was pale, still sore from his battering, but her face looked almost normal. There was no discoloration, no outward sign of her terror and hatred of him.

Can you do this? she asked her reflection. Can you marry Fraser, take his name, let him touch you? Lie with you?

She put a hand to her throat and thought of Bea's neck, of Fraser's man putting a knife against it. . . . She closed her eyes, praying for strength. She'd go through with this sham marriage, get her mother and Bea to safety elsewhere.

Fraser would have to sleep sometime. And then she'd kill him.

Chapter Twenty

Fraser came for her at noon, his hair gleaming, his clothes pressed and clean. He looked handsome, pleased with himself. And his eyes showed his approval when he saw her dressed and ready.

"It's time, Ellen," he said.

They walked silently to Netherby chapel, two men armed with muskets, swords, and pistols behind them. Fraser had two pistols in his belt, a gleaming sword at his hip—reminders, if she needed them, that he was determined to see this through. The day was lovely, the sun bright but not too warm, the breeze lifting the leaves, then letting them fall, making a soft rustling sound that sounded like the murmur of ghostly voices.

The walk to the chapel was much too short.

Several of Netherby's staff waited in the chapel, their eyes wide and questioning. Six, Ellen counted. The cook and two of the kitchen maids, two footmen, and her mother's maid. Four women, two men. Not enough to stop this mockery, even if the men Fraser had brought would let them. Two more of his thugs met them just inside the chapel. And two more stood in the second pew, just behind her mother, who, pale and shaking, met Ellen's gaze across the small church. Her mother's mouth trembled, and she pressed her lips together in the gesture Ellen knew so well. Rose was terrified. Bea was not there.

The priest, a man she'd never seen before, met them at the altar, his eyes shifting from her to Fraser, his expression calculating. He had to know this was not a happy occasion. How much, she wondered, had he been paid? Was he even a priest? He handed Fraser the marriage license and asked them both to sign it.

Ellen read it several times, her mind refusing to absorb the words that said that Miss Ellen Graham of Netherby married Cecil Fraser of Dundee this day. She signed it with a shaky hand, and the priest laughed, saying something about bridal nerves. Fraser laughed with him and took Ellen's hand, tucking it under his arm.

They faced the altar together.

Sunlight filtered through the stained glass windows, tinting the air indigo, but Ellen did not see the streaks of blue that lined the aisle and draped across the pews, across her mother's shoulders. She saw the small eyes of the man who pretended to be a man of God, felt Fraser's blue eyes watching her. The priest laid the license aside and lifted his hands, asking all gathered to join him in prayer.

Ellen took a deep breath. Her wedding had begun.

She did not hear anything the cleric said. He talked for a while, said some prayers, and waited for her to do something. She stared at him, and when Fraser pulled her up, she rose to her feet. The priest reached for her hand. He spoke to her, then again, sharply, his voice very quiet.

"Your fingers, please, Miss Graham. You must put your fingers out."

Ellen looked down at her hand. She had been holding her fingers tightly clenched and stretched them out now, watching with a roaring in her ears as Fraser put his hand on top of hers.

The priest put one of his hands beneath hers and the other on top of Fraser's, saying another prayer. Fraser smiled at her and turned his hand, palm up, to receive the ring the priest placed there. The priest lifted Ellen's hand.

"Repeat after me," he told Fraser. " 'I give you this ring as a symbol of our union.' "

"I give you this ring as a symbol of our union," Fraser said.

She did not hear the rest of the words, nor feel the ring that Fraser slipped on her finger, pressing it to the base, his hand tight on hers. She started to sway, feeling her head spin; Fraser grabbed her by the waist and held her against him.

The priest took her hand and turned it over, placing a plain gold ring on her palm. Ellen stared at the ring. James had given her his ring. Where had she left it? In her drawer, she remembered, tucked in her finest handkerchief, to keep it safe. She'd planned to send it to Neil, but had not been able to part with it.

James.

James should be here at her side, not this monster. She began to explain it to the priest, that this was all wrong, that this was not real.

The priest squeezed her fingers. "Miss Graham," he hissed. "Repeat after me, please. 'I give you this ring as a symbol of our union.' "

Ellen looked at the priest, then at Fraser. She took a deep

breath and tried to control her trembling. This was real, and she had no choice.

"I give you this ring as a symbol of our union . . . ," she whispered.

She repeated the rest of the words without hearing them. The priest held Fraser's hand out to her, and she slipped the ring over the tip of his finger, then paused.

"Do it!" Fraser said between clenched teeth. "Do it, Ellen!"

Ellen slid the ring down his finger, pressing it to the base.

James stared at the house. Netherby Hall looked the same, but no one was in the yard, no one had called a greeting or challenge as they rode up the drive. He sat for a moment and listened, then slid to the ground and threw Neil his reins.

"Where is everyone?" Ned asked as he came to stand next to James.

James shook his head. The door stayed closed; no one came around the side of the house. He walked quickly to the steps, taking them three at a time, Ned at his heels. James paused at the door, reaching for his pistol, but Ned flung it open and stepped into the foyer, calling a greeting. His voice echoed in the silence.

Ned turned to James with wide eyes. James put a finger to his lips and gestured for Ned to draw his pistol and follow. They walked through the rooms on the ground floor. Someone had been here not too long ago, and someone was expected to return. The dining room table was set for a meal, with four places. The house was empty. Where was Ellen? Where was everyone?

James called twice, then turned as Neil and Duncan

joined him. Ned ran upstairs, and they could hear him shouting Ellen's and Britta's names.

"No one's here," James told them.

"They're all somewhere," Neil said.

"Aye, but where? And why would they all go?"

"What's that?" Duncan asked. "Did ye hear it?" He went to the door, then turned to them. "There's a lass running up the drive, screaming! It's Britta!"

James moved out on to the top step, Neil and Duncan behind him, watching as Britta ran forward, waving her arms. She stopped at the foot of the stairs.

"Help me, please, sir, I need—" She looked at James and screamed in terror, taking a step back. "Oh, God, protect me!" Then she looked at Neil and screamed again, turning to run. "God protect me, there's two of them!"

James pounded down the steps and caught her, turning her to face him. She squeezed her eyes closed and screamed again. He shook her shoulders. "Britta! It's James!"

She opened her eyes. "You're dead!"

"No, lassie, I am not. Where's Ellen?"

"There are two of you!"

"My brother. Both of us alive, Britta."

"We thought you were dead! I thought you were a ghost."

"Aye, I ken. Where's Ellen?"

"She's getting married. Oh, sir, you must stop it! They're forcing her. I could not stand to watch! I snuck away—I was on my way to get Mr. Grant when I saw you ride in here, and oh, please—"

Ned bolted through the door and down the steps, pushing his way between Britta and James. Britta clung to him, then turned to James, pointing wildly to the pathway that led around the side of the house.

"You must stop the wedding!" she cried. "Hurry!"

"Where?" James shouted. "Who's forcing her? Where are they?"

"In the chapel! It's Fraser—"

James waited for no more. He spun away from her, giving Neil and Duncan a wild look, then leapt into the saddle. Britta was still pouring out her story as Ned led her to his horse, Neil and Duncan a footstep behind him. James whirled his stallion around and took the path to the chapel.

He paused in front of the chapel, hearing the voices inside. His horse danced in a circle while he thought of the layout of the church. There was one aisle down the center, pews on either side. And only one doorway, with double wooden doors, built to fit the Norman archway. Tall doors that opened inward. He smiled. He could do it. He leaned low over the saddle and pressed his heels against his horse.

The doors burst open under the pounding of the stallion's hooves. James had leaned low over the horse's neck when they went through the door, but rose to stand in his stirrups as soon as they cleared the choir stalls above. The handful of people in the pews screamed and cried out, but he did not spare them a glance.

Ellen stood at the altar, her back to the church, a blond man at her side, a priest in vestments before her. The blond man turned.

James met Fraser's gaze. And drew his sword.

Ellen turned at the explosion of sound from the back of the chapel. There was a banging on the doors, then they slammed back against the walls, swinging to crash against the stone. A form filled the opening, huge and black, silhouetted against the sunlight outside.

It was a big man on a very large horse. The man straightened as he came into the chapel, his dark hair blue in the light from the stained glass windows, his expression fierce. He stared at her.

James.

Her heart began a wild pounding. James. But it could not be James. Neil, then. Or a dream from which she'd wake. The horseman lifted his arm high, his sword catching the light. He looked at Fraser for a moment before staring at her.

"Ellen!" he roared.

The great beast leapt forward, taking the aisle in a few strides. Neil bent low over its neck, reaching for her, and Ellen lifted her arms. He caught her around the waist with his left arm, pulling her almost onto the saddle. She wrapped her arms around him.

This was no specter. The man she clung to was real, his body warm, twisting under her arms as he whirled his horse around. The priest and Fraser scrambled out of the way as the animal rotated on the altar steps.

James gave another roar, this one of triumph, then bent low over Ellen and raced back down the aisle and out of the church. He stopped a hundred yards away, letting her slip to the ground, then dropping beside her.

"Oh, Neil!" she cried. "Thank God you came! How did you know?"

He lifted her chin and crushed his mouth on hers, pulling her against him, pressing her breasts against his chest, her hips against his. He bent her back over his arm and deepened the kiss, probing and capturing her mouth, his hand running down her spine to hold her even closer. She met his fire, then pulled herself back from him, her hand on her mouth, her eyes wide.

"Neil?" Her voice was a whisper.

He shook his head. "No, love, it's James, no' Neil."

She stared at him, then lifted a hand to cup his cheek. "James? Is this really you? Am I dreaming?"

"Nay, Ellen, I am real enough."

"I thought you were dead," she whispered, her eyes filling with tears.

"Aye, Ned told us. That's why I'm here."

She stroked his cheek as her tears fell. "James. Oh, thank God. James."

He caught her hand and brought it to his lips, kissing her palm, then catching sight of the ring on her finger. Fraser's ring. "Are ye married to him?"

She nodded, her tears falling now. "He said he'd kill Bea and my mother if I didn't."

"The swine!" He looked into her eyes. "Did he touch ye, lassie?"

"No. It's not me he wants, James. It's Bea's land."

"Bea's land? Is he mad?"

"He wants the income. He thought to marry me and gain control of the property. I think he was going to let the world know about the marriage. And then . . . then I'd have an accident. He was going to kill me, James. I'm sure of it."

James looked to the chapel, where the Netherby staff was pouring through the doors, the men pushing the women before them. Ellen followed his gaze.

"My mother is in the chapel, but he's holding Bea somewhere. If he doesn't give the order otherwise, she'll be killed an hour after the ceremony started."

"Then we ha' little time left."

Shouts came from the church.

"Fraser has men with him," Ellen said.

"So do I," James said, turning her so she could see Neil,

Duncan, and Ned, with Britta clinging to his arm. "How many does he have?"

"Six. All armed."

She looked toward the chapel when the Netherby staff gave a collective gasp and stepped back. Fraser, dragging her mother by the arm, came through the doorway, brandishing his pistol at anyone who came close. Rose looked terrified as he yanked her to his side and glared around him. His men gathered behind him, watching the Netherby staff with drawn pistols.

"Stay here, Ellen," James said, reaching for his sword and pistol.

He moved forward, a weapon in each hand. The staff watched in horror, frozen in place, the maids clutching each other and crying. When James stopped ten feet in front of Fraser, Fraser aimed his pistol at James's chest.

Neil and Duncan moved to flank James. Fraser's men crept away from him, fanning out along the front of the church, facing the Highlanders with drawn swords and loaded pistols.

"Let her go," James said to Fraser.

Neil stretched his arms out, pointing his pistol at Fraser; Duncan did the same. Ned waved Britta to Ellen, then ran to Duncan's side. Fraser laughed.

"So, the MacCurrie twins together. I can shoot one of you."

"Aye," James growled, "but the other will kill ye."

"You're outnumbered, MacCurrie. I have six men with me. There are only four of you."

The two Netherby footmen moved forward to stand next to Neil, who passed daggers to them. "Six, sir," one of them said to James.

James grinned. "Odds are even now, Fraser."

"Not quite. I have seven men with guns, you have four. And I have her." Fraser pointed his gun at Rose's head. Ellen's mother flinched but did not move. James took a step forward.

"Stay where you are, MacCurrie," Fraser said. He nodded to his men to fan out even more, which they did. Neil swiveled to face the two who tried to move behind him. Duncan and Ned held the three on the right.

Britta bolted to Ellen's side. "Miss Ellen," she whispered. "Are you all right? Did he harm you? I knew you wouldn't marry him by choice."

"No." Ellen gave Britta a squeeze. "I'm fine."

Britta leaned closer, her hand slipping into Ellen's. A moment later Ellen felt the handle of a pistol, the metal still warm from the girl's touch. "It's your father's pistol, Miss Ellen. I thought we might need it."

Ellen gave Britta a relieved smile. "Bless you, Britta. How did you know to bring it?"

Britta raised her chin. "I know what it is to love, Miss Ellen. I knew there was something horribly wrong if you were marrying Cecil Fraser. If I couldn't stop it, I was going to come back and kill him myself."

"You're wonderful!" Ellen whispered. She held the gun before her. It was loaded, and she hefted its weight.

James took another step forward.

"MacCurrie, stay where you are!" Fraser shouted.

James moved forward again. Ellen caught her breath as Fraser rotated his pistol to aim at James again, his eyes narrowed. Behind him, the priest appeared in the doorway of the chapel. He looked at the Highlanders, then scurried along the edge of the church and around the corner. No one paid him any attention as he made his escape.

Ellen moved forward. She wasn't sure what she'd do, but

standing and watching while Fraser pointed a gun at James or held it to her mother's head was not a choice.

"Fraser," James said, his voice calm and steady, "I ha' waited for this day."

Fraser pulled Rose in front of him. "MacCurrie, you were lucky in the clearing. How the hell did you get out of there?"

"I'm smarter than ye are, Fraser," James said with a wide smile. "Yer men were makin' enough noise to raise the dead."

Fraser laughed. "Not the best choice of companions, I'll grant you that. Stay there, Ellen."

Ellen stopped moving forward and looked from his icy blue eyes to her mother's warm ones.

"Release her and put the gun down, sir," James said.

Fraser shook his head. "So you can kill me? No. Step back, MacCurrie. You might shoot my mother-in-law by mistake."

"She's no' yer mother-in-law," James said.

"My ring is on Ellen's hand. We're married. She's my wife."

"Soon to be yer widow, Fraser," Neil said.

"Ye're no' legally married," James said. "Ellen and I handfasted. This ceremony was a farce."

"Your handfasting was a farce, Highlander."

"Drop the pistol, Fraser," Duncan said.

"Go to hell, MacKenzie," Fraser said. "Back off, MacCurrie."

James let his arm drift down. Fraser narrowed his eyes and leaned back, shifting his pistol to his left hand, keeping it against Rose's head as he reached for his sword. James took a step back.

"Another. Tell your brother to do the same."

James said something in Gaelic to Neil. Neil laughed and replied, but did not move. Duncan moved to Neil's left, his pistol pointed at Fraser's head. Ellen caught her breath. If either Duncan or James shot at Fraser and missed, her mother would die.

James laughed softly, then seemed almost to relax. Fraser watched him with a frown. "Where d'ye have Ellen's Aunt Bea hidden?"

"Oh, let me tell you at once," Fraser said with a sneer.

One of his men leapt forward, rushing James, but Ned shot him before the man could move four feet. Ellen gasped, and Britta shrieked.

"Odds are even now," James said quietly.

"Not quite," Fraser said. "The boy will have to reload. You only have three armed men." He pulled Rose with him as he moved to his left, his pistol dipping for just a moment when she resisted.

With a roar, James leapt forward, his sword flashing through the air.

The air was suddenly full of noise. Ellen heard the gunshots, then the screams and shouts from the watchers, momentarily hidden from her by the smoke. Fraser's pistol fell to the ground, and her mother's skirts dipped as though she was falling, but Ellen could see no more as the group of men surged forward, then back. Two of Fraser's men fell under Neil and Duncan's assault; a third was wounded by the Netherby footmen. Ned, sword drawn, fought with another of Fraser's men. Britta screamed.

James was still alive, battling with Fraser, their swords ringing against each other, blade shivering along blade, the air violent with the sound of their strikes. Her mother lay in a heap on the ground, but she was alive. Two of the Netherby women leaned over her. Fraser's gun lay on the ground near Rose, James's nearby, both ignored now. Ellen raised her father's gun, trying to get a clear shot at Fraser.

Neil dispatched Fraser's wounded man, then watched as Duncan and Ned subdued the last one. Fraser was the only one left.

James thrust with his sword. Fraser parried, then swiped through the air under James's outstretched arm. James jumped back, then leaned forward again. Fraser evaded the next blow, stepping sideways. But James had anticipated Fraser's move and used his advantage to strike.

He slapped Fraser's arm aside, knocking Fraser's sword from his grasp and plunging at Fraser's throat, stopping the steel before it pierced Fraser's skin. The blond man sank to his knees, then looked up at James. There was silence for a moment before Fraser spoke.

"I didn't think you could do that," he said.

James raised his arm, his blade catching the light as it moved.

"No!" Ellen screamed. "James, no!" She ran forward, grabbing at James's arm, ignoring the shouts of protest from Neil and Duncan.

"Bea," she cried. "He has to tell us where Bea is!"

James took a deep breath and nodded, lowering his arm slowly. He pressed the tip of his sword against Fraser's throat. "Where is she?"

"Go to hell, MacCurrie," Fraser said.

James lifted the sword and sliced the tip along Fraser's cheek. "Where is she?"

Fraser grunted but did not flinch.

Neil leaned over Fraser's last man. "Where is she?" he demanded. He pressed his sword through the man's shirt. "Where is she?"

The man screamed, writhing away from Neil's blade.

James turned to look at Neil. Fraser pushed against James and leapt to his feet, whipping a dagger from his belt and swiping at James's middle with a vicious lunge. Ellen screamed, James jumped backward, his kilt sliced where Fraser had hit. Fraser brought the blade back toward James.

Ellen raised the pistol and shot Fraser in the head.

James stared as the blond man sank to the ground, then turned to Ellen. Ellen met his gaze, then looked down at the pistol she still held in her shaking hands. Fraser was dead, his blue eyes staring into the sky. She loosened her fingers and let the gun fall to the ground, the horror of what she'd done overwhelming her.

James reached for her, pulling Ellen into his embrace, enfolding her in his arms.

"Where is she?" Neil demanded of Fraser's man.

The man looked at Fraser. "At Mr. Stuart's house. In the cellar."

"Alive?"

The man nodded.

"Guarded by how many?"

"None, sir. It's just her."

Neil told Ned, "Go get her." The boy nodded and bolted away, Britta at his heels.

The Netherby staff cheered, but Ellen did not hear them, did not see her mother step forward with tears in her eyes. Ellen heard only James's tender words comforting her, saw only his eyes shining with love.

Chapter Twenty-one

Ellen Graham married James MacCurrie in the flower-filled chapel at Netherby, on a brilliant August afternoon.

In the morning her mother, Bea, and Britta dressed her, the three women fussing over every detail. She wore a green silk bodice and overskirt, a soft color that her mother said always reminded her of new growth, of new beginnings, over a creamy white underskirt.

The lace on her bodice was white as well, her hair caught back in a simple wave and threaded with the tiny white flowers that her mother grew, the dark curls loose on her shoulders. Ellen watched Britta tuck in another flower, then she stood, basking in her mother and Bea's approval. She moved to the center of the room, swirling her gown as Flora had done all those months before.

"I'm getting married!" she cried, catching Britta's hands.

Britta laughed. "You look so beautiful, Miss Ellen! Like a princess!"

"Like a woman who is marrying the right man," Bea said. "Make sure you marry James and not Neil."

Rose smiled, her eyes full of tears. Happy tears this time,

Ellen knew. Yesterday, after they had come back to Netherby from the chapel, Rose had blessed this marriage, had begged them to forgive her for not allowing it before.

Ellen had embraced her mother, and James had smiled at Rose, although he told Ellen later that nothing would have stopped their marriage again. Nothing.

James burned the license that Ellen and Fraser had signed, watching with grim satisfaction as the paper turned to ashes, his expression as savage as when he'd taken the ring off Ellen's finger and thrown it into the grave with Fraser.

That was yesterday, Ellen thought, as her mother put a hand on her cheek and smiled into her eyes. She wished her sisters could be here, and that her father, John, and Evan could somehow be here as well. But she could change none of that, she thought, and today was not for sadness. Today all was joy. Today she was marrying James.

When the last curl was placed, the last ribbon tied, Rose and Bea wiped their eyes, laughing and crying at the same time. Britta was so excited that she could not keep still. Ellen smiled at them all and led the way. James, she thought, I'm on my way.

Ellen paused at the foot of the aisle, then walked slowly toward the altar, toward James and their future together. The groom was resplendent, his linen snow white under the blue silk jacket, slashed to show the white silk lining.

His plaid was blue and green, the colors echoed in the jewels of his brooch. His hair, pulled back against his neck and tied with a ribbon, gleamed darkly, catching the rays of light that streamed through the stained glass windows. He smiled as she walked toward him, his eyes very blue. His smile widened when she reached him; he tucked her arm in his and turned to face the priest.

James said his vows without hesitation, his rich voice filling the small chapel. Ellen repeated her vows, her voice trembling with emotion. James slipped his ring on her finger and wrapped his hand around hers, looking into her eyes.

"Forever," he whispered.

"Forever."

The priest blessed their marriage, pronouncing them man and wife. James kissed her, a soft, lingering kiss that held the promise of more to come. Ellen MacCurrie smiled at her husband, then turned with him to face the church and their families.

Outside in the sun, Neil wrapped his arms around his brother, then embraced Ellen, kissing her cheek and wishing them a lifetime of happiness. Duncan hugged her, saying he was delighted to be related to her at last. Ned told her she was beautiful, and that he was going to marry Britta if she'd have him. Ellen told him she was sure Britta would.

Bea claimed them then, embracing Ellen, then James, demanding a dance later with the groom. James laughed, promising he would save her several. Then he turned to Rose, who smiled into his eyes and patted his arm. James grinned at her, careful not to hint of the roar of triumph in his head. Ellen was his.

Ellen sighed with pleasure and stretched out in the big bed. Miss Ellen Graham no more. She was now Lady Ellen MacCurrie, wife of the most splendid man who had ever lived. James was still asleep, his lashes dark against his cheeks, his naked chest moving softly with his breathing.

Had there ever been a man more handsome? More wonderful?

Their wedding night had been all she could have hoped for. James had missed her as much as she had him, that much was evident. They'd not rushed their union, but savored it, exploring each other slowly, thoroughly.

Marriage seemed to agree with them both.

And now? The world would not leave them alone for long. James would return with Neil and Duncan to the army, to war. She pulled the cover over her shoulder. Her thoughts had chilled her, not the temperature this lovely summer morning.

James sighed in his sleep, and she looked at him again. The stubble was thick on his cheeks, his hair in tangles around his head. He was beautiful. My husband, she thought. My love. How can I let you go again? She stroked his cheek, feeling dangerously close to tears.

James opened his eyes and reached for her with a smile. She slid into his arms, letting his warmth comfort her. He kissed the side of her neck and pressed himself against her, his readiness apparent.

"Again?" she asked.

"Ye had better get used to it, Ellen. I ha' no intention of missing a moment wi' ye." He kissed her mouth, then pulled back, brushing her hair from her face. "I intend to spend most of our marriage in bed wi' ye, lassie."

She caught his hand in hers and kissed his palm. "Who knows what will come?"

He laughed, the sound rich and content. "I do. Fifty years of peace. Others may no' ken what's to come, but we do."

"The legend," she whispered.

"Aye. I dinna ken how each part will be fulfilled, but I

ken it will be fifty years of peace, Ellen." He grinned. "I may be weary of ye by then."

Ellen smiled. "I'll see that you're not," she said, stroking a hand down his chest. "We'll make our own legend, my love."